W9-AEF-332

Pinto and Sons

Also Available in Norton Paperback Fiction

Richard Bausch, *The Fireman's Wife and Other Stories*
Simone de Beauvoir, *All Men Are Mortal*
The Mandarins
She Came to Stay
Heinrich Böll, *The Casualty*
Anthony Burgess, *A Clockwork Orange*
Mary Caponegro, *The Star Cafe*
Robert Coover, *The Origin of the Brunists*
Rick DeMarinis, *The Coming Triumph of the Free World*
Sharon Dilworth, *The Long White*
Leslie Epstein, *Pinto and Sons*
Montserrat Fontes, *First Confession*
Mavis Gallant, *Overhead in a Balloon: Twelve Stories of Paris*
Francine du Plessix Gray, *Lovers and Tyrants*
Ron Hansen, *Desperadoes*
The Assassination of Jesse James by the Coward Robert Ford
Janette Turner Hospital, *Dislocations*
Ward Just, *In the City of Fear*
Ivan Klíma, *My First Loves*
R. M. Koster, *The Dissertation*
Mandragon
The Prince
Thomas Mallon, *Aurora 7*
John Nichols, *A Ghost in the Music*
The Sterile Cuckoo
The Wizard of Loneliness
Anthony Powell, *The Fisher King*
Jean Rhys, *Collected Short Stories*
Good Morning, Midnight
Wide Sargasso Sea
Joanna Scott, *Arrogance*
Josef Skvorecky, *Dvorak in Love*
The Miracle Game
Daniel Stern, *Twice Told Tales*

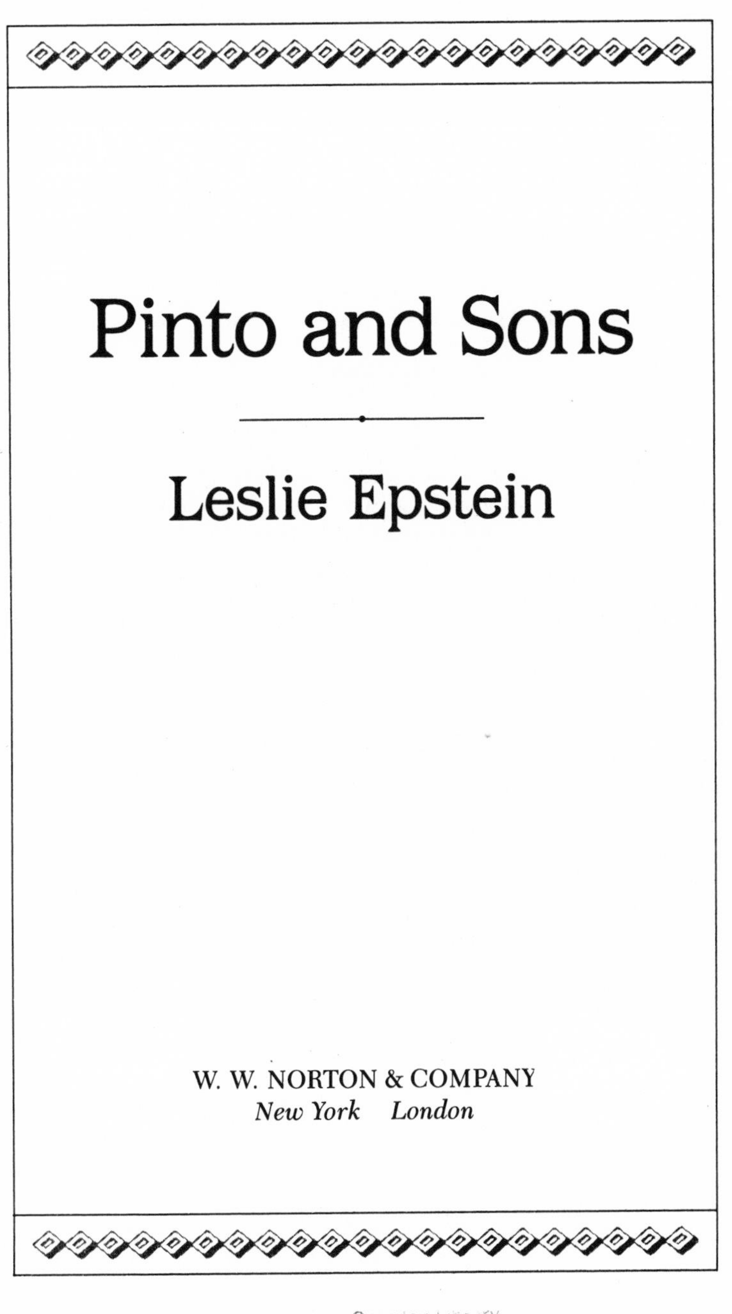

Pinto and Sons

Leslie Epstein

W. W. NORTON & COMPANY
New York London

First published as a Norton Paperback, 1992
Reprinted by special arrangement with
Houghton Mifflin Company

Printed in the United States of America

"Life Without Pain" first appeared in slightly different form in the *Atlantic Monthly*, and a portion of "The Discovery of Neptune" appeared in very different form in *Triquarterly*.

Library of Congress Cataloging-in-Publication Data

Epstein, Leslie.
Pinto and sons / Leslie Epstein.
p. cm.
I. Title.
[PS3555.P655P56 1992]
813'.54—dc20 91-37314

ISBN 0-393-30846-4 (paper)

W.W. Norton & Company, Inc.
500 Fifth Avenue, New York, N.Y. 10110
W.W. Norton & Company Ltd.
10 Coptic Street, London WC1A 1PU

1 2 3 4 5 6 7 8 9 0

For my own sons, Paul and Theo
And for my daughter, Anya

Misled by fancy's meteor ray,
By passion driven;
But yet the light that led astray
Was light from heaven.

"The Vision," Robert Burns

Contents

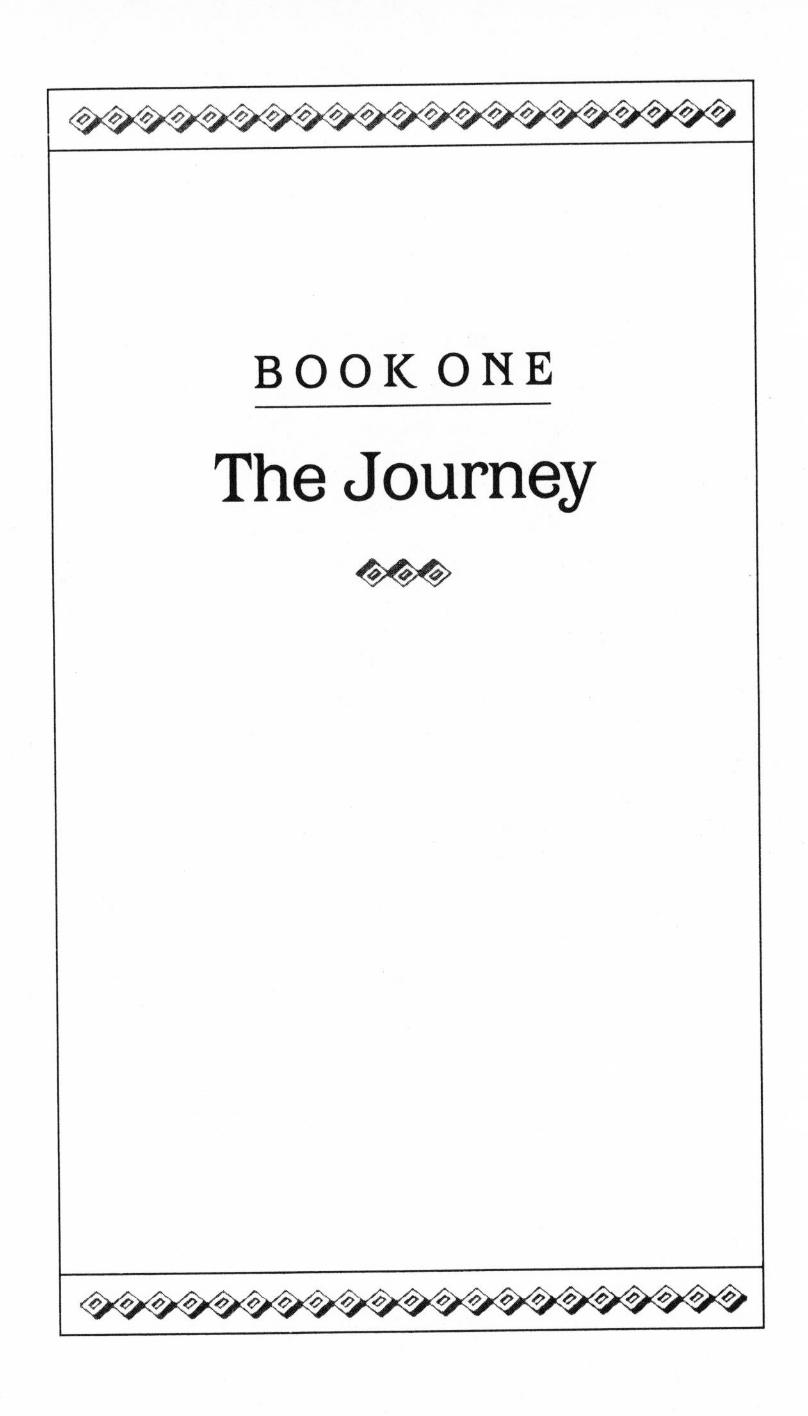

BOOK ONE

The Journey

BOOK ONE: THE JOURNEY

CHAPTER ONE

Life Without Pain

1

THE LEGEND IN OUR FAMILY is that on the very day Columbus left Spain for the west, the Pintos, with thousands of other Jews, were forced to sail eastward from the port of Cadiz. Doubtful. Fanciful, even. Only this much is certain: the banished Pintos wandered throughout the Ottoman lands, settling here, settling there, before moving northward, into Hungary, where they struck roots near the old city of Pressburg. In all likelihood their name had then been not Pinto but *Pintor* — "painter," in the sense of house painter. Or else it had been shortened from *Pintojo* — "spotted, stained," in the manner of a mottled fish or a horse. Indeed, like many such Jews, the Pintos tended to birthmarks. I myself, Adolph, have moles on my back and upper arms, together with a round, soft, dark one on the cheek beneath my eye. It is the sole reminder, in a face otherwise pale, of the fierce burning sunlight of Spain.

Three and a half centuries after Columbus — in the fall of 1845, to be exact — I, too, crossed the ocean, in order to study the science of medicine at the Harvard Medical College. One year later, at the Massachusetts General Hospital, I witnessed an event that changed the rest of my life. There I sat, in the top row of the surgical theater, watching the breeze blow the last of the morning clouds away from the high glass dome. At age fifteen, with thin legs, with narrow shoulders, I was much the youngest in that crowded room. On my lip there was no more than a hint, a haze, of moustache. In my throat an Adam's apple looked, in profile, like the blade of an ax. Dark eyes, long nose, dimpled chin. Under my hat, however, my hair was pomaded, and two black curls were slicked down on my forehead so that they never moved.

Dazzlingly, the river's reflection began to dash along the inner surface of the rounded glass. I continued to squint upward at the play of light, not once looking toward the floor of the room, where the surgeons were waiting. Above, in the blue patch of sky, a gull flew by like a pair of silent scissors. The amphitheater had grown quiet. We could hear the far-off cries of the dock men as they hauled in the lines of the ambulance boats. In those days many of the hospital patients arrived by way of the Charles. And left in that manner, too, if the rumors — that paupers' bodies were simply dropped through trapdoors into the tide — were true. Awful thought! Enough to make one tremble. With a shudder I forced myself to look down.

In the well below, old Dr. Warren stood off to one side. The patient, Abbott by name, a printer, was already half reclining in the surgical chair. Even from my high perch I could see the tumor, gnarled, raw-looking, like a wen on the trunk of a tree. It was attached to Abbott's neck and jaw. The roots, as Warren had already demonstrated, went right through the jawbone and lay buried under the poor fellow's tongue. A second shudder went through me. Delay! More delay! We were waiting for a dentist, a Dr. Morton, who claimed a great thing: painless surgery. Warren had announced he would make the test there, that very morning. Alas! It had been clear from the doctor's voice, and from the laughter greeting it, that the printer could not hope to lose his tumor without suffering like all other men.

Frank Townsend, sitting two rows below, turned round to face me. He said simply, "Wells." Cole, also a student, laughed lightly at the word. I knew the reason. Some two years before, another dentist, this Wells, had persuaded Warren to let him gas a patient during the class. Halfway through the operation the sleeping volunteer had uttered a yell, a real bellow, and knocked down old Bosworth, lecturer in materia medica, with a kick to the chest.

"What a shame you missed it, Adolph," said Townsend. "A piece of theater! A grand farce!"

I did not dare answer. My own jaw, out of sympathy, perhaps, with the patient's, had begun to ache.

Cole chimed in: "And Wells was only removing a tooth!"

Both students remained turned in their seats. The sunlight streamed through the dome, onto their faces. Townsend said, "It makes one wonder about our celebrated surgeon. To go through it again — and with another dentist!"

"Getting old. Past seventy, I'd say." Cole tapped the side of his head. "Forgot the test with Wells ever happened."

Townsend, eyes narrowed against the light, continued to stare in my direction. I was certain he could see my trembling limbs. "What do you say, Adolph? About your hero? Going soft?"

Again, for fear my quavering voice might betray me, I did not trust myself to reply. Was I truly the only one in the room with shaking knees? How calm the doctors seemed. How carelessly they — Hayward, Parkman, the balding Bosworth — chatted among themselves. And my classmates, in their neat white collars and black neckties, seemed merely bored by the delay. Abbott was actually smiling — smiling! — though now they had strapped him down.

Standing apart, Warren snapped his pocket watch closed. He leaned over his instrument box. Impossible not to note how rounded his shoulders were, and how, where it stretched over them, his worn black cloak shone. It was no secret that the old man spent the whole night before an operation praying, fainting, vomiting even — all because he had to show up in the morning at the bedroom of his patient. Time, now, to offer a prayer of my own: *Lord, when Abbott starts screaming, do not let me throw my hands to my ears!*

Warren chose a knife. His cheeks had sunk, his skin was pale. "Since Dr. Morton has not appeared," he declared, "I presume he is otherwise engaged." The students laughed, just as they had before.

Cole did not join in. "I knew it. The idea was a hoax. A dream."

"A dream, indeed. *That's* the only example of painless surgery we shall ever see." Townsend thrust out an arm to point not at the patient but at the Egyptian mummy — Paddy, each new class always called him — standing in his open coffin, against the right-hand wall. "Everything's gone. Bowels, heart, liver, lungs. They even sucked the brains out through the nose. Excellent surgeons! Paddy never felt a twinge. What a model for us all: kill them and cut them and stuff them with cotton!"

"Shhh!" Cole had a finger to his lips.

Two men had rushed into the room — one, surely Morton, with a glass globe in his hand. Warren, with his knife raised, on the very verge of cutting, stared at the intruders from under his shaggy brows. Then he stepped back. "As you see, sir," he said to the dentist, "your patient is ready."

Morton, a hearty man, ruddy-cheeked, with long sideburns and a strong, grinding jaw, took Warren's place next to the chair. He told the printer what we students already knew — that he had discovered a preparation that would save him much distress during the operation. He added that his companion had already tried it and could testify to its powers. Everyone turned to the second fellow — Frost, his name was — who nodded at Morton's words. The dentist put his hand on Abbott's bound arm. "Are you afraid?" he asked him.

The patient spoke for the first time. "I am not. I will do what you say."

No laughter now. No mocking. The students leaned forward, as pale, as motionless, as Apollo the Healer, whose marble statue stood across from the mummy at the front of the room.

Morton began. He took a bottle from his pocket and poured its contents onto the sea-sponge at the bottom of his rounded flask. From that glass ball two tubes projected, at nearly right angles. Morton pressed the larger of these to the patient's lips, and told him to breathe through the mouth. Abbott did, inhaling the vapors that were in the globe. How quickly the man was affected! His face grew red, practically crimson, and his arms jerked upward, as if pulled by invisible cords. Then his eyes dropped shut and he fell asleep. Morton removed the glass. He bowed toward Warren and repeated his very words: "Sir, your patient is ready."

The doctor acted at once. With one hand he seized the knot of veins; with the other he made a cut on the neck, upward, toward the tumor. There was a gasp throughout the room; but the scream I had dreaded, the cry of pain, did not sound. In fact, Abbott hardly stirred. Warren pressed forward, probing among the vessels and nerves. Still no outcry. The thin hair on the printer's brow was wet and matted, like that of a sleeping child. Below, dark blood dripped from his jawline. The aged Bosworth spread his own handkerchief across the patient's chest. With his needle, Warren wound the thread of the ligature around the base of the tumor, and squeezed. At this the drugged man lifted his foot a little. The doctor compressed the purple mass all the more. Now Abbott groaned. Both his legs began moving, as if he intended to run away.

It was clear to me, high in the amphitheater, that the experiment was about to fail. Yet to my amazement the activity below — the thrashing movement of the patient's legs, the groan that rose from his throat — did not affect me at all. It was almost as if I were watching a scene from a play. A thick, bittersweet smell rose from the floor to the uppermost row. Like oranges, I thought. Then I giggled. Why? Because I had seen how, inside the mummy's coffin, with its pictures of bird-people and snakes and animal-headed men, Paddy himself had given me a definite wink. Nonsense! Impossible! The eyes were blank shells. Now I laughed aloud: the buck-toothed mummy had winked again.

Even as I continued to chuckle with mirth, a separate part of my brain knew full well what had happened. The vapors in Morton's bottle had risen to the top of the amphitheater and collected there in a pocket of gas. The smell was familiar — reminiscent, oddly, of the soap works, the factory of old Papa Pinto, on the outskirts of Pressburg. Was that scent oranges? Yes. With something underneath, like the smell of India rubber. What was it? What? No matter: how gay the scene was below. The black-skinned mummy was turning his head. His mouth opened and shut. Was this not a splendid thing? Morton was the god, the Apollo! And so was Warren! "Ho-ho-ho!" I laughed loud enough to cause the nearest students to turn about. These doctors could bring dead men to life!

There was a clang, an echo, and all heads swung back to where Dr. Warren had just thrown the tumor into a galvanized pail. The operation was done. Abbott was sitting upright, with the white handkerchief like a napkin around his throat. The mummy, of course, made no motion, uttered no sound. Suddenly all present, doctors and students, began talking at once. Above the hubbub of voices, I could hear the great surgeon ask his patient if he was now fully awake. Abbott touched his sewn-up wound. He nodded.

"Tell us. Did you feel pain?"

The reply, though slurred, was clear enough: "No. Only a pressure. Like the stroke of shaving."

Warren turned — not, as you might think, to his colleagues, but to us, the row upon row of young men. How his eyes gleamed!

How his eyebrows twisted and writhed! What he said then each of his students would remember to the last day of his life: "Gentlemen, this is no humbug."

As one, the whole room — including the very students, Gill and Parrott, Buffum and Chaffee, who had driven Wells from that spot only two years before — stood cheering. "Hurrah!" I cried, louder than all the others. "Hurrah!" Then I dropped into my seat and burst into tears.

No one paid heed. Down the steep aisles the students excitedly tramped. They ran for the exit doors. Of all the class, only I, with my two companions, remained.

"It was real," Cole said. "No dream."

Townsend lifted the camera, the wood-and-leather Giroux model he carried wherever he went. "And I missed the moment."

"No. There was too much movement. And not enough light reaches the well."

"Whose fault is that? You are the chemist. You said you'd develop a formula to bring out the image. Now we've — what's that weeping?"

Townsend twisted about and peered up to where the tears were washing down my cheeks.

"Why are you crying?" asked Cole.

"Poor people," was all I could manage to say.

Cole gathered his coat and muffler. "What people?"

"The ones who lived in the past! Who have come before this day. Think of them. The thousands, the millions! How they suffered! This did not have to be."

There was a sharp laugh, like a bark, from Frank Townsend. "Ha! Ha! Now we'll all have our teeth out. We'll ask to be mummified! Thanks be to the dentist!"

"Mr. Townsend!" I exclaimed, wiping the tears with the silk sleeve of my jacket. "Mr. Matt Cole! Do not laugh! Do not mock me! You know how much I wish to be a physician. How to pursue this ambition I left my *Gymnasium* classmates, my family, my native land. Now I will make a confession. I was about to renounce this life of a doctor. Not from choice — never from choosing. But what was I to do when some suffering man begged me to stop? Or when a child cried, *No, Mr. Pinto, you hurt me, no, no, no!* A child! I have tried to make myself hard, to feel no emotions. But always, at each operation, my heart fails. I tremble with fear!"

In the sunbeams, Cole's blond curls made a halo over his brow.

"We know that," he said. "You shake half the rows with your knocking knees."

Townsend, frowning, looked down into the nearly deserted well. Abbott was just departing, walking off on his own feet to the ward. The last of the students had swept from the room. Only the doctors remained, clustered in a knot around Morton. They were arranging to repeat the demonstration on the following day. Warren was off by himself, with his arm, and his blood-stained hand, thrown over the back of the surgical chair. Frost, Morton's companion, was explaining to Bosworth how he had once inhaled the gas from a folded cloth. "On an ordinary handkerchief," he said. "In three breaths I was unconscious. When I woke, the tooth was gone. I have it at home in a box."

"And you, too, felt no pain?"

"None. I swear it."

"A miracle worker!" That was Townsend, who muttered the phrase under his breath. Suddenly he got to his feet and strode down the aisle to the well. Cole followed, while I, light-headed still, brought up the rear.

Townsend went straight for the dentist. That man — and here is a sign of how quickly the events of that morning had happened — had never removed his greatcoat, with its brown fur muff. His face, seen closely, was covered with a film of sweat.

"Dr. Morton?"

Everyone turned to the short, muscular student.

"May I assist you?" Morton, not unkindly, replied.

"Do you know Dr. Wells, of Hartford?"

"I do. For a time we practiced together."

"And do you know of his experiment, in this room, with nitrous oxide?"

Here one of the doctors, Parkman, moved forward, reaching for the student's arm. Townsend stepped easily aside. Unruffled, Morton responded: "I know that he failed."

"Would you tell me if you have just used the identical agent?"

Frost spoke first. "What is your name? It's not for you to ask that question."

Bosworth squinted nearsightedly through the half-lit room. "It's Townsend, isn't it? Don't I know you from the College?"

Cole stepped close to his friend. "Come, Frank. We'll go."

Morton held up his hand. "I will answer him. I have not applied nitrous oxide."

Quick as a flash Townsend said, "Then what is the name of the liquid you poured on the sponge?"

The doctors reacted to the forbidden question with all the energy they had expended in not asking it themselves. "The devil!" Frost cried, jerking backward, as if from a blow.

"Be still!" said Parkman, this time taking a firm hold on Townsend's arm.

Professor Hayward, his monocle flashing, murmured, "Shame!"

"Who are the fellows?" That was old Bosworth, patting his pocket in search of his spectacle case. "Is that you? Mr. Cole?"

Through the disturbance, Morton had continued to smile. "Let them be. I'll tell the man what he wants to know. I call my discovery Letheon."

"What *I* should call it was the meaning of my question. I cannot ask the chemist for a compound by that name."

"Soon you shall."

Townsend wrenched free of Parkman's grasp. "Yes, after you have secured your patent. I suspected this the moment you started. Why else would you disguise your potion with oil of oranges?"

"I have a right to be rewarded for years of effort. Think, will you, of the risk I took today. If the patient had not survived, I might now be in jail, manslaughter the charge. I know the risk Dr. Warren and his staff took with me. This hospital, I promise you, will never have to pay a royalty fee. Do not say I am ungrateful! Never say I wish to profit from mankind's pain!"

The dentist began that speech with much dignity; yet at the finish he was shouting, and had raised the glass vessel over his head. Who knows? Perhaps he might actually have hurled it down, had not a new voice interrupted. I clicked the heels of my high-tops together and made Dr. Warren a stiff little bow.

"Herr Doktor! Greetings! And heartfelt thanks! I am to have a career! I will help people and children! You have done this, sir! The greatest thing accomplished in Boston! No, not Boston! In all the world! Sixteen October, 1846 — history's greatest day!"

From the great surgeon, no response. He turned on his heel. So, in fact, did I, making for the doorway. Behind my back I heard, from Cole: "Catch him!" Then he and Townsend followed in my wake.

Morton, with Frost and the others, remained behind. Upon reflection I believe we can say there was little chance the dentist would have thrown down his glass globe. After all, it had been made to order; there was no other in the world. The following day he would use it to cause his next patients to fall into a sleep so deep that not all the tools of the doctors — the knife, the needle, the saw — could make them wake.

2

Outside, on Fruit Street, on Blossom, the life of the city was going on as before. The wind whipped along the avenues. Sycamore leaves spun by like darts. Everywhere men hurried this way and that, the tails of their coats lashing the backs of their legs. Bounding along, loping up Temple Street, I felt my head must burst from the pressure of the knowledge within it. *A remarkable discovery! Our lives are changed!* I wanted to shout out these words, like a boy crying the news. Up ahead a carriage had come to a halt at the entrance to Bowdoin Square. I ran to the spot, determined to share my secret with the passengers inside. *Dr. Warren has performed an operation! He cut Abbott's neck! No sensation! No discomfort!* Three men, with pink faces, biting cigars, stepped out. I came to a halt, my woolen muffler blowing out from my throat in lieu of the stream of words.

Shy, tongue-tied, I continued to trot: through the square, through the Stoddard Alley, to Howard, to Somerset Street. With every step I was climbing, as if the great secret, swelling like a balloon inside my brain, were drawing me higher and higher. In a moment I came to the pinnacle of the city, where the top of the hill had been lopped off so that the dirt could be used to make new land out of the river. Breathless, clutching my half-wool hat, I scrambled to the top of a knoll and surveyed the scene below.

To the north, beyond thousands of rooftops, ships moved in the harbor and whitecaps slipped off the waves. Leftward, at the edge of the Charles, was the hospital, with its gleaming glass dome. On the far side of the river, in Charlestown, I saw the shaft of the monument to Bunker Hill. These Yankees! They moved mountains. Made revolutions. Turned the world upside down! For an instant I felt as if I were rising yet higher, lifting right off the hilltop and floating above all these roofs, these spires, these wisps of smoke. A hum, like the sound of bees, rose from every point. I took a deep breath; there was a sweet smell, like honey. *"Ja,"* I murmured aloud. *"Dies ist ein Paradies."*

A laugh, short, abrupt, made me whirl round. "Mr. Townsend! Mr. Cole!"

Indeed my two classmates were there — Townsend, hatless, coatless, with the heavy box of his camera slung over his shoulder, and Cole by his side.

"You followed?"

"Yes. Right from Fruit Street. All the way up to *Paradies*!" Cole laughed. "Boston! A paradise!"

"Yes, I admit that was my thinking. I see it in the faces of people. Mr. Cole, I see it in your face, too." And how could I not? On the head of the older student the ringlets were piled like stacks of coins. His face was clear, unmarked, with no signs of age. Eyes blue. Cheeks rosy. In short, the face of a child. "In this new world, in my opinion, is a new kind of man. Here we start fresh, yes, like babes!"

But Cole scowled. "Fresh! New! Why, everything about this country is borrowed and stale and old. Look, will you, where we spent the morning. That amphitheater: a mummy from Egypt, a statue of a pagan god. The very building — Bulfinch's dome, the arches, the columns: it's all been stolen from Greece and Rome. There's not an original idea in our culture. Everything — the science, the music, the shape of the spoons we eat with, the words in our mouths: it's all been shipped over the ocean in a boat like that one." Here Cole waved contemptuously toward a far-off brig, which was beating, with a rocking-horse motion, toward the wharves.

"Nein! What happened this morning was new, new! *Life without pain!* Only America could think such a thought. And to bring it about — to make earth into heaven!" My tongue had not only been loosened, the words came pouring out. I turned, so that the message, the tremendous news, would carry over the American city. "No more pain! No pain, friends! Paradise!"

Townsend, who had been staring silently at the ground, now raised his head. "There is money to be made from it. Millions. Tens of millions."

"What money? Made from what?" asked Cole. "From the invention?"

Townsend did not reply. The wind flattened his hair, short cut, reddish, against his scalp. His forehead was so contracted with thought that a furrow, in the shape of an omega, seemed carved upon it. Then he spoke in a rush. "Under the terms of a patent, Morton can license his discovery to anyone he wishes. What if he grants the exclusive use of his preparation to one man out of every ten thousand in the population? What if his fee — a modest one, oh, he'll be modest! — is one hundred dollars? That is more than a thousand dollars in royalties from the city of Boston alone. A single city! And for every hundred thousand citizens elsewhere there's a thousand dollars more. Do you know the population of the country? Twenty million, is it not? That means Morton will realize two hundred thousand dollars for the first year's license. But a patent is held in this country for fourteen years. Can you multiply? In your heads? I can! I've worked it out. Two million, eight hundred thousand dollars, *not* allowing for increase in population, *not* considering the English patent, *not* counting in royalties from around the world. It is a fortune!"

Cole, who had bent down, out of the whistling wind, now sank right onto his haunches. "Can this be true? *Millions?*"

My own head was spinning with the numbers. "What are you saying? Please repeat. How can a person make a patent from a natural fact?"

"He can do it, and will."

Still holding my hat, I stepped down from the knoll. "But this is not possible! Here is a question: could your Benjamin Franklin patent electricity because his kite made a spark? Ho! Ho! Such an idea! What if the great scientist Priestley had held a patent on oxygen? Would we pay a fee in order to breathe?"

So narrow was the line of Townsend's mouth that it looked as if he'd swallowed his lips. His eyes were as fixed as the mummy's blank shells. "What I resent was the way he tried to trick me. With his smell of oranges!"

"But 'exclusive use.' You said 'exclusive use.' Does this mean only a licensed man can perform a painless operation?"

"Within his county or district it means just that. And he can charge whatever the traffic will bear. He'll have his investment back the first time a man walks in with an impacted molar."

"And the patients who cannot walk? Who cannot afford such charges? Are they to suffer? I cannot think it!"

Townsend shook his head, smiling. "I can."

Cole stood up once more. "We can prevent him. We can protest. Dr. Warren will back us."

"It cannot be done, Cole. Haven't I thought and thought? As for Warren and the rest, you've seen what their price is: a simple royalty fee!" Townsend waved his hand in disgust, then turned to leave.

"Wait!" Cole exclaimed. "Where are you going? Is there nothing we can do?"

"It is almost twelve. Twelve is Professor Webster, Webster on sulfur. Why should I miss it? At one, Wellington is to demonstrate the valves of the heart. I have a ticket for that lecture, too. I'll beg Hayward — on my knees if I must — to admit me to his class. So that I'll learn how to grope in a bladder for a stone. And I'll beg Morton as well. *Forgive me! Forgive me, sir!* Oh, not because I want to learn about teeth and gums. I am a medical student. What I want is a license to dispense Letheon myself."

During this exchange I stood mute, both eyes shut. By this means I was attempting to recall the scene in the amphitheater: there were Abbott, Warren, Morton, together with the mummy, winking, moving his leathery jaw. Once more I picked up the smell of the compound: ripe oranges, and the second scent, the under-odor — like pink rubber, with rubber's spice, rubber's tang. The next instant I had it — the soap works! The vats! That's where I'd smelled the aroma before. "Maria Theresa!" I cried.

"What's that, Pinto?" Cole asked.

Townsend said, "The old queen? She died ages ago. We'll get no patent there."

"No, no! You do not understand me! This is the name of the soap! Made by the family Pinto!"

Townsend hoisted his camera onto his hip. "Enough of this. I shall be late for Webster."

"Not comprehending! Excuse my excitement! My heart is beating! Listen, friends: I know the scent in the bottle. Upon the sponge!"

Cole: "As do we — oil of oranges."

"Not oranges! Sulfuric ether!"

"Ether! That's mad! Half Harvard College has breathed it. It's old news. I've taken the fumes myself. They gave me a headache."

"Matt, be still a moment." Townsend moved toward me, until he stood one step away. "Go back a bit, Adolph. Be calm. The soap, the soap works. What has all that to do with Morton's secret?"

"Here is the method of my grandfather, old Papa Pinto. Cheap bars are melted, the fine perfume is added, the new bars are formed. Ether is used to draw the scent from the buds, the flowers. The Maria Theresa brand was the first to be made by this process. Even Vienna came after. Do you now comprehend? Here is the vat, what you call a still. The flowers — rose petals, orange blossoms — are placed in the center, high on a rack. Up rise the vapors, only to fall back in drops through the flowers. This is repeated, again, again, like the percolation of coffee."

Townsend snapped his fingers in his impatience. "Everyone knows ether is a solvent. This is nothing, Pinto."

"But the smell! I recognize it! With my sensitive nose. India rubber! Mixed with orange essence. It is ether, I will swear!"

Townsend turned to his companion. "Cole?" he said.

Cole was frowning. "I know my chemistry. I've worked with ether. I didn't pick up the scent."

"Not just the scent. There is more! In the finest soap bars we use ambergris, from the whale. Many times I would soften it with my fingers. Squeezing and squeezing. For hours. At the end, when I removed my hands: cuts, scratches, bleeding. This was from the beaks of the squid, the octopus, that the whale had eaten."

Townsend: "So? So, Adolph? So?"

"No pain! No feeling! Only numbness! It is the same with all who work in the factory: father, uncle, old Papa Pinto himself. It is the fumes. Now I see it! The same as the printer's jaw!"

Now Townsend struck himself, first on the chest, then two, three, four times on the thigh. "Ether! Ether, then! My God!"

"Is it, Frank? Is it?"

"Yes! It has to be! The same smell — the same insensibility to pain!"

A broad, foolish grin stretched across Matthew Cole's face. A flush spread on his skin. "Ha-ha! I'm sorry — can't help it! Ha-ha! I'm laughing against my will!" Hugging himself, the young man staggered off the lot onto the road. "We know! No one else does! No one in the world!"

"Besides Morton, you mean."

Cole stopped laughing, as abruptly as he had begun. "And Frost? What about him?"

"No. I think not. Why should the dentist let him in on the secret, any more than Abbott?"

The next voice was my own. "Here is a theory: the beaks of the squid, family Loliginidae, irritate the whale, which then secretes the ambergris as a lubricant, like oil. It is a sign of sickness, of disease."

Neither Townsend nor Cole heard my words. The latter had begun giggling again. "Then it is true! Only we know!"

Townsend hissed him to silence. His brow was stamped even more deeply with the omega mark. The wind alternately lifted and flattened the short strands of his hair. "The whole world will know soon enough if we fail to act. Morton means to repeat his experiment in the morning. He'll apply for his patent the minute he's done. That means one of us must leave for the capital tomorrow. I'll find the fastest way — perhaps at the Western Railway. Or we'll use coaches if we must. But first we must prove that it really is ether. Pinto: fetch an animal. A cat. A dog. A lamb from the Common. Anything alive. Cole: you're the expert among us. Go to Burnett's for ether. I'd swear that's where Morton got his. If you have to, distill it yourself from the alcohol and acid. We'll meet again in an hour. Sooner if we can. Where? At your house, Cole? Pemberton Crescent? No. Your family will be there. And not in Cambridge either. There's not a room at the school without some fool of a student in it. Do you know the hotel on Scollay Square? The east side? Yes: the Lafayette! The first of us back, take a room. In the name of Wells. Ha, Wells! So! We are partners. It is a great venture. You agree? Yes, agreed? Then go!"

Cole whirled and ran for Somerset Street. Townsend raced downhill pell-mell. At once I made to follow, but the toe of one blucher caught on a root, pitching me face-first to the earth. The gravel, the small pebbles, ground into the meat of my hand. Here was a revelation: the little accident pained me more than my hands had in Pressburg when the vat of ambergris had scraped them raw. These palms stung me more than Abbott had suffered from his jaw. I got to my feet and brushed the dirt away. Strange not to have made the connection between the solvent and painlessness earlier, in childhood, in the soap works. After all, had I not often wondered why my hands had gone numb? Yes, yes. That meant I must have come close — "within a whisker," as they said in this land — to making the discovery.

Then the thought struck me: not only had the role of ether been all but revealed at the soap works, who else but I, Pinto of Pressburg, had provided the spark, the flash, the lightning bolt of inspiration that had solved the mystery now? I performed an about-face; I returned to the very top of the knoll. Why should my friends and I go to Washington, capture animals, and distill the solvent from acid? Our first task was to inform the one person who above all others deserved to know the secret: Dr. Warren! I knew where the old man lived. From my perch I could make out the block — yes, and the very rooftop — on Park Street below. Imagine how surprised the surgeon would be to hear the news:

> It is ether, sir. The liquid on the sponge. Only ether.
> Are you certain? How can you know this?
> I suspected the truth in the city of Pressburg, when only a weenling.
> But you are a mere lad at this moment.
> True, sir. But I have been trained in the inductive method. I am a disciple of Bacon. An heir to the work of Harvey.
> And why, son, have you brought the formula to me?
> So mankind will benefit from it. You and I will offer it to them. As a gift. No payment. No royalty fee.

Then the famed doctor — I saw this as distinctly as I had seen the wink of the ash-faced Paddy — removed his long, dark cloak and draped it over his student's shoulders. *You are the one to wear my mantle,* he said.

That daydream stopped of a sudden. It was noontime, and in one church, then another, the bells began striking the hour. Gulls, cawing, and wrens, lifted off all the spires and wheeled in the gusts of wind. These sounds, with the humming of the great hive of the city, rose upward, past the hill, past the knoll where I was standing, and into the sky, from whose vast blue vault Bulfinch, and the Romans before him, had taken the plan for their domes.

An hour later we three students gathered at Scollay Square. Cole was first. He registered as Horace Wells, of Hartford, and left word to give any person who asked the number of his room. Townsend came next. Hunched over, with one arm out of my smoking-style jacket, I was third to arrive. Cole pointed to the brown, corked bottle on the wooden mantel. Townsend spread a timetable, Boston to Washington, by way of Providence and the ferry. Then I threw open my coat, so the others could see the pigeon clutched to my bosom. The bird strained toward them, striking over my hand, then drew back its head. Its green mane puffed like a lion's. No one, in all that time, had said a word.

The room was on the second floor of the hotel, facing an alley.

The windows in the bank building opposite had a view of our chamber. Cole drew both sets of curtains over the unfastened glass. The light in the room grew thick and dim. Townsend reached for the bowl of the lamp on the dresser. Cole stopped him.

"No. Flammable." He said this hoarsely, in a whisper.

For some reason Townsend whispered, too. "Very well. We have light enough to begin."

Beneath my fingers I could feel the beat of the bird's fierce little heart. "But what are we beginning?"

We three conspirators looked at one another. Townsend acted. He stripped the quilt from the bed and shook one of the pillows from its cover. Then he uncorked the ether and sprinkled the liquid over the linen case. Immediately the smell filled the room. Cole brought his handkerchief to his nose. Townsend lifted the slipcase, which was drenched right through. He held it, stretched open, in my direction.

"All right," he said, in a near normal voice. "Drop it in."

Should I do it? Could I? With a pang I thought of how I had captured the bird. A row of three pigeons had been standing on a flat stone cornice, with their tailfeathers to the wind. The gusts made them look blown inside out. I'd held a bit of muffin in my palm. Two of the birds flew off at once, but the third turned in a circle and pecked at the crumbs. I'd netted it with a swirl of my jacket. Just as easy, I realized, to free it now. All I need do was cross the room — two strides, no more — and thrust the pigeon through the drapery, into the air. I felt its tiny legs push against my chest. "Shhh," I said, so as to calm it. Then I plunged the bird to the bottom of the sack.

Instantly Townsend clamped the top and held it against the horsehair mattress. The bird flapped wildly within. One could see it, as if in relief, whenever it hurled itself against the clinging walls. A whole minute went by. The solvent did not seem to be working. If anything, the pigeon's efforts to free itself grew more frantic. Once the entire pillowcase rose from the bed, half flying. The wet linen yanked and jerked and writhed.

Cole was horrified. "It's enough, Townsend. We've made a mistake."

I moved to the window, for air. "Gentlemen, please. Permit it to go."

Townsend hung on. "There's no mistake. We'll see it through. Look now! It's taking. He's slacking off. It's taking!"

This was true. The movements in the sack were growing feeble, and in seconds entirely stopped. The linen lay limp, with a dark, damp bulge in the center.

"Done, by God!" said Cole. It was as if his voice — high, excited — had never broken. "Hurry! Open up!"

Townsend upended the pillow slip, and the bird, with a dozen loose feathers, tumbled out. We three students leaned over the bed. The pigeon was on its side, its head bent into its iridescent breast. Cole poked it with a finger. No response. Then he extended a wing and let it drop. It did not fully close.

"Sleeping," he said. "As sound as Abbott."

It was I who lifted the head, so they could see the single drop of blood, like a ruby, on its beak. "Dead. Of heart burst."

"No," said Townsend, quite calmly. "Suffocation."

Cole pushed us both aside. "Dead? Don't say dead. I tell you it's the coma. I'll stick him. He'll wake from that." With the pin from his collar he actually made a stab at the bird. Half flinching, I knocked his arm aside.

Cole turned on me. "It's your doing, Pinto. You've cheated. Brought a pigeon! An *animal,* you were told. Something large, something warm-blooded. It's the same childish fear you showed in the theater. You'll die from fright someday!" The next thing I knew, Cole had pushed me off my feet, onto the bed.

Townsend stepped between us. "Stop it, Cole. What's come over you? The dose was too large, that's all. It's one of the factors we're here to learn. You'll get your chance to cut and stab."

"No," said I, pulling myself upright on the bed. "I am to blame. Coward! Cowardliness! This was my thought: from a pigeon there will not be a scream."

Townsend moved to the double curtain and pushed it aside. He stared into the alley below. "Cole: look. There is the fire door on the side of the building. Wait for me there. Give me fifteen minutes. When I pound three times, let me in. You shall have your beast, large, warm-blooded, and all." By the time he'd finished these instructions, he'd crossed the room and stepped into the corridor of the hotel. His short, sharp laugh echoed in the hall.

Cole pursued him. "Frank, are you laughing? What is the joke?"

But Townsend was already trotting down the rear stairs. The next moment, as I noted from a crack in the window curtains, he had made the alley and was heading for Scollay Square.

What the joke was Cole discovered when, some ten minutes

later, he heaved the iron door open and Townsend came rushing through with a brown-and-white bulldog. "It's Caesar!" he cried, thunderstruck.

And so, moaning and whining and shivering with delight, it was. I, too, smiled at the sight of the Cole family dog. The humor lay in the contrast between the sturdiness of the build and the mildness, even cravenness, of its manner. Cole, of course, was not amused. He stood, his skin damp and blotched, against the room's whitewashed wall. "Does my father know? Does my sister? How was it done?"

"Oh, no one knows. I came round the front of Pemberton Crescent and saw the family having their tea and dessert. I brought the dog through the garden in back. I am sorry, Cole. I didn't do it for a joke. It's the only way I know to continue."

The bulldog, meantime, was moving from one of us to another. Its corkscrewed tail, the hindquarters, indeed the whole rear half of its body, was aquiver.

Townsend laughed. "He's such a cur!"

Caesar, mistaking the words for an invitation, began to grovel by Townsend's feet. When I knelt, the animal turned toward me, thrusting its large head, its protruding jaw and hanging skin flaps, into my Jewish lap. The dog groaned with pleasure.

"Hold him, Adolph!" Townsend said this over his shoulder. He was pouring more ether onto the pillow slip.

Cole's tie had come loose and hung in strands down his shirtfront. "You're not going to put his head in the sack, are you? I can't allow that."

"No," Townsend replied. "We'll go back to the tried and proven." He displayed the linen, which he had folded into a bulky square.

All the while I grappled with the dog. It pulled backward, trying to slip its head from the collar. The furrows in its brow, the whole wrinkled face, made a mask of worry, as if it knew what was about to happen. Townsend, to our amazement, began to croon.

"Come, Caesar, brave Caesar: such a brave fellow, so strong, so handsome, so smart . . ."

The bulldog, thrilled, thrust its head toward him, directly into the fume-filled cloth. Townsend dropped on the animal, clamping his arms around the powerful body. I grasped the collar with both hands. The dog twisted, but Townsend forced the wet linen over its flat black snout. The struggle did not last a moment.

First the dog's bladder let go, soaking the carpet and the cuff of Townsend's pants. Then, with a shudder, its legs buckled and it collapsed to the floor.

"Not too much. Isn't that too much?" Cole had not yet moved from his place by the wall.

"To the count of ten," Townsend responded.

I released the leather collar. The smell of the urine, of the ammonia in it, was as strong as the sulfuric ether.

"Enough! Enough! Enough!" Cole shouted, as the seconds went by.

Townsend lifted the mask; the subject was clearly sleeping. Its lips were withdrawn, smilingly, showing the pink-and-black gums. Its tail wagged once, still trying to please. The three men in the room breathed more heavily than the dog.

"A knife! Damn! Why didn't I think of it?" said Townsend.

Who, of all people, took out a penknife, small and silver and shining? The Hungarian. Instrument for the cuticles and nails.

Townsend grasped it and knelt by the animal's rump. He seized the little tail with one hand and with the other sawed it through.

"By God. By God." That was Cole.

"He did not blink," I murmured. "Not the lash of an eye."

Blood trickled from the remaining stump of tail. Townsend pressed his own clean handkerchief to it. The bleeding stopped. For a moment the room grew still. We three listened to the even, unruffled respiration of the sleeping dog. Outside, in the corridor, someone was walking from one end to the other. The closed curtains rose and fell, as if they were breathing, too.

Without a word Cole stepped forward and held out his hand for the knife. Townsend gave it to him. Cole drew the sharp edge through the dog's ear. It caught in the nap of fur. He slashed again, until he had carved the tissue in two. Then he held the little ear up, like a trophy. From where they crouched on the floor, the two students turned. Their gaze was directed at myself. I stared back at my friends. They were bloody, their hands red with it, a separate spot shining on Cole's cheek and one on Townsend's chin. They grinned at me, their mouths half open.

What, I wondered, to do? Should I run? That was one option. The other was to join them. Cole was holding the knife out. I took it. I turned the dog's massive head, to get at the unwounded ear. It was, on the inside, as smooth and pink and curving as a mollusk shell. My own ears rang, the very air drummed against them, as if to protest the deed. I cut the flap cleanly. I used such force that the point of the blade went through the carpet and stuck in the floor. From the expression on my friends' faces, I knew that I, no less than they, was grinning.

Cole said, softly, dreamily, "We can do anything."

After a pause, Townsend replied. "Yes, anything."

The animal moaned. It panted. The wet tongue lolled. Then its legs began to move, all four of them, as if in its mind, rising toward consciousness, there still lingered the dream of catching a cat or a hare.

3

The same wind that had scattered the morning clouds blew up new ones late in the afternoon. Near dusk the first drops of rain started to fall. In the Harvard Yard students ran this way and that, protecting their heads with jackets and textbooks, as if they feared the brains inside might dissolve. A group of three or four huddled together beneath the dark green umbrella that covered the fruit-seller's cart; but a bolt of lightning, with the thunderclap that followed, sent them flying to the solid stones of University Hall. That left only the dark blur of Lewis, the orange peddler, standing upright behind the pencil lines of falling rain.

Cole and Townsend, who had both attended the College, knew the old man and his wares, as did generations of students, going back nearly to the days of the Revolutionary War. Indeed, he had been at the College so long — had *always* been there, it seemed — that no man alive could say whether Lewis was his given or his family name. Cole's father, class of 1818, still spoke of waking in the morning to find the Negro in his doorway — he had been "Lewis" even then — plunging a potassium stick into a bottle of acid, making a tiny blaze. For a penny, the black man, with the famous Instantaneous Light Box, could spare any scholar from having to bank up coals for the night.

From the day he arrived in Cambridge, Lewis had limped. His story, told over and over to every class, was that he'd been wounded when, a boy of eleven, he'd been struck by a shell at the battle of Yorktown. He had been a drummer under the command of Lafayette, and had helped turn back Cornwallis's retreat during the French barrage. All the Harvard men had heard how the artillery had aimed over the town, into the British fleet. Lewis himself had put down his drum at the sheer beauty of the sight. In the river, flames jumped from the mast of one ship to the mast of another. White columns of water shot upward like the spouts of whales. The clouds in the sky, he told the students, had been on fire. That was when a volley of howitzer shells fell short, cutting through the ranks and sending slivers of metal through the black boy's foot.

After the surrender, Lewis had found himself in one of the hospital tents of Washington's troops. Each day the commander in chief walked the aisle. From his cot Lewis could have touched his coattails or his scabbard. *Well, boys,* said the general to his soldiers. *You have felt the bullet's sting and heard the bullet's whistle. It hurts, but there is something charming in the sound.*

A lieutenant, a senior at Harvard, brought Lewis back to Cambridge as his valet. When the officer took his degree, Lewis stayed on, teaching himself to read, even attending classes. He had always lived in the wide, low-ceilinged attic under the roof of Hollis. With the years, and the sharp, stinging pain in his foot, it became almost impossible for him to make the nightly climb up the stairways of Stoughton and Harvard and Massachusetts halls. The class of 1820 bought him his two-wheeled cart, and there he stood, year in and year out, in good weather and bad, until each day's meal in commons was done.

In his first years at the stand, Lewis used the bottle and sticks he'd always carried from room to room. But when friction matches came in, the students began to light their own grates with the new lucifers. That was when the Negro began to sell oranges. Wherever he got them — from the Caribbean trade or the southern states — he always seemed to have a year-round supply. Even in January his cart was piled with the round balls of fruit. In the winter months he made fires in metal drums to keep his wares from freezing. They were dessert for the students after their meal.

In only minutes the autumn shower worked itself up into a full-fledged storm. The sky lowered. The clouds collided. Rain blew across the Yard, under Lewis's flapping umbrella. We three medical students watched from an archway as the old man pulled his collar about his neck. We were wet through ourselves. Water dripped onto Townsend's shoulders and his wooden camera top. Cole carried a large leather medicine bag, which he'd taken from

Hayward's surgery while the professor was holding class. It shone like licorice beneath the beating rain. Clutching the ether bottle, I peered through the slanting shower. All I could see of the black man was the shine of his teeth and the white woolly horseshoe of his hair.

"Is that the gentleman? The man with the wounded foot?"

Townsend put his hand on my shoulder. "You'll see. When he walks."

"But why does he not leave now? On such a night? Surely no person will buy his fruit at this hour."

Both students smirked. Cole said, "You need not worry about his making a sale."

At that moment, from the side of the darkened quadrangle, a woman rushed to the umbrella. She wore a white blouse; her black skirt reached her ankles.

"Who is it? Curse the rain! Goody Peacock?" Townsend swiped at his eyes with his damp sleeve.

"No. Younger. Goody James."

"I do not understand. Who is this woman? Is she wearing a costume?"

Townsend still had hold of my shoulder. "She is a servant. As is Peacock. That is what she wears when cleaning the rooms."

"Tell him the rest, why don't you? Those men, Pinto — the ones who stood under the umbrella. Do not suppose they were seeking to buy Spanish oranges. They want ten minutes with a servant woman. That's what the haggling was about. Lewis controls the trade. He sells the friendship of the college servants."

A sudden wind bore upon the distant figures, whirling over the cart and the billowing umbrella. A second person, also female, with hair bound up in a bun, darted forward, from the direction of University Hall. Just as she arrived the umbrella collapsed, shedding water in an arc. The two women struggled to secure it, as Lewis rocked the cart wheels out of their muddy ruts.

"Do you see? I knew it! Adolph, look!"

I saw, indeed. The Negro, retreating across the Yard, lurched behind his wagon, so that the foot he dragged after him bore none of his weight.

"We've got him!" Townsend exclaimed.

"Come! This way!" Cole plunged over the walkway toward Hollis, with Townsend and me no more than a few steps behind.

We reached the hall ahead of the Negro and waited for him on the landing of the stairs. We heard the thump of his walk, and then a hollow clicking, well before we saw him pull himself up the banister rail. The click was the sound of his teeth, still strong and white; they chattered from the chill. He saw us by the fading light at the casement windows.

"Mr. Cole, sir! I am very pleased to see you. And Mr. Townsend. A pleasure to see you as well. And this—" He poked forward his large, straight nose, not like the nose of a Negro, and hauled himself up another step. "This is not a Harvard man."

Cole did the honors. "This is our friend Adolph Pinto, from the Habsburg Empire. He is the most promising surgeon in the Medical College."

The banister was on Lewis's left, so he held up his right arm to shake my hand. How thin the old man was! How delicate! Surprising to see how he winced from my grip. An odd thought: if the man hadn't been black, you could have seen right through him. A faint mist of steam rose from his clothes, as it did from ours. But there was a smell to it—like a flower-stem odor, I thought, when the flowers have been left in the vase too long.

"The young men are still dining at commons," said Lewis. "Have you come to visit a friend in Hollis? There are a number here who intend to take up medicine."

Cole said, "No, we've no friends here."

"Is it one of the ladies? That is a pity. None is here now. And each has an appointment later tonight."

"The fact is, Lewis," said Townsend, "we've come to see you."

I could not suppress the words that came next: "It is because of the foot. We are able to help. We will treat it without causing the least sensation of pain."

"We've seen it grow worse, Lewis, over the years. There may be lead there. A poison in the bloodstream." Townsend leaned down to where the black man was standing some steps below. "We are prepared to perform an operation now, at this moment, in your room. In an hour you might be cured."

Lewis smiled, but his face seemed a shade lighter. "Mr. Townsend, I understand you wish to help me and put into practice the things you have learned. I thank you for your kindness. But this cannot be done. How could you cut me when I cannot touch myself? When I cannot bear even to remove my shoe?"

Cole squeezed between us to speak. "You did not listen, Lewis.

There won't be pain. This is a new thing. We have seen it for the first time this morning. The patient slept through the cutting, and so will you. The vapors in that bottle will make it impossible for you to feel so much as a pinprick."

The old Negro rubbed his long, dimpled chin. The whites of his eyes were actually butter-yellow.

Something, a sensation of sobbing, was working its way up my throat. "Mr. Lewis. I have learned from my friends how, in the fight for freedom, you received your wound. The fire. The bombardment. The suffering of many people. Finished with that! Finished! We are going to remove such pain from the earth. And you will help us to do it!"

But Lewis shook his head. "I have borne it this long. I believe I will bear it the little while longer."

"And you hardly strong enough to climb to your room!" Cole exclaimed.

As if to dispute this, the old man began to heave himself past us, half hopping upward, step by step. We watched, not interfering. In seconds he stopped, sagging against the banister rails, which seemed to be the only support for his otherwise boneless body.

Cole started toward him, but Townsend pushed by, reaching the black man first. "Poor Lewis. The pain. Poor Lewis. It hurts him. It hurts poor Lewis." Amazing to hear this: he was speaking with the same tone he'd used upon Caesar, the dog.

"I am well. I am not hurt," Lewis said. He pulled himself to a seated position, to see what the former Harvard man would do.

Townsend continued crooning, always on the note of the Negro's name. But the little penknife, the one we'd used on the bulldog, was in his hand. With one swift motion he slit the cracked boot from top to bottom and twisted it off the dark, swollen foot. Lewis cried out. Half his rotted stocking had come away too. Cole and I leaned back, away from the rising stench. But Townsend bent nearer, wiping his own damp brow with his sleeve. Then he snorted. "It's what I thought. What I always thought. A fraud!"

He held the big foot up for us to look at. Even in the dimming light we could see how the toe had been lacerated by the ingrown nail.

Cole guffawed. "Higher. Get the light on it. It's nothing but the nail!"

No laughter came from my lips. "It is not true? You were not at the famous battle?"

Lewis's yellowish eyes bulged from pain. "I could touch him. I was close to him. I smelled the powder in the general's hair."

Townsend said, "He's told the story so often he thinks it's true."

At that moment, well below us, the first of the Hollis men were returning from dinner. They crowded into the entry, laughing because of the rain.

"Would you help me to my room?" asked Lewis.

I saw the chance the same instant Cole did. We said, in chorus, "You will let us?"

"He will!" laughed Townsend. "He wants to keep his secret." With that he threw the old fellow's arms over his shoulders and then, as easily as if Lewis had been made from his own potassium sticks, lifted him upon his back. He trod with his burden up the rest of the stairs.

Cole followed, with the medicine bag. Cringing a little, I picked up the slit boot and brought up the rear. Down below, the stairwell was echoing with the laughter of the Harvard men, and their ringing footsteps, and their shouts.

The low attic ceiling was barely high enough to allow us to stand. The room had three windows, two round ones that flanked a rectangle; but night had fallen and they gave neither light nor — as Cole discovered when he tried to force them open — air. For a time we stood choking from the rank odor that filled the space. Slowly our eyes adjusted to the light of the whale-oil lamp that burned, feeble and guttering, on a nearby beam. The room was virtually empty. Two coats and a pair of limp trousers hung from nails driven into a rafter. There was a bed with metal springs and a thin horsehair mat, and near it one table, one chair. On the round tabletop stood a white clay pitcher, a white clay mug, an orange, and an egg. Also one book, its pages gilt-edged, bound in black leather. The rain beat loudly, as if the roof above were made from tin.

Cole shook his head. He retreated toward the door. "We can't continue. No air to breathe. No light to see by."

Townsend walked to the lamp and turned it higher. "We'll have the light."

Lewis lowered himself to the straight-backed chair. "What is the matter?"

"It's fire, Lewis. In these close quarters the compound might explode if brought near the flame." Cole was actually at the door. "We must put everything off until we can find another space, or at least until daylight."

"What is your opinion, Mr. Townsend?"

"My opinion is that the risk is small. We ought to operate now."

There was a pause. Lewis leaned his head on his hand and stretched his leg out, so we each could see the swollen, clubbed-looking foot. "And you will be the one to remove the nail?"

"No," Townsend answered. Then he pointed at my narrow chest. "He will."

And why, I reasoned, should I not be the one? Everyone knew I was the best surgeon, not only of us three, but of any in the dissecting class. Yet fear surged through me, and my skin felt as if it had been rubbed with ice.

The black man looked me up and down. "Will you take long?"

"Nein!"

"How long?"

"Drei Minuten!" Then, more softly: "Three minutes only."

There was another pause. It almost seemed that the man had dozed off, his cheek on his palm. Then, from that position, he said, "Well, I have memorized each poem in my book."

Townsend sprang forward. "Good! Cole, quick, your handkerchief. Good, good! Pinto! Unstop the bottle. Come, no trembling! Not at the historic moment!"

But tremble I did, so much so that the ether was churning to froth. Townsend snatched it from me and soaked the handkerchief. In no time the fumes mingled with the smell of festering in the room. But the flame in the lamp held steady. Cole, seeing that, giggled from relief. Townsend spread the wet cloth and held it to the black man's face. He told him to breathe through his nose. Lewis did so. In seconds the lids of his eyes dropped shut. Overhead, the sound of the rain was like the beat of a drum.

Cole loosened the old man's pants and pulled them off his body, over the remaining boot. Then he and I laid the patient on the bed, while Townsend kept the handkerchief over his mouth and nose. Cole swung the hurt leg out from the mat, to the wooden seat of the chair. It was like a long, ash-colored stick.

I now chose a knife from the medicine bag and walked, nearly on tiptoe, to the propped-up foot. At the head of the bed Townsend raised the damp cloth. The patient sighed once. His head dropped to one side and his mouth hung open. My thoughts? First of the sleeping dog. Then of the pigeon. I could feel, on my skin, the push of its rubbery feet.

Cole seized the suspended shin with both hands, as if to wring it. "Cut!" he commanded.

Here was a phenomenon: I still trembled, my whole body shook; but my hands, like those of a completely different person, were steady as stone. I drew the knife across the toe, below the curl of the nail. The flesh broke beneath the blade.

"Wait." I made another incision, this time at the joint. Then I raised my head toward my companions. "No blood."

Cole released his grip and peered down at where his fingers had been. They had left no impression on the flesh.

I placed my own hand on the spot. "Cold."

"Try the pulse," said Townsend.

Cole placed his fingers at the curve of the ankle. "None. There's none!"

Townsend again: "Pinto. Another incision. But higher."

I hesitated, suddenly afraid that with this cut the patient would scream. Then I brought the knife down into the skin above the ankle. No sign of bleeding. Grimly, I plunged the blade into Lewis's calf. It was like cutting a crumbling cheese. Horrified, I let the knife drop from my hand. There was a moan — from Cole, not the Negro. "It's terrible. It's terrible."

"Now listen. Do what I tell you. Pick up the knife. Go higher. Still higher."

I obeyed. The next cut was a long curving line a hand's width below the knee. The dark blood oozed from the severed vein.

"*Ja!*" I cried, in triumph.

Townsend half rose, looked, then ripped one of the coats off its rafter nail. He held it out to Cole. "Tie it here," he said, demonstrating on his own thigh where the tourniquet was to go.

But Cole stood frozen with the black jacket in his hands. "What are we doing? What are we thinking of? We're only to deal with the toe!"

"We've no choice. You see the gangrene. Now our achievement will be greater than Morton's. Greater than Warren's. It's a piece of luck!"

"Luck!"

"For Lewis, as well! If we hadn't arrived, he would have died within thirty-six hours. So tie! I tell you, tie!"

Cole bent to do it. The Negro's thigh was so thin the sleeve of the jacket went round it twice. The student twisted the ends together. The blood flow stopped as neatly as if he had closed a spigot. Cole squatted there, keeping the pressure firm.

Meanwhile I searched through the bag for the instruments required to cut off the limb. I chose a larger, semicircular knife, and a saw. *Do not think,* I told myself. *Do not allow feeling. Become the machine.* Thus did I attach the ligatures to the curving needles and pin them to my lapel. After all — so ran my thoughts — what happened here, in Hollis, would be no different from what was daily done at the Braman's Baths, at the anatomy sections. I had seen a dozen amputations at the thigh. I had practiced myself on corpses. The Negro's gray skin was much like that of the cadavers; and he, like them, would not feel a thing.

"Why are we waiting?" Cole asked. "Are you dreaming? Why do you smile?"

Was I smiling? At such a moment? If so, the reason was this: I had just pictured myself with one of the red wool caps the students wore in the dissecting room. Here was the little joke everyone told: *to soak up the bloody thoughts underneath.*

It was Townsend who said, "Amputate."

The greater part of Lewis's leg was suspended between the chair and the bed. I pressed my left hand to the knee and with the right made a circular cut, completely around the thigh. The two halves of skin pulled away from each other. I repeated the action, digging well into the meat of the groove. The muscles parted in the same way, as if strong men were pulling from either side. The arteries and veins were practically dry. I put the knife in my mouth, the way Hayward, and Warren too, did with their patients, and tied the vessels off, leaving a series of dangling threads. The sciatic nerve, glistening and white, was still intact. I pulled it downward and cut with the tension still on it, so that the top half burrowed upward, like a worm into its hole. How much time had gone by? A minute? A minute and a half? Warren could sever a limb in fifteen seconds, and that with the patient writhing, screaming, and three men to hold him down. A great man! Great surgeon! I gripped the knife again and plunged it down as far as it would go.

"Hurry!" said Cole.

"Yes, faster," said Townsend.

With bare hands I forced the flesh simultaneously up and down the broomstick of bone. But before I could take up the saw we all heard a sound that chilled us through. It was the click of the Negro's teeth striking together.

"He's waking!"

"No! Reflex!" But to take no chances, Townsend loosened the stopper on the ether bottle and moved the damp cloth near to hand.

I placed my instrument on the femur, but did not dare saw. Inside the room, the wick, half consumed, threw shadows across the walls. They were like hands, waving, applauding, or like dark wings. I thought of the gull flying over the dome top. How blue the sky was! How the light danced and rippled upon the glass! When had that been? Only this morning? Hours ago? Not years and years? I tried to catch the call of the dock men and the splash of waves. But all I could hear was the rain striking the rooftop, as if a drummer were perched there with his drum. *Boom! Boom! Trum-trum-trum!* The sound grew louder and louder. I knew this much: once I began sawing, that sound in my ears, the drumbeat, would never cease.

But I sawed. The blade skipped across the slippery surface of bone.

"Oh! Oh, God!" Cole, in his anxiety, was twisting the tourniquet into a knot.

I tried once more, pulling the blade toward myself, raising it, settling on the same spot again. The teeth caught and dug a track. I sawed faster, in both directions. The dust fell in a stream to the floor.

"That's it! That's it!" The shout came from one or the other of my companions. "Saw harder!"

This I did, back and forth, like a woodsman, until the grinding sound of the blade was joined by the unmistakable drone of the patient's voice. We three turned. Lewis was sitting up, eyes closed, declaiming a poem.

> "Come to my arms, my Katie, my Katie,
> An' come to my arms and kiss me again!
> Drunken or sober, here's to thee, Katie!
> And blest be the day I did it again."

Here were words that struck us with terror. Cole let out a hysterical laugh. "It's Burns! Ha-ha-ha! Bobby Burns! The nigger is reciting from Burns!"

For a moment I was certain the fumes were causing another

illusion. It was as if the mummy, moving his jawbone, had at last found his voice. Then I realized it was Lewis, not I, who was dreaming. "More ether!" I was able to shout.

But Townsend, unaccountably, was not by the bottle. I whirled round. There he stood, five feet off, under the guttering lamp. He turned the wick upward.

"No!" screamed Cole.

"Quiet! Don't you see I need the light?"

Here was an unbelievable sight: Townsend had propped his camera upon the table and inserted his silvered plate. Now he stooped, so that only the top of his skull, with its damp red hair, showed behind the gleaming lens. "Hold still!" he ordered. "I am taking the image. Not a movement! Not a word!"

At that instant Lewis, as if in obedience to the white man's command, suddenly stopped chanting. He also opened his eyes. His gaze was fixed on his half-severed limb. No one spoke. No one moved. Then the Negro took a breath, as if to recite again; but instead of the lyric, a dark stream of vomit came out of his mouth.

Confusion! All was confusion! Townsend forced Lewis down with the wet rag of ether. Cole clutched his own head and broke into tears. At a loss for anything better to do, I resumed sawing. Now the worst came for Lewis. The debris of the vomit had lodged in his windpipe. He gagged and writhed. The black skin of his face turned a purply blue. His body, twisting and jerking, so loosened the tourniquet that all three arteries of his upper leg began to disgorge their load of blood. Cole lost his nerve completely. "He's dying!" he cried, and leaped from his station. Bumping his head on the rafter, blinded by tears, he began to grope toward the doorway. Townsend paid no heed. He forced his fingers into the Negro's mouth, probing for the dregs of the spew. In four strong strokes I sawed off the bone at the thigh.

At that instant Cole reached the door and threw it open. Old Bosworth, lecturer in materia medica, stepped into the dimly lit room. "Madam Peacock! My dear! I have been thinking of this moment all through the day!" In his hand there was a bunch of flowers — daisies with soft yellow centers, and dahlias. "For you — a bouquet! I have come early so they would not wilt." For a moment the professor remained in the doorway, smiling, nodding, peering nearsightedly about. He did not see his three students, or the sufferer on the mattress, the blood still spilling from his stump. Then he patted his breast pocket, where he kept his spectacle case. He took out his glasses and placed them on his nose.

4

Anesthesia: without feeling, loss of sensation, artificially induced insensibility to pain. One more thing borrowed from the Greek — though the word was first applied to surgery by an American, Oliver Wendell Holmes, who later became dean of the Medical College. I had not been mistaken in saying that the idea of life without pain was itself American: nothing done here before or since has proved of such worth to the world. How strange, how ironical, that this blessing, which has spared so many from pain, should bring nothing but misery to those who discovered it. Perhaps not so strange. History likes such jokes. Even the great Columbus, the admiral himself, was finally brought back to Spain in chains, like one of his own Indian slaves.

Briefly, then. Wells, the Hartford dentist, the man who came so near the prize, was arrested in New York City for throwing acid on streetwalkers there. He had done this while under the influence of the chloroform that, as an experiment, he'd deliberately inhaled. Once in his jail cell, he breathed an even larger dose of that same anesthetic and, in the instant before sleep overcame him, slashed his thigh with a razor. He bled to death.

And so with Morton. His patents, little honored, much criticized, were not renewed. He spent the last years of his life in a bitter struggle with a Dr. Charles T. Jackson, who insisted the dentist had stolen the idea of ether from him. Morton's breakdown also occurred in New York, soon after he read an article that backed his rival's claim. Physicians were called to his bedside, but he fled them, whipping his buggy up Broadway and into Central Park. There he ran to the boat pond and thrust his head, hot with humiliation and fever, under the water. It was not quite the end. The doctors ran to him, but again Morton broke free. He dashed up the meadow, leaped over a fence, only to drop unconscious on the other side. His heart stopped some two hours later.

Dr. Jackson, no less than the others, seemed the butt of the ironical prank. He was admitted to the very asylum in Boston where he had tested both ether and chloroform upon the inmates. Years later he died in the place, a madman himself.

The lives of all the others involved in that day, that night, of debacle were to remain inextricably linked — even the lives of the assistant, the fellow Frost; the monocled Hayward; and, for that matter, Caesar, the mutilated dog. For the moment, however, the careers of us three students were hopelessly shattered. Cole and I attempted to continue at the Medical College; all too soon the threat of scandal forced us to withdraw. Townsend departed at once, moving back to his home at Charleston. There he joined his family's shipping line, as a plain seaman at first, then as a purser, and even as ship's doctor. He made the run up the coast to Baltimore, New York, Boston, and then over the Atlantic to ports in England, Holland, and France.

Lewis did not bleed or choke to death, and there was no further sign of the gangrene that, had his limb not been removed, must surely have killed him. He did not suffer from the shock of the operation itself, since all he remembered of it was a dream in which he was drumming in the Revolutionary army, as he claimed to have done some sixty-five years before. Nor did he bear any hostility to the Harvard students. He would point to his black leather volume, the works of Burns, and say that even the best-laid schemes go astray. In time he was back in the Yard, selling his oranges and moving about on the fine ivory leg that one of the three students had bought him.

Last of all, Professor Bosworth. He retired from teaching that term, moved from his lodgings on campus, and never returned to the hospital or the Harvard Yard. He had always served as an informal guide, almost a chaplain, to the students and staff of the Medical College. Now he took a more definite religious turn, studying for the ministry proper. He was assisted in this task by Goody Peacock, who by the first snows of that winter had become his wife. Now she brought him his meals, built his fire, and saw that his clothes were mended. Through the long nights the old man read to her from the difficult texts, some in Latin, some in Greek. These languages meant no more to the former college servant than the green snakes and jackal-headed men that were painted on the walls of Paddy the mummy's tomb.

CHAPTER TWO

Soldiers with Scalpels

1

THE YEAR 1848 began with two earthshaking events. In Europe, in Paris, a crowd gathered both to celebrate the birthday of George Washington, first of presidents, and to demand an extension of the right to vote. When the people were fired upon, the barricades went up. In just two days, on the twenty-fourth, Louis Philippe was driven from his throne. The February Revolution — in many ways the second American Revolution — had begun. Once this torch of freedom had been lit, there was no putting it out. All of Europe went up in flame. In every capital, kings tumbled, tyrants fell. Kossuth, the Thomas Paine of my country, declared Hungary an independent nation. In Vienna, the emperor was chased through the streets by crowds waving the American flag. And in the old city of Pressburg, the young people, the technical students, sang out while under bombardment: *Yankee Doodle, keep it up! Yankee Doodle dandy!*

Meanwhile, in America itself, something no less momentous was already taking place. In January — that is, one month before the overthrow of the French monarchy — a man named Marshall discovered gold in California. What happened was that he noticed a number of round pellets shining in the mud of his millrace: when he hammered one out, it did not break; it only got thinner, thin as a leaf, thin as air. Impossible to keep the secret. By the spring thaws hundreds of men were panning the American River; in midsummer they dotted the creek banks like flies about a honey pot. Before long the city of San Francisco had no more than 150 people left in it. The very newspapers that carried word of the finds were forced to shut down, because all the typesetters ran off to the sites. Prisoners walked from the jailhouse and were soon working claims alongside their former jailers. Even soldiers deserted, as did whole shiploads of sailors. Every soul in the territory had come down with the yellow fever.

Dwelling alone in the city of Boston, I knew nothing of the upheaval over the ocean, to the east, or the one so far off in the west. Indeed, by the hot summer months of 1848 I hardly knew what was happening under my own feet or — since I was then living below ground, in a small cellar room — over my head. What a room that was! At the harbor. A mere thirty feet from the wharf. What I remember best is the walls, which in those summer months sweated saltwater like human skin. In winter the same surfaces glistened with thin sheets of ice. And everywhere, in all seasons, the four sides bulged and groaned, as if they were bulkheads about to burst under the weight of the flood. Sunshine? Fresh breezes? Not to be thought of. The only window, a non-opener, was a thin slot at the level of the gutter, through which I could see, moving this way, moving that, the rush of countless feet.

There I lay, on a hot, airless morning in the month of July. If you had crouched own, peeking through the grime-covered glass, you would have recognized the fellow within. Pale, still, with the old mole on the cheek. Heavy-lidded eyes. Hair-free lips, alas, and a whiskerless chin. One difference was that I had grown taller, an actual six-footer, so that the knobs of my wrists and the balls of my ankles poked through the sleeves of my smoking-style jacket and the cuffs of my gabardine pants. Thinner, too. A skeleton, to be frank, with a long, curving nose that stuck out like an eagle's beak and ribs you could feel, or run a stick across, the way boys did to the iron fence around the Harvard Yard. "Ho! Ho!" The bitter laugh burst from my lips, though there was no person to hear it. "I am dying from hunger!"

Dying? From hunger? All too true. I could barely raise my head from my straw pallet; and when I swallowed, my Adam's apple filled up my throat like one of those pears or peaches that is squeezed into a narrow-necked bottle of schnapps. But how could I starve when once each month there would arrive from the family Pinto a twine-bound package in which were six gold coins and a pastry treat: a *Gugelhupf*, an *Austerlitztorte,* or one of those *Kokosbusserln* that I had so often seen my mama pull from the oven, each little kiss in its own paper cup? These gifts I would eat, devouring them all like a tiger. Yet I would not spend an ounce of the gold on my needs. The reason was simple: those six coins were meant for my student fees, my Medical College tuition. *Greetings to Surgeon Adolph!* So read the accompanying note, signed each month by the Pressburg Pintos: parents, grandparents, uncle, mute cousin Sigmund. Every penny of this allowance went for the pure ivory limb upon which poor Lewis now stood when selling his oranges in the Yard. Coward! False son! Dissembler! Not once in the last twenty months had I informed my dear family of the scandal that had ended my medical career.

There was a second family, before whom I was even more ashamed to admit my disgrace. This was the community of scholars I had left behind in Pressburg. It was while wearing the uniform of a *Technisches Gymnasium* student that I had first come to believe in the inductive method and the values of the Enlightenment. Indeed, it was under the tutelage of the Herr Doktor Professor F. Busch that I first formed the idea of becoming a surgeon. Not a day had gone by in the New World that I had not thought of that far-off classroom, with its tall windows overlooking the Danube, and of the rows of young, idealistic pupils, each in his dark trousers, his flannel coat. Every morning, in their high, fresh, innocent voices, they sang the stirring words of F. von Schiller:

> *Alle Menschen werden Brüder,*
> *Wo dein sanfter Flügel weilt.*

All men will be brothers! Under the soft wing of joy! I could hear those words in Busch's baritone, and see him too: tall, with spectacles, and the fluff of an imperial-style beard under his lower lip. What wonderful experiments we had done together! Even in this dim cellar, through half-closed eyes, I could see the *Oberstudienrat* at the front of the room, passing clear liquid into clear liquid, creating a surprising beaker of purple; or proving to us skeptical students that a metal needle could float. *Question:* so Busch, in his Socratic manner, would ask. *To what principle may we ascribe this effect?* Then, from a dozen, from two dozen throats, came the eager reply: *Prinzip der Oberflächenspannung!* Surface tension!

What a genius, the Herr Doktor Professor! Once he had shown us — it was this sight, in the microscope lens, that had convinced me to become a doctor — what the great Harvey had proved but had not lived to see: the blood in a tadpole's arteries as it was about to flow, in a perfect circle, back to the veins. *Der Kapillarprozess!* In the same way, the professor astonished his class with the proof, made by mathematics alone, that beyond the orbit of Uranus an eighth planet must someday be found. He had known an invisible body must be acting on the visible planet, just as Harvey had known that the blood was impelled in a circular orbit by the heart.

Alas! His faith in the heavenly body — for the new planet of Neptune had been seen at last — had been better placed than his faith in me. Doctor? Surgeon? How could I explain to those old classmates that my only connection to my chosen profession now was the tutorials in Latin I gave to Buffum, to Parrott, and to the other medical students? Or the floors that I mopped at the dissecting hall, where only a short time before I had been the star pupil? Even these last links to medicine had been broken by the ongoing rumors of scandal. Thus the Latin students had constantly mocked me — Tiberius Augustus becoming, for instance, the Emperor Thighberius — while the anatomists at the Braman's Baths, where the dissections took place, never stopped playing tricks. Only last spring a group of these students, each in his traditional red woolen cap, had motioned me near.

"Here, this way!" called Ben Piper, the chief anatomist's son. The smell of mint leaves, which all the apprentices chewed to keep off the stench, was on his breath. "Come closer!"

As I drew near, the students lifted the rubberized sheet. Chaffee made the joke: "Do you see? We have saved the leg, the whole of the femur, for you!"

Without even the pennies I used to earn from these menial tasks, I languished in my cellar, surviving like a plant on little more than sunlight, plain water, and air.

On that July morning my thoughts were interrupted by a thud against the door. I had barely the strength, or the will, to respond. A minute went by. No knock. No call. With a groan I rolled from my pallet and crawled on what felt like bare bones — points of elbows, knobby knees — to the door. I pulled it wide. A parcel, not a person, was there. It was from Pressburg! From the family Pinto! I was saved!

I dragged the package indoors and tore at the wrapping, the cord. The top of the box came off. Inside, for padding purposes, were layers of newsprint. Ravenous, I tore through them all. Finally I came to the waxed tissue that covered my dainty desserts. I ripped it away and brought the delicacy to my lips. Error: here was no coconut kiss but instead — first I detected the rose-petal smell, next tasted the alkali, then saw the portrait of the dowager empress — a bar of my family's Maria Theresa brand soap.

"Ah! Ah! *Mein Gott! Meine Mutter!* Save me!"

What could be, for this cruel joke, the explanation? Carefully now, I went back through the wrapping papers. Here was the familiar packet of six gold coins, along with the customary note of greeting: *Herzliche Grüsse an unseren Chirurg!* "Greetings to our surgeon." What followed, however, was a complete surprise. Because of the insurrection, my mother wrote, the barricades, it was impossible to obtain either butter or flour. Instead of an *Austerlitztorte*, these bars of soap would have to do.

Insurrection! Barricades! What, I wondered, now fully awake, fully alive, could these words mean? The answer was in the columns of newsprint, especially those from the famed *Prager Tagblatt*, in which the gift had been wrapped. Now I learned, all at once, in a matter of minutes, not only of the February Revolution in France, but of the revolt in Hungary, Kossuth's declaration of independence, and of the counterrevolution, the determination of the Habsburgs to keep the Austrian Empire intact. This news, I realized, was already six weeks old. The besieged Pressburg might long since have surrendered. What of the family Pinto? And the family of *Gymnasium* students? Had they fallen? Or repulsed the foe?

Even as I asked these questions, I knew that whatever the outcome of the distant battle, the real victory was mine. I had won something more precious than *Kokosbusserln* or any other food to eat: a reason for living! Now I could return to my homeland. And when I did so, there would be no hint of shame, of scandal. This was because I would at one and the same time help struggling mankind and practice my profession anew. I would be a fighter for freedom *and* a physician. How? In what manner? By caring for the wounded. By treating those who had fallen on the field.

"A soldier! A soldier!" I cried aloud. "A soldier with a scalpel!"

Question: how was I, the penniless Pinto, to return? I spent the rest of that morning at the shipping agents'. Imagine my dismay when I learned that the cheapest ticket to Europe was $165. That was close to the value of all the gold coins I had received in the previous twenty months! By the time I could hope to save such a sum the battle might well be over, with the hated Habsburgs back on the Hungarian throne. There was only one thing to do, and, exhausted as I was, staggering from lack of nutrition, I proceeded to do it. That was, of course, to request Lewis to return to me the gift of his ivory limb.

I found the old fellow at noon, selling navel-type oranges from his two-wheeled cart. His leg, the false one, was hidden by his trousers. On that summer day there were no students about to interrupt us. I explained my plan. I made my request.

The Negro turned away. "What has the war in Hungary to do with me? That is your homeland, not mine."

"But you were at Yorktown! You fought with Washington there!"

"You believe that yet, Mr. Pinto?"

"Ja!"

"I was the drummer for the general."

"You may be still! The citizens of Paris fell in his name. This is his revolution, too — it is the same battle you fought as a youth. For *Freiheit!* Yes, freedom!"

There was a pause. The open umbrella creaked in a gust of wind. Saliva dripped from my lips — not because of the balls of fruit, the sharp aroma, the bright-colored peels, but because of a thing I could neither see nor smell. The hidden leg. It was all I could to do prevent myself from falling to the earth and pulling the artificial limb from its straps. "Will you, Mr. Lewis? Allow me to sell it? So I might be a fighter, too?"

The old man bit his purple lip. I saw in a flash that he had decided against me. But I could not have guessed the reason why.

"I am sorry, sir. You are my leg now. What will happen if my doctor crosses the sea?"

There could be — I could see this in the set of the black man's stubble-haired jaw, in the yellow tint of his unblinking eyes — no argument.

Where to turn now? My only hope was to ask my two friends, my fellow conspirators, for assistance. Townsend, I knew, was then purser aboard the *Lightning*, a three-master that belonged to his family fleet. He may have been closer that moment to Liverpool, in England, than to the city of Boston. Matt Cole, however, was still at his home at Pemberton Crescent. The sum I required was, for him, no more than a trifle.

It took much of my strength to cross back from Cambridge and climb Beacon Hill. At the Crescent, running the length of Cole's mansion, stood a brick wall. A stout wood gate blocked the way to the yard. I fumbled, fruitlessly, with the iron bolt. A sound, like garden shears, came from the far side of the wall. Overhead, the thick leaves of a chestnut tree, *Castanea dentata*, stirred in the freshening breeze. No hope, in my weakened condition, of forcing open the lock. With painful effort I hauled myself to the top of the brick. There was no gardener on the lawn within. Yet the sound of the trimming shears sounded once more. Under the tree, in the deep shade, something shook. I strained toward the curtained windows, the closed door, of the house. "Hola!" I shouted. "Mr. Matt Cole! Here is A. Pinto!"

The answer came in an instant: a cough, a growl, a roar. All these noises originated from near the trunk of the tree. There was a blur there, a movement. And then, bursting from the shadows, into the sunlight, came a pair of jaws, a glistening snout, and two burning coals in place of eyes. Also: fur, claws, the stump of a tail, and half of two ears. The bulldog! Caesar! The scissors sound was in fact the snapping together of the animal's terrible teeth. At the last possible moment I lifted my legs, and the fangs of the beast — had he shed his fearfulness, his fawning, along with his tail? — closed on empty air.

"Help! Assistance! It's an attack!"

The house, however, remained lifeless and shut. The animal, springing upward on his four bowed legs, rose once again toward his foe. The eyes flashed fire. The jaws gaped wide. This time there was a ripping sound and a sickening tug, which could only mean that one of the sharp lower canines had caught the cuff of my gabardines. I fell backward, to the safety of the street, while the furious animal continued to hurl himself against the bricks where his former tormentor, his torturer, had perched.

Wearily I trudged downhill, back to the harbor. But I had no thought of returning to my hovel. Instead I turned leftward, seaward, onto the planks of the deserted dock. I squinted into the late afternoon light. Out in the bay a fishing boat was tacking back and forth in the faltering breeze. Gulls wheeled about it. Slowly I moved to the very end of the pier and crouched upon the rounded top of a piling. Despair gripped me like a palpable hand. I leaned out to where the water, green and greasy, lapped only a few feet away. The sun, striking my head, bowed me lower still. Egyptian pomade ran from my scalp, like the melting matter of my brain.

Just then a shrill call rang out. The gulls, I saw, were battling over the approaching boat. One of the birds, family Larinae, had snatched up a fish, or a part of a fish, that had been thrown from the vessel's stern. Now it skimmed over the harbor, its bill clasped upon its silvery prize. As the gull neared the wharf, a second bird swooped down from above. The first veered, and uttered a foolish cry. The catch flew from its open beak, landing no more than a yard from where I sat.

I turned. I gaped. Here was a whole plump fish head, its eyes round and black, reflecting the afternoon light. Gift from the gods! Mackerel from heaven! It took but an instant to leap up and hook a thumb through the bubbling gills. A soup, perhaps. Or fish cakes, deep fried. Why not all of the head roasted over the grill?

But before I could take a single stride toward my dwelling, a problem arose. Or, rather, descended. The gull that had released the fish dropped down before me, barring my way. It hissed with anger. The second bird, the pursuer, fell like a stone just behind. It opened its wings, white and wide, and with its sharp beak made a rush at my ankles. Next, with a noise like whips, the rest of the flock settled upon the pier. Besieged! Surrounded! A terrible thought passed through my mind: that these creatures, cawing, craning, had descended upon me to avenge the poor pigeon I had suffocated in the sack. The animal world was fighting back! With a yell I dropped the fish head and leaped to the piling. The birds fell on the carcass, dragging it in one direction, then another. Screeching now, they picked at the flesh, shredding it, tossing the silver scales into the air.

What the gods give, thought I, swaying upon the tilted timber, *the gods take away.* I raised one hand to my throbbing head, the other to my shriveled stomach, through which ran a pain like a stiletto. blade. It was as if the razor-sharp bills were pecking there, stabbing and stabbing, the way the eagle of legend attacked Prometheus with beak and claw. Like that hero of Athens, I had desired but one thing: to bring knowledge to mankind, to aid my fellow creatures, who yet stumbled in darkness, and ignorance, and pain.

At that very moment—difficult to say whether this was a purposeful act, or simply the result of bodily weakness—I tumbled from the top of the piling and fell with a splash under the eagerly lapping waves.

Down I went through the fathoms. My limbs thrashed. Bubbles came through my mouth and nose. At one end of my body, my Adam's apple sought to bob upward like a buoy; but at the other my heavy bluchers might as well have been lined with lead. Thus did I sink even further, through the cold green sea, while the currents swept me away from land, toward the harbor's bottomless depths.

At such times, it is said, a man sees his entire life pass before his eyes. Of that thesis we may say: *not proven.* For in my own case I remembered but a single incident—and this is not from my own life but from that of old Papa Pinto, my grandfather, who used to tell me how, when only a weenling himself, a little Ludwig, he had once watched the great Maria Theresa float down the Danube upon her royal barges: one filled with musicians, another with candles and torches, and the third with schoolgirls throwing petals of flowers. As I twisted and tumbled through the green waters, all I could think of was that nighttime scene: those vessels, with their dripping oars; the sound of oboes; the rose-petal aroma; the plump profile of the empress, just as it appeared on the waxed paper enclosing the soap. Here was a new idea! Those barges, melting in the Danube currents, surrounded with the scent of roses, supporting the torchlit figure of the empress: what were these but the cakes of Maria Theresa brand soap? Yes! Yes! How clearly I saw everything now! The bars turned out by the factory were my grandfather's memories. Thus was our every work and endeavor nothing but the attempt to recapture childhood and youth. Alas! For Adolph there would be only adolescence. With that final thought I surrendered myself to the cold grip of death.

But the hand that touched me had five fingers. The hip that

knocked against mine was made from flesh and bone. I opened my eyes. The rays of the sun just penetrated the depths of the olive-green sea. I saw, floating beside me, the pale form of a fellow human. I stared again. This was a female figure. A young woman. Without a shred of clothes.

"Pardon!" I uttered, before gallons of water poured into my throat.

No reply. I thrust my hands toward her. She turned to face me. How pale, how white the skin of her face. How dark her flowing hair. The small breasts of a maiden. I strained forward, mouthing my words.

"Ho! Ho! Non-swimmer!"

Again, no response. She continued slowly to rotate, until, in what seemed a gesture of disdain, she had turned her thin back, her shrunken buttocks. Only then, surely too late, did I realize that the poor young girl was in despair — worse than despair: she wanted to die. This was a suicide victim!

Heedless of everything, I now cried aloud: "No, no! Don't give up hope! My dear! You must live!"

Odd the nature of space and time. It seemed to me that from the instant I had leaped into the half-fresh waters of the harbor an hour at least had gone by; surely I had been swept out to the all-salt sea. But in truth everything had taken place in some fifty seconds; and when I grasped my fellow sufferer's arm and kicked my way to the surface, I found myself not well out in the deep but only a yard or two away from the very piling from which I'd fallen.

The danger, however, was far from done. One may drown in a foot as well as a fathom. Moreover, the weight of the wench, my bare-skinned burden, threatened to pull me down.

"Help!" I cried, and in fact went under.

Amazing how such a thin figure, more emaciated, even, than I, could weigh so much. Amazing, too, the sudden power of my own desire to live, which only moments before had been quite extinguished. Hence I kicked again, I clawed skyward, hauling the limp lady behind. Once more we broke the surface in a spray of foam. Hopeless! Helpless! The wharf was still out of reach.

Down I went again, drawn under by my companion's eerie avoirdupois. This time I did not think I possessed the strength to rise again. The only hope of saving myself lay in releasing the poor maiden I clutched in my grasp. Could I? Should I? I glanced at her again — at her wretched, wasted form, at her dark, floating hair. No! Never! With a wild beat of my bluchers I propelled myself to the light.

I was at my last gasp: no breath in my lungs to call for assistance, no force in my limbs to stay afloat. Then, as I was about to sink for the last time, the fatal third, an object, a stout stick, an alabaster rod, appeared before me. I looked up. There, lying prone on the dock, was Lewis! With both hands he held out — how dazzling it was in the sunlight, like a shining shaft of ice — his unstrapped limb. I seized it with one hand, even as, with the other, I kept the drowning damsel in tow. Thus did the black man draw the two of us to the pilings, from which I crawled onto the dry wooden planks of the pier. Together Lewis and I hauled up the frail female form. Immediately I bent over my sister in suffering. Poor creature! She lay with her eyes open and her thin lips clasped in a bitter line. Her hair was full of ringlets. Her girlish breasts neither rose nor fell.

"Tot," I murmured. *"Das Mädchen ist tot."*

Only then did I notice — and this was the reason why such a wasted body could have been so weighty — the two lead balls tied, like grotesque ornaments, round her ankles. On both were the clearly stamped words MASSACHUSETTS GENERAL HOSPITAL. This was no suicide; nor was she a victim of drowning. Cause of death: tuberculosis. Here was a pauper. Thrown without pity to a watery grave.

I turned to the man who had saved my life. He was leaning by the piling, propped up on his natural leg. The artificial one I still clasped in my hand. I held it up toward its owner. "Take it, Lewis. Put it on."

The old fellow frowned. He shook his head.

"But it belongs to you!"

The Negro spoke — but only after a lengthy pause. "I can, Mr. Pinto, stand on wood as well as ivory."

"What does this mean? A change of mind? You now agree? To sell the limb?"

Lewis's thick lips spread in a smile.

"*Wunderbar!* And you will give me the proceeds, to buy my passage? You no longer insist that your doctor — I, no other — remain by your side?"

"Ah! But you will, Mr. Pinto. My parents crossed the ocean as slaves. I will return a free citizen — to bring freedom to others. Do you understand? I intend to join the struggle. We shall fight side by side. Together!"

2

So it was that one month later two men, one pale, the other dark, set out one night upon the Charles in a small blue skiff. Our destination was not the continent of Europe — at least not directly; instead we floated toward the large mossy timbers upon which the outermost section of the hospital jutted over the river. The fact was, we were no nearer our goal than in the month of July. The ivory, once we sold it, fetched only $40 — and this when we required two tickets, not one. To save money, the two of us had moved in together in my subterranean den. Lewis sold his oranges to the fishermen, while I, braving the taunts of my former classmates, returned to mopping the floors of the Braman's Baths. At the end of four weeks we had, with our earlier savings, the sum of $65. At this rate it would take more than a year, perhaps even two years, to reach the front.

Meanwhile the first refugees from the '48 Revolution had begun to arrive on our shores. The tidings they brought were grim. One by one the new, free nations of Europe were overcome by the imperial armies. Even in France, the cradle of the revolution, hungry workers were fired on by the soldiers of the republic itself. Worst of all was the news that the defenses of Pressburg had been broken and that the Austrians had shelled the very banks of the Danube where the *Technisches Gymnasium* was located. In my mind's eye I saw the rows of lindens in flame, the rubble of brick and glass and stone, and the voices of my schoolmates calling out, *Doktor! Helf uns! We need a doctor!*

It was out of desperation, then, that I hit upon a plan that would advance not only our cause but that of science as well. The key to its success was the little craft that Professor Bosworth had once used to sail back and forth to his home in Cambridge, and which had lain at the ambulance dock ever since he'd retired. While I made arrangements at the Braman's Baths, Lewis pried up the floorboard where we hid our tiny treasure and took fully half our savings to the marine warehouse close by the mast yard.

There he purchased a De Groot brand diver's suit, together with air hose and line. To this he added a whale-oil lamp and a curved oyster knife. The two of us met at the hospital dock at the end of day. The hawser of Bosworth's boat was rotted and the sail blown away. But the oars were intact, as was the well-caulked hull. In the half-light we entrepreneurs climbed aboard and severed the last strands of rope. Lewis took the oars, pulling us into the current that soon brought us beneath the General Hospital. We tied up to one of the massive pillars. Awkwardly I donned the rubberized suit and screwed on the bulb of the helmet. Then the two of us waited.

An hour, two hours, went by. The life of the hospital rumbled away over our heads. The floorboards creaked and thudded. Now and then a panel would open and a shaft of light pierce our murky grotto. Lewis would seize the oars while I slammed shut the round glass mask — only to have a bucket of slops or a bucket of sewage pour through the open trap onto the river surface. The wait resumed.

The night was a cold one. Through my vulcanized garment my fingers and toes were going numb. Lewis, trembling himself, wiped the stinging salt spray from his eyes.

"Mr. Pinto. My hands are frozen. Even the wood in my leg is aching. I fear we must return."

At that very moment, twenty yards off, a new panel opened, larger than any of the others. I cut the line. Lewis snatched up the oars. The boat moved forward. Lewis glanced round. "Look," said he. I stared through my porthole. Down from the hospital floor, in beams of yellow light, came a kind of cage, slats of wood nailed together, like a trap for lobsters. But this box was bigger, wider, and completely filled with what looked like a huge silk cocoon. From that white mass protruded a human foot, a human arm, each weighed down with a metal ball.

"Ah," said I, just before shutting the glass. "The poor pauper."

We sat, watching, as the cage dropped lower. Then, just as it seemed it must strike the water, one side sprang open, and the dead soul within tumbled to the Charles.

A moment's confusion: the cage drew up; the panel closed; and our dinghy rocked side to side. Then, of a sudden, the corpse in its shroud shot under the hull and, sinking rapidly, entered the main river channel. Lewis pulled after it, bending his oars in the current. With a splash, boots first, I went over the side. This time no sun penetrated the deep. The only light came from our whale-oil lamp, which Lewis had attached to our stern. I groped in the inky waters. The sound of my own labored breath filled my ears. Then something white, like the underbelly of a fish, crossed my porthole. The sheet! The winding cloth! I grabbed for it. The body, a blur, slipped away. I snatched again. Nothing: mere liquid. A third attempt: here was a bare, bony limb. I clasped it close and pulled on the line. Lewis hauled the two of us upward, hand over hand, until we broke the surface in a geyser of bubbles and air. It took but a moment to bring the corpse on board. Clumsily I followed, clawing at the helmet that encompassed my head. Then my partner held up the glowing lamp. Here was no mermaid, no undersea maiden. A male, approximate age 60, approximate weight 140 pounds. Also a consumption victim.

The hardest work, the most difficult physical labor, lay ahead. By then the skiff had drifted almost into the harbor reaches. Lewis and I took turns, bending our backs for stretches of ten minutes at a time. Thus we rowed upstream, past the hospital, all the way to the Braman's Baths, where the professor of anatomy had agreed to meet us.

About our scheme little was new. For some fifteen years all the cadavers for anatomy classes had had, in one way or another, to be smuggled to the dissecting hall. That was because the use of human subjects was banned by commonwealth statute. A whole industry had evolved, with ghastly coach rides over the borders of neighboring states. One schooner ran a regular route, Baltimore–Boston, loaded with corpses and ice. At the prices charged — up to $50 for a single cadaver — the college could afford to conduct no more than one or two classes a week. That was why, near midnight of a cool, late summer evening, Professor Piper and his son awaited the arrival of an old man and a youth at the back of the Braman's Baths.

"You are late," called the head of the anatomy section, a man so thin, so gaunt, one would have thought he had been driven to demonstrate his craft on himself.

"Have you got him?" asked young Ben, from dock's end.

"*Ja!* For certain!"

The blue dinghy struck the wharf. Ben Piper, only a few years older than I, seized the line. He held a lamp of his own. His hair, cut long, was free of his woolly cap. "Hand him up."

Lewis reached for the corpse, while the dissector bent to receive it. Awful the way its mouth fell open, as if it meant to protest. Professor Piper threw down four silver coins.

"*Moment,* sir. Did we not agree to a sum of six dollars?"

"I have made a deduction," the older man replied. "You neglected to remove the weights. Each is stamped with the mark of the Massachusetts General Hospital. That is a danger to us all."

Then Ben Piper threw the rope into the dinghy and, bracing himself against the side of the landing, kicked the craft and its crew back into the flow of the Charles.

The Charles? That river might have been the Acheron, the Styx: over the next six weeks we two boatmen, like old Charon on his raft, ferried scores of the dead to the dissecting halls at the baths. On some nights we waited in vain through the wee hours; on others, particularly after the start of the cold fall weather, we hauled as many as three pneumonia cases on a single trip upstream. Then, at the start of the new year, 1849, the Charles froze down to the Cambridge Bridge and we beached the boat at the shore. Our earnings came to something over $200, leaving us with a debit of $100. The next step was all too obvious. Why not do as others had done before us? That is, take the dead from their earthen graves. Nothing stood in our way but ignorance, superstition, fear. "And the frozen ground," Lewis remarked.

"We shall let others dig for us," I responded, tapping the side of my head in the international sign for intelligence. What I meant was that my colleague and I should disinter the dead on the day — the night, rather — they were buried. Even I was surprised at how easily this was done. On Winter Place, next to the Masonic Temple, was a small mortuary, which listed the names of those to be buried, much as the title of a sermon is displayed in front of a church. Every other day, on average, a small procession formed in front of the temple, then marched behind the black hearse down Tremont Street to the burial ground at the Common's edge. The firm of Lewis and Pinto, the one partner limping, the other in ankle-high bluchers, drew up the rear. Afterward, in the darkness, it was a simple matter to locate the grave, dig through the loosened earth, and carry the fully clothed corpse — disguised, when need be, as a drunken companion — through the deserted streets to the landward side of the baths.

Thus passed the long winter days. It was not the numbing

weather alone, the bitter blasts, that froze my spirits. The deeper chill came from Europe. The fact was, whenever there was no funeral I would prowl the docks in search of foreign journals, stuffing the scraps of newsprint — each containing worse news, more setbacks, than the one before — beneath my clothing, against the biting wind. It seemed more and more certain we would never reach Europe in time.

However grim the tidings, Lewis refused to despair. His one great hope was to address the great European Parliament at Frankfurt. He wanted to explain his own scheme of government — or non-government — which he called the Invisible Assembly. As best I could understand it, the African's vision called for the revolution to continue virtually forever. Thus, just as the kings and emperors had been forced to cede power to the parliaments, so those bodies must voluntarily abdicate to smaller and smaller governing units, down to the level of the individual factory, or farm, or apartment block. All signs of central authority would simply melt away.

"Think of it," the old fellow declared one morning as, chilled through, distraught, I returned from the docks. "No armies. No guardsmen. Not even a policeman upon a horse. Mr. Pinto: can you imagine the city of Boston governed this way?"

Bitterly, I shook my head. "The only place such a society will be found is on the Isle of Utopia."

Slowly the black man — I could see where his dull razor had scraped his rough skin, and the yellowish tint that surrounded the pupils of his eyes — stood on his ill-matched legs. "No. Utopia will be made on this earth. Here is the conclusion of the address that I shall deliver at Frankfurt: 'When each man is responsible for his own life and controls no other, then will he discover that all men are his brothers. On that day the Goddess of Liberty will reign in the land. Music will fill the air, as will a golden light. In a free nation, all men are dancing.' "

But this speech, so noble, so full of ideals, only increased my anguish. "Brotherhood! Dancing! Golden light!" Now I began to pull the newsprint from under my shirtfront and throw the scraps about our freezing room. "Here is brotherhood! Here is dancing! Instead of fighting the Imperial Army, the Czechs are fighting the Germans, and the Magyars the Slavs!" Nor was I done. The cruel words poured from me, as if the ink in the papers, with all its sad syllables, had seeped into my skin and infected the blood. "The

Habsburg emperor, the same who was driven from the streets of Vienna, has now returned. To the cheers of the very workers who manned the barricades! Mankind! It takes a step forward only to take two steps back! It is like the paradox of Zeno. Nothing arrives at its destination. No goal is ever reached!"

"No, no," Lewis objected. "Consider the two of us. Soon we shall stand on the soil of Europe."

"Never!"

"But we have saved almost the whole cost of passage —"

Now, out of despair, I began to rave like a madman. "It has nothing to do with money! Even if we could sail on the Great Western steamer, we would never make land. Haven't you logic? Haven't you sense? In order to cross the full ocean we must first cross the half; and in order to cross the half we must first cross the quarter, and then half of that, and so on, *ad infinitum*. A half of a half of —"

But, as in proof of this very theory, I never concluded. The old man came limping toward me. "The flaw," he said, "is in your logic, not mine. Your thinking would mean the sun itself could never rise to the zenith. Look, Mr. Pinto. Do you see?"

Here the cripple threw open the door to our underground room. The sun, blazing and brittle, was indeed at the high point in the sky.

Lewis: "It is no different with the revolution. The march of progress is slow, but it is sure. The dawn has already come. Have faith, Mr. Pinto. We shall see the bright day."

Slowly. Surely. That was how we continued our own daily and nightly rounds, until one brisk morning in March. On that day we two make-believe mourners stood, as always, at the corner of Winter Street and Winter Place, where the cortege for the latest funeral was forming. Just as Lewis and I were about to take our place at the end of the line, a sound — voices, tramping feet — came from the bottom of Tremont Street. I stepped forward to peer down that avenue. A group of latecomers was rushing toward us. Lewis saw them as well. "These are not mourners," he said.

All too true. This crowd hurried en masse up the slope. Those in the vanguard swept right by the intersection, ignoring the little parade of the bereaved. At Park Street they turned and, trotting, running, made for the State House on Beacon Hill. Before either

I or my companion could react, we found ourselves in the center of this pack. Now more and more people rushed from the side streets; they dashed from the buildings. Even those in the funeral procession began to join the throng. Everyone — men, women, some children, too — was pushing forward, up the street, through the muddy reaches of the Common, to the sunlit dome on the hill.

"Lewis! Lewis!" called I, clinging to a lamppost while the mob streamed by. "Where are you?"

"Mr. Pinto! My friend!" I turned. Above the others, the head of my partner, with its circlet of tufted hair, was bobbing along. He waved once, and then allowed himself to be carried away. I hesitated. What was occurring? Inauguration of the governor? Declaration of war? Had America joined the struggle abroad? Even as I debated the matter, my grip on the lamppost loosened. The next thing I knew I, too, was being swept upward, drawn into the funnel that led first to the steps of the State House and then into the rotunda itself.

Beneath the great dome the crowd was slowly revolving. Silent, hushed, it seemed to move according to some physical law — perhaps the same that governed the action of whirlpools — in a narrowing counterclockwise circle. Looking left and right for my colleague, I shuffled with the others toward the vortex. Once there, at the center, I was struck by a blinding light. My first thought was that the noonday sun had moved to a spot directly over the Bulfinch dome, so that its rays were glancing through the window at the top. But an instant later I saw that the illumination came from below, from a clear glass box, inside of which was a fist-sized nugget of gold. How that rock, in all its facets, gleamed! I could not help but think this was a kind of lodestone, a magnet, drawing the rays of sunlight down from above, just as the maelstrom sucks in the beads and bubbles on the tide. More onlookers pressed round, gaping, pushing, as if they too were being pulled to the very center.

Then, of a sudden, I saw a thing that made me jerk back, aghast. Just opposite, on the far side of the clear cabinet, was my dear companion. His dark face, crushed against the glass, was distorted — the thick lips spread, the eyes bulging wide, the cheeks pressed flat. All ten fingers were splayed against the transparent surface. To my horrified gaze he appeared like a man who was drowning, though his chest heaved and his lungs sucked in the gold-tinted air.

3

In this manner, a full year and more after Marshall had found his shining pellets, I learned of the gold strike in the west. Nor was I the only one who had remained ignorant of the great event. As far as the rest of the country was concerned, the discovery in California might have occurred on another planet. In the first place, it took months for the news to reach the eastern cities; and even when it did, the citizens took no more than passing notice. Only at the start of 1849, when President Polk told Congress that the rumors of the find were accurate, did the full force of the mania strike the States. What a thunderbolt then! Suddenly no tale — nuggets a man could sit on, for example, or gold flakes one pulled from the mine shafts like bark — was too tall to be true. At about the same time the Philadelphia mint assayed the samples sent round the Horn: they proved out at very near the standard for United States coinage. It was one of those samples — behind glass, glittering, full of light — that my companion and I discovered beneath the State House dome.

DREAM OF CORTEZ REALIZED: so read the headline of the *Boston Record*. The *Herald* said, "The coming of the Messiah or the dawn of the millennium could not create more frenzy among our citizens than this stone of California." These were the papers that old Lewis read and reread, with as much avidity as I had perused the scraps of the *Prager Tagblatt*. There was no denying that the black man had succumbed to the frenzy. He spent all day, every day, on Beacon Hill, until the traveling exhibit, the lemon-sized nugget, moved on to another city. Then he repaired to our subterranean chamber, not once stirring out. He no longer spoke about universal suffrage or the Invisible Assembly or our impending journey. Indeed, he hardly uttered a word of any kind. It was as if he had been struck in the head not by the stone from California, as the *Herald* called it, but by a rock from the surface of the moon.

Clearly something had to be done — and that quickly. For not only was Lewis crazed, all of Europe seemed to be going mad. The news I read at the docks was more discouraging than ever. In the French plebiscite the revolutionary parties had been rejected by hundreds of thousands of votes. Prince Bonaparte, the new Napoleon, was now president. Then, on a warm, windless, spring-like day, I came across the worst news of all: the Hungarian emperor had abdicated, only to make way for another tyrant, his young nephew Franz Joseph. The Habsburgs would go on forever!

Even as I stood on the India Wharf, the newsprint clutched in my hand, I came to a decision. I knew that our treasure consisted now of some $300 — enough for two tickets at the cheapest rate. Without a second thought I strode to the shipping office at the end of the wharf and booked passage on the *J. Q. Adams*, bound for Cardiff and Brest. The shipping clerk pointed her out: a small, trim clipper, anchored well out in the inner harbor, by the number-five buoy. Half of her sheets were down, hanging slack, unruffled by the slightest breeze. Nothing moved in that dead air, not even a gull. A lone side-wheeler picked its way among the marooned sailing ships. According to the clerk, the *J. Q. Adams* had in fact been scheduled to leave the previous day but — a stroke of luck for Lewis and me — had been stranded in port by the calm. She was fully loaded and would depart at the first wind. It was fair warning. The clerk would inform the purser to hold our berths; it was up to the passengers, once we had paid the fare, to get to the boarding ladder on time.

With giant steps I loped the half-mile back to our cellar. There was little to pack, no business to conclude, nothing to prevent us from boarding the tender within the hour and rowing directly to the waiting vessel. "Lewis! Mr. Lewis!" I called, while stumbling down the stairs to our abode. "Great news! We have passage! We sail with the wind!" I flung open the door and stepped inside. "The ship is the *J. Q. Adams*! Named for the sixth president. Foe of slavery. Founder of the Smithsonian Museum. And a Harvard man!"

No reply. "Friend Lewis!" I cried out again. Still silence. The room was deserted. Not only that: the floorboard, the one under which we'd hidden our fortune, was wrenched upward and the money itself, to the last hard-earned penny, was gone. "Help! Thief!" I shouted, and dashed back to the street.

The search for the missing man lasted all morning. I went first to the rotunda, thinking that perhaps a new exhibition had replaced the one that had departed. Then to the hospital area — the ambulance dock, the Braman's Baths. Still no Lewis. Next back to the harbor, in case my partner had returned to the cellar. Nothing had changed: the floor gaped wide, and no one was home. I searched through the room to see what else had been taken. Only the money, together with the leather-covered volume of Burns. Over and over I racked my brains. One thought, and that a dark one, kept returning to mind: that robbers had broken in, taken the treasure, and dropped the old man in some secluded spot, wounded or dead. Dead? That was it! I struck my forehead, where the dull wits were stored. The Masonic Temple! Winter Place! The funerals! Why had I not looked there from the start? With no further delay, I climbed the familiar stairs for the very last time, and set off across the center of town.

It was mid-afternoon by the time I approached the Common. Before arriving at Tremont, I found the way blocked by a crowd. What was this? Another cortege? The closer I drew to the thoroughfare, the greater the numbers became. Over the heads of the men and women I could see a number of high, rounded shapes, moving, swaying, one behind the other. For one mad moment I thought, *Elephants, Indian elephants,* such as I had viewed at the Circus Prague. With sharp elbows I pushed to the curb. Here were no members of the order Proboscidea, but numberless oxen, horses, mules. These beasts were pulling a long line of high-bedded wagons, whose closed tops I had seen sailing above the crowd. There was writing, crude painted signs, on the stretched canvas. ATLAS CO., one read. Another: SPARTAN BAND. A third, oxen-drawn, was surrounded by musicians playing flutes and drums. The name was on a board hung from the back: ROUGH AND READY.

The whole procession was moving downhill to the Common. Many of the onlookers had started to run there as well. I'd just made up my mind to join them when a loud cheer broke out from further up the incline. Down the road now, with sparks flying from the iron-clad wheels, came a cluster of four covered wagons. Even before I saw the sign—JOHN HARVARD CO.—I realized that here was a band of professors and students. They had turned themselves into what seemed a military unit: gray uniforms, with a stripe down the pants. Each man carried a rifle, a revolver, a sheath knife. The professors, like officers, wore sabers at their belts.

The first of this group went by, to shouts, to cheers. "Hello, Pinto!" came the cry from the second. I looked up. High on the driver's bench, cracking a whip over the heads of the oxen, was the blond-haired Matt Cole. The wagon swept by. The brakeman,

I noted, was Parrott, one of my Latin pupils. He was striving to keep this second wagon from running up the back of the first. Beside him, wearing a saber, was Professor Piper. Next to the vehicle ran Chaffee, red cap and all, who was pouring water over the smoking wheels. Bouncing, careening, steaming, the wagon swept down the hill. Seated within the puckered arch was none other than Professor Bosworth, now retired, with the former Goody Peacock, his wife.

I stood aghast while the caravan continued to lumber by. Had the entire faculty been stricken with the fever? The students as well? At the front of the third wagon I saw more familiar faces — those of Buffum and Gill and Hayward, all red-faced, excited, as if they had been drinking. At the back, poking through the drawstrings, was a swivel gun. Ben Piper was seated behind it, his long black hair curled at his shoulders. Now the fourth Conestoga, half out of control, teetering, rushed past. The oxen slipped on the cobblestones. Here, too, students trotted by the side, throwing water on the wheels. Just then I suffered a terrific shock. For standing upright beneath this last wagon's arch, clinging to the hickory rib, was none other than Lewis! He wore his own cloth coat, his familiar white shirt; but the trousers were gray, with a crimson stripe. Company issue! Filled with alarm, I dashed into the roadway and ran downhill.

At the Common the parade had turned into something like a fair. The gold-rush companies were literally selling themselves. Some had drawn into circles, as if to protect the train from marauders. Others had slipped canvas from the wooden ribs to reveal their appointments — like staterooms, some of them, in ocean-going ships. The members of John Harvard had drawn up in military order and were marching like Hessians back and forth below a crocus-covered knoll. Lewis, hatless, his woolly arc of hair showing clearly in the gathering twilight, was among them, hobbling along as best he could.

I sloshed across the muddy Common toward my friend. The Bostonians, all raucously shouting and shoving, made it difficult to reach him. All around people were attempting to buy places aboard the expeditions or, failing that, shares in the gold-mining ventures. It was like a great outdoor auction, with the buyers waving their money and calling their bids. Finally, I elbowed my way through to the John Harvards and seized my partner's thin arm.

"Lewis! Mr. Lewis!" I said.

Just then, at the edge of the crowd, there was a fresh commotion.

"A redskin!" somebody shouted.

The throng parted and Professor Hayward walked toward us, carrying what looked to be a living being. I peered more closely: this was a pasteboard person, an Indian, with a scowling mouth and black pupils in wide, staring eyes. Hayward, his monocle flashing, propped the life-size brave against the dark dirt of the knoll. Then, closer by, the elder Piper barked a brief command: the students — Buffum, Chaffee, Parrott, and the rest — dropped to one knee and raised their rifles to the shooting position. At the back of a nearby wagon, young Piper turned the barrel of his swivel gun until it pointed at the scowling savage.

"Gentlemen," Piper shouted, lifting his saber in the air. "A Pawnee!"

There was brief pause. I stood on the toes of my bluchers for a better view. This was not the first Indian I'd seen in my life. Once, when I was a child, age five, age six, my grandfather, old Papa Pinto, had taken me to the traveling troupe of the Circus Prague. A sideshow had the name *Die Drei Wilden Indianer Führer*. The three chiefs stood dark-skinned, with frowns. At the sight, I, the puny Pinto, had burst into tears. *"Feuer!"* I'd howled. *"Flamme!"* I'd thought the feathers of the bonnets were flames coming out of their heads.

"Shoot him! Shoot the redskin!" Thus came the cries from the Yankee crowd.

I was no longer a child of six. I knew full well that this Indian was no more real than the three painted gypsies at the Circus Prague. "Ho! Ho!" I laughed, pointing to the firing squad. "That is only a paper Pawnee. And those are mock weapons."

At that instant Piper dropped the point of his saber and the rifles, real ones after all, went off in a terrific explosion and a flash of blinding light. The Indian, with his painted feathers, his staring eyes, the black line of his frowning mouth, vanished in a wisp of vapor. Then even this plume disappeared on the breeze.

A shout went up from the students, from the gathered crowd. They gave a cheer.

But I stood thunderstruck. *The breeze!* No doubt about it. The smoke from the volley had also blown off. A chill gripped me, though it was not caused by the setting of the sun. This wind would doom us! "Lewis! The calm has ended! Come, friend! I have passage on the *J. Q. Adams*. The ship is about to depart."

Lewis withdrew his arm from my grasp. He shook his head. "I am sorry, Mr. Pinto. I cannot accompany you across the sea."

"Not accompany? What can you mean? What has occurred? Were you robbed? Who has taken the money?"

Slowly the old man reached into his jacket pocket. "Money? Here is the money." What he withdrew was not our actual savings but a receipt, a piece of parchment, for that sum. It identified the bearer as a member in full of the John Harvard Company, required to share in the tasks of the three-thousand-mile venture, and entitled to a fraction of the profits at journey's end.

"But this is not possible! You are an *Afrikaner!*"

Lewis smiled. He turned aside. Even as he did so I saw once more how his eyes, round the pupil, the whole of the sclera, had turned the color of gold.

Now I heard a flapping sound. I looked about the Common. Everywhere the wagon tops had started to billow, like so many sails. The end of the lull! "Lewis! Do you hear? There is not a moment to lose!" But when I turned back I discovered that the Negro had disappeared into the crowd.

By the time I reached the riverbank, the thick of night was upon me. The only way I could think to reach the *J. Q. Adams* was our old wooden skiff. The little craft was where we had beached it months before, hidden by an outcropping of the shore. Inside were the oars, the whale-oil lamp, the suit of vulcanized rubber. Also water, gallons and gallons of it, sloshing about the hull. A leak? Puncture? Or merely residue of snow and melted ice? The latter, since the dinghy, once bailed, did not refill. I stepped over the gunwale and cast off. The skiff darted into the stream. There was little to do but dip an oar into the current, and with that rudder keep the course. Quickly I sped under the Cambridge Bridge, past the General Hospital, and into the harbor's ebbing tide. The water turned from fresh to salt. The wind, blowing stronger than ever, swept me further out, into the deeper, darker water.

At the shore, the waterfront was all lights and motion. Figures ran on the docks. The black bulk of cargo rose in the air. Shouts floated over the water, with snatches of singing, the rattle of chains. A hundred ships, it seemed, were about to set sail.

Through the din came the clang and clank of what I judged to be the number-five buoy. To reach it, I'd have to row against the wind. Five minutes, ten, went by. A cold sweat broke out on my face. Blisters burst on my fingers. Still the buoy's din seemed no nearer. Suddenly, off to one side, a sleek schooner loomed out of the darkness, bearing down from forty yards off. The three lanterns on her mast seemed to be almost directly above my tiny craft.

Time to row in earnest. The dark ship hissed by, half swamping the open dinghy. I heaved on the oars until the outline of the cone-shaped buoy came near. I drew near the tilting metal cage and, after a half-dozen failed attempts, lit the wet wick of the lamp. *3*. That was the number that covered the side: *3*. *Dong-dong*, I heard off to the south: *dong-dong-dong*, like the chimes on a clock. What choice but head in that direction? Off I launched, into the dark. After a long haul the round red bottom of the buoy, like a bobbing apple, hove into view. On it, etched quite plainly, was the number 2.

"Ho-ho-ho! *Zwei! Nicht fünf!* Jolly joke!"

From the harbor, from the dark city of Boston, not a word. Instead, from all around, from every compass point, I heard a chorus of clanging. Which way to go? I imagine all the idiot buoys, floating under their pointed dunce caps, their clappers lolling like bright red tongues. *Dong-dong-dong*, they went, meaning, mournfully, *verloren, verdammt; verloren, verdammt:* lost and doomed.

Then, to the right, I heard a different sound, a hollow tin rattle, and saw a series of lights. Lanterns! Portholes! A ship! With all the strength left in my arms I rowed toward what had to be the number-five buoy. After an exhausting quarter-hour I drew up behind a tall three-master. It was obvious — from the shouts, from the pounding of feet on the decks — that the *J. Q. Adams* was about to sail. Indeed, as the skiff came round the bulging black wall of the stern, I heard the click of a winch, hauling the forward anchor. At the rear, a second chain stretched into the water; the skiff drew up beside it. "Ahoy! Brave sailors!" I called, while balancing upright in my pitching vessel.

No answer. The ship dwarfed the dinghy. A single lamp hanging from the taffrail rattled noisily as it swung along the pitch-coated planks of the stern. Then the winch started again and the chain that angled over the skiff grew taut. "No, no! Stop!" I gripped the dripping metal links, as if by main strength alone I could stop the anchor from rising. Amazingly, I did. A man peered down from the distant rail.

"Who's out there? What do you want?"

"A son of freedom! Who wants to sail with you!"

"Ship's full. We're weighing anchor. Get yourselves clear!"

"But I have a definite booking. Passenger Pinto. Bound for Brest. Here I am: just in time!"

The crewman laughed. "Brest? You mean the *Adams*. She left hours ago. At dusk."

At these words I felt myself grow light, like a piece of flotsam on the swell. Between my rowboat and the massive hull the churned-up waves made a choking sound. Not the *J. Q. Adams!* Then what could this vessel be? Before I could ask, the swinging lantern moved across the face of the stern. The light from its aperture lit up these peeling letters:

LIGHTNING

Charleston

"Lightning! Of the Atlantic Freight Line? Liverpool route?"

"What of it?" the crewman demanded. "I told you we've no places. Not a berth. We've got men asleep on the deck."

The brig, with one anchor up, wallowed heavily. The tossed-up spray stung my eyes. "Wait! Your medical officer — Mr. Frank Townsend. Call him. I must speak a word."

"Townsend?" said the sailor, moving aside. "He's already here."

Only then did I make out the tiny spot, hot and glowing, a few feet down the rail. What was it? Cigar!

"Mr. Townsend! Is it you?"

"Here I am, Adolph. And have been the while."

"Take me aboard! From friendship! From *Kollegialität!*"

The red tip brightened, faded. "Why do you want this? What are you after?"

"New career! Fresh start! A chance to join the struggle!"

Now the sailor interrupted. "How can we do it? Where would we put him? There's not a hammock aboard, even if he has the fare."

My fare! My passage! Only then, fool that I was, hapless Hungarian, did I remember what had become of our treasure.

Townsend, high overhead, lost in the darkness, barked out a

laugh. "Never mind. I'll find a place. Bring him up." With those words my friend crushed out his cigar: a shower of sparks spilled downward, winking out in the spray. In their wake came a hemp ladder, dropping like the one in biblical lore, out of the sky. With my raw, blistered fingers I grasped the first rung: the first step, I thought, in a new life.

No sooner had I boarded the *Lightning* than I was fast asleep. That is, I simply collapsed on the floor of the little room — it seemed a kind of surgical closet — to which Townsend led me. I heard the rattle of the anchor chain and felt the jolt of wind in the sails: oblivion next. I woke before dawn. For a time I lay disoriented in the dark, pitching cabin. It wasn't the sounds I heard — the creak and groan of woodwork, the tinkling glassware, the *thud-thud-thud* of the hull striking the sea — that confused me, so much as the noise I did not: the steady buzz of the snoring Negro. Lewis! I sat bolt upright. This was the first time in eight months I had not slept in the same room with my partner. I groaned. Poor old friend! Not to be able to cross the ocean as a citizen, as a free man! How could I have abandoned him? Could I not have seized him? Taken him on this journey by force?

At that moment the light of dawn touched the porthole. The sun! Its beams had never failed to fill the aged African with hope, with cheer: *we shall see the bright day*. I rose. I left the room and made my way to the narrow, turning stairway. If my companion could not stand before the Frankfurt Parliament, I would deliver the speech in his stead.

Once on deck I saw that the sun was well up in the sky. The ocean was aquamarine. A half-dozen gulls slipped back and forth over the path of our wake. The first thing that struck me was that of the great number of people aboard, filling every free foot of space, hardly a person was female. Then I realized that these men, too, were refugees, exiles, who had vowed to return to the fight in their native land. Everywhere on deck they were gathered in groups, playing cards, singing songs, reading to each other from books. Here and there sat a solitary fellow, knees clasped, staring up to the sky or out to sea. My heart surged at the good cheer, the camaraderie. I spread my arms to speak:

"Brothers! We may be leaving the home of freedom, but we carry the idea of freedom back to our home!"

A man looked up. Another shrugged. The boat rolled easily on the swell. One fellow took out an accordion; another stood on a hatch top and did a jig. A third leaned over the rail, staring at a distant spur of land.

Land! No mirage! An island! I strode forward on my sea legs to the nearest group of refugees. "Tell me, gentlemen. What is that spot?"

A thin man in a straw hat was the first to reply. "There, to starboard, that's Martha's Vineyard. In that mist to port, that's the island of Nantucket."

A second man joined in. "Last land we'll see today. Unless this wind holds to Block Island."

And a third: "Tomorrow, though, we'll be well down the coast. You'll catch the tip of Long Island before dark. That's called the Montauk Point."

I stood frozen, stunned as much by their accents as by their news. "You are not Hungarians?"

The chap in the boater gave a snort. "Myself, I'm from Buffalo, New York."

"Buffalo? New York? But why would you wish to flee to Liverpool?"

"Liverpool!" the second man exclaimed. "He thinks we're bound for Liverpool!"

Then the rest took up the cry, calling the word from man to man over the tilting deck of the ship. Even the gulls, motionless now, as if tied to strings, cawed out like the others: *Liverpool! Liverpool!*

Quickly I cast my eyes into every corner of the ship. These men were not carrying the weapons of freedom fighters. Not rifles. Not bayonets. Instead each had with him a pick, a shovel, an ax. What sort of soldiers were these? Next noted were the pens, with more cattle in them — calves, sheep, and pigs — than could ever be needed on a voyage west to east with the wind.

"Frank Townsend!" I shouted — for I had seen my former colleague leaning against the railing, near where he had stood the night before. "Is this not the *Lightning?* Are we not crossing the Atlantic Ocean?"

Townsend's arms were crossed on his chest. He grinned. "It is the *Lightning*. But like most ships on the Atlantic run, she's been refitted. In two months we'll reach the Horn and pass through the Strait of Magellan. Then it's up the Pacific, for two months more.

Adolph! You are going to California! So are we all. A new career, you said. A fresh start. So be it! This summer you shall be panning the rivers for gold!"

4

LATEST DEVELOPMENTS IN THE FIELD

> Our correspondent in the north reports the next boom town may be at the settlement of Yreka, near the Oregon frontier. No other topic is being discussed but the richness of the deposits there. Some of what he has heard defies the imagination. One story, widely in circulation, is that Mr. James McAdams, while washing his stockings one day at the Greenhorn Creek, fell asleep, leaving his hose to rinse in the stream. When he woke they were as shiny and golden as a babe's gilded shoes! One may question the particulars of that report, but there is no doubt that McAdams has not been alone in bringing down pure nuggets as big as any babe's fist; and no doubt either that the multitude, which thirst for gold from dimpled childhood to wrinkling age, will soon be crowding those parts from far and near. You may read developments here.

This story, a small one, at the bottom of the second page of the *San Francisco Chronicle*, affected the course of my life far more than anything I had read in the newspapers from Europe. The account of the northern gold strike appeared in the issue of January 5, 1850, just three days after Townsend and I had arrived in the city. The journey, you will note, took more than twice as long as my colleague had predicted. Not only that: we did not arrive aboard the *Lightning*, or, for that matter, any other sailing vessel. The reason was the storm, a three-day typhoon, that struck us in the Pacific, south of the Galápagos Islands. Until then the voyage, even the dread passage of the Horn, had been uneventful. Each June day was marked by fresh breezes; high, harmless clouds, flimsy as doilies; and calm, unruffled seas. At night, stretching behind us, the sea spread out in a phosphorescent wake.

"Look, Adolph," Townsend would say. "That is a boulevard of gold."

The storm struck unexpectedly, at night. We ran before it for hundreds of miles. The water flew over the bow in a divided stream, lifting, like the claws of a hammer, the planks of the deck. From where I'd lashed myself down in my tiny cabin I heard the longboats break from their moorings and crash into the hull. The cattle pens split and the calves and sheep, all lowing, slid into the deep. Every loose object rocketed about me, shattering against the walls. It was as if a crazed man had entered and set about with a poker. At the height of the blast the mizzenmast snapped and the *Lightning* went on her side. The swollen seas came down like an avalanche upon us. The poor ship trembled on the waves, like the little silver needle that the Herr Doktor Professor used to float in a pan of water. *Prinzip der Oberflächenspannung.*

Even at that moment of crisis Townsend refused to take cover. Indeed, throughout the storm he moved about the ship with his new camera, a metal Voigtlander, strapped to his chest. He came to the cabin — whose bottles were filled not with medicines, as I'd supposed, but with the chemicals of his craft — only to expose his plates to mercury vapors. At one point, during a lull, he drew one of his old copper sheets from a cabinet. Even in the light of the swinging lamp the reflection was blinding.

"What have we here? *Ein Spiegel?* A mirror?"

Townsend laughed. "Yes. A mirror with a memory."

Then, to my astonishment, he thrust the plate into my hands. "Turn it," he said. "Tilt it. You'll see."

I did as he directed. As if by magic an image appeared on the shining metal: a dim room, with three blurred forms inside it. "What is that place? I can't make it out."

"Look again."

No need to do so. Already a spasm, a tremor, was going through me, as if my body were the needle of a galvanometer and the copper plate, still clutched in my hands, conducted a current. Nor could I tear my eyes from the plate. There, emerging from its silvery mist, were three recognizable figures: myself, saw in hand; Matt Cole, twisting a tourniquet; and of course Lewis, staring wide-eyed, open-mouthed, at his half-severed limb. Hollis Hall! The experiment with ether!

"Ha! Ha!" Townsend laughed. "Your friend the nigger has come with you, after all."

I felt at this sight a terrible pang. This was worse than having to remember. It was as if I — and Cole, and Lewis, too — were being forced to live through the moment of agony again.

"Your camera! It is a time machine! It recaptures the past!"

"On the contrary. What you see is the future. The day will come when the camera will be present at every event. Nothing will go unrecorded: not the day Warren operated without causing pain, nor the moment Marshall discovered gold, nor even the normal events of daily life. If our ship goes down, its image will remain. On a score of plates! It's immortality, the dream of the Egyptians: to make the flow of time halt, to preserve the bodies of men and women just as they were, for a thousand years and more. But not in Paddy's rags!" Here Townsend, laughing, broke off, and pointed to where I clutched the daguerreotype in my arms. "No! On shining metal!"

There was a thunderclap. The ship shuddered as a wave struck it broadside. Townsend whirled round. "Ha!" he exclaimed. "Here's my light!" Then he dashed toward the upper decks. He spent the rest of the night attempting to capture the ship and the storm by the flashes of lightning that streaked across the sky like Lewis's potassium sticks inside the instantaneous Light Box.

By morning the storm had blown itself out and the sun shone bright. There was not a shred of canvas for what was now our single mast. The wind, however, was steady, and out of the west, so that we were able to limp back to Panama City with sails sewn from our clothes. Thousands of people were already packed into the tin shacks of the town, and hundreds more, gold-seekers all, arrived every day from across the isthmus. I descended into this throng, possessed only of the De Groot rubberized suit; the two bars of Maria Theresa rose-scented soap that I had found in the pocket of my belted jacket; and a ticket, issued by the Atlantic Freight Line, for passage on the steamer *Cherokee.*

That side-wheeler arrived on her regular run, San Francisco–Panama City, just three days later. A mob of forty-niners—prospectors, merchants, gamblers—was milling at the pontoon dock. When Townsend and I showed them our tickets, the men roared with laughter, and displayed theirs. Yet the steamship was already dangerously crowded. The identical scene was repeated as, day after day, week after week, each new vessel arrived. Three and four times as many tickets were sold as there were places.

Thus it was not until the end of that year that we two former students could find passage. Townsend, meanwhile, secured a room in a long, low, tin-covered building. After a week's fruitless search for lodgings, I moved in with him for the duration. It was only then that I discovered the daguerrian was sharing the space with a girl, a maroon-colored native. She wore a man's pants, baggy as a Turk's, and had tied a bright band of cloth across the top of her bosom, so that the breasts themselves, purple as plums, as aubergines, hung free. The name of this youthful female was Antoinette. During the night she and Townsend lay together in the room's only bed. The sight of her flashing teeth, the swish of her harem pants, filled me with agitation. Inside my chest my heart swelled to the size of a Polish ham.

In the morning this maiden, round-cheeked, with a knob of a nose, served oranges and coffee. She peeled the fruit and set it before us. She poured the hot black liquid into metal cups. Then, while I watched, she sat squirrel-like, gnawing on the end of a stick. Finally she leaned forward and spat the juice of the cane into the coffee. "Ha-ha-ha!" she laughed. "Sweet sugar from Antoinette!"

At the end of the month of December the three of us — Frank Townsend, myself, and the female Panamanian — secured berths on the steamer *Unicorn.* A mere four days later, on the second of January, we stood at the starboard railing while all around our fellow voyagers cheered, danced, and threw their hats into the air. Naturally there could be only one reason: ahead, on the horizon, the coastline of California had risen, shimmering in the haze.

It seemed that another four days must go by before we could actually reach the wharves of San Francisco. The harbor was filled with deserted ships, their sails in tatters, their hulls rotting through. Throughout the day the *Unicorn* was forced to maneuver inch by inch through what looked like a forest of masts and booms and spars. For those on board the delay was too much to bear. Well before our anchor went down the crew began to go over the side. They lowered the longboat. They rowed off in the dinghies. At that sight the passengers, in a frenzy to reach the diggings, began to leap into the shallow waters.

For the space of an hour I remained alone aboard the stock-still ship. How grim and full of discouragement was the prospect before me! For this jewel of the west, the metropolis of legend, seemed more primitive, even, than Panama City. The dwellings were made of paper and canvas, with roofs of tin, of zinc. In the twilight one could see candles shining through the walls. Lower down, near the bay, people were walking on the planks that had been thrown over the sticky mud. Garbage, refuse, dead animals even, were floating like a foam on the tide. And above, across the face of the various hills, chalk dust, swirls of it, little tornadoes, was blowing in the perpetual breeze.

Mr. James McAdams, while washing his stockings one day at the Greenhorn Creek. . . . In truth this little stream might have been named for the prospector in belted smoker, high-top bluchers, and checked gabardines, who, at the crack of dawn, knelt on its muddy shore. Here were the other accouterments he carried about him: woolly blanket; flat, shallow pan, like a frying pan without a handle; knapsack with bread loaf and bacon; shovel, pickax, box of wax candles; and a soft felt hat with drooping brim. The season was winter still, and the brisk morning air stung the fingers and numbed the toes. What was a greenhorn to do? Like thousands before me I knelt at the water's edge, filled up the pan's bottom, and swirled it around. Nothing showed but silt. I waded deeper, over my rolled-up cuffs. More sludge. More slime. On I went, hour after hour, along the slippery shore. By noontime, with the sun overhead, steam rose from my clothing, and I had become as black as a man who'd been tarred. There was no glitter in the bottom of the pan. *"Gott! Gott!"* The cry came by itself, unbidden, from my throat. No reply. No echo. No sound.

Thus, along the edge of this muddy gulch, in which not even worms were living, did I spend my first day at Yreka. The problem, I realized, was those thousands before me. If McAdams had ever passed that way, it had been long before. This became all too apparent on the next day, when I tried my luck at Humbug Creek. Humbug, indeed! The stream was bone dry. Not only that: shovel blades, worn-out shoes, rusted sardine tins, and tins for cheese or soup kept turning up in the dirt. The bed had long since been picked clean. Nonetheless, I slid down the bank and scooped the powdery earth onto my blanket. Then I tossed the corners until the dust blew away. I repeated the process for hours, stooping, standing, shaking, like a farmer winnowing wheat. But no golden grain appeared in my woolen threads.

Day three. South of Yreka. Hardscrabble Creek. Here, in the dry streambed, I found an open shaft. Leaving my tools behind, I scrambled down. The earth was braced with timbers to the bottom. After that a horizontal tunnel branched away. I followed by candlelight. After a time, crouching, finally crawling, I came to a spot where the ground dipped sharply to a pool of water. On impulse I plunged down and, on all fours, sucked in the drafts. An animal, perhaps a goat, perhaps a deer, had come that way too. Lifting my head, with the water streaming from my tiny moustache tips, I saw its white bones. Poor beast! Unable to climb the steep drop that, in its thirst, it had descended. And was I also trapped in that cavern? With a yelp, a yell, I went leaping up the incline, through the tunnel, and up the crumbling handholds of the shaft. At ground level, next to my knapsack, stood my partner, Frank Townsend. Grinning, in shirtsleeves, he put out his hand to help me to my feet.

"Come, Adolph! Hurry! I've found our fortune. I've staked our claim at Soda Creek!"

On the opposite side of Yreka, some two miles north of the town, a cluster of foothills, or, more correctly, a group of cinder buttes, rose abruptly into the air. The largest of these hillocks, Mount Etna by name, was not rounded off like all the others. Instead, the top seemed to have been sliced away, and in its stead was a wide, shallow depression filled to overflowing by a hidden fountain. This underground stream must have passed over molten rock, since the waters of the pond, milky white, bubbling, were sometimes hot to the touch and sometimes, more rarely, cool and crystal clear. The overflow from Etna Pond, running down the eastern flank of the butte, had carved out a gorge, which, because of its foaming, chalky waters, the miners called Soda Creek.

What a sight, when Frank Townsend and I arrived at the foothills, met my eyes! Many men were at work on the sides of Mount Etna, digging potholes, sinking shafts, sifting the earth and cinders. Many more — hundreds, it seemed — were spread out on the shores of Soda Creek, wading in the alkaline water or along the churned-up banks. The pickaxes flashed in the sunlight. The dirt flew in the air. The miners shouted to each other. They sang snatches of songs. Under my feet the earth actually trembled from the repeated blows. Townsend drew me along the edge of the gorge, where a series of tents — in reality only pieces of clothing or blankets stretched over sticks — had been erected. Upstream, where the river slipped over the hillside, on a wedge-shaped plot of land, Townsend's own jacket hung across four poles. "That's our claim," he explained, pulling me toward the spot. "Do you see? It stretches from there, by the coat, to there—where I've turned the soil. That's the practice: as far as a man can throw an ax."

I halted. "Who," I asked, "are those men?" Out of the multitude spread along both banks of the stream, two were briskly at work in the center of Townsend's plot.

"Those are the rules at Soda Creek. Any claim may be worked by any other claim holder, as long as the actual owner is absent. There is no actual owner, in fact—there's only the energy, the labor, that goes into the digging. Do you see these shirts? These coats and pants? The idea is, when the clothing rots through, and no one's been by to patch it, the claim is released outright. It belongs to the next man who comes along. The land is for those who will work it, the gold for those who will dig. That's what lies before us, my Adolph: work, and more work!"

I attempted to take this in. We owned the land and did not, both at once. It was as if we were leasing our claim from the rest of the Soda Creek miners and paying the rent with our labor. "But Mr. Townsend," I said. *"Das ist Kommunismus!* Who made such rules?"

My partner, however, had already resumed his trot down the sloping side of the hill. "We did!" he shouted. "There is no one else. The Mexicans have been defeated. The territory is not yet a state. Even if it were, there are no soldiers, no police, no judges. Why, there aren't even women. No children either. There is only the miner, with his pick, his pan, his courage. Do you feel it, Adolph? We are free. As free as men have ever been!"

I stood motionless, staring after my friend. The two anonymous miners were still at the water's edge, tipping a wooden box back and forth on its runners, as if they were rocking a cradle. Indeed, for the moment, all these men, wading, shouting, splashing, digging into the soil, seemed like hundreds of children at play upon the shore. They sang as they worked. How full, how clear, their strong-throated voices. With half-shut eyes I imagined I could hear the words of J. C. F. von Schiller, as sung by the comrades of my youth:

Alle Menschen werden Brüder,
Wo dein sanfter Flügel weilt.

With that sweet sound still echoing about me, I bounded down the incline, into the bubbling stream. My laced-up bluchers sank into the soil at the bottom. Like the fabled socks of McAdams, they would soon be covered with gold.

That same night you might have seen me pouring the contents of my gold sack upon the zinc bar top of the Sazarac Saloon. "Schnapps!" That's what I shouted. "Schnapps for everyone!" The crowd pushed close, while the barkeep wet his fat fingers and began to measure the pinches of dust. I glanced up, above where the row of bottles stood like soldiers, each with its little silver helmet, to the gilt-edged mirror. There, beneath the floppy brim of a hat, was a reflection that could only be my own: drooping eyes, long nose, mole on cheek, cleft on chin. The work in the sun had barely darkened my pale white skin, but the thin pencil strokes of a moustache now clung vertically to the space above my upper lip. The lip itself was thick and puckered, as if sewn from too much cloth.

My gaze now drifted higher, to where the painting of a plump, naked woman hung upon the wall. This pink figure lay on a grassy field, floating, it seemed, upon the tip of an elbow. Her hands supported the back of her head, with its loose golden tresses. A wisp of something — it might have been silk, it might have been smoke from the gentlemen's cigars — passed over her full breasts and round belly and the ruddy flesh of her thighs. The genius of the artist was such that wherever one sat, at the bar, like myself, or at the faro tables, or in the pit for rouge-et-noir, the eyes of this lady seemed to be gazing solely in that direction.

In confusion, I, a non-drinker, reached for the whiskey glass. I threw the dark liquid down my throat. On the balcony a fiddler sawed at his fiddle, while below, on the saloon floor, a piano player pounded away at his ivory keys. The gamblers stamped their feet to the tune. They banged their tumblers on the table-tops. People whooped and shouted. The gas flames among the chandelier's crystal lozenges glittered and glowed. A thought, like a fly, kept buzzing inside my brain. Why did this scene, and these happy people, seem so familiar? When, where had I been in a place such as this? Before I could think of an answer, the music suddenly stopped and the whole room, so full of noise, of animation, grew still.

Then the violinist tucked his instrument under his chin. It wasn't a jig this time. It was a slow, sad tune. " 'Lily Dale,' " murmured the barman, folding his thick arms on his barrel chest.

For a moment the miners merely listened. Outside the night was black. No moon, not a star, showed through the windowpanes. The sad song floated down. Then, when the piano player joined in, one man put an arm on another man's waist. That second man lifted his arm to the first man's shoulder. With clasped hands they turned. A new couple formed, partner bowing to partner. The musicians came to the ballad's end and played the notes once again from the start. The floor filled with dancers. They glided and turned. The next thing I knew a tall man with a full beard and yellow suspenders came to the bar and held out his arms. All befuddled, I stepped within them. The miner's hand gripped the small of this greenhorn's back. Together the two of us, the grown man and the youth, turned in a circle.

Then, of a sudden, I knew why this room, the Sazarac Saloon, seemed so familiar. Surely this was the vision, the Frankfurt address, of old Lewis: the lights, the music, the plump form of the golden-haired woman, who might have been the Goddess of Liberty herself. This dance floor was crowded with a new species of person — brave, free, modern-thinking men. Tears came to my eyes and fell on the cloth of the stranger's jacket: tears, first, of sorrow, that Lewis could not be here to see his dream's fulfillment; next, tears of joy for myself. Now I knew I had not boarded the wrong boat after all. I had sought the revolution, and here the revolution was, the new order, the Isle of Utopia. Again the pianist stopped; the violinist broke off. The only sound in the room was the squeak of the dancers' shoes, the steady *thump-thump* of their boots on the dance floor. In silence, with no melody, they continued to circle, each of them looking — *Alle Menschen werden Brüder* — into his brother's eyes.

CHAPTER THREE

The Discovery of Neptune

1

FROM THE AGE of the Greeks, and certainly since the discoveries of Copernicus, of Kepler, it has been clear to all freethinking men that the solid-seeming earth is in fact a ball of boiling gases, spinning around the even hotter sphere of the sun. On the edge of the continent, in what was soon to be the thirty-first state, every Californian knew that the crust that separated him from fire, from molten rock, was as fragile as paper, and nearly as thin. In the spring of 1850, for example, the whole of Etna Pond began to bubble and fizz, and by the end of April had boiled away to a series of stagnant pools. Soda Creek, of course, dried up on the spot. The miners hoped to pump the water from Greenhorn Creek to their claims; before the first length of pipe could be laid, however, even that muddy trickle had vanished. That was when a good number of Yrekans moved on — south, some of them, to the Mad Mule mine, or the Milkmaid at French Gulf; others to the Oregon seacoast, where, they had heard, the gold flakes were washed onto the beach by waves that never ran dry. As for the rest, the majority, they had no choice but to abandon their workings and either fan outward, off to the Siskiyou Mountains, off to the alkali plain, or move doggedly inward, following the hint of a lead into the streets of the town, sinking their pits and shafts beneath the foundations of the Metropolitan Hotel or in the alley behind the Sazarac Saloon.

No dancing now within those wooden walls. No music, either. The forty-niners stood at the bar, or sat slumped in their ladder-backed chairs. A green light, a reflection from the gaming tables, hung over the pit. Cigar smoke curled through it, the way water does in a glass of absinthe. Yet few of the miners bothered to lay down bets or swallow the drinks at their elbows. They were too busy passing from man to man — this was the real currency of the Sazarac — the news of the latest strike: those gold-washed beaches at Astoria, for instance; or a gigantic nugget, boulder-sized, dug up from under the snowcap at Shasta; or the tree, on the outskirts of Brandy City, whose trunk and branches had been petrified not into stone but sulfites of silver. Who in their right minds could believe such fantastic tales? Not a soul. But the bankrupt Yrekans were as gullible as any child turning the pages of the Brothers Grimm.

And what of those prospectors, Pinto and Townsend? My partner remained at Soda Creek longer than any of the other miners. Indeed, far from abandoning our wedge-shaped claim, he began to work the deserted land along the edge of the gully, and then to follow what he felt — by hunch, by instinct — must be the trail of the mother lode back up the slopes of the cinder butte. One need not be trained at the Harvard Medical College to recognize here the first symptoms of the fever that had gripped poor Lewis, along with so many thousands of others. Soon enough, Townsend began to buy outright what he thought were the most promising sites. To raise cash for these claims he rented a series of upstairs rooms at the Sazarac Saloon, and, after chopping a skylight into the roof, opened a studio for daguerreotypes. The forty-niners lined up in the hallway for portraits to send back to the States.

While Townsend was the last miner to remain at the buttes, I was among the first to depart. The whole month of May I spent in Yreka, gathering what was to be the inventory for my next venture — bolts of cloth, tins of food, sacks of beans and sacks of coffee, along with windup alarm clocks and needles and thimbles and pins. When my sack of gold dust was nearly depleted, I went to the Sazarac, whose owner, Judge Steele — not really a judge, though some said he had practiced that profession in the States — had advertised in the *Ingot* that he had a mule for sale. The animal was tied up in the alley at the back of the saloon. I stared through the shadows at the coal-black beast: a pair of eyes, dark and liquid-filled, stared back. I saw the long cat's whiskers and the thick, rubbery lips.

"What a darling! Such strong incisors!" So saying, I threw my arm around the mule's neck, with its coarse mane, its twitching ears. "Judge Steele! Name please your price!"

The rest of that warm June day was spent going back and forth between my room at the Metropolitan Hotel and this handsome hybrid. On each trip I carried another item from my stock of goods — a side of bacon, for example, or a pile of gold-washing pans. Finally, at nightfall, I slumped on a bar stool at the Sazarac Saloon. Why, you will ask, did I not simply bring the mule to the hotel and load it there? Because both my enterprise and my exit from town had to be secret. For the same reason, I did not dare leave the Sazarac until the last of the patrons had gone to sleep for the night.

Little did I suspect that the delay would last to three in the morning. The drinkers and gamblers seemed never to tire. When one game was over — whether rouge-et-noir, or faro, or vingt-et-un — a new one would begin. At midnight the Yrekans began to amuse themselves by teasing the Indian, Two-Toes Tom. That old fellow stood barefoot, wearing a calico shirt and a pair of trousers cut for a much larger man, waist size 40 or 42. Tom himself was skin and bones. His head, his forehead, like those of all grown Modocs, had been artificially flattened, so that it receded sharply into his shock of black hair. Trinkets, some of them shiny gold nuggets, hung from his ears. More gold was strung round his neck. He was grinning, smacking his lips, shifting his weight from his five- to his two-toed foot. Both hands, I saw, were busy: the right gripping a goblet half full of pink, foamy liquid; the left holding the waistband of his pants. The red man knew a few words of English. "Cherry cobbler," he said, draining the dregs of his glass.

"One dollar," said big Jeff Ruggles, the barkeep. He shook his silver canister so that the contents, the cobbler, splashed inside.

The Indian, already tipsy, paused. Then, slowly, he bent down, placed his empty goblet on the floorboards, and fished in the pockets of his pants: first the right pocket, then, awkwardly, the left.

"Broke!" he said. "Goddam!"

The white men laughed. One of them threw a coin at Tom's feet. Then all fell silent, intent on what the old man would do.

The Modoc bent at the waist, staring at the shiny silver. Then he picked up the coin and held it out toward the barman. "More cobbler," he demanded.

Ruggles, large and moustachioed, shook the canister once more, whipping the cocktail to a froth. But when he removed the top, there was no place to pour the contents.

"The glass," he said.

With the coin still in his hand, Tom turned round. He studied the problem: three objects; two hands. The Yrekans broke out in guffaws. Their faces, from ne plus ultras, from brandy smashes, were as red as the Modoc's.

"A philosopher!" shouted Arch Osborne, the stable owner. He pointed at the puzzled native.

Judge Steele laughed. "No wonder the redskins never discovered the wheel."

This was a factual statement: the Indian tribes dragged their belongings behind them on pairs of sticks. Nevertheless, it is unlikely that the face of the wheel's inventor, that first engineer, shone more brightly with the light of his inspiration than the wrinkled features of Two-Toes Tom now lit up with his. He leaned over the goblet, with the silver coin in the palm of his hand. Then he dropped the latter with a gay tinkling sound into the former: that is, the dollar into the wineglass, which he now picked up by its slender stem and thrust over the bar.

The white men laughed. They applauded. While they did so, the big barkeep plucked out his payment and filled the goblet to the top with the pink, pleasant brew.

The Modoc licked his lips. "Taste good," he said. "You betcher!"

I turned from this scene to look about the saloon. Above the mirror the golden goddess, the Venus, lay with her tresses flowing, her arms clasped behind her head. The crystal lozenges in the chandelier were gleaming. Across the deserted dance floor, on the far side of the room, a handful of gamblers were playing in the pit. I could hear the faint click of balls in the roulette chambers, and, in the keno cages, the sound of the tumbling cards. To my left the plush-covered staircase led to the rooms on the balcony level. Even at that hour a half-dozen miners were standing on line outside the daguerreotype shop. They wanted their portraits: an image of themselves, a fantasy in slouch hat and buckskins, with pickax and pan, to carry with them in the sad caravans that, heading eastward, already matched in numbers the wagon trains heading west.

And why — this was the thought that now struck me — should I not have my own likeness transferred to the memory mirror? After all, this was the last day, the last hour even, in which I could truly think of myself as a digger for gold. I had not contacted my family since the debacle at Hollis Hall. Now I could send them a portrait — yes, with the double wisps of a definite moustache — which they, in turn, would show all their neighbors in Pressburg: *Hier ist ein treuer Neunundvierziger!*

Ahead in the line was a man I recognized: the tall, bearded miner with whom I had once shared a dance on the floor of this very saloon. The color had faded from his gay suspenders. He stood with his hands tucked into his armpits; even his head was bowed. From fellow feeling I addressed him:

"Greetings, friend! For what person do you seek this portrait-souvenir? Mine is for Mother, for Father, for old Papa Pinto!"

Before my acquaintance could reply, the studio door opened and the previous sitter, Alf Meek, a miner, came out. At once the tall dancer ducked inside. My turn next. The wait was a short one. In less than a minute the second entrance, only a few feet down the hallway from the first, sprang open and the subject, a stranger, walked out. I strode by him, shutting the door behind. On the instant I knew something was amiss. Near darkness. Near blackness. Only the gleam of a single candle. Impossible to make out the tripod, the camera, the winking lens. I looked up, to where Townsend had cut a gap in the ceiling to let in the light of day. Not even a star. Not even the moon.

"Ho! Ho! Such a dunderhead! How could a portrait be accomplished in the dark of night?"

No sooner had I spoken these words than a chill went through my spine. What, then, were these men, the downtrodden forty-niners, waiting for? Why were they standing in line?

This question was answered by a voice that came out of the darkness, at the level of my knocking knees. "Hello, Jim! I love you. You love me?"

At once my Adam's apple leaped upward, like a trout seeking a fly. I could hardly utter the following words: "Who is it? Who's there?"

Two black hands emerged from the darkness and seized the rubberized waistband of my checkered pants. "What you want, Jim? Want to stand up like a horse behind Antoinette down like a dog?"

"Antoinette!"

Slowly the pupils of my eyes dilated, so that I could discern, upon a plain pallet, the Panamanian's naked form. "So! You are the daguerreotype model! Eh? Unclothed: like Venus of Milo."

Unlike the statue, however, this female figure had arms. She used them to pull my gabardines to my ankles, together with my shantung silk drawers. At once my testes climbed upward, to the safety of the abdominal zone. A terrible truth had dawned: this was no artist's studio; it was a house of assignation.

"You like love me a lot, good-looking Jim?"

"*Nein!* No thank you, mademoiselle!"

With that I turned, twisted, and like an athlete made three large hops to the door. I yanked it open and stumbled into the hall. There was — at the sight of my nakedness, my confusion — a burst of laughter. Caught in my clothing, I made mincing motions to the second portal, which I threw wide. With a jump I was inside. Alas! This chamber was as dark as the other. Another taper burned. Worse, another female, also undraped, with bosoms, lay on an identical pallet.

"You come here," she said, in a deep growl of a voice.

I tried to speak, but the *glandulae salivarius,* whose function it is to lubricate the mouth, the throat, had dried up completely.

The woman — it was an Indian, a squaw, flat-faced, with nipples on her dusky twin breasts — raised herself upward. "Five dollar you special."

"Not possible," I croaked, gesturing down to my gold sack, which was as empty as the one that had contained my gonads.

"You love Mary," said the squaw, grinning wide, so that her teeth flashed and her pink tongue spread on the floor of her mouth like a rug.

An amazing thing then occurred. A wave of heat, like that from a plaster, spread over my body. Then my testes descended, and, like a lever responding to the weight of those stones, my male member rose. I glanced round toward the door. I wanted to flee in that direction. Yet the half-step I took, and the half-step that followed, were forward, not back. I was like a fish, hooked on the end of my own stiff pole. Another shuffling step. And another.

Miss Mary lay back, with her arms raised, and her legs raised, too. She was like the dark puddle, the liquid, that draws the dousing stick, that twitches the divining rod. Hobbled, I hopped, dropping directly upon her. Fingers twined round my neck; ankles locked over my hams. From that moment it was no longer possible to say with precision where the dark pagan ended and the pale Pressburger began.

"So," said I. "We enter now the realm of erotics."

For some moments we moved pleasurably together. Then I experienced a definite sensation, in places that had never undergone feeling before: the hair ends, for instance, the nails of the fingers and toes. My body felt as a catapult must when those who man it twist ever tighter the thick hempen ropes. In my ears the hot breath of my partner made a whistling sound; the candle tipped and toppled; and the strands, the strings that held my body together of a sudden let go, casting me into the world. *"Liebchen!"* I cried, embracing my co-worker with all my strength. "Solution to the mind-body problem!"

How long did we lovers lie motionless in each other's arms? A minute? An hour? Hours more? Difficult to say. All I knew was that when I at last drew up my trousers and tiptoed from the chamber, the Sazarac was empty and the chandelier, together with all the other lamps, was out. Two-Toes Tom alone remained on the floor. He was slumped over a table, snoring in his sleep. The glasses, once filled with cobbler, were all about him, some upended, some on their stems, like mushrooms sprung after a storm.

In the alley my four-footed friend was waiting, under the weight of her burden. Joyfully, she whickered to see me.

"Shhhh! Hush, you sweetheart!" I admonished, a finger to my lips. Then I transferred several of the heavier bundles onto my shoulders and untied the halter from the hitching rail. Slowly, carefully, I led the beast out of the alley, onto Main Street, and then, heading east, onto Miner. All was dark, quiet, still. The peat-gas lamps at the intersection were out. The stars overhead were covered by a layer of cloud. Nonetheless, we moved with care. "Hush, hush, you darling!" Thus did I repeat my warning. With every step the pots and pans that hung from the load banged together, while the teapot lids rattled like castanets. I cringed. It seemed to me that the whole population of Yreka must hear.

On we went, past the factory for lemon syrup and the burned-out shell of the Hotel de France. Even after we had left the last buildings behind, and the road had given way to the dust of the alkali plain, I continued to hunch over, casting quick looks behind to see if a light had come on, or if the head of some Yrekan had appeared at a window. Surely, I thought, someone must hear or see. How much noise we made! And how brightly my face burned with shame. Shame at what? At my failure as a prospector, a miner? Never! At having engaged in the act of love? Certainly not. Here stood A. Pinto, former medical student, a fighter, a brave pioneer; yet here was I now, plodding under a peddler's pack, for all the world like any medieval ancestor, a hump-backed Jew.

2

Up came the June sun, beating upon mule and mule skinner as we trudged eastward across the alkali plain. How slow our progress! Time and again the hybrid halted, turned about, and set off resolutely in the direction from which we had come. When I attempted to draw her onward again, she would dig in her hooves and stare wistfully at the high, empty heavens back to the west. I could not help but think of how Herr Doktor Busch would peer through the night at the vacant place in the constellations where he had calculated his missing planet to be. "Come! Come, you dear one!" I exhorted my dawdling companion. "Come, you Neptune!"

On we plodded, through the day, into the night, and, after the briefest of sleeps, on into the dawn. Our problem was water. I had taken only enough to last what was supposed to be the two-day trip to Milk River, where a gold camp, with women in it, and even children, had long since been working the shore. My hope, of course, was to sell the goods — the calicoes and cook pans, the fishhooks and threads — to the settlers. At our pace, however, the journey took twice as long as planned. By the time we finally drew near our destination, every drop of liquid, including the tinned fruit's sweet syrup, was gone.

Imagine our horror, then, when we discovered that this wide stream, like Hardscrabble, Soda, and Greenhorn creeks, like Etna Pond too, had gone dry. There was not, on its chalky bottom, even a pool, a puddle. On the far shore was the ghost town. The population, in fleeing, had left not so much as a thimble of water behind. At once I dropped to my knees and began to dig, among the pebbles of the riverbed, a sinkhole. At a depth of two feet it was dry. At three feet, after an hour's wait, we found an inch of seepage — salty as seawater, and a faint seawater green. Into that pit Neptune, her legs splayed wide, thrust her hairy head.

What to do? The nearest settlement, Yreka itself, lay some thirty miles behind us. We knew all too well there was no water between ourselves and the town. The only sign of life, a thin strand of smoke, lay in the direction we had been going, at the edge of the alkali plain. According to the maps there was water there, at Tule Lake; but the distance was as far to the east as Yreka lay to the west. As for the smoke, it rose from a near-extinct volcano. The Modocs called the cone Wigwam, the home of the Grandfather, first ancestor. They believed that the Old Man had woven the world from that spot — outward, in coil after coil, the way Modoc women wove baskets from tule. Then, with the hairs from his armpit, he had peopled his creation.

"Ho! Ho!" Thus did I, in a cracking voice, utter a laugh. "Think of that, you darling! Armpit hairs!"

But Neptune did not raise her head from the hole her master had sunk. She snorted, sending the white dust over her whiskery muzzle and mane. Then her tongue came out — there seemed to be inches and inches of that bright pink ribbon — and with it she licked the bottom of the cistern. Empty! Barren! Bone dry! Time to make the decision. Should we retreat, hoping that a mad dash might bring us to Yreka? Or advance, on the chance that we might find an uncharted stream, or meet an emigrant train that had strayed from the Oregon Trail?

Neptune, naturally, cast her vote for the former option. She stood steadfast, her head pointing back. Nonetheless, I suddenly made up my mind to continue on. With a grunt, a grimace, I swung her round. Not even I could explain this choice — unless it was some distant memory, a buried recollection of how, in ancient times, my own ancestors had also wandered the desert in search of the earth's one center, the basket's bottom, their only home.

"Come, you beauty!" So saying, I pulled on the halter, dragging my four-footed companion toward the horizon, where the dark strand of smoke was rising. "You see? No need for worries! That is the cloud that will lead us by day!"

It did not take long, mere hours, for that faith to wither. There was no sign of water; no wagon-wheel tracks. The worst part of my error was that it could not be corrected. Nothing to do now but push on. Poor Neptune! Her head drooped lower and lower, until her wiry whiskers scraped the ground. She made, in her throat, a whining sound, less like a donkey than like a dog. Her eyes had lost their luster. I leaned toward her, but my words — of encouragement, apology, endearment — were garbled and slurred. My mouth, because of my swollen tongue, felt as if it had been stuffed with a Turkish-type towel. Ahead, the black line of smoke rose like a snake, swaying in the atmosphere as if to the notes of a Hindoo's flute. No: it was a rope, a hangman's noose, into which I had thrust my head. I continued to plod toward it, though with each step I could feel its rough fibers tighten about my parched throat, my drooping neck.

Finally we two travelers halted. The last of our strength was gone. Behind us now, the sun was rapidly falling. Ahead, our shadows grew and grew. Impossible not to recognize that here, on this spot, my long journey had ended. How far from the family Pinto! The sparkling Danube! The half-salt waters of the Charles! I looked about me. Nothing to see but the flat plateau, with its sage, its scrub. And when, years hence, men came across this soft felt hat, the smoking-style jacket, the gabardine pants, would they know that the bones they covered, like those beneath the rags of the Medical College mummy, belonged to a Harvard man? A moment, and more than a moment, went by. The mule sank to her knees. Painful to see how, beneath her shaggy skin, the muscles twitched, as if she were being tormented by swarms of flies. In pity I reached toward her, to loosen the straps of her pack.

At that moment, just as the sky grew dark, a breeze sprang up. So did the moribund mule, catching my arm in the cinch. Both of us had sensed, on the evening air, a peculiar odor — something like burning boots, or the eels I had seen in my boyhood, washed up on the Danube dike. "My beauty! What can such a scent be?"

No answer. Neptune twisted her wide-nostriled snout. She twitched her ears, long as a rabbit's. Then, without warning, she bolted ahead, dragging her poor master by her side.

"Halt, miss!" I croakingly cried.

But the animal, if anything, increased her speed, flying headlong, with myself, A. Pinto, skip-skipping, hop-hopping, in tow. Where had the mule found such powers? Toward what goal was she heading? And how might I stop her? Careening wildly between the beast's fleeing flanks and the hard, gritty ground, I tried repeatedly to throw a leg over the animal's rump. No success. I gathered my strength for a final try. *"Houp-là!"* I shouted, gripping the mane with my free hand and hooking the heel of a blucher over the mule's tossing croup. In that manner, though my head hung down and the stars above writhed in agitation, I managed to cling to my mount.

Neptune never faltered. Her hooves drummed steadily across the flat terrain. Half swooning, I held on for dear life. At one time it seemed the steed was racing downhill, over the edge of the high plateau. At another I could have sworn we were flying through air. Yet again, the element about us felt liquid, as if we were fording a river or swimming the sea. Too much blood to the head: that was my diagnosis, made at the instant I fainted away.

When I woke I saw at once it was still night. How did I form this opinion? First, by the darkness. Next, by the sight of an orb, round and shining: undoubtedly the moon. The problem was, this glowing disc was hanging mere inches from my open eyes. Then I understood that this was not the moon but, rippling, undulating, all aglimmer, the moon's reflection on a body of water. Water! Only now did I hear the *lap-lap* of waves, together with the sucking sound, the gentle splashings, of Neptune's lips, Neptune's tongue, as she drank her fill. It took no more than a second to loosen the cinch round the animal's belly, so that I fell into the cool waters of what turned out to be a vast, tule-bordered lake.

What nectar! Such honey! I swallowed huge drafts of the liquid, gargling with it, squirting it up in a fountain. How I then frolicked! I dove like a porpoise. I slapped the surface like a beaver. Like a muskrat I let the water dribble from my moustache's perceptible tips. At last I sat in the shallows, pouring hatful after hatful of the precious element — more valuable, far, than silver, than gold — upon my streaming head. In short, I was drunk on the non-alcohol brew. Finally I rose and stumbled through the thick tules to the solid earth of the shore. There I slid off my pack and undid my oilcloth. Inside was a mattress, a B. F. Goodrich, which I now filled with air. On this puffy pallet I lay. A last waft of the breeze, stinking still, blew by me as I plunged headlong into sleep.

* * *

I woke at dawn, to the sound of the wind — no, to wind instruments: oboes, it seemed, a reedy bassoon, even one of the modern clarinets. Fearfully I opened my eyes. A band of Indians, Modocs all, were stretched out about me, each one snoring away at a different pitch. Every brave lay on his back, hands clasped on his chest, like the carved figures on medieval tombs. Except that these statues shivered, their teeth chattered in the early morning chill. Some were nearly naked, with little more than the paint on their cheeks, their chests, to keep them warm. Others were dressed in odd pieces of clothing — broadcloth trousers, denim pants, a worsted vest, mismatched shoes.

I, too, shivered — but from fear. My pack held no weapon. There was not even a pickax to ward off the savage horde. I thought, and with envy, of how on the Boston Common Professor Piper had raised his sharp sword. One minute there was the Pawnee, with his painted scowl, the black pupils in the wide eyes; the next moment nothing — not even a feather. My sole hope was to steal away while the natives were sleeping. Close by, chomping on the tule tops, was my steed. If I could reach her, mount her, spur her on, we might escape unscathed.

Carefully, inch by inch, I raised myself upward, to my elbows, to my knees. Suddenly, at that very instant, there was a rude noise:

Fuh-rapp! Fuh-rumphh!

The inflatable B. F. Goodrich was emitting the air through its rubber lips.

In a flash, a twinkling, the Modocs were on their feet. They grinned. They rubbed their eyes.

"Ho! Ho!" piped I. *"Guten Tag!"*

The tallest of the group stepped forward. His brow had been flattened, and beneath it glittered two black, pinpointed eyes. His shoulders were wide, his jaw thick and massive. "Big Ike," said the Indian, pointing to his outsized sternum. "You gotta happy birthday present for Ike?"

With that more Modocs pressed forward. They surrounded what they could not know was a pale-faced Jew. They touched me. They poked me with their mustard-colored fingers. One of their number reached into my trouser pockets, turning them inside out. Another plucked at the pockets of my silk-lined smoker, reversing these too. A third dug after the contents of my waistcoat, my vest. Soon I was covered with the little sacks of inverted pockets, as if I were the victim of an eruptive disease. The first of the burrowing redskins pointed at a fellow tribesman. "Shacknasty Jim!" he declared.

That Modoc nodded toward the speaker: "Shacknasty Jake!"

"Brudders!"

"Live inna ugly house!"

The two men broke into laughter, a sound full of clicks, like whirring clockwork.

A third Modoc, blue-lipped, shivering, said, "Humpy Joe bloody cold!"

The fourth, a gap-toothed fellow, shivered too. "So is goddam One-Eye Mose!"

As if in anticipation of that complaint, the giant, Big Ike, stepped back from a heap of crisscrossed tules, which burst into lively flames. Then he began to throw wooden boards — not juniper bushes or rough lumber, but hewn planks — onto the fire. The blaze, the whoosh of sparks, seemed to dispel the last of the nighttime gloom. I looked about. Behind me, through the tunnel of tules I'd tramped down in the night, I could see the lake stretching off toward the north, its waters a deep shade of blue. The reeds stuck up all around it, to the height of a man and more. Odd shadows, like rippling waves, moved over the surface: the wind, the reflection of clouds, I assumed, until I made out the low humming sound and realized that swarms of flies were zigzagging quickly through the air.

In the opposite direction, to the south, was the volcano, with smoke rising from the top: proof, for these Modocs, that the Grandfather was still at home. Old lava had spilled from the cone's cracked northern face, and lay frozen like a huge black glacier. Its gnarled fingers reached to within a few hundred yards of where we stood, at the edge of the lake. And there, on a smooth black expanse of obsidian, was a sight that made me rub my heavy-lidded eyes: a line of three wagons, prairie schooners, their canvas tattered, shredded, and no mules, no oxen, in sight.

"*Mein Gott!* Can this be?"

For stretched across the rent canvas of the middle wagon were the words JOHN HARVARD. Here was the company from the Medical College! Colleagues! Fellow students! Without thinking, I started across the plate of smooth stone toward the encampment. Immediately the Indians moved to cut me off. A young brave, the only one whose forehead was not flattened, held up his hand. "Stop. You listen to Jack. You no wanna see."

At this my fear returned, stronger than before. What terrible fate had befallen my former comrades? Why were the wagons deserted — without oxen, without smoke, without the least hint of life? Dead, then! Worse than dead: murdered! Butchered by this roving band. Half swooning, with a chill sweat on my skin, I looked at the savage faces. How sharp, how strong their teeth. How fierce the warpaint. Had the binding of their heads, the flattening of their brows, destroyed that part of the brain where conscience and fellow-feeling are formed? In a quick movement of panic, I broke toward the line of wagons. But the young brave, no older surely than my own nineteen years, jumped in the way: "Feller go to wagons soon gonna die!"

There! Out in the open! Worst fears confirmed! Suddenly I realized where the odd smell, the stench of rot, came from. The bodies of my friends! Not only that, I now knew the source of the tribe's odd wardrobe — the pair of braces on one Modoc's shoulders, the silk underwear worn by another, the nankeen breeches on a third. Plundered from the John Harvards! Stripped from the bodies of the dead! Picture my horror, then, when the smiling brave, square-jawed, crop-haired, and with a full, bulging brow, reached out for the brim of my soft felt hat.

"Pretty topper! Look good on Dandy Jack!"

The words were like a sentence of death. And not for me alone. Down in the lake, Neptune, too, was surrounded. A trio of Modocs were pushing and pulling at her piled-up cargo, the way they had at my pockets. Meanwhile the others had set up a large kettle over the fire's leaping flames. The boards that fed that blaze had undoubtedly been pried from the abandoned wagons. I thought I could see the stenciled *H*, the letter *A*, on one of the planks. As for that pot, that caldron: no doubt now what lay in store for man and beast. This was why there was no sign of the company or its oxen. Eaten! Devoured by the cannibal tribe!

Suddenly a cry went up from the lake. The Indians had found what they had been seeking. With a shout of jubilation they came bounding back toward the fire. Dandy Jack, the full-browed brave, uttered an answering whoop. He moved to the fire as well. The whole band of Modocs gathered round, repeating a guttural chant:

"*Coffeecoffeecoffee*."

"Coffee?" I echoed. "*Der Kaffee?*"

The broad-shouldered Modoc lifted the ten-pound sack of mocha. "Big Ike," he said. "He find 'em!" With his bare hands he ripped the burlap asunder. Thousands of beans spurted out.

The tribe had seized another treasure: a green coffee mill, product of Holland. Shacknasty Jake scooped up the spilled beans and dropped them into the hopper of this machine. His brother, Shacknasty Jim, turned the handle. The dark stream of powder poured into the boiling urn.

The Modocs pressed round, licking their lips, patting their bellies. The hot steam, the sharp, pungent aroma, rose into the air. Slowly, one after the other, the tribesmen sank onto the ground, their arms around their drawn-up legs, their chins on their knobby knees. Silently, as if mesmerized, they stared at the fire, whose flames, reaching upward like the throats of hungry birds, were so much redder than their own bared skin. Why red man? Why redskins? To my eye they seemed more like Chinamen — black-haired, almond-eyed, their flesh stained the color of nicotine. And, too, the way they gazed at the fire, entranced, motionless, under a spell, made me think of the Celestials inside their opium dens. Were they fire-worshipers, then? Addicted to coffee? To the alkaloid of caffeine? No matter: here, I realized, was the chance to make off unseen. Carefully I edged from the fire, the drugged natives, the bubbling pot.

What now? What next? My only thought was to reach the line of wagons. Perhaps I could hide there until nightfall and then, under cover of darkness, run to the field of frozen lava. With smooth, gliding steps that belied my racing heart, I made my way up the black plate of obsidian, which lay between me and the twisted crags of stone. The middle wagon, the one with JOHN HARVARD across the torn top, loomed only a short distance away. Suddenly, from behind me, a new shout went up. I glanced over my shoulder. The Modocs were leaning over the pot, scooping the dark, scalding liquid into their mouths. *Attention! Beware!* the doctor in me was tempted to shout. *You will damage the esophagus zone!* Still the addicts continued. They dove like ducks into the boiling brew. They paid no heed to the fact that their flesh, their entire digestive tissue, must be suffering second- and third-degree burns. Were their throats forged from metal? Were they superhuman?

In a panic, I ran pell-mell for the Conestoga and threw up the canvas flap.

"*Gott!*" This cry came from my own throat. "*Im Himmel!*"

There, sprawled upon the wagon bed, was a body — no, two bodies; no, three in sum. I started, agape. It was as if this canvas were a curtain that had been lifted at the end of a tragedy, revealing a corpse-littered stage. But these were not actors. The first victim's hair was cut short, in the German manner, and a monocle was still in his eye: Professor Hayward, of the Medical College! The next was thin, lanky, tall: the anatomist Piper! Nor was the third man a stranger: Frost, Morton's assistant — the man who had lost his tooth!

"Oh! Devils! Villains!" I shouted, shaking a fist at the murderers below.

It was my nose, a long one, that now detected something amiss. The smell of burnt rubber, of freshwater eels, was still in the air. But it did not originate from these bodies. If anything, it seemed to come on the breeze out of the east. From my higher ground I looked off in that direction. Something bright and silvery was shining amidst the tall tules of the shore. I blinked. There, made out of twigs, out of mud, like birds' nests turned upside down, were the huts of a Modoc village. I could see movement: dogs running, with children, in and out of the squat, round dwellings. Women, a dozen kneeling squaws, were beating their clothing against a circle of stones. Just to the north, four men stood together, shooting arrows into the lake. They pulled fish after fish out of the water — bullheads, surely, family Cottidae, the only species that could survive in this alkaline flood.

The stench, I realized, came from the fish. So did the silvery glint that had first caught my eye. The Modocs had spread the bullheads on the roofs of their huts — to preserve them, most likely, and perhaps to keep them from the milling dogs. The bones of the vertebrates lay everywhere; their scales shone in the light of the rising sun.

A cry, a ululation, came from the shore. The washerwomen had risen. I saw they wore little straw domes on their heads, like miniatures of the huts they lived in. The more modern among them had skirts of cotton wrapped at the waist. All were pointing directly at the spot where I stood. Some had begun to shout in their click-clacking voices. From the village huts, through the tules, the braves came running. No doubt about it: I, the observer, had been observed.

I whirled round. The crags, the fingers of lava, were no more than a quick sprint away. With my long legs I could reach safety before the pursuers waded through the stretch of shallows. Why, then, this hesitation? Answer: Neptune. The darling! The innocent girl! How could I abandon her to the savages who even then had started to splash into the rippling waves?

"Neptune!" I cried. "Take heart, honey!"

Far below me, hip deep in water, the quadruped glanced round. How sweet she looked, how comely, with a cattail dangling from the corner of her mouth. In an instant I was bounding downward, past the startled band of coffee addicts and onto the trampled tules. The next thing I knew I was in the water, with my arms about the shaggy muff of the animal's neck. Poor creature! Dumb brute! Not once in her life to entertain a logical thought. Worse: this female, like all hybrids, was sterile. For her, no joy of motherhood. Never, for her, the hope of immortality that even simple life forms hear in their offspring's cry. Tears welled in my eyes. They coursed down my pale, Pressburger's cheeks.

"Ah! Ah! Sweetheart! How short, how filled with sorrow, your life!"

At that the animal craned backward and, with her pink tongue, licked my face. Oh, do not I think I suffered illusions: all mammals need to replenish their bloodstream with the element contained in my salty tears. Still, as the sound of the attackers reached us over the *slap-slap* of the waves, I was in some measure consoled by this kiss.

The attackers! The natives! They were now no more than one hundred American yards away. What to do? Neptune turned westward, as was her wont. I swung her round. With the reins in my hand I advanced upon the foe.

Ahead, the Modocs halted. A murmur ran through their ranks. Then the tribe slowly retreated, moving a step backward with each step I advanced. And who could blame them? A primitive people, a Stone Age folk, they saw striding forward, with pots and pans clanging, a modern man, from the age of copper and iron and brass. In a matter of moments the Indians had withdrawn all the way to the eastern shore. The braves and squaws ran off to the stands of tules. I paused. Up close, the stench of the drying fish had become difficult to bear. I could see the fumes, quivering in the atmosphere; I felt, on my skin, an oily film. For a brief spell I reeled, overcome by the noxious gas. Then, resolute, determined, I tramped through the ankle-deep waters to the muddy shore. Here I halted. I undid the load from the back of my faithful companion. I spread out, just beyond the reach of the little lapping wavelets, my wares.

"Meine Damen und Herren! Gute Damen!" I called. Silence. No movement. Only the dogs, yellow ones mostly, ran back and forth along the shore. "Nice things to buy!"

No response. The sun on the fish scales made the little domes, the mud-and-twig huts, shine as if covered with silver leaf. *Yap-yappity-yap!* went the mongrels, working themselves into a frenzy. From my collection I seized a bolt of gingham.

"Look, ladies! Cheap! A bargain!"

There was a stir in the reeds. Quickly I unrolled the stuff, wrapping it about my hips in the style of a sarong. "Attention! Here is the latest fashion! In Prague, in Vienna! The thing to wear!"

Before the women could react, a man, a Modoc, strode forward, from between the closest huts. He was short, thin, with oddly curly hair above his flattened forehead. His chin was pointed, and so were his elfin ears. Except for his ornaments and his painted skin, this native was completely unclothed.

"Doctor!" he shouted, pointing at his own bare breast. "Curly-Headed Doctor! White feller make sick! Goddam you gotta go!"

The Modoc gestured toward the tules. At once something appeared in the air, rising above the cattail tops. Up, up it went, into the sky; then it turned over and dropped with ever-increasing speed to the ground, where it violently vibrated an inch from my high-topped bluchers. An arrow! Immediately a second shaft flew skyward and, describing an identical parabola, fell next to the first.

"Ho! Ho!" I managed a laugh. "Are you still fishing, friends? Look here. Do you see? Imported. First quality. A tin of sprats!"

There was a loud twanging sound and the whole eastern sky filled with arrows, so many that they clicked together like teeth in their flight. Then they fell point first about my mule and me, ripping through the oilcloth, drumming on the tinware, making what looked like a whole new stand of quivering tules.

Now the braves prepared to shoot again. But instead of the hiss and hum of feathered shafts, I heard a different, deeper sound. It was a low rumble, like thunder. I looked up. Another Modoc, tall, with a full brow, and wearing a white man's dress shirt, had stepped in front of the naked medicine man. He held a tin washboard whose corrugated surface he scraped with a stick. It made a roar. The dozens of Modocs fell back, murmuring, "Washboard Bill."

This newcomer moved forward, splashing through the shallow waves. "Chief want pants," he said. "Give 'em to Bill."

That was the signal for the others, the men and women, to come trotting ahead. For a moment I stood there, unable to take my eyes from the tall Indian's face. It was pitted, pockmarked, in what was for any physician an unmistakable manner. Smallpox. The chief might have been named as well for the scars on his face as for the implement in his hand.

The rest of the tribe arrived. Half eager, half timid, the menfolk surrounded me. They reached with their dirt-colored fingers toward my clothes. They patted the material, fumbled at the buttons, and dug into my pockets, turning them wrong way out. The women, meanwhile, had gathered at the display of goods. One squaw, with a bone in her nose, a part in her hair, seized the sarong and wrapped it numerous times about her hips. A second squaw was pulling at the loose end of the material, attempting to don it herself. Now the remaining women, like shoppers everywhere, joined the spree. They unfolded the blankets, pawed through the beads, and fingered the raisins and figs.

Off to one side, three or four squaws upended a carton, spilling a score of powder-puff compacts onto the ground. With a whoop, the ladies fell on the prize. They cracked open the cases like the shells of clams. They gaped at the sight of themselves in the built-in mirrors. Then they took out the puffs, tossing the little cushions from hand to hand, the way Mexicans make tortillas. Clouds of dust rose into the air. The rest of the women crowded round, sniffing at, even tasting the cakes of powder. Then they began to apply the colored dust to their cheeks, their throats, their bosoms.

Pushing through the crowd, I approached the scene. "Ladies! Form, please, a queue. Now we pay for these items!" To one and all I indicated my portable scales.

The squaws paid not the slightest heed. Behind me, one group of braves had found a box of phosphor matches, and had set about lighting these tiny torches one by one. Another band, the fisherman quartet, had opened the box of alarm clocks. They held the ticking instruments to their ears. Several clappers began to sound between brass bells.

"Friends! Friends! What about money?"

Washboard Bill seemed to understand. He held up his pair of denim breeches and gave a command in his own tongue to his fellow tribesmen. Immediately one of the fishermen came forward and began to stuff a bullhead, whiskery and bug-eyed, into the pocket of my vest.

"Nein! Kein Fischfleisch!" I pointed to the twin dishes of the empty scales. "Here. Gold please. Money. Wampum. *Geld!*"

The redskins nodded. Smiling, they rushed to pile the silvery creatures onto the metal pans.

"Ha-ha! Damn fool Modocs! Stinking Indians don't know goddam thing!"

We all, salesman and shoppers, turned to the speaker. It was the full-browed youth, Dandy Jack. On his feet, I now noticed, he wore a pair of wing-tip shoes. Whether because of this finery or his unflattened forehead, it came to me that he must be the son of the chief, Washboard Bill. He reached once more for my hat, seized it in fact, and set it upon one pan of the scale. Then he turned to the nearest brave, a thin flathead with a protruding lower lip. "Split-Lip Sam dressed up too much," he said, taking away the older man's bracelets, and the nuggets round his neck. "He just a stinking Modoc."

Now Dandy Jack began to place the ornaments on the scale. I watched, we all watched, speechless, as the glittering pile grew larger, forcing the leftward pan lower, while the felt hat on the right rose up and up, until both halves settled, trembling, in balance.

"Sold! Ho! Ho! Ho! Sold!" I shouted. I reached down and swept the pan's contents into a large burlap sack. What a phenomenon was here! A plain soft hat worth — not as a figure of speech but literally, at $16 an ounce — its weight in gold!

Now the real trading began. The women, squealing, shouting, crowded round. Into the right half of the scale went, in turn, thread, needles, scissors, followed by loose raisins and coffee-bean piles; into the left went more dust, or gold leaf, or nuggets. The women tore the ornaments from around their necks and the flesh of their arms. They pushed each other, they lashed with their elbows, in the attempt to get to the ribbons, the calicoes, the trembling scales. Most prized were the powder-puff cases, each of which had cost me 65 cents. These shoppers were paying, in the form of precious metal, the equivalent of $42 for every one. Nor was the frenzy limited to the weaker sex. The men purchased fishhooks, fishing sinkers, and handfuls of Havana cigars—which, with their friction matches, they lit up at once.

I stood, grinning, bowing, in a kind of trance. Had I died and gone to heaven? Was this not the sight that every Jew hopes to see in paradise? No need, however, to give myself a pinch. I knew I was awake. How long had these Modocs been plucking these nuggets from the creekbeds and streams? For decades? No: centuries! There was no reason this wonderful bazaar should ever come to an end!

This, of course, was not to be. Standing apart, with such a scowl on his face that it seemed he had donned a mask, Curly-Headed Doctor had gathered a group of fierce-looking braves. Together they had dragged from the huts—surely this had also been seized from the unfortunate caravan—a metal washtub, with mechanical mangle. Now they began to turn the handle, making, with the rubberized rollers, a roar, a rumble, far louder than anything produced by Washboard Bill.

Very well. My goods were gone. My burlap bulged. Time, therefore, to depart. Quickly I dragged my treasure away from the crowd, to where Neptune stood waiting in the lapping waves. With a wink, a finger to the lips, I heaved the sack atop her back and turned the willing animal about. Thus with the reins in my hands and my wealth on her withers, we began to make our way to the west. Behind us the roar of the mangle continued. I took a last glance over my shoulder. The Modocs, buyers and sellers, the warriors on the shore, even the four-footed dogs: all were lost in a thick haze of Havana and the dust from the powder puffs. "Darling!" I shouted. "We are rich! Rich, you sweetmeat! You lamb!"

But we were not yet to make our way home. Moving through the shallows, hugging the shoreline, we soon came to the spot where we had bathed the night before. Here we turned landward, walking along the path of trodden tules. From behind a tall stand of these rushes there came a familiar voice.

"Our Fadder," it said.

There was a long pause. Then another voice, also familiar, said, "Fool brudder! Dumb Indian! Got no brain!" That, clearly, was Shacknasty Jake. He finished his brother's sentence:

"Our Fadder in de oven!"

Carefully, cautiously, I poked my hatless head through the wall of tules. The little band of Modocs, mocha-lovers, was standing together near a mound of the dark, moist earth. Joining them, alive and untouched, were a number of John Harvards: my classmates Ben Piper and Parrott, together with Bosworth's bride, the former Goody Peacock. Bosworth himself was there, with wild white wisps of hair blowing about his scalp and forehead. His wire spectacles were on his nose, and a book, a Bible, was in his hand. He was looking encouragingly at Shacknasty Jim, who screwed up his eyes in thought and chewed the indigo slab of his lip. Like a schoolchild, the gap-toothed One-Eye Mose raised his hand. His breath made a whistling sound as he responded: *"Hollow Ed your name!"*

Humpy Joe took a turn: *"The dumb king come!"*

The giant, Big Ike: *"The well be down in earth."*

All turned again to Shacknasty Jim. Poor fellow: the sweat rolled down his receding brow. He pulled on his nose repeatedly, but no answer came out. Once more his brother answered for him: *"Ass eat a seven!"*

Then each took his turn. Humpy Joe: *"Give ass bread!"*

Big Ike: *"And give ass four horses of pisses —"*

One-Eye Mose: *"Against a horse piss on ass!"*

Then all broke into their click-clacking laughter. The next words came neither from Shacknasty Jim nor from any of his fellow tribesmen. They were in the sweet young voice of a girl: *"And lead us not into temptation —"*

I strained to see. A child, no more than four years old, or five, was standing between the Bosworth couple. Another child — her sister, clearly, her twin — was beside her. She spoke next:

"But deliver us from evil."

Together the two girls, blond-headed, braided, finished the prayer. Then everyone, the white men and women, and the Indians too, said, "Amen."

Professor Bosworth closed his Bible. "Excellent. Very well done. I thank you all. And now we must lay our friends to rest."

With that the crowd stepped aside, and I saw, stretched out on the earth, the same John Harvards — Hayward, Frost, the elder Piper — I had seen inside the wagon that morning. Nor were these the only corpses. Buffum and Chaffee, my classmates from the Medical College, lay there as well. What a massacre, a slaughter, had occurred on these shores! The cruel Indians had left hardly a person alive! Indeed, at that very moment I noticed that yet another body was being brought down from the lava crags, past the three wagons, toward our spot in the rushes. Two men, each with a handkerchief over his face, carried the dark thin form. Peeking over the tule tops, I stared, struck with amazement. Then I broke from hiding and began to dash toward the bearers and their burden.

"Lewis! Dear man! Oh, Mr. Lewis!" I cried.

It was in truth my old friend. I had recognized the stiff tapered form of his man-made leg, and the white horseshoe of hair, like sheep's wool, about his black scalp. His bared body was thinner than ever, and there was a kind of dust, like purple powder, on his skin. His hands, on his chest, were clasping the leather volume: *The Poetical Works of Burns.*

Suddenly, from the crags, there was a roar. The washboard! No, louder: the rubber rollers! The Modocs had circled above us. Surrounded! I glanced up toward the lava. From the volcanic stones an object on four squat legs was charging downhill at a tremendous rate of speed. There was a flash of fangs, a malevolent glint of eyeballs: the bulldog! The fury-filled hound! It was hurtling at breathtaking velocity straight for its age-old antagonist, its hated foe.

Then one of the pallbearers pulled the bandanna away from his mouth. It was Matt Cole. "Caesar!" he commanded. "Go to Polly! To Nan!"

The roaring beast veered, sweeping by me to where the twin girls waited with open arms. Its master turned toward me. "Adolph!" he exclaimed. "Can it be you?"

"*Ja!* A. Pinto!"

The second man, also disguised like a bandit, pulled the mask from his reddish face and sandy moustache. This was Gill, also from the Medical College. "What are you doing here?" he asked.

"You see a poor peddler! And what of you? Have you strayed from the Oregon Trail?"

"Yes, we've had misfortune."

"I know this. Your caravan, the John Harvard Company: did it not number more than one hundred pioneers?" I paused, looking back toward the little band standing at the gravesite. "Now you have remaining only a handful of souls. Could so many be killed by *die Indianer?*"

Gill shook his head. "I wish it were the redskins. Then we might have fought back."

"It was cholera," said Cole. "It wasn't the Modocs. If anything, we've brought the sickness to them."

"Cholera? *Cholera morbus?*"

"It began on the *Avalanche,*" said Gill, "out of St. Louis. Four cases at first. All in one night. Then eight. Then eleven. Think of it. A ship full of doctors, of medical students, and nothing we did could stem the spread of the disease. In the morning the dehydrated patients would lie on the decks. They'd defecated whatever was in them; even the linings of their intestines had come out. The ones who could crawl made for the paddlewheels, to catch the spray."

Cole took up the tale. "The epidemic followed us onto the plains. We could not outrun it. Each company that had gone before us was forced to forage for grass in a wider arc than the ones that had preceded them. By the time our turn came, the animals had fouled every spring for a half-mile in either direction. When we reached Fort Hall, we'd already lost half our number."

"Half! But what of the rest? Those still alive? Where are the poor people now?"

"We spent the winter at the fort," Gill replied. "But in spring, when the passes cleared, a number turned back the way we had come. Still more went south, to Salt Lake City. My wife is there now. The rest of us took those three wagons onto the Oregon Trail. Then — well, it was as if the plague had taken a cutoff and was waiting at the lower elevation. The cholera returned. We made a detour for this water and have been here close to a month, waiting for the sickness to run its course."

I stood silent. Everything was now coming clear. The three men in the wagon had succumbed to disease. So had Buffum; Chaffee and Lewis, too. The Modocs, the coffee-drinkers, had been converted to the Christian faith. And the others, the tribe of redskins: no wonder they had fallen back at my approach. They must have feared I would bring the contagion to their village.

"Look close," said Cole. "Where the rushes are cut away. There are four more graves, each as large as this last."

I scanned the lakefront. I saw the spots. But I had noticed something else: the tops of the remaining cattails were weaving. Neptune, with my treasure upon her, was trampling through the vegetation, heading for the west. Instinctively, I bounded off in her direction. Then I halted. I turned. Slowly I approached the black, burned-looking body of my close companion. I touched his limbs. The wooden leg was warmer than the one of flesh. The points of his pelvis, the wings of the ilium, thrust against the tightened skin like the edge of a broken plate. Inside my chest, where it hung like a fruit on its tree of ribs, my heart was bursting.

"Poor fellow," I said.

For a keepsake, a memento, I gripped the book of poems and pulled it from the deadly grasp. At once I dashed back to where my last friend on earth was just thrusting her rubbery lips, her whiskered snout, out of the rushes, into the light of day.

Between, to the east, the tule-bordered lake, the field of lava, and, on the west, the start of the plateau, the alkali plain, stretched a thousand feet of open earth. I caught Neptune's reins a mere thirty yards after she'd left the reeds. Matt Cole overtook the two of us at the midway point. With a water keg slung over his shoulders and a company rifle in his hand, he was prepared to walk all the way to Yreka. The three of us started along the zigzag trail that led up the steep wall of the plateau, the same one that Neptune and I had plunged down the previous night. At the first turning, suddenly, startlingly, an Indian stepped into our path. Dandy Jack. He grinned beneath the brim of my soft felt hat.

"Give fancy coat," he commanded.

He was, I saw, pointing at my belted smoker.

"What's this?" Cole asked, alarmed. "What does he want?"

The chief's son answered for himself. "Washboard Bill got boiled shirt: make dirty skin white. Jack gotta fancy topper, make head real smart. Now Jack gonna get jacket."

He paused to take the coat that I'd slipped from my shoulders. Immediately he turned the sleeves inside out, and held up the garment, lining first. He buried his face in the fabric. "Smell good! Smell sweet! Not lika fish! Make Jack smell good too. White man gonna say, *Look at that helluva feller! Gentleman Jack ain't no stinking Modoc!*"

"*Ja!* You are welcome to this. No charge!" What else, I wondered, did the Indian want? My gold? My scalp? My life? But there was nothing else. The well-dressed Modoc started down the cliff side, as our tiny party resumed the upward trail.

Ten minutes later we reached the top of the plateau. We paused there for a last look back. Southward, to our right, was the smoking cone of Wigwam; then the fantastic shapes, the deep gullies, of frozen lava; and, extruded from it, the jet-black field of obsidian that led downward, to the left and north, all the way to the edge of the lake. Across that rippling surface the flies darted back and forth, like flights of opposing arrows. There were the three sway-backed wagons. Far off, the huts of the Modoc village, the fishbones and fish scales, glinted in what was now the noonday sun. Last of all, directly below, I saw that the Indian lad had donned his new jacket. Only then did I remember — more's the pity — that Lewis's book, the volume of Burns, was still in the pocket. Worn inside out, the red material of the lining rippled across the Indian's shoulders, looking, in the sunlight, like a jockey's bright silks.

3

Bound for home, there was no holding the mule. She would have traveled all night had we not hobbled her forelegs. As it was, we covered the sixty-odd miles in less than that many hours. At dusk, approaching Yreka, a strange thing happened. Neptune shied from the town and turned north, toward the series of buttes. No argument, no pleading, availed. She wouldn't be budged. When we gave her her head she trotted straight for old Soda Creek, and then up the south slope of Mount Etna. Townsend, the sole prospector there, was just finishing his work for the day. He stared at Cole from the side of his pit.

"Think of it," I declared. "We three together once more!"

Neptune, meanwhile, had continued perhaps three fourths of the way up the incline, until she reached a boarded-up tunnel gate. Cole was the first to notice. "Look at that. The animal's found a shaft."

"Silly girl! That is the mine of Judge Steele. Ho! Ho! She thinks she has come home."

Cole frowned. "No. Look. Do you see?"

The ex–Harvard student pointed to where the animal was hurling herself against the wood planks, head first, the way one goat might attack another.

"I knew it!" Townsend exclaimed. He jumped from his hole and began to scramble up the side of the butte. He paused to wave us after. "All these months I swear I knew! I've sensed the lode beneath my feet since the day we arrived. My legs have been trembling like the sticks of a divining rod. Come! Come on! I feel gold in my limbs!"

Cole had no trouble dislodging the planks with the butt of his company rifle. At once the mule dashed within, disappearing in the thick, mysterious gloom.

Lighting candles, we comrades of old came after. The tunnel dipped downward, inward, its jagged walls narrowing on every side. Townsend darted from one surface to another, scraping with his knife, kicking at outcrops with his boots, even pressing his cheek to the warm rock, as if he expected the vein of gold, or the secret vault, to whisper its whereabouts. "Nothing! Nothing!" he muttered at each new test. "Damn it to hell. Nothing still."

Now Cole hung back. "I don't like the place. We're under the very mountain. Don't you sense the weight? Look at the candles, how they flicker. We'll be crushed. We'll run out of air."

When Townsend merely laughed, his classmate threw down the rifle. He stretched both arms to the tunnel roof, like a blond-headed Samson—except that he hoped to hold up the walls, not tear them down. The hot wax from his candle ran over his arm.

Then, from the dark depths, Townsend shouted: "Come. I've found something. A vein!"

All caution was now cast to the winds. Cole and I raced each other to see who could reach the strike first. Together we came upon Townsend, holding his candle to the ceiling and wall.

"What is it?" asked Cole. "What have you found?"

"See for yourself," Townsend replied. He raised the flame higher. There was a splash of white against the dark rock, almost as if someone had emptied a bucket of milk.

Cole: "But what does it mean? Is that the gold?"

Once more Townsend placed his face against the wall. He sniffed at the soapy surface. Then he licked it, as if the grains glittering there were sugar or salt. We held our breath, awaiting the verdict.

"Quartzite. Low grade. The lead won't pay."

"That is why, surely, Judge Steele abandoned the shaft."

Townsend said not a word. He was trembling. That old knot, the omega-shaped wen, throbbed at the center of his forehead. "I don't understand. I could swear, even now, there's a vein nearby."

At that moment, from the deepest part of the corridor, came a tremendous thud. It echoed about us, reverberating more and more loudly, as if the winding passage amplified the sound. The walls shook. Pebbles broke loose from the ceiling.

Cole dropped his candle. Townsend's was snuffed by a fall of dust. Out of the blackness, the thud reverberated again. "It's collapsing!" Cole screamed. "We'll be crushed!"

Again the gravel rained down and dust filled the air. Shielding the last precious source of light, I peered through the powdery haze. Two orange-tinted gleams reflected the wavering flame. I knew them: the wide-open eyes of the mule. For what seemed a full minute they gazed at the huddled humans. Then the animal's head dropped down and her rear legs shot backward, against the tunnel's far wall.

"Neptune! Think, darling! Don't be foolish!"

"Damn the brute!" Cole cried, groping back along the floor of the passage for his weapon. "I'll shoot her. I'll kill her before she kills us!"

But the hybrid, heedless, was quicker than he. Again her head ducked between her front legs while her rear ones shot back. There was a loud, sharp crack, and a flash of light — not from the gun muzzle, but from the shattering wall of stone. Then a quick breeze, an air puff, rushed the length of the excavation and blew the last candle out. Only then, wildly, aimlessly, did the gun go off with a loud report and a flame of its own.

Silence. We three colleagues stood gaping dumbly. Each of us had seen the bright flash of light where the wall had given way. It was as if the animal's metal-shod hooves had struck against flint in the stone. But the light had been brighter, more intense, than any spark. Cole, softly, spoke first:

"Did you see?"

"Ja! Ein Licht."

Frank Townsend found a match. He struck it.

"Oh!" Such was our astonished cry. Then we started forward. Cole was first. He stepped through the broken wall into a cave, an underground cavern, whose sides glittered and glowed with innumerable facets of light. We followed. It was like entering a church where thousands of candles burned at the altar. Or as if the mule, instead of merely kicking through the crust of rock, had raised the very top of the hill, so that we inside could see the heavens, filled with burning stars. The match went out.

"Yes. I told you. I knew." Townsend's voice came from the dark.

"This is no quartz," said Cole. "Nor pyrite either."

"Hier ist das Gold."

Townsend struck a new match and touched it to his candle. We saw each other's crazed faces, each other's dazzled eyes. To me, the entire chamber seemed to be spinning, circling, like a steam carousel with revolving mirrors.

"Adolph, have you a balance?" Townsend asked.

"Why must we bother?" asked Cole. "Do you doubt your eyes?"

But I was already pulling the scale from my sack of gold. Townsend, meanwhile, pried loose a nugget the size of a quarter of walnut meat. We gathered at the scale. Townsend placed the nugget on one plate and balanced it with three silver coins. Cole removed the top of his water keg and submerged the even pans. The silver rose; down dipped the golden nugget. Instantly Cole plunged in his hand, seized the specimen, and set it on a rock. Like one possessed he began to beat it, hammering it over and over with his rifle butt. It spread like butter over the stone. Townsend squatted. He peeled away the flattened foil.

"Go on. Speak, why don't you?" That was Cole. He was panting from his exertions. "Is it gold? Or is it not?"

Townsend said, "The mint makes none finer."

At those words, we three prospectors went mad with joy. We hallooed. We hollered. Cole and Townsend leaped on each other and began to roll on the ground. I danced like an Indian, war-whooping, high-stepping, making exclamations in my own guttural tongue.

Cole was the first to recover his wits. "What shall we call her? The Harvard, eh? The Etna? No. Here's one that fits best: Lucky Strike."

"No, sir. No, my comrade. That is not fair. That is not just." I bolted to where Neptune stood waiting. I threw an arm round her sweat-stained neck. "Gentlemen! Dear friends! Equal partners! Here is our heroine. Our benefactor. All our fortune we owe to her."

Hee-haw! went the steed, to signal assent.

But Cole had turned aside. "Look," said he, pointing to where Townsend had continued to roll from side to side, over the floor of the chamber. "Hold him! He is having a fit!"

No need. The seizure, if such it was, ended. Townsend rose — first to his knees, then to his feet. Cole stopped in mid-stride. I stood as if paralyzed. Even the dumb beast shook her head and bared her yellow teeth at the sight. Quartz dust had caught in the man's hair; crystals clung to his clothing. His very skin was aglow, like that of the famed El Dorado, whom untutored Indians painted with gold.

"The Neptune!" said he. "This is the Neptune!"

Then all three of us shouted together: "The Neptune Mine!"

Night had long fallen by the time we three millionaires emerged from the underground passage and began to wend our way down the side of the butte toward the town. Overhead a thick bank of clouds covered the stars and moon. But below, in Yreka, the peat lamps were burning on Main Street, and the whale-oil lamps shone through the windowpanes. At the distance, in the surrounding gloom, the settlement looked like a gold piece shimmering at the bottom of a deep, dark pool. The breeze carried the faint sound of the place: snatches of singing, muffled shouts, a horse's neigh, a man practicing notes on a horn. Beneath it all was a steady clank, a regular rumble: the *Ingot* presses, running off the next day's edition. Hearing that, I gave a secret smile. Soon this machinery would have to stop. A new headline, in giant type, would take the place of the old: STRIKE AT YREKA! And underneath, in letters almost as large: HARVARD MEN UNCOVER BONANZA.

As for that Harvard trio, we, with our lucky mule, went straight for the Sazarac Saloon. That was where, in his gambling pit, at his keno cages, Judge Steele was sure to be found. The plan was for Matt Cole, a stranger in town, to strike up a conversation with the mine owner and offer to pay him his price for the claim. Townsend, meanwhile, went round to the alley in back, to wash off the telltale dust, while I brought in my sack filled with gold.

The saloon was much as I'd left it at the beginning of the week. On the dance floor a number of miners were at the old game of teasing Two-Toes Tom, who was dancing—in truth, rocking from foot to foot like a sailor—while clinging to the dark, plump arms of Antoinette. Judge Steele was at his usual table, smoking a thin cigar. When Cole approached him, he said that his claim was not up for sale. Upon hearing those words, I could not help but speak out:

"But the shaft is abandoned. Not worked. Empty. We could claim it ourselves."

Kane, the faro dealer, shook his head. "Those laws don't apply to underground diggings."

The other gamblers nodded assent.

I looked toward Steele. His eyes were pale and protruding, even when, at this moment, he squinted through the smoke of his cigar. "How do you know it's empty? Have you broken through the gate? Have you gone in?"

What could I say? "In? Into the excavation? Ho-ho! The tunnel, you mean?"

"Yes. Did you?"

The Yrekans, gathering round, as if viewing the play at rouge-et-noir, tittered aloud. I thrust my hands into my gabardine pockets and grasped the nuggets I'd taken from the cavern walls. Heaven forbid that, in their trembling, their tinkling together, they give our scheme away.

To my surprise, Townsend came up to our table and gave a forthright reply. "We did go in."

"I thought as much. How far? Halfway?"

"Yes. Halfway."

"And beyond?"

"To the end of your diggings. Right up against the rear face."

"And what did you find there?"

"You know," said Townsend, "what we found."

"You are mistaken. I do not. Tell me."

The entire saloon, even the customers at the bar, as well as those at the gaming tables, fell silent. The only sound was a faint drumming, a rattling — the balls in the roulette chambers, the cards in the keno cage. The crowd leaned forward, to hear what Townsend would say.

"Oh, first the low-grade ore you left in the lead. And then the spot where the vein pinches out."

"That is all? Nothing more?"

What, I wondered, would my partner do? Lie outright? And what of myself? Was not the question addressed to me as much as to the others? Was not silence a kind of equivocation, abetting the crime of fraud? Townsend, I saw, was having similar doubts. He lifted his hat, in order to scratch — it was a worldwide gesture of perplexity — his scalp. I let out a gasp. My friend's hair was shining! It glittered with crystals of quartz!

At this threat my tongue came untied. "My good sir! Look here! At our offer. A burlap bag! Inside, fifty pounds of genuine gold. This is in dollars more than ten thousand. Twelve thousand, in fact! So much money for an empty mine!"

Now the crowd burst out in laughter, in exclamations. The town butcher, Poland, who'd lost a fortune of his own, took me by the arm. "We been over those buttes with fine-tooth combs. You couldn't find gold there to buy you a shot of whiskey."

Townsend placed his knuckles on the table, and leaned close to Steele. "I've told you, we've been in your tunnel. You know the vein we've seen. The ore in your lead won't pay more than two dollars to the ton. It would take you years to pull eight hundred ounces from the diggings. That's what we're offering you now. Are we madmen? Very well: madmen. But we have a scheme to make the butte pay. We're going to bring in machines: a stamp mill, a flywheel, an amalgamation ditch. Raising the capital, finding a boiler to run the works—those are our problems. Yours is whether to accept our offer. There is the gold sack. It's a decade of profit for you. Do you accept, or do you not?"

On either cheek Steele's hair formed a hatchet. The twitch of the muscle beneath made the blade seem to fall. "Gentlemen," he said, "it is done."

There was a pause. Townsend sank into an empty chair. In triumph Cole thrust a fist into the air. And I, the triumvirate's third? A single tear of joy rolled from my eye. I felt it roll over my circular birthmark and into the sparse hairs of my demi-moustache. Then I threw back my head and shouted:

"Schnapps for everyone!"

There was a cheer, three cheers, and a rush for the bar. I soon had to push my way through the crowd. I took my hand from my pocket, with a nugget clenched in my fist. Straining forward, I threw the bright stone onto the zinc-topped counter. It rang true. Like a crystal. Like a tiny gong. "Come! Fellow Americans! Here is the first fruit of the Neptune Mine!"

Jeff Ruggles picked up the nugget. He bit it, as if it were fruit indeed. Then he nodded. "Gold. Through and through. They've made their strike!"

There was, at this declaration, a terrific hullabaloo. Shouts. Oaths. Exclamations. In a delirium of happiness, I climbed onto the bar top and began to hand out wineglasses to the men below. Then I turned. Just above was that Venus, the white-skinned beauty, with gauze over her bosom, gauze on her thigh. She gazed at me with a smile on her ruby lips. Yes! Gazing at me! A man worth millions! A man with a moustache!

Just then I heard the rumble of Ruggles's voice. He said, "Hold on."

"Something wrong, Jeff?" asked someone in the crowd.

The big barman, his pink skin showing through his sweat-stained shirt, was squinting at the yellow rock. He held it to his eye. "U-R-I," he said, spelling out a strange string of letters.

"Uri?" I echoed.

"No. *URIBUS*."

"Uribus?"

"That's what it says. Here. On the gold. N-U-M. Says that too. Must be a secret message."

"The writing's no secret." That was Arch Osborne, the livery-man. He dug into his own pocket and took out a coin. "I've got the same words on this double eagle: *E Pluribus Unum!* That's what you Boston boys are — one out of the many who bought themselves a salted mine!"

Now the men, the rough miners, started to laugh. Perched still on the zinc platform, I said, "*Selz?* Chloride of sodium — NaCl?"

Poland, gasping, wiping his eyes, struggled to explain. "It's not salt. It's gold. Gold out of a shotgun! Fifty dollars' worth of filed-up gold pieces! After that, even a dungeon would look like Solomon's mines!"

Ruggles was doubled over as well. "Ha-ha! Ha-ha! That trick is as old as the hills!"

Now the saloon, from end to end, rang with laughter. The Meek brothers, Alf and Dick, and the other prospectors beat their fists on the bar; they slapped each other on the back. Ruggles just managed to gasp, "You've been swindled. Bought yourselves a worthless mine."

Cole cried out, over the melee. "It cannot be! We found the gold by chance! The mule kicked down the wall."

"Trained to!" yelled Osborne. "That's how she earns her oats!"

Kane: "Judge Steele, he's sold that mine twenty times!"

Now the miners, so gullible themselves, most of them bankrupt, danced about, stomping on the floorboards. They almost choked on their laughter. From where I stood I clearly heard, through the tumult, the raucous shouting, the most painful laugh of all:

Hee-hee-hee! Hee-hee-hee. Hee-hee-hee: HAW!

At that I dropped down. I forced a path through the crowd to the door. All was dark, save for the yellow light that poured through the windows. I strode over the walkway to the hitching rail. There stood the merry mule, with her wiry whiskers and coarse black mane. What a pang I felt at the sight of those dark eyes, the long yellow teeth, the flattened ears. "Faithless woman!" I cried, choking back the sob that rose within me. "You have broken your master's heart!"

CHAPTER FOUR

General George

1

THE MOST VISIBLE RESULT of my venture, and the most permanent, too, was the two-story building I put up on the south side of Miner Street, well east of Main. This structure — transformed, it is said, into a firehouse — still stands. Fitting: since it was in those days the only fireproof, indeed the first brick building, in all of Yreka. A metal shutter closed over the plate glass window, and a good portion of the dry goods — the clawhammer jackets and jackonettes, the velveteen vests and nankeen trousers — hung from wooden poles that jutted from the brick facade. The ladies' accessories, the haberdashery for men, together with the textiles and bedding, were heaped on shelves within. The Jew's slop shop is what the townsfolk came to call it. That strong, solid building meant an end to my life as a peddler. Instead of A. Pinto traveling to customers, customers would come to A. Pinto's.

How, you will ask, did I, who owned nothing other than a double-dealing mule, raise the funds to build such an impressive structure? Not from Judge Steele, although he did offer to buy back his mine at fifteen cents on the dollar. Townsend refused. He swore, still, that there was gold, a thick vein, a rich vein, beneath the claim. He spent his every moment at the butte, hacking away at the floor of the salted cavern. Not only would he not sell his own share, he bought up his partners'. Cole sold all but ten percent, in return for a fraction of future profits; I gave up the whole of my own, and gladly, for $300 in cash.

Townsend handed over the money in the month of July. We

met at the Kittle and Moffet depot, where he and Cole were about to board the weekly stage for Weaverville and Red Bluff, from where they intended to book river passage to San Francisco. Townsend's plan was to salvage the boiler of the abandoned *Unicorn*, and to use the huge cylinder to drive the stamp mill he intended to build at the butte. I could not, upon hearing this scheme, hold back misgivings:

"This journey is, in my opinion, a foolish notion. You are planning a gold mine before you have found the gold. You wish to bring back the ship's boiler before you have found the ship. Cart before horse!"

Townsend shifted his Voigtlander strap from one shoulder to the other. "We shall," he said, "find both."

"And if you do? Locate the *Unicorn*, let us say? Easier to raise the gold from a sunken galleon than that steam-making boiler. How will you do it? How transport it? On your backs? On the backs of Chinese coolies? You would do better to dig up the butte and move it to the harbor!"

Cole, at the depot doorway, signaled that the coach was about to depart. It was he who addressed me:

"We intend to float it. First in the *Unicorn* herself. Then on a barge to Red Bluff. After that on rafts to Shasta."

"Yes? And then? Across dry land? Over the plain? Perhaps you will roll your machine? Ho-ho-ho: like a barrel of beer!"

Cole, however, was already moving down Main Street. Townsend remained within, measuring the light through the window, as if deciding whether to take a last daguerreotype of the town. "Do you remember?" he asked. "The laughter? The mockery? At the saloon?"

I nodded.

"It is no memory for me. I hear it still. It rings in my ears at this moment. One thing can overcome it: the hiss of steam; the crash of iron machines; the grinding of rock to dust. We are going to make the earth, and these people on it, tremble."

In the street, on his high box, the coachman gave a shout. His whip cracked in the air. I grasped my friend's sleeve, to detain him. This strange speech was surely the result of the long hours spent digging within Mount Etna. I doubted whether the owner of the mine had slept at all since the debacle at the saloon. False assumption. From what Townsend said next, it was clear that he had not only slept but dreamed:

"I have a kind of vision, Adolph. It comes back a dozen times in the course of a night. The image is of a serpent. Milk white in color. It moves, in the dream, through the black earth, the way a serpent moves in water, the curves of its back clearing the soil. You know, do you not, what that snake represents?"

I did. Here was the mother lode, the great vein of quartz that stretched the length of California, at some spots diving deep in the ground, hundreds of feet, perhaps even thousands, while at others it rose to the surface, breaking the crust in a spume of boulders and rock.

Townsend pulled free of my grip. "More trembling, Adolph? Do you fear this serpent shall swallow you?"

"*Nein.*"

"Or me?"

Again I shook my head. It had not been the idea of a snake that had made me shudder. What had come to my mind unbidden was the image of Lewis: rather, the taut white nerve, the sciatic fiber, as it twisted beneath the dark skin and dark flesh of the Negro's leg. This project — the boiler, the mill, the mine itself — would be no less the fiasco. "I repeat. This is a delusion. You are suffering from the fever. The gold is ersatz. It does not exist."

Townsend gave a laugh, his sharp, sudden bark, and then ran after the stage, which was already starting to roll away, over the dust-filled road.

For the whole of that summer I baked the bricks for my building. Neptune, as if to make amends, dragged the hardened mud behind her to the Miner Street site. The actual cash I put into inventory, which began to arrive before the shop was done. We raced to complete our work by Christmas, 1850. For the opening I chose a frock coat, black wool, a double breaster, and — here was an indulgence — a Mexican-style hat. This headgear, also black, and high-crowned, had a dozen tassels in the form of round cotton balls attached to the brim. For the owner of A. Pinto's, no slouch hat, no floppy felt! Only such a sombrero, with chin-strap, with silver chasing, would do.

The opening on the holiday was a success. After the initial rush, however, there was a lull. One quiet evening, just before closing, two new customers drove up, sitting back to back in a dogcart. *Old* customers, I should say, the oldest, since facing forward in the cart was the son of the Modoc chief, Gentleman Jack. Leaning against him, facing the rear, was a squaw, wrapped round with blankets against the chill December day. The two Modocs guided their shaggy pony to the front of the deserted store. They debarked from the two-wheeled cart and crossed the walkway to where I was standing, rubbing long surgeon's fingers, wearing a merchant's smile.

"Greetings, friends!"

The Indians said not a word. Stone-faced the one, scowling the other, they pushed into the shop. Had they — this was my fearful thought — come to reclaim what they had given? The sackful of gold? Once inside, the woman sat on a hard wooden chair, her hands on her wide-spread knees, her belly propped on her lap; the young man, resplendent in the reversed silk of my former smoker, simply dropped cross-legged onto the floor.

I moved round to my spot behind the counter. "Might I offer cups of English tea?" No answer. *"Mit* cream? *Mit Zucker?"* The squaw stared ahead. Her breasts were only half hidden by the loose folds of her blanket. Suddenly, at the glimpse of the nipples, like darkish dunce caps, I knew her: Miss Mary! Paramour! She was, in the light of the slop shop, far plumper, with more flesh, than I had remembered. I fought back the urge to embrace her, to kiss her undimpled cheek.

The silence grew. The teapot began to whistle. The clock on the wall ticked off an entire minute. I could contain my fears no longer. "What can I do, friends? What do you wish? Not possible to return the gold horde. Finished. *Kaputt!* As easy to lift from the ground this building of solid brick!"

At that Miss Mary stirred, raising an arm from her kneecap. She leveled a finger at Dandy Jack. That lad shifted, he groaned; then, as if he were being hauled upright by an unseen winch, an invisible block and tackle, he rose by slow inches to his feet.

"Chapeau!" commanded the squaw, in her familiar deep voice.

Jack swept the headgear, my old wide-brim, aside. His hair, I saw, was damp, and a blot of perspiration, in the form of a maple leaf, spread on his silky shoulders. For a moment he stood, shifting his weight from shoe to shoe, turning the hat in his hands. Still nothing happened. The clock ticked away. The kettle urgently whistled. Suddenly the Indian threw back his head, so that his gaze was directed at the pressed tin ceiling, and opened his mouth.

"*Wuh, wuh, wuh,*" was what he said. His jaws hung open, as if the letter *W* were lodged between them. "*Wuh, wuh,*" he repeated.

Then, clenching his teeth, he went, "*Eeeeee.*" Finally, with effort, he combined the two letters:

"*Weeeee!*" he wailed.

Then he dropped again to the floorboards, crossed one leg over the other, and said, "Gimme cuppa hot tea."

Pity the poor Modoc lad: his task was not yet completed. Once more his taskmaster, my erstwhile lover, held her arm aloft. Jack, as if tied to that appendage by a filament, a string, rose to his feet again. Now he hissed like a snake:

"*Ssssss.*"

Next he put all three sounds together, "*Weeeessss,*" and added a fourth: "*Ullll.*"

Again he stood silent, suffering written upon his face. He grimaced, he groaned, he rolled the balls of his eyes. With his hands he kneaded the crown of the hat like a baker softening dough. For a moment the only sound came from the kettle, whistling for attention, rattling its galvanized lid. Then, with a sudden, violent motion, Dandy Jack threw back his head. Like a confused rooster, heralding dusk instead of dawn, he began to crow:

"*Weesleekitcowrintimrousbeeeessssstieeeee!*"

I, the paleface, stood petrified. Was this a war cry? In Choctaw? Chinook? The savage stood grinning, like a tenor who has completed his song. The female, a basso, joined in:

"*Oh, what a panic's in thy breastie!*"

"Pardon?" said I.

Gentleman Jack: "Word inna book. All about mouse."

"Poem," boomed Miss Mary. "Poem from Burns."

"Ah! Mr. Robert Burns! Poet of the common man! Definite supporter of the French Revolution!"

The squaw struggled to her feet. She reached inside her blanket and produced a worn leather volume. Lewis's! The one I'd left in my pocket! "You look," she said, in her low, rumbling voice. "Real pretty book!"

The tome fell open to the work in question. The first line was hardly legible beneath a layer of palm prints and smudges:

Wee, sleekit, cowrin', tim'rous beastie —

"You have learned this? Through self-study? You have read such words yourself?"

"Jack smart! Smart inna head! Know plenty! *A. B. C.* Ha-ha! *L. M. N. O. P.* Jack know that, too!"

Now the heavyset squaw shuffled to where the autodidact was standing. Arm in arm they walked toward the door. The woman, flinging her blanket, capelike, about her shoulders, addressed the shopkeeper:

"You! Jew feller! You teach. Jack learn. Learn alla word inna book. Brudder gonna talk smooth lika white man. Gonna change damn fool Indian life."

Brother! And she was the sister! I looked, with something like family feeling, toward the son of the chief. From his place on the walkway, he had the parting word. "Poor mouse. Scared. How come he scared? Jack say: ain't gotta house to live in."

That visit took place on the next to last day of the year. The next occurred on January second. I heard the rumble of the springless dogcart, the snort of the little shaggy pony, and the quick step, on the covered walkway, of the wing-tip shoes. Before I could move from behind the counter, Jack-a-Dandy burst into the store and gave a shout:

"Thouneednastartawasaehasty —"

It took the two of us the remainder of the afternoon to sort out, with the help of a Webster's *American*, the garbled line of verse. And still, when darkness fell, we were sounding and spelling the words. The squaw, Miss Mary, sat in her chair, breathing heavily through her mouth and nose. Jack sipped tea from a teacup. His broad brow, smooth and unflattened, was on this occasion etched with deep lines of thought.

"*Na,*" he said. "*Na.* Letter *N.* Letter *A. Na.* Why Bobby Burns say *Na* if he wanna say — what he wanna say?"

"*Not,*" I explained.

"Yes. Good. *Not.* Letter *N.* Letter *O.* Letter *T.*"

"This is *der Dialekt.* Dialect. The way white men speak in Scotland."

"Scotland?"

"The north zone of Britain. Land of Mr. Robert Burns's birth. Described in well-known novels of Sir Walter Scott. Example: *The Fortune of Nigel.* A dashing tale."

There was a pause. The lines in the Indian's forehead grew deeper. He placed a thumb on the poem. "There. Look there. Why Bobby Burns say *awa?* Letter *A.* Letter *W.* Letter *A.* This the how-you-call-him? *Dialekt?*"

"Correct! Gold star! The Scottish farmer speaks to the Scottish mouse. He uses a language the rodent can understand."

Dandy Jack, who had been leaning over the manuscript, stood upright. He hurled the teacup and scalding tea to the floor. Then he strode, with his sister waddling behind him, to the door. "Mouse! Mouse! A mouse!" With this cry he began to strike his fists against his temples. He knocked a spray of tears from his eyes. "Mouse know *Dialekt!* Mouse read Bobby Burns! Mouse smarter than stinking Indian! Than dumb Dandy Jack!"

The slam, the bang, of the slop-shop door was like a fist striking a blow at my chest. For a moment I stood motionless, as if my rib cage, with the heart trembling inside it, had been shattered into as many pieces as the porcelain cup.

My distress, however, was replaced by delight when, at high noon of the following day, that stout door burst open, and the same Indian stood inside.

"Wi' bickering brattle!" he exclaimed, having deciphered each word of the third line on his own. Nor was he, as he stood beaming on the threshold, done. "*Wi.* Letter *W.* Letter *I.* This is *Dialekt.* What Bobby Burns say? Jack tell you. Word *with.* Simple! Easy! Even dumb dog unnerstand!"

"Bravo!" cried I, raising like a prizefighter my hands above my head. "This is *prima!* Grade A!" Behind me, on the stovetop, the teakettle began loudly to whistle, like a spectator with his fingers in his mouth.

Now the two Indians returned each afternoon. Clearly the pair were not reaching Tule Lake, which was at least a day and a night's gallop away. Instead, the brother and sister were camping just east of town, where they would study the dog-eared text by the light of a kerosene lamp. Each night a new line was put to memory; each day the siblings arrived at the slop shop so that the proprietor and his pupil might master its meaning, working out with the aid of our Noah Webster the sense of *stibble* and *dribble, hald* and *cauld,* and of *O' foggage green!*

So the chill gray days went by. At times the Indians would depart sad and speechless as the shape of the rhymed tale became clear — the rodent's preparations for weary winter coming fast; the gathering of leaves and twigs for the cozy abode; and the crash of the cruel plow blade through all its hopes and expectations: *"Thy wee bit housie, too, in ruin!"* If, on the next day, the dogcart was late, I'd pace back and forth on the walkway, peering eastward, until I could see, beyond the far end of Miner Street, the patch of red silk, glowing in the dim light of early dusk, and hear, above the pony's hooves, the grinding of the unoiled wheels, the slight burr of the Modoc's tenor: "Mister-r-r Pinto! Mister-r-r Pinto! Gentleman Jack is here!"

Then one day toward the end of February the two Indians did not show up at all. I tramped along my covered walkway, beneath the jackets and trousers that hung like the victims of a lynching party from their wooden poles. No sign of the Modocs. Out I leaned, into the street, where a fine rain had been falling all day. No sounds either, save for the mechanical clank of the *Ingot* presses. Then, from Main Street, from approximately the location of the Sazarac Saloon, shouts and laughter rose in the air. I remained, squinting into the slanting rain. Around the corner, where the noise of celebration continued, someone fired a gun. A horse whinnied. There was a snatch of song. Impossible to bear the suspense any longer. I jumped from the walkway and began, in my tasseled hat and checked gabardines, to slosh through the puddles that had formed in the road.

At the intersection I turned south and paused. There, tied to the Sazarac's hitching rail, was the very dogcart for which I'd been waiting. No mistaking that vehicle: the seats that faced in opposite directions; the high, spoked, springless wheels; the same undersized pony, whose winter coat now hung damp from its flanks. On the instant I broke into a trot. A crowd spilled through the saloon's bat-wing doors and onto the gallery planks. Cigar smoke billowed over their heads. Inside, people were shouting, singing. I pushed my way through.

Half the town, it seemed, was there. The Yrekans stood three deep at the bar and packed the gambling pit. The dance floor was full of people shuffling to the strains of the violin. I saw, at the center of one group of waltzers, the Panamanian, Antoinette. She was dancing with four men at once. They held her arms. They gripped her waist. They pressed her from behind. A second group was revolving left, revolving right, in the manner of an Old World polka. Then I realized that the hub of this pinwheel was the fat form of the Modoc squaw. Mary! She stood unmoving, like a plump maypole, while the men rubbed against the soft rolls of her flesh.

Where, then, was her brother? There! Standing on top of the bar! Judge Steele was below him, striking a spoon against a glass. To that tinkling sound no one paid heed. The noise of laughter, of gambling, the thump of the dancers' heels, drowned it out.

Dandy Jack was as pale, almost, as the white man below him. He wore, in addition to his usual felt hat, inside-out smoker, and wing-tip shoes, a pair of spotless white gaiters. When the Indian smiled, I noticed another new item — a gold tooth, left central incisor, glittering in his mouth. The young man threw back his head and started to speak.

"To a Mouse," he began, or so I imagined. The noise was so great it was impossible to hear a word. The Modoc continued to mouth the words: *"On turning her up in her nest with the plough."*

Once more Steele beat on the glass. "Quiet! Quiet!" he shouted. "We're going to hear a poem!"

Bit by bit the large room fell silent. The drinkers drained their glasses. The bettors put off their bets. On the dance floor, all movement stopped. Everyone turned toward the bar, toward the bottles, the mirror, and the spot on the wall above the mirror where an American flag, with tricolored bunting, had replaced the gauze-draped muse.

I now posed to myself a question: what was this day's date? The answer flew into my sombreroed head. February 22! Of course! What could be simpler? The flag, the bunting, the celebration: this was Washington's birthday! Anniversary of the February Revolution!

"Wuh," said Jack, into the air of the silent room. *"Wuh-wuh-wuh."*

The Yrekans looked at each other, then back to the finely dressed youth. His smile had vanished. The lines of concentration had returned to his brow. Beads of sweat ran from under his wide-brimmed hat.

"Pssst!" The prompter was Pinto — that is, I, myself. *"Wee!* Remember? *Wee beastie!"*

"Wuh," Jack repeated.

Just then there was a commotion at the center of the dance floor. Without partners, without support, Mary had dropped down to her haunches. She squatted there, with her woolly blanket hiked well above the fat flesh of her knees. She breathed noisily, raspingly, through her mouth and nose. A ripple of laughter ran through the room, but whether it was directed at the clumsy squaw or her tongue-tied brother I could not determine. Jack, the gentleman, remained on the bar, his arms wrapped round his torso, as if to squeeze the lost words from his chest. He chewed, with his old teeth, with the shiny new one, on his lower lip. No doubt now: the crowd was laughing openly at the mute Modoc. Stack, the postmaster, pointed at my protégé. "Haw-haw," he guffawed. "They think a redskin can talk!"

I now raised my arms in the air. "Friends! Americans! Patience! I assure you this former savage knows by heart the work of the bard!"

But the tide of laughter, far from abating, actually swelled. "Your savage!" Alf Meek called out. "He's wearing spats!"

"Do not, friends, mock this child of nature. True, he is *ein Primitiv*. But what of that? No man is born so low he cannot be raised, or is so ignorant he cannot be taught. *A man's a man,* declares Mr. Burns, *for a' that.* Let us listen politely."

But the native merely stood there, as if under a douche bath of his own perspiration. Audibly he ground his teeth together. No: that sound did not come from the Modoc's molars. It grew into a low growl, a rumble. People looked around.

"It's the storm," said Poland. "The rain and thunder."

But the noise was too strong and steady for that. It continued to grow in volume.

The greengrocer, Voorsanger, gave a shout: "A tremor! I feel it!"

So did I, and all the rest: a trembling, a drumming at the foot soles. The crowd began to rush fearfully through the double doors. They gathered on the walkway, peering one and all to the south. Swept up in the surge, I stood with the others, straining to see what it was that drew near upon the mud-filled road.

Straight up Main Street a mule train was hauling, on rows of rolling tree trunks, a gigantic physical object. The animals, the drivers, the underside of the thing itself, were so bespattered they looked like shapes cut from black paper. Only I, of all the crowd, knew what was coming. It was Townsend. And with him the *Unicorn* boiler.

Now the Yrekans ran into the street, to get a closer look. Some waved their arms, shouting, "Stop!"

But the juggernaut could not stop, or even slow, without sinking into the mud. The moment a log came free at the rear, someone — it was Townsend himself — seized it with a grappling hook. With a yoke of two mules he brought it round to the front, where a companion — the dirt-daubed Matt Cole — inserted it at the head of the series. The impact of this movement was indeed like that of an earthquake. The heavy weight, the turning tree trunks, made the matchstick town of Yreka, with its false facades and flimsy buildings, shake and sway. All the glassware in the Sazarac Saloon was tinkling. The windows shook in their frames.

How far, I wondered, had they gone in this fashion? At this pace? Even the thought made me weary. Forward I dashed, calling to my friends. "Mr. Townsend! Matt Cole! Is it you?" Both men, in a kind of blackface, their clothes draped in dark clay like crepe, marched on. But the look Frank Townsend cast upon me with the whites of his glaring eyes stopped me dead in my tracks.

For a moment I stared upward, while the enormous hollow cylinder rolled by. It seemed to me an enormous beetle, a gigantic bug. The rain settled down on the flattened top, which itself resembled a pair of closed, copper-colored wings. At the bottom a number of pipes stuck out, jointed and tangled, like spindly legs, or broken antennae. Stout ropes stretched from the surface to the halters of the mules, as if those poor struggling creatures could prevent the mammoth insect from flying away.

"Doctor! Doctor feller!"

The shout came from the walkway, in front of the saloon. There was Two-Toes Tom, a foaming cobbler in his hand. He repeated his cry: "Doctor! Run quick! You come!"

Then Poland leaned from the gallery. "Pinto! You're the doctor he means! Come inside!"

I whirled. I rushed back to the saloon. The large room was nearly empty. For an instant I thought I was needed to tend Dandy Jack, who still stood on the bar top, silent, motionless, as if he had gone into shock. Then I saw that the few customers who remained were gathered round the form of the squaw. She sat where I had last seen her, on the dance floor. But between her bent legs, spreading out from under the wool of her blanket, was a dark stain, as thick as oil. Voorsanger stood closest to the patient. He pointed to the blanket. "Lift it," he said.

I did so, and saw, in the center of that coffee-colored puddle, the newborn boy. The cord, still attached, hung loosely round the neck. The afterbirth lay to one side. A cream — it looked like a shaving lather — covered the infant, from top to toe. He was not moving. He did not breathe.

"Dead," said Voorsanger, above the rumble that still echoed from the road.

Kane, the faro dealer, took a quick look. "Stillborn. Strangled in the womb."

Now I was the one in shock. Fool! Idiot! How could I not have known the woman's condition? The swollen belly. The mammaries. The shortness of her breath. Was I a blind man? I might have saved the child!

Someone pushed me aside, making for the grayish babe. "God-dam!" said Two-Toes Tom. Then he seized the blue-veined cord and gnawed it in two. "Bloody bugger!"

No use. Too late. The infant did not move. Now I came forward and leaned over the little creature. What a strange-looking fellow! How big the head was — far too large for the tiny wrinkled body or the thin stem, no bigger than my own thumb, of the neck. The little hands were curled, like those of any sleeper, under the chin.

Miss Mary moaned. But what help could I offer? I picked up the boy in the palm of one hand and turned the face upward. The eyes were hidden under the delicate eyelids. The mouth hung slack. I bent my head, bringing full, thick lips down to thin blue ones. I inhaled through my nose and blew a warm stream of air into the cold body. Nothing happened. I breathed again. I felt — did I hear it, too? — the invisible sac of the lungs snap open. A third breath. Through my fingers, the palms of my hands, I felt that bag, and the bony bellows of the chest around it, expand.

How quiet everything had become. No rumble from the street. No sounds from the crowd. But here was an odd event: atop the bar, at long last, Gentleman Jack had begun to recite the poem, the field mouse saga, almost as if my repeated efforts had given him breath as well. On and on the Indian droned, without error, without forgetting a rhyme. No one listened. All eyes were fixed upon me, the physician, as I lifted my mouth from the child's. The chest of the infant rose and fell on its own. A tiny fist waved in the air. Then a sound, a weak wail, came from the open mouth. The babe was crying!

Those in the crowd, the rough miners, the Yrekans, broke into smiles and gay laughter. The whole creamy body of the newborn began to writhe: the feet kicked, the fists shook, the head twisted on the reedlike neck. And still the wail continued, louder now, a bawling, a sorrowful sobbing, almost as if the child in some mysterious fashion had heard, and comprehended, the sad tale of homelessness and ruin and dashed expectations that was being recited behind him. Indeed, the Modoc, while performing, had to raise his own voice to compete.

> "But, och! I backward cast my e'e
> On prospects drear!"

Here Jack, for an instant, paused. As he did so, the wet, wailing infant opened his tightly shut eyes. Large and dark, they seemed to focus upon the face bent above him: my own. The bawling trailed to a whimper, and ceased altogether. There was nothing to hear then but the sound of his breath, catching in his throat. His eyes, still fastened upon me, as if upon a strange, slightly moustachioed mother, did not blink once. The head, with its bulging brow, turned slightly. Those watching swore that he did so in order to hear Dandy Jack, as that smartly dressed Indian completed the last lines of his poem:

> "An forward, tho' I canna see,
> I guess an' fear!"

2

The rains soon stopped, and for a few days in March, there was a false, fleeting spring. Birds sang. At the bottom of Etna Pond, the Etna Fountain erupted. Shoots of wild onion, of desert buckwheat, pushed up from the ground. Alas: no joy of the season for me. That was because on that same night, Washington's birthday, February 22, the dogcart had rolled out of town, carrying with it Jack-a-Dandy, his sister Mary, and General George — which, naturally enough, was the name the townsfolk had given the newborn babe. Time and again I mounted my mule and rode into the alkali plain. I started eastward, hoping to see the dust from the cart, the silk patch of the reversed smoking jacket, or to hear the wail of the papoose. But there was no color, no movement, no sound, save for the balls of prairie weed rolling back and forth at random, as far as the eye could see.

Finally, well into the month of May, when I had almost abandoned hope, the three Indians reappeared, driving their little wagon down Miner Street to the two-story shop. My curving nose picked up their smell, the familiar stink of the bullheads, even before they'd stepped onto the walkway. Then the door flew back, and the young brave stood in the frame, his gold tooth shining, the volume of poems in one hand, the Noah Webster in the other. He threw back his head — round his neck, I noted, was a new haberdashery item: a maroon cravat — and began, in his tenor tones, to recite:

> "My bonnie lass, I work in brass.
> A tinker is my station —"

Before he could finish, his sister, now in a light calico skirt, pushed him aside. On her back was a cradle board, inside of which sat General George. Only his head, wobbling on the straw of his neck, was visible above the tightly woven cone of the basket. A thin fuzz of hair had sprung up above the unknit bones of his skull. The boy's features — the wide, dark, staring eyes, the narrow nose, the almost lipless mouth — were pinched together between a large, swollen-seeming forehead and the sharp point of the chin. How, I wondered, would the tribe flatten this bulging brow? The head extended backward as much as it protruded at the front, as if bursting with the matter of the brain.

I ached now to bend close, to touch the top of the skull and, through its tiny, trembling window, the pulse of the fountain below. But the stench of fish oil drove me back. "Wait, friends!" I exclaimed. "*Moment!*" Then I opened the trap to the cellar storeroom and let myself down. When I came up again it was with a large tin basin, together with a small, hard object some five inches long, three inches wide. Yes: you have guessed it! The last bar of Maria Theresa brand soap!

At once the squaw, Miss Mary, seized the scented cake and began to rub it over her hefty bosoms and under the pits of her arms. I turned from where I was pouring cool water into the tub.

"No, no, madam! You see? First we remove the bar." Carefully I undid the black-and-gold wrapper. Mary held the slick paper, with its lightly embossed portrait of the empress, to the window light. "Fat lady!" she declared.

"*Ja!* Queen of Bohemia. King of Hungary. Friend to farmers of the realm. Also, mother of sixteen children. Including well-known Marie Antoinette of the country of France."

Now Jack came close, staring at the semitransparent tissue as if all the facts of history were printed upon it. "Poor Indian!" said he. "Dumb Indian. Gotta whole lot to know."

Now the teakettle started to whistle and, in its impatient fashion, rattle its lid. I strode to it and began to pour the steaming contents onto the cooler water inside the tub. Then I returned to the squaw, seized General George by his bare, bony shoulders — a baby bird, surely, had more flesh on its folded wings — and lifted him from the conical basket. Immediately the babe started howling. He waved his fists and kicked his feet, which were balled up like fists as well.

"Ho! Ho!" I give this merry laugh while averting my face and holding the burden at arm's length, as if it were indeed the rotting bullhead it smelled like. "A sitz bath for you!"

Then I plunged the little fellow, ruby red with rage, into the round tin basin. There was a moment of astonishment, of silence; then the mouth of the infant gaped wide, in order to let out a deafening scream. Dropping to my knees, I pushed up my sleeves and began, with the pink-colored soap bar, to work up a lather.

"Wasser!" I cried. The Indians leaped to comply. Dandy Jack filled the kettle, while Miss Mary stirred the juniper bark in the stove to a hotter flame. For the next moments all was chaos: the thrashing, the caterwauling of General George; the water dashing over the sides of the tub, while geysers and sprays, as if from a miniature typhoon, flew in the air; and, through it all, the maddening one-note whistle of the neglected kettle. Gradually, however, soapsuds started to rise, shining, shimmering, swelling. They collected on the skin of the bather, clinging, in balls of iridescent light, to his chest, his chin, his outstretched hands. The howling ceased. A gummy grin spread over his face. Soon the child disappeared within the mound of bubbles, becoming a hundred children, like an image caught in the multiple chambers of an insect's eye.

"Eins, zwei, drei," said I, an Uncle Adolph, as I playfully punctured the glistening orbs. *"Vier, fünf, sechs!"* Slowly the flesh-and-blood boy reemerged, gasping at each tiny explosion. With the fingers of his right hand he clutched, one after the other, the fingers of his left. *"Sieben, acht, neun, zehn!"*

Now, as if each bursting bubble had released the essence of a perfume, the sweet smell of rose petals wafted through the air. Jack-a-Dandy looked up from the kettle. He sniffed. He snorted. Suddenly, in a blur of motion, he began throwing aside his white man's clothes — hat, coat, shirt, cravat.

"Attention! What is this you are doing?"

From the Modoc, no reply. The pants came down. Away flew the wing-tip shoes. The next thing I knew, the young Modoc had plucked the infant out of the water and stepped into the tepid tub himself. There he stood, stark naked, scooping up the soapy water and throwing it over his head, his shoulders, his back. He grinned. His gold tooth flashed.

I fetched a yard of worsted, in which I wrapped the aromatic infant. How the heart of the lad raced, tripping palpably through the cloth. Mary took him. He was still clutching his fingers, each in turn, and drawing his breath in gasps — as if every such sigh marked a bubble's expiration.

"Mister-r-r Pinto!" exclaimed the brave, now in a squatting position, knees under chin. I gave a start. It seemed to me that the Indian, so dark before, so dusky, was now several shades lighter — though whether this was because of the soap's cleansing properties or the glow of the idea that now lit his features, I could not say. Fairly beaming, he continued: "Mister-r-r Pinto! Jack gotta smart idea! Sell fancy soap cake to stinking Modocs. Make 'em smell good! Like French fellers. Like Mr. Beau Br-r-rumel!"

Sadly I shook my head. "Alas. You have in those waters the very last bar."

On the instant Jack's face was transformed. A look of dismay, of horror even, passed across it. He began to splash in the basin, to grope on the tin bottom. "Where soap bar? All gone!" he wailed. "Alla bar gone. Got stolen!"

"Ho! Ho! Not stolen. Dissolved!"

"Dissolved?"

"There! You see?" I pointed to the side of the tub, where — this was an unfortunate defect in the Pressburg process — only a sliver of the original cake remained.

The native peeled the pink scrap from the tin and gazed mournfully at it. Then, totally from memory, he started to speak:

> "Pleasures are like poppies spread,
> You seize the flow'r, its bloom is shed."

The instant I heard this rhyme, a notion was born in my head. I began, in excitement, to shout: "Poppies! Blossoms! Poppy blooms! Wait, please. *Moment!*" The next instant I was through the slop-shop door, leaving the three Indians — two sweet-smelling, one foul — alone. In no time I returned, arms laden not with poppies but with the pale whorls of desert buckwheat that had pushed up between the planks of the walkway; and, from where it clung to the brick base of the building, a spray of owl clover.

"My friends! *Voilà!* You see here flowers! Petals of flowers.

From this we shall distill the sweet essence. We shall make a perfume. Rare as the scents of France!"

Now spring, the true spring, with its bursting blossoms — yellow-throated monkey flowers, bright red mountain paintbrush, leathery-leaved penstemons — passed into summer, with its hard, dry, near-Arabian winds. No vegetation, apart from mustard and sage and the colorless, scentless sneezeweed, survived on the plain. Luckily, we had thought to dry great stacks of the earlier crop. From these flowering plants we distilled our aromas.

The apparatus was entirely makeshift, built from pressed tin and rubberized tubes. All day long it bubbled away in the basement, sending up clouds of steam and emitting, ultimately, from its curved sugar-pot spout, a few drops of amber-colored essence. These were mixed not into a perfume, strictly speaking, but into a toilet balm: alcohol and water in equal measure, with the oils of buckwheat or wallflower or clover at a concentration of just two percent. Daubed on the body, even splashed over the skin, the scent was not quite powerful enough to mask, on the two grown Indians, the ingrained bullfish stench. General George, however, soon came to smell like the sultan of Persia. A musky fragrance, like precious civet, rose from his tiny body, from his tightly stretched skin; and even his breath smelled less of his mother's milk than of sesame — native, no less than the rarest ylang-ylang, to Asian climes.

Each week the two Modocs, with General George crouched in his cradle board, would drive to Tule Lake with a single bottle of this eau de cologne. On one such occasion they took me, Pinto, the *parfumier,* along. The John Harvards, of course, had long since departed, and their wagons had been taken away by the tribe. From where the dogcart stopped at the eastern edge of the plateau I could see the braves, dots in the distance, moving about the shore. They were not fishing. Nor were the squaws weaving their baskets. Some were singing, so loudly in fact that the words drifted all the way to the top of the cliff. Others were performing a tottering dance. Slowly I began to grasp what should have been obvious from the start: there was not a sober Indian in sight.

The truth was, I was perhaps the last white man in Yreka to realize that the whole tribe of Modocs had become intoxicated. More and more natives were riding to town, bent on the worst kind of mischief. Alf Meek and his brother, working their mine shaft at Hardscrabble Creek, were among the first to be harassed: picks stolen, a mule driven off, their tent shot through by an arrow. West of town, Arch Osborne's haystacks were set afire, and a section of fencing was torn from the livery corral. At night, under the cover of darkness, someone shattered Simpson the barber's plate glass window. As the summer wore on, the disturbances spread. Bands of Modocs, unmistakably drunken, began roving about, begging from citizens, pilfering the shops, lying across the walkways in a stupor.

The great question was, where were the redskins getting their liquor? Not from the Sazarac: even Two-Toes Tom was turned away from that, and every other, saloon. Naturally enough, the Yrekans thought next of Gentleman Jack, who continued to go back and forth between the slop shop in town and the Modoc village. But when a group of miners surrounded the dogcart on one of its eastbound journeys, they found that the Indian, his sister, and nephew had nothing with them but a single whiskey bottle — and that filled not with liquor but with lavender-colored water. They tried again, this time on a trip back. But the little wagon carried only mustard plants and a pile of the common hawk's-beard. "Dandelions!" said Osborne, the liveryman, as he scattered the puffy heads to the wind.

Then, at the end of the month of August, Poland found a Modoc in his butcher shop, snoring away in a drunken trance. The brave's pockets were stuffed with dressed quail. The vigilantes dragged him outside. The poor Indian got his name, Scarface Charlie, from the beating he received that morning. The white men knocked him down. They struck him with their gun butts and kicked him with their boots. They walked back and forth on his buttocks, his back. Finally the Yrekans hauled him to his feet one last time. Everyone in that crowd watched while the thief raised his arm and, bleeding, trembling, pointed to the drygoods shop of the town's only Jew.

Not five minutes later that same battered native limped through the door of the fireproof building and repeated his gesture, this time pointing not at the shop itself, or its frightened proprietor, but at the squaw and her sleeping papoose. Immediately a group of white men — Osborne, Jeff Ruggles, Poland, Steele — followed him through the door.

"Gentlemen!" No need to explain who uttered this greeting. "Something in seersucker, perhaps?"

Then Dandy Jack poked his head out of the cellar trap and General George, waking, started to howl. Poland strode to the hole in the floor and rudely, as a man might do to his dog, pushed the Indian aside with the toe of his boot. "There it is!" he shouted, ducking down to peer into the room below. "A regular still!"

Ruggles, who had remained by the entrance, barring it with his bulk, now lowered his long-barreled musket toward the Modoc male. Osborne moved to the squaw and pulled her off the chair, to her feet.

"What are you doing?" I demanded. "Why are you here? Mr. Poland, what is it you want?"

Instead of replying, the butcher joined the liveryman. Together they held Miss Mary's arms. Now Scarface Charlie moved behind her and in one swift motion lifted the swaddled infant out of his woven cradle. The mother twisted round to reach her son, but the men held her fast. Now Steele came forward and reached into the bottom of the basket. His hand, when he withdrew it, held a half-pint bottle, corked and full.

"Was," I inquired, *"ist das?"*

From the doorway, Ruggles gave a shout. "The whiskey!"

Poland: "That's how it's done!"

I stared at the bottle, at the amber liquid within. *"Nein!* Not whiskey! Eau de cologne!"

"Perfume, is it?" said Steele, digging once more into the cradle's bottom — a false bottom, in fact, full of empty space that the papoose's drawn-up legs should have filled. He withdrew a second bottle, a third, fourth, and fifth. Each was identical: tightly corked, filled with a fragrance half of whose volume was ethyl alcohol, C_2H_5OH. In other words, one hundred proof!

I rounded now on Dandy Jack. "What have you done? Smuggled, sir? Committed a crime? Were we not partners together?"

The Indian's gold tooth flashed in a smile. "Jack smart! Make lotta money! Play good joke!"

Suddenly, surprisingly, Mary broke free from the grasp of the two Yrekans and bolted for the door. By the time her captors could react, she had reached the walkway. In two more steps she crossed it and leaped into the dogcart. Tipping, careening, the little wagon sped down Miner Street in a cloud of dust.

Now the squaw's brother attempted a similar escape. One moment he was smiling, half in the cellar, half in the shop; the next he had vaulted from the trapdoor and was running headlong into the trio of Ruggles, Osborne, Poland. He bowled them over as if they were no more substantial than the three spindly legs of Townsend's tripod. Then he, too, dashed through the door, over the walkway, and into the dust cloud that still swirled in the street.

But his flight had a different ending. Only a second or two after disappearing into the dust screen, he emerged, walking backward, his hands in the air. Ben Piper had the barrel of his swivel gun pressed to the Indian's chest.

I was the first out the door of the shop. "Mr. Ben Piper! Why are you here? I thought all the John Harvards were at Mount Etna. At work on the mine machines."

"I work for Townsend, all right. But these drunken Modocs have made the same mischief at the butte as in town."

The gunman, in speaking, never broke stride. He pushed his captive onto the walkway, then down the covered planks. The others — the five white men, along with Scarface Charlie, still with the papoose in his arms — came after. They marched down the promenade, then right, and right again, until the whole group gathered at the back of my solid brick building. They stood General Jack against the windowless wall. Ruggles snatched away his soft-brimmed hat. Poland settled one of the half-pint bottles on top of his head. Then both men sprang backward, leaving Jack standing in a spread-eagle stance.

All of this had happened so rapidly, and wordlessly too, that by the time I realized this was to be a shooting, a summary execution, the executioner had seated himself a score of steps distant and was sighting along the long barrel of his swivel gun.

"No! No! *Nein!*"

Too late: the blast from Ben Piper's weapon drowned out my words.

There was a single scream — not from the victim, who lay crumpled at the base of the wall, but from his infant nephew, whom Scarface Charlie, an instant before turning on his heel, had thrust into my frock-coated arms. Charlie himself disappeared around the corner of the building.

"Let him go," said Steele, as Arch Osborne started after. "Pick up that one. Hurry."

The liveryman halted. He went back to the wall, where his companions had already grabbed Gentleman Jack by the armpits and were hauling him to his feet. There was no wound on his body. No blood. Not a scratch. Once more the Modoc stood against the brick, rubbing his stinging eyes. Poland, unbidden, balanced a second vessel on his doused, dripping head. From Piper's lips there hung — this was the mark of the anatomy student — a sprig of mint. With a laugh, he lowered his cheek to the stock of his smoking weapon.

This time the bottle seemed to shatter even before the rifle's report. The knees of the native buckled, but did not give way. The smell of rosewater spread over the scene.

Everything was quiet, save for the rattle of the gunman reloading his gun. Even the babe stopped his wail. Without a word, Poland placed a third container where the two others had been. Then Ruggles shook his large, wax-moustachioed head.

"Enough," he said.

"Not enough," said the sharpshooter, and pulled the trigger again. The bottle collapsed, like a tiny glass building. The scent sprayed through the air.

"Another," said Piper.

The butcher hesitated, looking toward Steele. The latter nodded. Poland set up the target and took a step back. Osborne pointed at the redskin.

"Look at him. How he's smiling. Hell, it's like this was a game."

The others stared. The young man's skin, his shiny silk lining, were drenched. Bits of glass glittered in his hair. His eyes were tightly clenched — not in fear, but because of the sting of the spirits, the smart. But the smile on his lips stretched from ear to ear. If anything, it grew even wider as Piper blew the next bottle to smithereens. The pale pink liquid spilled over his face, his shoulders, his clothing. Now he broke into laughter — and gaily continued while, one after the other, as fast as the gun could be reloaded, the shots rang out and the bottles shattered on top of his head.

At that moment I felt a sharp pain above the ear. For an instant I feared I was wounded — hit by a ricochet, a shard of glass. Then I realized that with each new shot General George was tugging a tuft of my hair. He was counting the detonations. He only stopped when Ben Piper ran out of bullets. Then, in the dying echo, the stretching silence, the infant began his long and pitiful wail.

From Dandy Jack, however, there came a gleeful shout, a triumphant cheer. He knew that he was banished. But he also knew that the perfume which had bespattered his clothing had also soaked so deeply into his skin, his body, that no amount of water could ever wash it away.

3

General George did not stop howling. His cry went on night and day. Those living on Miner Street were kept up for hours. Even those who never seemed to sleep, the gamblers in the Sazarac Saloon, the late-night drinkers, could hear the high-pitched wail, like a siren, through the shut windows. Who would have thought — so said the miners — that such a little fellow, hardly able to hold his head up, could make such lusty sounds?

No one suffered more from the hullabaloo than I. During those first nights I wrapped my head in worsteds, and screwed cotton rags into my ears. Then, in desperation, I ran into the street and howled myself. Next, in a panic, I shook the lad, turning him upside down, as if the source of what pained him might, like a burr from under a saddle or a hairball from a cat, be shaken out. But the Indian boy, writhing, weeping, lifting his knees — did he think he was still in his conical cradle? — only wailed the more.

Finally it occurred to me that the belly of the abandoned infant must be empty. But how, and with what, to fill it? Siskiyou County was virtually milkless. The only wet nurses — that is to say, the unhappy lad's mother and the other Modoc squaws — were sixty miles off, on the shores of their fish-filled lake. The white women nearby, including Goody Peacock, Bosworth's spouse, were as sterile as the oxen that had survived the trek across the plains.

That night, driven to distraction, with a ringing noise in my ears, I ran round to the east side of the building, where Neptune stood in her sheet-metal shed. She was, at the moment, chewing a wisp of hay. "You female! You darling!" I cried, throwing my arms about her coarse-maned neck. "Give me a cream drop! A milk flow! Make the effort!"

Moments later, I, the crazed foster father, made the same request of the crowd at the Sazarac Saloon. Everyone had a different idea: at the bar, they trickled cherry liquor down the babe's throat, followed by licorice-flavored spirits, and finally spoonfuls of crème de menthe.

Waa-a-a! screamed the infant, unceasing, relentless, until green-colored bubbles appeared at his mouth. Soon the rough miners, the hardened gamblers, were fleeing the room. One of these, Richard Meek, returned, leading a she-goat that the brothers kept at their claim. Quickly the miners spilled out a bottle of wine and filled it one third with the animal's milk. A strip of flannel — they tore this from Jeff Ruggles's bar rag — was twisted deep into the narrow neck, so that soon it was soaked with white fluid the way a wick would be with kerosene. But the boy would not take it into his mouth. He jerked his head back, grimacing, spitting, letting out an ear-splitting bellow. It was all the miners could do to refrain from seizing the saturated cloth and gagging the black, gaping mouth.

Baggy-eyed, baleful, I returned to my upstairs bedroom and bed. But after two more sleepless hours, during which even Esquimaux-style earmuffs proved of no avail, I appeared once more before my whiskered mule. This time I drew on her halter, threw a blanket over her back, and rode with my screeching stepson through the night's blackest hour out of the town.

There was still light left the next day when we approached the Modoc village. We smelled the bullheads long before we came to the edge of the high plateau. I dismounted. Off to the left was the trunk, leafless, nearly branchless, of a lone juniper tree. I laid the bawling boy beneath it on his back and turned resolutely aside. If the stench of the fish reached this far, I reasoned, the sound of the infant's voice would carry even farther. Jack-a-Dandy, back with his people, exiled from the world of the whites, would recognize that piping cry. He would bring the child back to its mother, to her swollen, milk-full breasts. And if he did not, let some animal, a she-bear, a coyote, feed the foundling, the way a wolf had suckled Romulus, builder of the city of Rome.

Such were my thoughts, cruel ones, worthy of a Habsburg, as, at a jolting trot, Neptune the mule bore me away. Then, just before I rode out of earshot, I realized that the howls of the babe had already ceased. Onward I went nevertheless — ten, fifteen, a score of yards. Then I stopped. Like a fierce Tartar, with lips curled back from my teeth, I yanked the head of my mount round to the opposite direction. Then I beat her on the croup, and raked, with my blucher bottoms, her flanks. In short, I sent her galloping as fast as the wind. With my head bent down to the flying mane, my breath coming in painful rasps, I sent up into the colorless sky, to the stern, unbending God of my people, the following prayer: *Do not let the savages be there! Do not let the Modocs find him!*

A moment later I reined in and slid from the back of the mule. There, not five feet away, was the blighted tree and, alone underneath it, in the exact place I'd left him, the large-headed child. I dashed to his side. The abandoned boy was staring upward, smiling liplessly, toothlessly, while he pulled, in a kind of milking motion, upon each of his fingers. Twisting about, I stared upward too. Above, in the bare branches, perched—*eins, zwei, drei*: I counted along with the child—a number of birds. Swallows, I thought, or jays, or blackbirds. The tears that started to my eyes made it difficult to tell.

"My son! My son! *Verzeih mir!*" I cried, scooping the swaddled infant into my arms. Quickly I mounted and trotted off to the west. I hugged the boy. I kissed his bulging forehead. Over and again, in a sob-filled voice, I kept repeating, "Forgive me!"

We arrived back in Yreka two nights later. Peat-gas lamps were burning in the street. More lights came on in the second-floor windows as the babe, howling at full strength once more, passed below. I drew up before A. Pinto's and dropped from the mule in a daze of exhaustion. Mechanically, I crossed the gallery and went inside. In the darkness, with the slow steps of a somnambulist, I moved over the floor of the shop, and then, batlike, as if guided by the pipings of the creature clutched in my arms, I climbed the stairs. Up we went, one step, another, to the top. Now down the hall. Now into the bedroom. Already asleep, my brain no more receptive to stimuli than the specimens pickled in jars at the Harvard Medical College, I took four giant steps and tumbled, with all my clothes on, even the tall sombrero, into bed.

A few moments later—not because of the infant's squalling but, on the contrary, because of the sharp shock of silence—I woke. A few stray moonbeams fell through the half-closed shutters, dashing against the wall, the bedstead, the coverlet. By that faint light I saw the naked form of the hungry infant pressed to the plump purple breast of Mademoiselle Antoinette. Even as I watched, the little fellow raised his bobbing head and took a deep breath. Instantly the Panamanian splashed a fresh white dollop of goat's milk from the long-necked bottle onto her chest. Then the boy, with a sigh, a smack of his hardly visible lips, plunged back onto the dampened nipple.

"Shhh," cautioned the wet nurse, whose form took up the greater part of the bed. "No talk, handsome Jim!"

In the next weeks it became clear that General George, gulping greedily, would not die of starvation. Yet he gained hardly more than a pound and grew less than an inch: it was as if that bony body, with its twiglike neck and tule-thin limbs, its knobby elbows and knees, had been stunted by the coils of swaddling, the way the skulls of the older Modocs had been forced backward by rawhide bands. Nor, to my dismay, and that of my fellow Yrekans, did the child's bawling cease. He only fell silent when he sucked at his nurse's breast, or fitfully slept, or when — pulling upon his fingers, as if they were abacus beads — he was counting. That was why I, his substitute sire, would often plunge him into the soapy waters of the galvanized basin. What relief! The bather would add up on his fingers the number of shining bubbles that burst round his shoulders, or escaped, shimmering with iridescent windows, into the air.

The trouble was, the soapsuds invariably came to an end. So did, at the Sazarac, the faro cards that Charlie Kane laid out before him, and the rings of smoke that Judge Steele blew from his lips, up toward the lozenges of the chandelier. No less finite were the slop-shop goods and the piled-up receipts I had earned from their sale. It took the tiny Modoc no more than a quarter-hour to sort the coins into gleaming piles of similar denomination, or pour a stream of gold dust into miniature mountains of ounces. It was during these reckonings that I discovered the method of the mathematical Modoc: an index finger for tens, the middle finger for hundreds, the ring finger for thousands, and, for all I could tell, perhaps the pinky for tens of thousands and more. But whatever the sum, once it was counted, General George would throw back his head and start to wail.

So passed the late summer, the early fall. Then, toward the end of a September afternoon, there came, through the wads of worsted stuffed into my ear canals, a loud clang and a booming thud. Instantly the entire shop — the chairs and table, the tin plates and teakettle top, the teacups themselves — started shaking. The windowpanes rattled in their frames. Dust flew off the shelves. On the floor the infant, his head tipping left and right, fell silent, listening. The percussion, the rapidly repeating thuds, came from some spot out-of-doors. At once I snatched up the trembling boy and ran upstairs to the bedroom. I threw wide the shutters of the window.

The air was clear. The sun, bent out of shape, as if it were being struck at full heat upon an anvil, sent up from the horizon its last rays of light. But the sound of blows came from the north. There, a mile and a half away, well up the side of Mount Etna, the mill of the Neptune Mine had started to grind. At the distance the factory, with its tilted chimney, tin-topped sheds, and oversized flywheel, looked like some landlocked ship, like the steamer *Unicorn*. Quite clearly, in plain sight, the great wheel turned, the dark smoke belched from the smokestack, and, with a sound audible for miles around, the heavy stamps, with their iron-clad shoes, crashed down upon the newly mined rocks.

Again I felt the sharp tugs at my neck hair. "*Eins, zwei, drei* . . ." I started to count, along with my wobbly ward. But since the far-off blows fell so rapidly, several times every second, I soon came to a halt. Down below, I noticed, the Yrekans had run into the street. They too stood listening to the unending thump, the ceaseless thud. Beneath their feet, the very earth quivered and shook. Now, at the window of the slop shop, the child in my arms raised one tiny fist in the air; with his other hand he drummed his fingers upon the stiff, smooth crown of my hat. Above the town, with its silent population, the mill went about its work, half in the growing shadows, half in the purple light.

END OF BOOK ONE

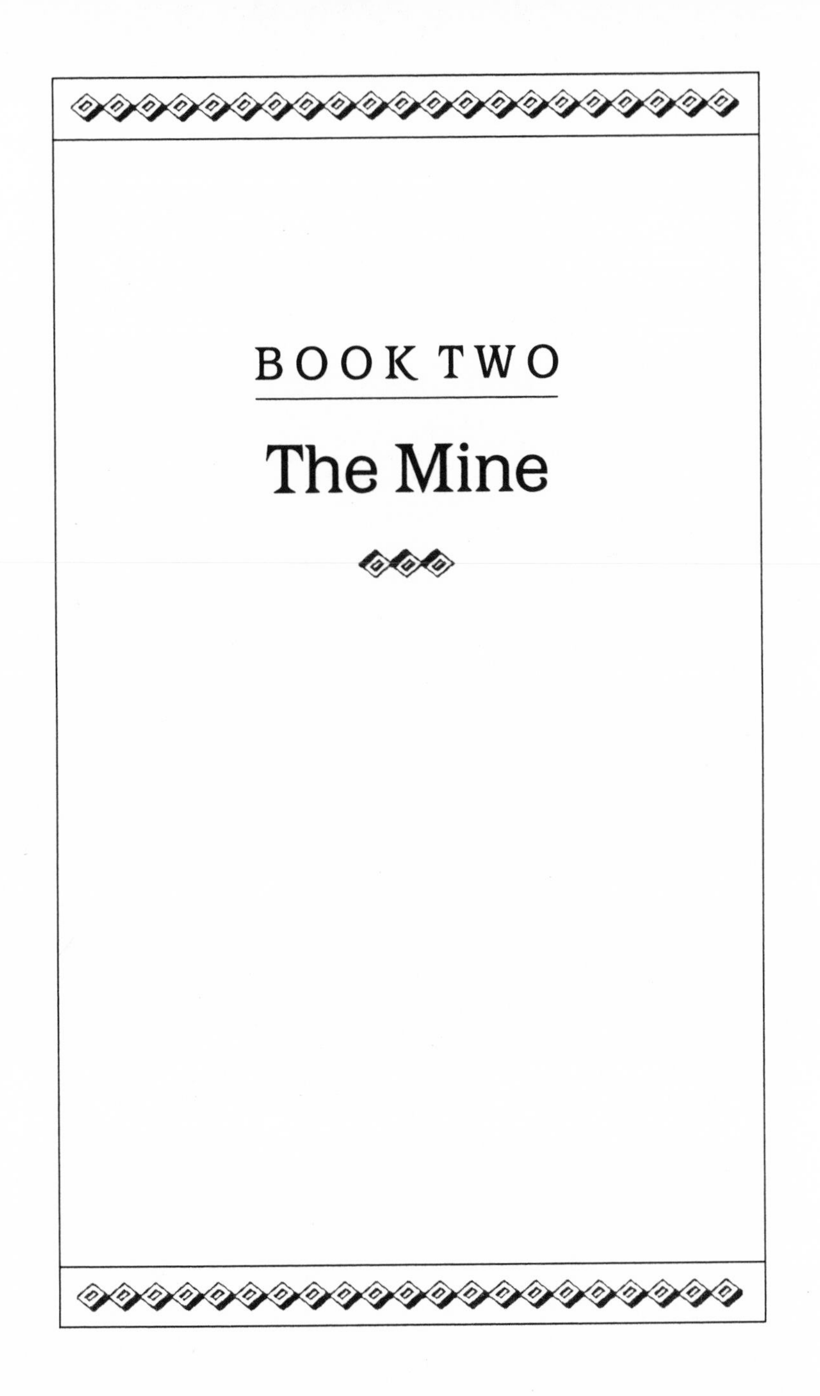

BOOK TWO

The Mine

BOOK TWO: THE MINE

CHAPTER ONE

Gravity

1

HOW MANY TIMES in Yreka did I gaze from my bedroom wi
dow to see the moon, its disk reddened by smoke, pass over tl
top of the far-off buttes? As often, most likely, as the moon i
those years turned full. Nor could I fail to note how little ther
was to distinguish the lunar landscape from that of the eartl
below. At night the charcoal fields, where juniper smoldered ii
dirt-covered ditches, made the hillsides glow the color of rustec
iron. The visible craters of Kepler and Tycho, of Copernicus and
Plato, were mirrored, as if on water, by the numberless pits the
Yrekans had scooped from the ground. The deserted terrain
resembled the pockmarked field of a battle. Alas, the vein those
diggers sought had cropped up only once, just where Frank
Townsend had always said it would: some thirty feet below the
floor of the Neptune Mine. Then it plunged straight to the
depths.

The moon, they say, is lifeless. No atmosphere to breathe; no
water to drink. Those vast oceans — Sea of Tranquillity, Sea of
Serenity, Mare Nectares — are illusions, angles of light upon empty
plains. Temperature by day, at the point of boiling; by night,
minus hundreds of Fahrenheit degrees. Not even a worm there,
not the smallest microbe, could survive. Fit planet, as the Modocs
believed, for the souls of the unburied dead. Unless, on the far
side, the dark side, men or monsters thrive. Who might guess, look-

ing toward the mine at night — a few dim lanterns hung from the hoisting frame; white steam-wisps curling over the open shaft; the shadowy flywheel endlessly turning — that beneath the dull, near-motionless surface men hurried about at unending labor, and a city of sorts, an inverted metropolis, teemed with life?

The clue, of course, would be the noise. From the earliest days, when the mine possessed but a single battery with two small, metal-clad stamps, the sound of the blows, the constant thud-thudding, echoed throughout the town. The ground never stopped shaking. In every cupboard, not merely those at A. Pinto's, the teacups, the tin plates, the cutlery, rattled. The chandeliers at the Blue Wing and Bella Union danced tipsily on their chains. At the Sazarac, the fixture's crystal lozenges, striking each other, cracked and finally fell, so that by the middle of the decade its flames burned bare. Inevitably, in the course of time, the ceaseless percussion, the unbroken boom-booming, the roar as mountains of stone were transformed into mountains of tailings, of trash, became for us a kind of silence, deeper than the hush that must pervade the airless reaches of the moon.

As far as I was concerned, the Neptune Mine might just as well have been on that distant satellite. Though I saw it plain, and had no choice but to hear and feel it, years would go by before I ventured to set foot on the site. The fact was, I could follow the progress of the shaft — both the proliferating levels underground and, on the surface, the ounces of gold wrung from tons of ore — from the confines of my shop. The relays of water wagons rumbled close by Miner Street, eight a day toward Tule Lake, eight a day back, until the empty bowl of Etna Pond was once more brimming with those alkaline waters. Even in the mid-1850s two of the wagons, like huge, flattened barrels, still passed back and forth, to replace the inevitable loss to the process of refining, and to the heat of the summer sun.

The town, of course, and the slop shop with it, had prospered in the mine's early days. All the new miners had outfitted themselves at A. Pinto's, on their way to the hiring shed. Townsend, remembering the laughter in the Sazarac Saloon, turned all the old Yrekans away. He had plenty of others to choose from, refugees from all the places — Port Wine and Brandy City, Monte Cristo, and, from the Oregon Territory, Yellowjacket, Olex, Cornucopia — where the lode had already pinched out. It was these men, Cornishmen mostly, with a scattering of Germans, Bohemians, Swedes, who had — at an overall rate of a half-inch to an inch an hour, or a foot to two feet in a twenty-four-hour day — sunk the shaft downward and tunneled sideways to the rich vein of ore.

From the very first months of operation there had been one great threat — apart, of course, from the very obdurateness of the quartz, the granite — to the vein's steady yield of between $300 and $400 to the ton: the heat underground. After a year, when the shaft had reached the three-hundred-foot level, the temperature had risen to a point where it could no longer be borne. The work in the Neptune came to a halt while a second shaft was sunk, higher up the mountain and parallel to the first, to which it was connected by tunnels, or drifts, at every level. Since the mouth of the new column was at the highest point on Mount Etna, that is, on the northern rim of the reservoir, the two shafts were actually connected to each other beneath the great basin of water. The downcast of fresh air was drawn into the new ventilator, ran through the various horizontal drifts, and came up through the original main shaft. An unexpected result of this flow was that steam began to form at the hoist works, especially in the evenings: the trapped air, hot and stale, rose to meet the cool air at the surface. As the main shaft dropped further, to over four hundred feet, a white plume hung over its mouth nighttime and daytime, in shade or sun. It was like the breath of a living beast, the flame of a dragon that seared the men in its belly before it expelled them, prostrate and trembling, upon the open ground.

And still the underground temperature rose. It was the ex-student Gill, the hoistman now, who thought up the next solution: an enormous sail, its linen white and bulging, which caught the constant breeze at the crest and funneled it downward with more force than a modern compressor engine, directly into the opening of the ventilation shaft. This device allowed the gasping miners to descend an additional ninety feet, and sent the ghostlike wraith of mist into motion, turning counterclockwise on its axis like a perpetual top. The sail itself, rising above the smooth cinder butte, looked — at least from the vantage of my far-off bedroom window — like a gay feather atop the kind of hat now called a derby.

No gaiety for those under the surface. The miners, after this last advance, had finally reached their limit. Even the Bohunks, the Bohemians, who stood the heat best, could not work a face for more than an hour at a stretch. They claimed the deep earth of the region had never cooled from its volcanic past, and that at any time they were in danger of breaking through to molten rock. One day, while the shaft was stalled near the five-hundred-foot mark, two men died from the heat — one underground, at the furthermost stope; the other, his skin white, dry, blistered, while still in the cage, hurtling toward the surface. After that, no matter how much Townsend or Cole or even Ben Piper exhorted the men to return to work, not a single miner would board the skip. "She's deep enough," they said.

It was then, on the third night of what amounted to a miners' strike, that Frank Townsend noticed, silhouetted by the glare from the charcoal ditches, the sole Indian employed by the Neptune Mine: Two-Toes Tom. The old man moved back and forth, dragging his rake across the smoking earth. Sparks flew up, sputtering, to settle on his shoulders, his hair, the knuckles of his hands. In the gloom, the mine owner saw something that made his breath stick in his throat: the charcoal tender was walking barefooted, like a fakir of India, directly upon the hot embers, the smoldering coals.

From that day on the Modocs began to work at depth in the Neptune. They alone could stand the heat of the underground stopes. At last I understood how the Christian converts, Big Ike and the rest, had been able to pour scalding coffee down their throats. It was as if, after living for centuries at the foot of the old volcano, they had become igneous themselves.

Soon the Indians began to arrive in Yreka by the score. They settled beyond the northernmost stretch of Main Street, between the upthrusting buttes and the town. Bullheads from Tule Lake sizzled on the tin roofs of their shanties, like so many cod in a skillet. Their dogs, the yellow curs, yapped in the Modoc Town alleys and ran out in the roadway whenever someone passed by on his way to the mine.

The natives brought their children with them. It was these — the boys, mere lads, too young to have had their scalps flattened — who began to show up at A. Pinto's. Not for clothes, not for coffee, but for instruction. I had already begun to teach the two Bosworth girls, who came by each afternoon for their lessons.

"John Anderson, my jo, John,
When we were first acquent —"

Thus would the twins recite. General George, while present, did not take part. He simply bobbed his oversized head — it lolled on his neck like a daisy upon its stem — in time to the verse, or the thud of the distant stamps, or, for all anyone knew, the beat of his own rapid pulse. Dumb George, the Yrekans had already begun to call him: to my growing dismay, my deepening sorrow, he seemed unable to pronounce a word. What sounds he did make were more like squeaks, or high-pitched pipings, than speech. But he loved, with his nodding head, to follow the pigtailed girls:

"Your locks were like the raven,
Your bonnie brow was brent."

The young Modoc students did not join us on their own. It was Washboard Bill, his face rough and pitted as ever, who sat them down in my makeshift classroom. The boys were glum. They scowled. They wouldn't speak any more than the light-skinned Dumb George. Nonetheless their numbers grew. The main reason for this was that the Modoc settlement continued to expand. By mid-decade fully half the tribe, braves, squaws, papooses, had moved from Tule Lake to the tin-topped shacks. All too soon the sole Indians left at the ancient site, long venerated, stretching back to prehistoric times, would be the old men, the old women: almost ancestors themselves.

It didn't take long, then, to collect so many students I had to hold classes out-of-doors. The fact was, no pupil, having once enrolled in the school, graduated from it. Love of learning? Perhaps. But the greater factor was Frank Townsend's rule that every male Modoc not in the classroom had to work a full eight-hour shift at the Neptune Mine. Even mere children, five-year-olds, were forced to squirm into the narrow drifts, holding cartridges packed with black powder. My youngest pupil, Elbow Frank, aged six, was already a veteran of the shaft. He was a round-headed lad, whose coarse, ungreased bangs were cut Chinaman style. To every question he responded by waving his arm — the left one, since his right was missing up to the elbow that had given him his name.

Nor was there any lack of such questions: all my lessons, whether on the Scotsman's couplets or on the dots, the dashes of the S. F. B. Morse system, were conducted according to the Socratic method I had learned at the feet of Herr Doktor Busch. Indeed, the influence of my late professor was felt in every aspect of the school, from the reliance on practical experimentation down to such details as the need for formal dress. The last requirement I met from my stock of surplus banker's clothes: striped pants, stiff shirtfronts, cutaway coats — even black top hats and glossy patent-leather shoes.

Let us go round to the field in back of the slop-shop building to see what, in the spring of 1855, a typical class was like. There, standing upright, the teacher. On his face, the old modest moustache, the thick, puckered lips, the round, raised mole. Also: six definite hairs on the chin. My age was then twenty-four. As for the young scholars, most had to wear their striped trousers with the silk cuffs rolled; the sleeves of the clawhammer jackets were held back with pins. Yet not all the students were, as the poet would put it, wee bairns. Kepler Jim and Bacon Jack were old enough to have had their skulls flattened in the traditional manner, while Boston Charlie, chewing a toothpick, was only a year or two younger than his instructor.

These three eldest students, and a fourth, the plumpish Cavendish Sam, had lined up on one side of our teaching device, two tin washtubs, placed vertically rim to rim. Neptune the mule was tied to the other. To begin the demonstration I employed a reversed bellows to pump out the air between the two fitted halves — a replica, of course, of the famed Magdeburg hemispheres — of the basins. Then I corked up the hole.

"Question!" I cried. "How long ago was this experiment first attempted?"

The answer came from a half-dozen throats: "Twa hoondred years!"

"Correct! Now we begin. Gentlemen: pull northward! Come! You honeycake! You darling! This way — to the south!" These last words were addressed to the hybrid, who, her hooves dug in, her neck straining against her collar, nevertheless managed to move not an inch. The four strong Modocs had no better luck. Sweat ran on their concave and, in the case of Cavendish Sam, convex brows. Still neither half of the globe gave way.

Now came a shout, a cheer. The rest of the class bolted forward, so as to join in. Some pulled with their classmates, some on the side of the mule. There was grunting. There was groaning. Neptune hee-hawed. Above everything came the high, piercing whistle, like the note of a piccolo, from General George. And for all that, the twin hemispheres remained together, stuck fast.

Now I raised my frock-coated arms. "Question! What natural force is here at work?"

One boy, sharp-featured, looked round. "Principle of the vacuum!"

Another: " 'Tis air pressure as weel!"

"Excellent! Gold star!" With these words, I uncorked the basins. With a bang like a firecracker the two sides parted, spilling the scholars to earth.

"*Voilà!* The original spheres, those of the great Herr von Guericke, withstood the force of sixteen horses!"

Exhausted, panting, the children lay tumbled upon the ground. In my eyes, the entire scene, with its springtime blossoms — buckwheat in yellow, orange sand-dock, the showy pink of flowering onion — looked like the celebrated garden of Athens where the scholars of old used to gather. Academy of Plato? Of Pinto! Except these Academicians lay among the shoots of larkspur and lavender they knew from their only textbook, *The Poetical Works of Robert Burns.*

2

All these flowers had long since withered by the time, some two months later, I led my band of natural scientists to the Neptune Mine. Indeed, it was in part to escape the torrid summer sun that I wished to meet atop Mount Etna. There, where the ventilation sail reached into the sky, a breeze always blew across the cooling waters of the man-made pond. But the chief motive in making this excursion — my sole visit to the butte in five full years — was that it was the only place we could perform the important experiment of the day.

The scholars, in their cutaways and collars, assembled early in the morning, together with the twins, in their pretty frocks. All climbed into my borrowed buckboard just as the far-off whistle sounded for the eight o'clock shift.

" 'Tis the signal!" cried Cavendish Sam. "Do ye hear it? Coom! Coom! Awa'!"

"Hurrah!" cheered the youths.

"On, Neptune!"

"Pull, ye beastie!"

"To the mine!"

Kepler Jim held the reins in his slender fingers; he looked back to where his instructor sat in the rear. I had prepared for the butte, with its pounding, its percussion, by jamming twists of cotton into both ears. On my lap I held two iron shots, one a regular cannonball, the other a one-pounder, no larger than the yolk of an egg. Already the surfaces of each, exposed to the rising sun, were warm to the touch. Clearly, before this day was done, the temperature of the air would rise almost as high as that in the depths of the mine. I lifted my sombrero to our driver: time to get under way.

Kepler Jim, hollow-cheeked, flat-headed, cracked the whip over Neptune the mule. The wagon lurched forward. The passengers laughed, steadying each other. With both hands General George supported his fuzzy-haired head, so that it would not, under the sudden acceleration, roll from the narrow shelf of his shoulders. From where I sat opposite, I noted how his pupils drifted to the corners of his eyes, then jerked back — only to drift off again. Nystagmus, that was the diagnosis: common enough among miners, although this patient had never been underground. At that instant the orphan's eyeballs snapped back in their sockets, catching my gaze. Dumb George smiled, gums glistening, and his whole head, from the point of his chin to his bulging brow, bobbed and nodded, like the motion of a faltering top.

It took only a moment to turn from Miner Street northward, onto Main, and then head out of town. A moment more and we were passing the Modoc quarter. Yellow dogs came yapping from the alleys. The Academicians waved to their pets, calling their names. The animals darted at Neptune's hooves, then slunk back to the village. The natives, the youths, had already turned away, wincing at the stench of the drying fish that rose from the sun-baked roofs.

"Ho! Ho! Am I not, children, a foolish fellow? To put cotton in my eardrums instead of my nose!"

As we continued, moving north-northwest across the plain, the buckboard passengers began to talk about the mine. Apart from Elbow Frank, the only student to have been below surface was Humboldt Johnny — and even he had gone no deeper than the long-defunct level number one. His grandfather, Steamboat Ed, who patrolled that abandoned drift, had shown him how the supporting timbers, a foot in diameter and more, had been compressed by the tremendous weight of the earth to half their original length. The workings, once a high cavern, had in this unrelenting crush shrunken to a lopsided dwelling for dwarves. " 'Twas black in that spot!" said the Modoc boy. "Ye cadna see your hand this far frae your face!"

The others listened in silence. The Bosworth twins held hands. Even Boston Charlie, the oldest, held his toothpick motionless in his mouth. The speaker continued the tale of his tour under the ground:

"Then I saw the lights: glowing here, winking there, yellow like the eye o' the black slinking cat!"

"Oooo," sighed the twins.

" 'Tis a lie!" declared Newton Mike.

Priestley Bill: "A trick o' fantasy!"

The boy was not done. "Mair! There is mair! On every tree was some live thing, bubbling and swelling, opening and closing. Like mouths! Like lips! Like tongues! I wadna fib: the tree trunks were breathing!"

Here both girls let out a scream and held each other fast. Bacon Jack buried his head in his lap. The dark skin of all seemed to go pale.

Humboldt Johnny: "D'ye ken what these be? Steamboat Ed told me: the souls o' the miners killed by cruel fate! Poor wan ghaists!"

"Ha-ha-ha!" laughed Boston Charlie, the only native who had not learned his English from the pages of Burns. "Dumb fool Modocs!"

Kepler Jim laughed as well: "Fie!" he said. "Fie!"

Indignantly the tale-teller burst out: "But I seen wi' my eye!"

There was, I knew, no reason to scoff. The strange sight in the drift, this growth of phosphorescent fungus, was caused by the fact that all the creeks — the Humbug, Hardscrabble, Greenhorn — that the Yrekans had once panned above ground had sunk beneath the surface. These subterranean streams had so saturated the land beneath the butte that the atmosphere of the mine had lost much of its cooling value. The main shaft temperature, which had increased at a steady rate of one degree Fahrenheit for each 180 feet in depth, now rose even more quickly. At the lowest levels — and by the summer of 1855 the Neptune was close to 1500 feet, driving toward the then unheard-of distance of a third of a mile — the water would shoot with tremendous force through the drill holes, scalding the Indians who stood near the face. A sump, simmering, steaming, had formed at the bottom of the shaft, and had to be pumped out with each new advance. The humidity was worst at the topmost levels.

Here, in a hothouse climate, the compressed, contorted tree trunks had begun to rot. Fumes rose from the dripping wood, and thick plants, like clusters of grapes, formed on the outer bark. It was these, and their exhalations, together with the lowering roofs, the constant creaking and cracking of the timber, that created such a strange tropical forest that even a rational man, a disciple of the method of Bacon, could believe in the shades of the dead.

The closer our buckboard drew to Mount Etna, the more the enthusiasm for our expedition waned. The Modocs craned round, staring at the butte, which loomed higher and higher. Even Neptune, whose ears twitched as if she understood the tall tales of the humans, slackened her pace. Now the two mine veterans began to swap stories about the dreaded fourth level, a full four hundred feet beneath the surface. Elbow Frank said that when he had worked there the ground had been so hot the skin of one's feet would become blistered through the soles of wooden shoes. That's why the men's hair was shaved: so it wouldn't, all by itself, spontaneously, catch fire.

Humboldt Johnny replied that he had heard that rats lived at that depth: "Rats wi' the beady eye, the lang tail, and whiskers as wide as my arms!" So saying, the boy stretched out his limbs. His fellow Academy members oohed and aahed. "No miner dare fa' asleep in that drift," the lad continued. "Else when he wakes he might find 'tisna foot on his leg! 'Tisna finger on his hand! A' the flesh might be gone frae his bones!"

In the frightened silence that followed, little Priestley Bill put his hand to his mouth to hide the missing teeth in his smile. "Was that the cruel fate of Elbow Frank? Maybe a rat gnawed off his arm!"

"Ha-ha-ha!" The scholars squirmed with glee. Even the victim laughed at the joke, waving the flap of his stump — which had been created not by huge, whiskered rats but by a fuse that seemed to fizzle, while at its hollow core the powder had in fact been racing toward the charge.

Once more it was Elbow Frank's turn. He began to tell his schoolmates about the fantastical bird, a vulture, that the Modocs swore came out at night, every night, in the chambers of the fourth level. The miners believed this black bird would snatch up a man the way an eagle at Tule Lake might snatch up a fish, only to drop him into the near-bottomless shaft. "Oft hae we heard, our salt tears trickling, the forlorn cry o' the soul while he falls down, down, down a thousand feet in the gloom-filled shaft. O sound abhorrent to the heart!"

Nan: "Can this be true? A vulture?"

Boston Charlie: "Goddam! Right down that bloody hole!"

Elbow Frank shook his round, Buddha-like head. " 'Tis true. A' true. The life of a man, 'tisna worth a farthing."

It was then that Neptune whinnied and drew to a halt. We had arrived at the base of the butte, not far from where Townsend and I had first staked our claim at Soda Creek. Off to the left was the great mound of tailings and, closer by, the amalgamation ditches, where broken-down mules strained to drag huge boulders over a pulp of quicksilver and pebbles. The mouths of these beasts were toothless, their hair grew in patches — not because of their years underground, but because of the mercury they absorbed through their hooves.

"Come, Neptune! You honeycake!" I cried. "Onward! To the top of the butte!"

Before the quadruped could respond, the twins, Polly and Nan, let out a scream. They put their hands over their eyes. I was as shocked as they by what now appeared. This was a group of eight men, clearly the first miners up from what had been the midnight shift, who came stumbling down the butte toward the edge of the dried-up creek. What struck me first was not the miners' bodies, which were, save for the mittens on their hands and the Dutch-style clogs on their feet, completely unclothed, but their color: pale, pasty, as if the heat underground, or the hot steam at the surface, had bleached the pigment from their skin. Had the Bohemians, I wondered, or the Cornishmen, returned? Then I looked again. The line of workers, each with his hair shaved close to his flattened skull, plodded closer. Already their skin was darkening, like the meat of opened apples. I recognized the men. Or, truth to say, they recognized me. One stepped out of line and took a step toward our wagon.

"Coffee feller," he said.

Another halted as well. "Mocha man! He don't forget his stinking friends."

A third miner remained a little apart, staring down at the lines he drew in the dust with his heavy clogs. The Modoc nearest to him shook his head in disgust. "Dumb brudder! Don't know nothin'! He wanna say he glad to see Jew feller a lot!"

It was beyond all question Shacknasty Jake. The other converts — his brother, Humpy Joe, One-Eye Mose — were also part of the shift. Big Ike, jug-eared, lantern-jawed, waved his hand and nodded his massive head.

Then a still more startling thing occurred. Two-Toes Tom, the old charcoal raker, came trotting down upon the band of miners. He was fully clothed, with a blue ribbon tied round his arm. He began to prod the naked men with a hard wooden stick.

"Goddam Modocs!" he shouted. "No talk! Stinking redskins gotta get inna ditch!"

Then two other natives, each with a blue ribbon about his arm as well, also descended upon the converts, pushing them toward the edge of the ravine.

I stood up in our wagon. "Wait! Gentlemen! Where are you going?"

But the officers, if such they were, began to strike the miners on their backs, on their shoulders, so that, even with the thick shoes on their feet, they broke into a shuffling trot.

"Goddam sonabitch!" shouted the first of the native policemen. I knew him, too: the tall Modoc, Split-Lip Sam. His companion was shouting as well:

"Goddam sonabitch bastard!"

Thus was the entire group herded out of sight, over the lip of Soda Creek.

"Ah, Mister-r-r Pinto," moaned Cavendish Sam. " 'Tis here an evil hour!"

I was, however, already out of the buckboard. Motioning my students to remain behind, I began to cross the thirty-odd yards between our wagon and the ravine. Before I reached the edge, I heard a shout behind me. Turning about, I saw a fresh group of miners, undoubtedly those who had worked a deeper level, staggering down the slope of the butte. They were as naked as the converts, though each man wore one of the old brass alarm clocks about his neck. With the Indian policemen prodding them on, they too dragged their way to the edge of the gulch. Then they went over, to the cracked, parched earth.

Fearfully, I approached, and leaned over the verge. The first thing I saw was Frank Townsend, bent over the box of his camera. The lens was aimed at the far wall of the gulch, where a number of naked Indians, perhaps two dozen in all, were lined up, their backs to him, facing the sheer side of the gorge. Another two dozen men waited at the near wall, just below where I stood. The last band, the ones with the alarm clocks at their chests, were advancing along the streambed. They split into two files, four braves lining up at the far wall and four facing my side of the gulch. The Modoc policemen, Split-Lip Sam and the rest, moved between the two ranks, stepping from stone to stone, as if the alkaline waters were still splashing by.

No one, in all this time, had said a word. Now Townsend stood up from his Voigtlander. This served as a signal. The miners squatted, clasped their shins, and began to defecate in dark streams onto the ground. The excrement ran in the old ruts of the bed. The guards waded in the dark liquid, stooping to rake it through with the points of their prods. From time to time a policeman would haul up one or another of his fellow tribesmen, forcing him to stand with his head between his knees, pulling the cheeks of his buttocks apart. Then Two-Toes Tom would come up.

"Goddam Indian!" he'd shout. "Got goddam nugget in asshole!"

Then Split-Lip Sam would stride forward and beat the offender on the back of his knees, on his hams.

Two-Toes Tom: "Shit two hundred dollar! Two hundred dollar!"

Above this scene I stood a moment, aghast. The next thing I knew I was stumbling down the side of the ravine.

"Stop! Halt at once!" I shouted, in what remained of my Pressburg twang. "This is California! A free state! You must not treat men like slaves!"

Townsend stood smiling at the edge of the stinking creek. "What are you saying, Adolph? Why do you shout? Haven't we the right to stop smugglers? Don't you know that if we didn't search them, the Modocs would sneak out half the wealth of the mine? We wouldn't have enough gold to pay the costs of digging deeper."

"Search them?" I panted. "Is this how they steal?"

"Highgrading, it's called. They swallow the nuggets as well. And whole handfuls of the dust. Ben Piper has a way of making them vomit. If he could he'd pick every tenth man and cut him open. He knows how to make an autopsy still. Their guts must be made out of gold. At sixteen dollars the ounce!"

I could not help — from the force of his words, from the reek of the streambed — but reel back. "No, no. You are making a joke!"

Unsmilingly, solemnly, Townsend shook his head.

Then one of the miners turned round and began, in his thick clogs, to march through the muck. It was a convert, One-Eye Mose. "Java man! You gotta happy birthday present?"

Instantly two of the policemen were on him, cursing, raising their sticks.

"No! Sardine Frank!" Townsend shouted. "Hooker Jim! Let the man be. He'll tell us whether or not he's a slave."

The guards stepped back. One-Eye Mose grinned. His breath, when he spoke, whistled through the gap in his teeth.

"One month," he said, "one dollar."

Now his fellow converts, also midnight shift members, turned about. They spoke up as well.

Humpy Joe: "One month, one dollar, you betcher!"

"Inna year make ten dollar!" That was Shacknasty Jim. He paused, looking at the ground. Then he lifted his head. "Or twenty dollar."

I was appalled. This was worse, almost, than the search itself. "One dollar a month? These are not wages! The Cornishmen earned twice that sum each day. How can these folk survive?"

Townsend: "Oh, they have no need of money. The mine provides them with shelter and food and clothing. Should they fall sick — well, here we are: students from the Harvard Medical College. I'll tell you what they do need. And what they want. It's to make a better life. To improve themselves."

At this, the converts nodded their heads. They all began talking at once:

"Drink coffee outta cup!" said Big Ike.

Shacknasty Jake: "Live inna house!"

"Wear fancy pants!"

"Get rich!"

"Get smart!"

Shacknasty Jim clapped his hands together, as if applauding his own words: "Smell good."

His brother summed up the outburst: "Feller dress up and smell good, he meet President Polk!"

Townsend laughed. "Won't that be a picture!"

"*Nein!* This is not right. It is amiss. Think of the village: all the men and women and children in it. The Indians have lived at

Tule Lake for hundreds of years. Are they all to move to Yreka? To work for twelve dollars a year? Here is the extinction of the Modoc tribe."

"What would you have?" Townsend replied. "Do you want them to continue as savages? In huts of mud and straw? Shall they go on painting their bodies and deforming their skulls? Tell me: do you want their children to worship spirits, and shrink at the sound of their witch doctor's evil spells? Evidently not, Adolph, since you have already begun to teach them the secrets of science. The mine is a teacher, too: these men will move in a bound from the Stone Age to the nineteenth century, from a primitive village to civilized life. Look at this group, your friends. Bosworth has made them good Christians!"

At that the converts began interrupting each other once again:

"Humpy Joe damn good Christian. Love Jesus a lot!"

"Lame gonna walk!"

"Last be first!"

"Poor be rich!"

"All stinking feller gonna smell good: get washed lika lamb!"

I hardly heard what these miners were saying. The reason was that I had just made out, from above, from up the butte, an all-too-familiar roar.

"Mr. Townsend," I said. "What is that noise?"

But I knew the answer myself. Above the pounding, the percussion of the stamps, there now came a dangerous grizzly-like growl. What could this be but the bulldog? With its cut-off ears, its cut-off tail!

Nor was I in error. Atop the ravine a cloud of powdered quartz rose in the air. That was where the tan-and-white canine, rushing upon us, had come to halt. Slowly, deliberately, it turned its head upon its powerful neck. The squashed-in face, the flattened features, looked as if they had been struck by the heavy stamps, or compressed, like the subterranean timbers, by the weight of the earth. Its crooked legs were tensed, ready to spring at the sight of its prey.

Then I saw a thing far more frightening than the dripping jaws or the wet black snout. General George! He had climbed from the wagon! He was toddling, teetering, along the edge of the Soda Creek gorge! For a moment I could only stare at the boy's beauty: how innocent he was! How fragile! His large ears were almost transparent in the morning light. The strands of his hair, standing out upon his head, looked like a dandelion's fluff. A breath of wind, or so it seemed, might blow his head away.

Then, with even more alacrity than I had descended the decline, I found myself scrambling and clawing back to the top.

"Here, sir!" I called to the crouching canine. "I am the person you seek!"

With a roar the blunt-faced beast swung round. It made straight for me. Its lower jaw hung open, as full of teeth as a shark's. Petrified, I stared at the bulging chest, the foam-flecked lips, the fury-filled eyes, much as an unarmed matador might stare at a charging bull. Just then, from the direction of the mine, a familiar voice rang out. Matt Cole was trotting down the slope of Mount Etna. "Caesar! Come, Caesar!" he cried.

No effect. No deviation. In three bowlegged bounds the animal closed the gap between human and hound, until, at the very last instant, it was brought up short by a piercing note, like that from a bosun's whistle. General George! He stood, with his head tipped back and his mouth opened wide. There could be no doubt: the mute Modoc spoke.

"Ceso!" he said. *"Ceso! Ceso! Ceso!"*

The bulldog halted, whipped about, and then trotted back toward the boy. Here the foundling faltered, dropping to his knees. The dog drew up before him, inches away. Impossible, at that terrible moment, to move a muscle. Beyond all my powers to utter a sound. The child, however, grinned; the canine shook the stump of its tail. Then it opened its mouth, with its curved, gleaming incisors, and the boy, in the manner of a lion tamer, leaned the thin shell of his skull toward the wide-gaping jaws. Before I could lift a finger, the animal thrust forward its thick red tongue and licked, repeatedly, the Modoc's hollow cheek, the paper-thin ear, the bulging brow.

"Look, Matt," said Townsend, as he climbed up the side of the creek. "Our classmate has made up his mind to visit the mine."

Cole was staring at the buckboard, where the older boys—Boston Charlie, Kepler Jim—were frantically waving. "Who are those two?" he asked. "How can grown men be part of your school?"

To those words I paid no heed. Tears were falling on my cheeks. Spots, like the tassels of my sombrero, danced before my eyes. I stumbled toward my former colleagues.

"Gentlemen! Old friends! Did you hear? He spoke! My dear

boy is a speaker! Red-letter day, sirs! General George has said his first word!"

As for my foster son: he stood now and squinted upward, toward the top of the butte. Then he raised his arm, long, thin, and trembling, like a compass needle pointing north. Immediately the once mighty Caesar, tame as a lapdog, started off in the direction his new master had pointed. Then I picked up the featherlight youth and rejoined the Academy of Pinto.

3

The air above the reservoir rim was shining, shimmering, full of beads of light. As our wagon drew up, I could almost see the molecules of water, the hydrogen element, the oxygen element, leaping upward, turning themselves into atoms of gas. Indeed, if this liquid were not constantly replaced, the whole of the basin would bound into the high, blue-colored sky. Principle of evaporation. I rose in my seat and looked down. Far off, miles away to the east, a column of dust was even then rising from the alkali plain. Surely this was one of the Tule Lake relays, returning to replenish the pond.

Caesar, awaiting our arrival, gave an impatient growl. We jumped from the buckboard and ran to the top of Mount Etna. Here, at our feet, was the wide circle of the man-made lake. All of us, even the dog, leaned out over the water. Our own faces shone back from the surface, as if from the quicksilver at the back of a mirror. Opposite, at the butte's northernmost point, the ground rose slightly. From this pinnacle the white sail lifted into the air. There, at the opening of the ventilation column, the experiment of the day must be done. We strode round the embankment to the spot.

In a matter of minutes Bacon Jack was lying flat on the ground, with Cavendish Sam gripping his ankles. The older boy's arms were stretched right over the dark, untimbered square of the ventilation shaft. The breeze, tumbling out of the overhead canvas, plastered his fine, loose hair to his scalp, as if he had dressed it, Modoc fashion, with fish oil. Downward, in a series of thumps and thuds, the rush of air continued, like a solid object careening against the earthen walls. There seemed to be no end to the fall: in fact, the column was longer than the actual mine shaft, whose entrance, with its hoist works, its derrick, began a third of the way down the opposite side of the butte.

Above the prostrate boy, at the very summit, stood Kepler Jim and Boston Charlie, holding on to their tall silk hats. They were waiting for me to give the signal: then they would swing the boom, with its great sheet of canvas, out of the windstream. The younger scholars sat cross-legged, cross-armed, also waiting.

"Mister-r-r Pinto!" said Bacon Jack, who was holding in his outstretched hands the heavy cannonball and the one-pound shot. "My arms grow weary!"

Now I took a last look about. From this peak one could see all the way to Oregon Territory in the north, with the hazy outlines of the Siskiyous; and, to the south, the great cone of Shasta, snow-capped, glittering, as if it were a mound of quartz-laced tailings. The wind whipped the cotton wisps that I'd screwed into my ears, which hung like the side locks of a pious Jew.

"Friends!" I began. "Pioneers of Progress! We are about to reenact the most famous instance of the experimental method in all of history, a great day in man's quest for knowledge. Question: in what year did this event occur?"

Ten hands shot upward. Ten voices rang out: "1590!"

"And in what far-off land?"

"Italy!"

"Ladies and gentlemen: the name, if you will be so kind, of the structure from which the demonstration was made?"

Once more, the shrill, high voices: "Tower o' Pisa!"

Humboldt Johnny declared, "Ane hundred eighty feet! 'Tis the length o' the tower!"

"High marks," I declared. "High marks for all!"

Bacon Jack, twisting toward me his head, uttered a low, painful grunt. "Now, sir? Let them fa'? I hae nae mair strength."

"Soon. Soon. *Moment.* First, the important question. Who will tell me the discoverer's name? The honor should go to our senior Academician: Mister Boston Charlie."

That young man hunched his silk-covered shoulders. Thoughtfully he turned the toothpick in his mouth. "Benjamin Franklin?" he said.

"Ha-ha! What a doylt!" cried Priestley Bill. " 'Tis Galileo!"

"Galileo!" the class cried in unison. "Galileo Galilei!"

For me, what bliss. I felt, at this performance of my pupils,

something of what Galileo himself must have experienced upon seeing his two missiles strike — contrary to the laws of Aristotle — the ground together. I gazed round at what such a short time before had been the faces of rude, untamed natives. *"Prima!"* I exclaimed. "Gold star!"

I was answered by the rapid chatter of the two iron spheres. The ten- and one-pounder were striking together in Bacon Jack's trembling hands. The youth, it was clear, could hold out no longer. I rubbed my own hands in anticipation. Was that the thudding of the stamps I heard? Or my own joyful heart?

"So. Very well. We begin. Here we have two ratios of ten to one: first, the weight of one sphere in relation to the other; second, the length of this shaft compared to the height of the Pisa tower. Question: will the heaviest projectile fall to the bottom ten times faster than the light one?"

A chorus of voices: "Nae!"

"Aha! Five times faster, perhaps?"

"Naeeee!" shouted the class.

"How much faster, then?"

The answer came in the manner the shots would fall: simultaneously. "Na faster at a'! Nane before t'ither! The same!"

"Correct! Next question: will the journey down this shaft of one thousand eight hundred feet take ten times longer than the fall from the tower of one hundred and eighty?"

"Nae!"

"No? *Nein?* And why not?"

Two or three hands waved in the air. "Acceler-r-ration!"

The sharp-witted Newton Mike outshone the others. "Twa an' thirty feet faster every second."

"Bravo! *Wunderbar!* Now we perform mathematics! How many feet each second were Galileo's spheres moving at the end of second number two?"

Cavendish Sam: "Easy! Four an' sixty!"

"Ah! And after second number three?"

Kepler Jim answered this one: "Six an' ninety!"

Priestley Bill rushed in with the answer to what he guessed to be the next query. "Nae problem! Hoondred an' twenty-eight!"

With that the whole group of arithmeticians broke into spontaneous applause — except of course, for the one-armed Elbow Frank; and for Bacon Jack, whose fingers were frozen into what seemed a death grip around either sphere. The tremors that

shook his arms passed in waves along his entire body. "Sir-r-r," he drawled in his Highland burr. "Hur-r-r-r-ry!"

I was too caught up in the lesson to respond. "Question! A difficult one. How many of these seconds did it take the great scientist's spheres to complete the journey of one hundred and eighty feet? Here we must use higher mathematics. Come, youths! Put on your thinking caps!"

The entire class seemed befuddled. They looked up at the sky and down at the ground. They bit their lips. They tugged their hair. Meanwhile, I was performing my own calculations. *Sechzehn,* sixteen, the average of zero and thirty-two: that must be the distance traversed at the end of second number one. *Vierundsechzig,* sixty-four, the average of thirty-two and sixty-four plus the sixteen feet already traveled: hence the distance covered at the end of second two. At that rate of acceleration, both the original spheres would move over two hundred feet before another second went by. "Ho-ho! No answer? No? Must I provide it? So! Between two and three seconds! From the top of the tower to the earth below!"

Newton Mike, chagrined, stood up to issue a challenge. " 'Tis nae mighty thing to make such a paltry sum. Wha' aboot the length o' time to drap the length o' *this* mighty shaft? Ha-ha-ha! E'en Sir Isaac canna perform that!"

My turn, now, to chew the moustache hairs above my puckered lip. Was I a physicist? No! A physician! Nonetheless, I concentrated my forces. *Zweihundertvierundzwanzig,* two hundred twenty-four, the average of sixty-four and ninety-six plus the sixty-four feet already traveled. Wait. Confusion. Was this the speed the missile traveled or the number of feet it had descended? And was it feet? Or meters? And what was the question? Not feet. Not speed. But time. How many seconds did this figure represent? Was it three? Was it four? This was not my forte! The numbers flew in my brain like crows in a cornfield.

Suddenly we heard a sharp growl. And a second and a third. All of us there, Pinto and pupils, turned about. On the slope between the ventilation shaft and the surface of the pond, Caesar was barking out a sum. Of course it wasn't the bulldog who was doing the figure. General George sat beside his new pet, with his spindly arm about the animal's meaty shoulders. The balls of the lad's eyes, instead of jerking forward and back, had rolled up under his lids, his lashes, so that his sockets were blank. Each time

he pulled on the animal's ill-fitting skin, slobbering Caesar gave another bark, and, like a trained horse or trained donkey, struck the ground with his paw. Six times. Seven times. Eight. What a feat of mathematics! Such clever calculations! All together the students counted the remaining number of seconds:

"Nine! Ten! Eleven!"

Then they clapped hands. That was the answer: it would take the iron shots eleven seconds to drop the length of the 1800-foot shaft.

From this mental magic to a mere Modoc, from Newton to the nadir: that is, to Boston Charlie, who all this time had stood scowling, his eyebrows brought together in a single dark line of concentration. Now he struck his plug hat and uttered a ringing declaration. "Fool Charlie! Dumb Indian! Ain't Benjamin Franklin! Hell, no! It goddam Copernicus!"

Such merriment! The scholars laughed aloud. Even Bacon Jack, writhing on the earth, perspiration streaming from him, risked a single guffaw. Priestley Bill shouted above the others: "Na thinking cap for Boston Charlie! A doonce cap instead!"

I raised imploring hands. "Please. Gentlemen. No cause for laughter. It is proper to mention here the name of the Pole. He it was who proposed a great theory that was not confirmed until Galileo made his invention. Question: what invention was that?"

The Pioneers of Progress grew suddenly silent. They stared, in their bankers' stripes, their velveteen vests, at the ground. Not one Modoc, though each knew the answer, would respond. It was Nan who thrust up her hand. "I know! I know! The telescope!"

"*Ja! Das Teleskop!* And what, through this invention, did the great Galileo see?"

Once more the Indians remained sullen, silent. Polly replied. "The mountains on the moon!"

Nan: "The reflection of sunlight from earth!"

Polly: "Stars of the Milky Way!"

Paracelsus Max stepped toward the twins. "Nae mair. Hush."

Truth to say, I failed to sense the shift in the Modoc mood. I proceeded to the next question: "What else did he see? The most important discovery of all? The one that proved that what Copernicus had said was true?"

Humboldt Johnny was on his feet. "Nae! Dinna say! Dinna speak!"

Elbow Frank tried to cover his ears with his one good arm and the stump of the other. "Dinna ask! I wadna hear!"

"Ho! Ho! Such nonsense, friends! You know the answer yourselves. Come, Mr. Newton Mike! What about you?"

The sharp-nosed, sharp-chinned youth grew pale. " 'Tis a lie."

"We know! We know!" The twins were jumping in the air. They waved their arms about. Their words tumbled over each other: "The moons of Jupiter! They were spinning around the planet! The way the moon spins around the earth and the earth around the sun. That was the proof. The *sun* was the center of the universe. Just like Copernicus said! It was the *earth* that moved!"

"So! Excellent! Grade A! For shame, gentlemen. You have let the ladies carry . . ."

My voice trailed away. At the top of the butte, Boston Charlie, with tears on his cheeks, and Kepler Jim, also weeping, were staring eastward. The other Indians were gazing in that direction, too. I turned, shading my eyes against the glare of the sun. There, far off, across the vast alkali plain, the sky at the horizon was darkened by a smudge of volcanic cloud. That was at Tule Lake. At Wigwam. The father of the Modocs, the ancestor of even these silk-trousered children, was at home.

Someone, it might have been Elbow Frank, murmured under his breath: "A fig for Copernicus!"

The others stood silent, staring unflinchingly toward the spot where, outward from the center, the way a basket is made, the universe had been woven from a single strand of tule.

"Oh! Oh!"

That cry came from the throat of Bacon Jack. He looked up, sweat-covered, from the edge of the shaft. "Alack!" he said, empty-handed. "I hae drapped them both."

In less time than it took the projectiles to fall a dozen feet, the class burst into frenzied action. Kepler Jim and Boston Charlie attacked the great boom, twisting the sail out of the prevailing breeze. The other scholars dashed to the shaft, throwing themselves down at the edge of the precipice. Even the powerful bulldog hurled itself recklessly forward, so that its loose jowls flapped over the pit. The Modocs stared downward, into the endless depths — out of which, because of the sudden reversal of draft, an odd, sour smell had started to rise.

"Ane second! Twa seconds! Three seconds!" The class, in its brogue, its burr, was counting. Down, down, down sank the invis-

ible missiles, into what seemed the center of the earth. With all the others, I leaned over the dark abyss.

"Question! What is the force that draws these two objects downward?"

"Principle of gravity!"

"Gold star!"

The natural scientists continued the count. "Nine seconds! Ten seconds! Eleven!"

Now the children stood breathless, waiting for the plummeting missiles, moving now at a rate approaching half the speed of sound, to make their simultaneous splash. Nothing. No impact. Silence.

"Twelve?" ventured Cavendish Sam.

Humboldt Johnny: "Thir-r-rteen?"

Silence still. What could this mean? Were the spheres to go on falling forever? Until they passed out the far side of what Columbus had proved was the spheroid of the earth?

Then, as if in answer to these unspoken thoughts, a wail issued from the reeking void:

AAAHH!

The scholars looked at each other, their faces drained of mustard-seed tint. The hair on the head of Priestley Bill stood out like quills; even the bulldog's hackles bunched themselves into a muff.

AAAAH! came the cry once more, echoing up from the walls of the shaft.

The Indians jumped to their feet. Trembling, they clutched each other. Elbow Frank shook his perfectly circular head. "Hark!" he warned. " 'Tis the bird! The vulture!"

"Goddam!" cried Boston Charlie, running to the edge of the pond. "Cannonball hit him! Wake him up!"

"Flee, laddies!" That was Humboldt Johnny. " 'Tis the Devil from hell! Flee for your lives!"

Pell-mell the scholars tumbled down the short slope to the reservoir's rim. Behind them the horrible howl sounded yet again from the chasm:

AAAHHDOLPH!

"Adolph?" repeated Bacon Jack.

That, quite clearly, was what the tomblike voice seemed to have said.

Now a second voice, above ground, rang out from the opposite shore of the pond. "Pinto! Come! An accident!"

I saw at once it was Ben Piper. He was beckoning with his arm. I followed my pupils to the embankment. Some ran around the pond to the right, some to the left: all converged on the white man who stood on the southern rim. Piper, breathless, pointed down, to the open girders of the hoist works. There the cage, the lift, was just coming to grass. The Pioneers of Progress gazed at the terrible sight. Even at the distance we could see that the platform was heaped with pale bodies. Only one man was standing. He was dressed in a shirt, in pants, in shoes. His hands were cupped round his mouth. "Aaadolph! Aaadolph! Aaadolph!" he repeatedly cried.

"Matt Cole!" I gasped. Then, with my long, loping strides, I bounded down the slope of the butte, with my pupils only a few steps behind.

The main shaft was located one third of the way down the side of the butte, close to where Neptune the mule had led the three Harvard men to the illusion of gold. Nothing from that long-ago day remained. The tunnel, the cavern, and all the earth above had been scooped away, creating an open-air ledge. Where the floor of the cavern had been, on the very spot where Townsend had rolled in the dust, there was now a rectangular hole that descended straight down for more than a quarter-mile. The whole of the great hollow column was timbered, so as to prevent the fall of rock. One part of the shaft was walled off to form a separate compartment. Here the enormous rods of the Cornish pump, each link of which was twice as tall, and thicker round, than a grown man, moved up and down at the end of a constantly bobbing arm. From the center of the main section a flat metal cable rose out of the ground to wind about an enormous horizontal drum. The drum itself was poised well up in the air, at the center of a tall, wooden derrick. There, too, sat Gill, the hoistman, red-cheeked, moustachioed, surrounded by levers and gears and signal bells.

To the Academicians, racing to the scene, the accident at the shaft looked even more dreadful than it had at a distance. The unconscious forms of the victims lay crisscrossed atop one another, much like some multiheaded beast, a hydra that had been dredged from the deep. Their dangling limbs had been scraped raw, blood red, against the timbering of the main shaft. By the time the Pioneers arrived, two of the guards — Split-Lip Sam,

Sardine Frank — had started to drag the first of the Modocs from the lift. I stepped forward, between the policemen and the pile of sighing men.

"What has happened? Why this catastrophe? Mr. Matt! Do you hear me?"

Cole was already off the platform. His clothes were drenched through. With every breath his chest heaved outward, as if it were being inflated with air. His eyes, dazzled by the surface light, were tightly shut.

"Mr. Matt!"

Still my old colleague did not respond. Sweat poured from his forehead, from beneath his gold curls, like water from a pipe.

Perched in the hoist works, Gill shouted back: "It's the sump crew — the last of the midnight shift. The gear slipped from the hoist taking them up. I could not bring the cage from the bottom. My God! Five minutes over that sump! Just ten feet above it! They're steamed alive! Steamed like oysters!"

"But Mr. Cole —?"

"We dropped him by rope," answered Gill, whose face, above his beard, was flushed and fleshy. "A hundred feet to the old first-level station. We stopped the cage for him there, but his weight made it sink again. He got a good dose himself."

I did not need to hear more. I stripped my frock coat from my shoulders and began to fan the comatose forms on the lift. Each had a round shiny patch on his chest where the brass clock had seared the skin. "We must cool them! Or they will perish!"

The schoolchildren, hearing this, followed my example: that is, each pulled off his jacket and whirled the clawhammer over the miners, making a pitiful breeze.

I paused to catch my breath. I saw how, from the direction of the changing shed, Two-Toes Tom was bringing along a fresh crew of Modocs. Frank Townsend, striding briskly, was in the lead. Meanwhile, Ben Piper had made his way down from the pond. "Take them off," he said to the guards, indicating the gasping victims. Then he raised his face to the lifting engineer. "Gill, here comes the first of the morning shift. You're to take them down. We're a half-hour behind schedule already."

The hoistman shook his head. "We've dropped a thermometer to the sump. The temperature of the water is a hundred and eighty-three degrees. The air in the drift above it is one hundred thirty. This mine has reached its limit."

Split-Lip Sam, approaching the cage, looked to Matt Cole for guidance. The white man's eyes were now open, but it seemed he still hadn't enough air in his lungs to speak.

Townsend, however, came striding up to take charge. "What happened?" he asked of Gill. "Lost the clutch?"

The hoist operator nodded.

"And is the line now engaged?"

Gill, whose face, where visible, was the color of his royal purple braces, nodded again. "It is. But you can't send another shift down. Even the pick handles are too hot to touch."

Townsend took Cole by the arm. "What are the assay returns? From seventeen hundred feet?"

Cole swept in a deep breath. He spoke slowly, slurringly, as if intoxicated. "Nine hundred and fifty to the ton. But the vein widens. It is getting richer. The yield will be a thousand dollars the next level down."

Townsend paused, glancing over the sickened men. It was not difficult to guess what he was thinking: the dozen-odd Modocs at his feet, shallowly breathing, must have weighed together close to a ton. "Clear the lift," he said.

"You wake up! You stand!" shouted Two-Toes Tom. He trotted up to his fellow tribesmen, prodding them with the end of his stick. "Damn Modoc trick! Sleep alla time! Don't wanna work!"

Split-Lip Sam bent to take one of the Modocs by the ankle. I grasped the guard's arm, just above the strip of blue cloth. "No! Do not touch, please! I am a medical doctor. To move these poor people is a peril to their lives."

The other guard, Sardine Frank, stepped forward and with ease pushed me aside.

Then someone — it sounded to me like Priestley Bill — cried out. "A light!"

Someone else, perhaps Cavendish Sam: " 'Tis winking! Bright as the dewdrop's twinkle!"

I saw it, too. A flash. A series of flashes, so dazzling that they lit up the faces of all those standing about. From under the broad brim of my sombrero I stared out toward where some thing, some object, was glittering, winking, beaming. Was this the snowy cap of Shasta, which, like a mirror, or polished metal, was reflecting the rays of the rising sun? No. Not possible. A second glance revealed that the source of illumination was drawing closer, to the base of our butte. Squinting, I made out through the glare the

shape of a pony, the flickering spokes of a wheel. "A wagon," I declared. "For *Wasser.*"

"Not water!" That was Gill, from his spot high up in the hoisting frame. "It's glass! A wagon of glass!"

Townsend smiled. Bits of quartz dust, of mica, were caught in his clothing, so that he seemed to be covered in a coat of shining mail. "Look close. It is ice."

Ice it was: slab upon slab of it, dazzling, dripping, cantilevered out over the back of an old, topless Conestoga. I knew that wagon: from the John Harvard caravan! Four Indian ponies were straining to pull the load up the butte's sloping grade. Suddenly the next shift of Modocs, wearing only their mitts and clogs, dashed to the schooner and began pushing at the sides, at the spokes of the high rear wheels. They surrounded the driver as well, touching his wing-tip shoes, his fancy trousers, the hem of his jacket's crimson silk. This was, with the reins in one hand, the old Noah Webster in the other, Gentleman Jack!

As the wagon drew near the hoist works, the miners used their tools to attack the ziggurat of frozen water, hacking away sharp slivers and jagged chunks of the opal-colored ice. Then they drove the points of their picks into a large, flat slab, levering it over the edge of the Conestoga, onto the ground. One after the other the half-conscious miners were dragged from the lift and spread on this vast, unyielding mattress. Their replacements in the next crew ran here and there, snatching up boulders of ice: with these burdens they staggered onto the emptied cage. Already they were goose-pimpled, blue-lipped from the cold. Freezing water ran down their thighs. Gill grasped the levers of the hoist. Rocking slightly, the lift descended with its frozen freight, into the inferno.

The Conestoga, meanwhile, with the bulk of its load still intact, continued to move past the gallows frame, the main shaft, the hoisting zone. Jack stood upright. With a broad, gold-toothed smile he nodded toward Gill. "Pretty braces!" he shouted. "Go good with what-you-call-him: smoker jacket!"

At once the engineer unbuttoned his clothing and threw the bright straps into the air. The smiling Indian, with rings flashing on his fingers, snatched the suspenders on the fly.

Still the wagon rolled on, turning onto the zigzag track that the water wagons had made in their trips to the crest of the butte. The Indian youths, the natural scientists, danced gleefully about

it, cupping their hands beneath the runoff and sucking on the shining chips. Caesar pounced upon the shards, grinding them in his teeth as if they were brittle bones. It took a good while for our procession to reach the summit, moving past where we had abandoned our buckboard and onto the embankment. Then the wagon maneuvered carefully around the rim of the pond to the ventilation column. Once there the children removed the exhausted ponies from harness. They arranged themselves behind the rear wheels and, inch by inch, forced the wagon up the incline to the very edge of the shaft.

"Attention! Pioneers! All ready?" I stood at the far edge of the shaftway, with one arm raised.

"Ja! Beginnen wir!"

I let my limb fall. The wagon teetered a moment, balancing over the abyss. Then, with a crack, the front wheels went over and the entire vehicle lurched forward and sideways, tipping into the dark, unfathomed well.

No need, on this occasion, to count the seconds. Some ten feet down the front axle struck the far face, ricocheted, and then lodged catercorner in the right angle of the walls. The tailgate ripped through the untimbered earth and also came to a stop. Thus, as intended, the entire wagon hung suspended on the diagonal across the chasm. Immediately Boston Charlie and Kepler Jim, old hands, leaped for the mast. They swung the slack sail back into the breeze. It filled, spilling its draft over the load of ice, forcing the chill to the furthest depths.

"Hurrah!"

That cry, repeated twice more, came from the hoist works down the far side of the butte. All the Academicians, and Gentleman Jack too, ran round the pond to the southern rim. Below, at the mouth of the mine, a mist, the condensing vapor from the ice, was rising like a tall, sheeted figure. Nearby, on the cold, milky slab, the heat-stricken Modocs were also moving, seeming to float like dark ducks upon the frozen surface of a pond.

We could see Gill stretch forward, to where the thermometer wire was wrapped round the winding drum. "One twenty-eight!" His shout reached all the way to the summit. "Down two degrees!" Yet another cheer went up, a loud hurrah. It was followed by a hollow, non-human echo.

This eerie wail sounded again. All of us atop the butte saw that it came from the throat of the fierce-faced bulldog. Caesar sat on

his rump, on his short, ravaged tail. His bowlegged forelimbs were planted on the ground. Back went his head. His mouth, with its jagged teeth, gaped open. Again he howled — to the sky, or to that part of it where a thin, almost transparent wedge of the moon was still aloft. To the dull-witted creature, it must have seemed a last sliver of the melting ice. For a third time, the last time, the wail from the beast rose upward, and faded away. But the moon, caught between one force, which would bring it crashing to earth, and another, which would hurl it into the outermost reaches of space, hung motionless in the morning sky.

CHAPTER TWO

Hydrophobia

1

ONCE EACH YEAR, late in summer, the prevailing wind shifted round, coming at Yreka out of the east, off the alkali plain and the distant beds of lava. So dry was the air, so hot and dusty the blast, that we townsfolk swore it issued from the mouth of Wigwam itself. There was no defense. If one shut the windows, caulked the doors, the temperature rose to something approaching the upper levels of the Neptune Mine. But in an open house the dust covered every surface. The only thing we could do was draw the blinds and take to our beds. We lived the way people do in the Orient, in Arabia, during one of those winds that are an excuse for any crime.

So it was that on the August afternoon of 1857 when the mad dog arrived in Yreka, the streets were deserted, and no citizen stirred. Actually, as we were to discover later that day, the attack began outside of town, at Hardscrabble Creek, where the Meek brothers were at work deepening a long-abandoned shaft — the same mine, the one with the goat's skull at the bottom, that I had stumbled across years before. What happened, Dick Meek explained, once he'd dragged himself back to Main Street, was that when he'd loaded his bucket with ore and jerked the rope for his brother to draw him to grass, there had been no response. He'd pulled again, three times, and shouted. He could hear the bell ring at the surface, forty-two feet above. Yet the nag, trained to start forward at the sound, did not move: the rope remained slack on the winch. Nor did Alfred answer his call.

There was no choice but to climb. This he did, using footholds,

hauling himself on the rope. At the surface, he saw that the winch horse had slipped its traces and bolted. Alf lay on his side, blood pooled around him, flies buzzing above. Then he heard a hacking, like a man with a cough, and turned in time to see, rushing forward, a black face, with red eyes and a long foam-flecked tongue. The lips were pulled back from the fangs.

Meek, in a reflex, jerked backward, tumbling head down into the shaft. A pain like fire flared along his chest, throat, and cheek, where the hemp he had clutched burned his skin; and across the calf of his right leg, whose tendons those same fangs had severed. Minute after minute the miner hung there, while the creature attacked the hoist handle, the drum of the winch, the frayed rope itself. Then, abruptly, the sounds ceased, and Meek pulled himself back to the land. On all fours, fainting and reviving, he crawled along the creekbed, and then over the hardened earth to the town.

By the time, at dusk, he arrived, Yreka was in an uproar. The animal had got there before him. It was all too easy to reconstruct its path. Leaving Hardscrabble Creek, the dog had swung north in a semicircle. Beyond the sawmill, where the west end of Miner Street ran to sand, stood Arch Osborne's stables. The horses, to escape the wind, had been lined up against the wall of the barn. The brute, trotting into the corral, slashed five of them, hobbling their legs, their hocks and heels, and gouging meat from their underbellies. Then, in its fury, it had bitten chunks from the fenceposts, as if the wood were flesh, too.

Gill, the hoistman, lived in a new two-story fireproof near the western edge of town. The beast's pad marks showed how it had swerved from the one side of Miner Street to the other, from horse trough to horse trough, gulping water, until it arrived at the stone steps in front of the sturdy brick house. An indigo curtain, hung across the open doorway, must have twitched in the steady wind. The animal hurled itself at the cloth.

Upstairs, Gill's wife rested in the bedroom. Their infant daughter was asleep in a smaller room two doors down. The woman thought the sounds she heard were part of a dream: the guttural gasp, the husky breathing, then a choking cough, like that made by a sufferer from croup. She woke at the child's scream.

What she saw on entering the nursery was the dark blue drape, the indigo curtain, in violent agitation. The animal, enmeshed in the material — only the whipping tail, the black, trembling hindquarters, protruded — was hurling itself about the floor. One such thrust struck the thin legs of the crib, which snapped. The naked infant tumbled out, upon the humped shape of the animal's back.

Elizabeth Gill threw herself forward, to snatch the howling babe. At that moment the slick teeth tore through the cloth; the jaws clamped on her forearm. The woman screamed and the bite relaxed. Then the entire head of the beast, swollen and snarling, broke through the rent in the cloth. There was a pause. The animal fell back on its haunches, snout upraised: for what might have been a full minute it remained there, panting hoarsely, ears twitching as if responding to inaudible sounds. Finally, ominously, it lowered its blunt black head.

The mother, with her child, had backed toward the window, determined to jump. But the animal did not make a rush: instead, through its open, foaming jaws, a stream of chocolate-colored liquid spewed to the nursery floor. Then it whirled, shredding the binding cloth, and darted down the stairs. The woman continued to clutch her daughter with her sound arm; her wounded one was open at the wrist. She turned to the window in time to see the shape of the brute, with its dark, matted fur, race down the center of Miner Street, toward the center of town.

"Wolf!" she cried, leaning well out the frame. "It's a wolf!"

No one on the nearby streets — not with the stamps pounding at every half-second — heard her call. For the next minutes the animal — not a wolf but an ordinary mongrel, swollen beyond normal size by its erect muff and full, distended belly — padded up and down the deserted boardwalks, crossing the road whenever it sensed a watering trough. From time to time it would stop to listen, to snap its teeth at the empty air.

Simpson, the barber, relaxing in his own leather chair, idly watched its progress. He saw how the cur chewed splinters from the wooden walkway and the stones from the road, and how once it even turned to devour its own liquid feces. Still the barber remained half dozing in his seat until the animal suddenly made a leap and, just in front of his shop, sank its teeth into the fetlock of a piebald pony.

"Hey! You mutt!" he shouted, foolishly showing himself at the door. The dog, whirling, sprang at him and laid open the flesh of his shin.

At the sound of the shout and the terrified neigh, Stack, the postmaster, rushed through the post office door. The pony's owner, Voorsanger, was just behind him. The dog swerved and jumped. Its teeth raked the latter's buttocks, through his combed cotton pants, then peeled the skin from Stack's pinkie finger.

Simpson stumbled back to his shop and seized his loaded rifle. When he returned to the walkway, however, the mad dog had already recrossed the road, to where a shimmering movement in front of the Metropolitan Hotel had caught its eye.

"Watch out!" the barber cried.

But two guests, along with the Chinese bellboy, a pigtailed elder, had already appeared among the swaying beads that hung across the door. Before they could do anything other than turn, the dog crippled two of them, slashing their hamstrings. Then it clamped its jaws about the tibia of the third, dragging the victim, the frail Celestial, off the gallery and into the road. Stack ran to the scene, a Colt's revolver in his bleeding hand. Simpson limped up with his rifle. Neither could shoot. The two antagonists rolled in a dusty cloud, making no sound in their struggle save for the snap of the Chinaman's bones.

Then, even in the midst of this attack, something else, something new, turned the sick beast's attention. This was young Christie, aged ten, who stepped out the door of the *Ingot* building, carrying a tray of type. Whether because of the sunlight, angling under the gallery roof, glancing off the faces of the font; or the sound of the type itself, clicking in its box; or the sight, the smell, the movement of the boy — the dog, distracted, dropped its former quarry and raced for the child. The postmaster fired his revolver, and missed. Simpson raised his rifle, but the bullet he fired struck the ground to the side of the bounding target. Christie halted, then turned to flee; but his boot caught on the rough boards of the walkway, and he fell on his back, amid the clattering type.

Stack, bracing his wounded hand with his sound one, let go a second round. "Got him!" he cried, noting the animal's sagging hindquarters. "Got him square!" But the numbness the postmaster had seen was caused not by his bullet but by the disease; hence the attacker hardly slowed. It was now at the walkway, ready to spring.

Instinctively Christie threw his hands over his face and drew his knees to his chin. The movement attracted the dog to the boy's head, which it lacerated repeatedly before seizing the nape of his neck and, in a scalping motion, peeling a flap of skin. Then Sid Christie himself, the *Ingot* editor, barrel-chested, bald-headed, burst through the door of his building, swinging a shotgun butt. The weapon struck the animal's rib cage, driving him off the gallery, onto the road. Then the others, their shirtfronts and pants legs soaked with their own blood, came hobbling forward to kneel round the boy. Voorsanger ripped off his coat sleeve and with this compress held the scalp in place. At that sight, or else from the delayed effect of his wounds, one of the hotel patrons keeled sideways, unconscious. But young Christie was awake. He tried to lift his torn head. "Where did it go?" he asked. "Where is it? He'll come back!"

"Don't worry," Simpson murmured, from near the boy's ear. "It's over now. He's run off. Clear out of town."

The postmaster, who had been sucking upon his flayed finger, removed it from his mouth. "He won't be back. We'll go after him. We'll hunt him down."

"Don't have to," said Voorsanger. "No need to. He's slunk off to die."

In the center of Main Street the mangled Chinaman sat upright. Bracing himself with his arms, he threw back his head and, in his own language — the Modocs would have said this was the voice of his ancestors, or even that of the beast which had drawn his blood — began to wail.

While these terrible events had been occurring, I, all unknowing, had been conducting my classes in the coolness of the slopshop cellar. We Academicians, chanting our verses from Burns, and shaking our iron filings onto an invisible magnetic field, heard no shouts, no gunshots, no cry of pain. It was Charlie Kane, from the Sazarac Saloon, who finally banged on the trapdoor above us. "Doctor!" he yelled. "Dr. Pinto! The whole town is bit!"

When I came out into the street I was surprised to see the full dark of night had already fallen. Ahead, at the crossroads, a sweet, honeylike smell rose into the air. It was, I knew, the odor of burning flesh. I could see, in the glow of charcoal embers, the silhouettes of a crowd. As I approached the *Ingot* building, a bright light flared on the walkway, accompanied by a sharp hiss, a curling puff of smoke. The Harvard doctors — Cole, certainly, and Gill and even Piper — were just then cauterizing the victims' wounds. The trail of gunpowder poured along the Chinaman's splinted leg had been touched off by a red-hot tong. Even as I watched, the other leg went off, sizzling like a fuse.

Two of the wounded remained — young Christie and Richard Meek, who had crawled to the intersection but a half-hour before. These were the patients who required the care of Harvard's best surgeon. I saw at once there was no way to apply the gunpowder cure to the boy's lesions. I called for ether. There was none. Nor chloroform. No choice but to proceed. Simpson, though bitten himself, shaved the youth's head. Then, as carefully as a jeweler at his clockwork, I seared the torn scalp and neck with the glowing end of a baling wire. With the makeshift instrument I sealed the stump of the postmaster's finger, which the others had thought prudent to amputate.

I turned next to poor Meek. The issue was which technique to use on his opened calf. Cole and Piper maintained that the heated wire, or certainly the red-hot tongs, would be sufficient. I reckoned that in a case of rabies, time was as crucial as the degree of heat — and the miner's wounds had occurred well before anyone else's. We settled, therefore, on the most radical cure. Cole packed the powder around the flayed flesh and into the cavity left by the retracted ends of tendon. The mixture, saltpeter mostly, with sulfur and charcoal, went off with a flash that lit up the faces of the surrounding Yrekans, even illuminating the false fronts of the buildings that lined the street.

In that sudden light I noticed how Elizabeth Gill stood with her naked daughter on her seared, blackened arm. I moved to her and took the child. By lantern light I ran, and reran, my hands over the infant's soft skin. Sound: unpunctured, ungrazed.

"Friends! A happy diagnosis! With this darling patient we need have no bad thoughts!"

Piper shook his head. "You can say what you will. That dog was rabid. There's no hope for anyone. The lot are doomed."

The Yrekans let out a groan. With a wave of my arm I cut them off. "No! Not so! We are optimists here. In our favor is the factor of time. We have cauterized the flesh before the infection could spread. Here is a definite prediction: recovery! Recovery in every case!"

I had spoken too soon. At that moment a horseman, with jingling spurs, rode down Miner Street from the west. The light from the saloon windows, the peat-gas lamps, fell on the rider and horse. Arch Osborne, the liveryman. Slung sideways across his lap was the body of Alfred Meek.

"Bled to death, looks like," Osborne declared. He lifted the miner's head by the hair, revealing the slash on the throat. "Got him by the juggler."

As if in response to the bloody sight, a woman let out a scream. Judge Steele, in the crowd of onlookers, cried, "The dog! It's at large!"

We all ran down the alley behind the Sazarac Saloon. There Antoinette, still in her dancing costume, was leaning out the rear window. She pointed down to where a washtub had been set outside, filled with dirty glassware — beer mugs, tumblers, shot glasses. The black beast, its ribs cracked, hindquarters immobile, had thrust its head into the soapy solution. The spilled water was stained a cherry red. Thus did the suffering creature attempt — by lapping the liquid, by chewing the glass — to satisfy both the passion of thirst, the instinct of fury.

Our sheriff was now Poland, also our butcher. He drew his revolver. Simpson aimed his rifle barrel. But Ben Piper strode to the dead animal and seized its stiff hind leg. He dragged the carcass out of the alley, into the Main Street light. The dog's mouth, and its red eyes, were open. The dust on its fur had turned to caked mud.

On the rooftops of all the town's buildings, like a line of ornaments atop antique structures, were rows of fire buckets, some filled with water, some with sand. Affixed to each corner building was a sturdy ax. Piper seized the nearest of these weapons and slit open the animal's belly. Particles of horsehide spilled out in the rush of liquid, along with a packrat's horde: stones, screws, pins, bits of wire. There were wads of paper and cotton and wool. It looked as if the animal had wanted to devour the very earth: clods of dirt mingled with horse dung and grass. The anatomist poked about in the mass.

"There! Do you see that?" he exclaimed, separating a part of the spew. He pointed to some beads, two carved bones, and a clump of half-digested straw. "Reeds. Tule reeds. You can still see the pattern of the weaving. It's a Modoc basket. And those are Modoc beads and Modoc bones. Here's the proof we need. This killer: it's one of the Indian dogs."

2

The roundup began some thirty hours later, just before dawn. At three in the morning a large group — more than half the population of Yreka — took up positions around the perimeter of Modoc Town. At first light Two-Toes Tom led his native police — by then we all knew their names: Rock Dave, Sardine Frank, Hooker Jim, Split-Lip Sam — into the suburb. When the main-shaft workers left the barracks for the 8 A.M. shift, another policeman, Scimitar Sal, stationed himself in front of the building's only door. Then the Modoc force, wearing their familiar blue armbands, moved through the narrow alleys. They rapped their sticks on the flimsy doors, and thrust their heads through the frames of the glassless windows. They shouted their orders: each family had only one hour to bring its dogs to the barracks. After that, any animal would be shot on sight. The white men posted around the quarter would kill any of the mongrels that attempted to flee into Yreka proper.

Well after the deadline had passed, however, only a half-dozen dogs had been shut into the crude kennel, and these belonged to the policemen themselves. As for the scores of mutts, those yellow curs that commonly roamed the pathways and alleys: not one was found. The Modocs had hidden the animals away.

Nothing, no one, could persuade them to give up their pets. Two-Toes Tom stood on the packed earth of the open square. He shouted through a tin can's cylinder to the surrounding shanties:

"You buncha dumb Indians! You listen to Tom! Ain't gotta fear! Ain't gonna hurt them stinking dogs! Put 'em inside! Treat 'em real good! Give lotta meat!" There was, to this, no response. The silent shacks might have been part of a ghost town. "Listen! Bring goddam dog! Or police gonna bang their heads with a stick!"

Hooker Jim raised his club. Scimitar Sal shook his long, curving knife. They both gave a shout. But there was not a movement, not a sound. The chief of the tribe, Washboard Bill, tried next. He pleaded with his people in the Modoc tongue. But his words, like the others', echoed emptily against the leaning walls of tin.

Finally, when the sun was well up in the sky, two more Modocs — Gentleman Jack, the son of the chief, with his nephew, Dumb George — came into the cordoned-off quarter. Just behind, at the heels of the boy, strode the bulldog, Caesar.

Jack-a-Dandy was by then one of the leading men of the town, as wealthy as Judge Steele, if not Townsend himself. He had begun his fortune with the ice — no one knew where, on that baking plain, or the fields of lava, its source lay hidden — that he continued to sell to the Neptune Mine. Next he had rented out balcony rooms at the Sazarac Saloon, into which he had moved first four, then eight, and finally a full score of Modoc squaws. The Yrekans, and white men for miles around, flocked to the dance floor. Gentleman Jack collected more gold dust on these women than Judge Steele did from the gambling pits and the drinks he sold from the bar.

Now the young Modoc, resplendent in his reversed silk smoker, in purple braces and maroon cravat, stood in the center of the deserted square. Gemstones winked on his fingers. An earring, with a pearl upon it, hung from his ear. A thin wedge of jet-black hair, like the goatee of a Frenchman, sprang from his chin. He cupped his hands about his mouth.

"You Modocs! Jack gotta lot of informations. It come from that Jew feller in town. What this is here is a what-you-call-him?" The Indian broke off and turned to General George. The little lad — it took all his strength to do it — held up the battered Noah Webster. Jack seized it, and flipped the pages. He continued:

"*Quarantine!* Means dogs gotta be alone a little while. Ten days maybe. Maybe two weeks! Make sure they ain't sick. Jack says you got his word. No bad thing gonna happen! Gonna treat 'em good! Feed 'em! Pet 'em! Ain't gonna kick 'em! Jack gives you the how-you-say-it? Goddam *guarantee!*"

No motion, no sound in the surrounding dwellings. Dandy Jack looked about. Small beads of sweat, one for each word of proper English, stood on his full, unflattened brow. With a handkerchief, fluffy, flower-white, he wiped them away. "Bring pets, if you please! After the, you know, the quarantine, they gonna come back. You nice Modocs! Be reasonable! Don't fuss about a buncha goddam yellow dogs!"

The jumble of lean-tos remained silent and still. Then General George started forward, trotting in the direction of the shacks. Caesar, no-eared, half-tailed, lumbered at his heels. As they approached the nearest shanty, a dun-colored mutt slipped into the open. Another came from the low window of the shack next door. A third, scrawny, bedraggled, crawled from under the porch of the neighboring hut. Within seconds, it seemed, the whole pack came from their hiding places and began to gambol behind the boy. Playfully they picked at the dragging tips of his clawhammer jacket. A few jumped high off the ground to nip at the wobbly brim of his hat. Like the pied piper of the folktale, Dumb George led the hounds round the square to the barracks door.

There stood Scimitar Sal. The policeman bent down and seized the bulldog by the loose skin at it shoulders. Before the animal could react, he gave it a terrific kick, sending it head over hocks through the narrow doorway, against the hard-baked bricks of the inner wall. At once Sardine Frank and the other guards moved forward, herding the rest of the dogs into the hot, airless chamber.

Dumb George, aghast, ran round the side of the building to the only window. Through the bolted shutters came a confused howling, a blind baying, as well as the distinct rumbling growl of the mighty bulldog. The boy turned then and opened his mouth to shout. No audible sound came out. For a moment he remained there, his heavy head tilted, teardrops falling from his eyes. Then he forced his gaze upward, girding himself once more to call for aid. This time everyone in the square heard the shout. But the words came not from the mute but from his mates. The schoolboys, all the Academicians, came running from the tin-topped shacks. "Mister-r-r Pinto!" they cried. And again, in the burr of the Highland bard, "Mister-r-r-r Pinto!"

The pity was, I, the leader of the Academy, could not hear my own students' plea. Nor had I been able to join the implementation of the very quarantine I had ordered. The reason for this was that I had spent every minute since the attack attending the victims, especially young Christie, whose condition had steadily worsened. At the moment the Modoc dogs were being sealed into the barracks, my poor patient lay inside the *Ingot* building, his pulse 135 beats a minute, his skin a ghastly white. The boy was only half conscious, slipping in and out of a condition of nervous shock. I prescribed what any physician would for depression of the vital centers: warmed, tightly wrapped blankets; elevation of the feet; and hot black coffee whenever the lad, a cold sweat on his lip, could take it in.

At mid-morning the boy's mother, a woman aged fifty, with red hands protruding from lacy sleeves and cuffs, dared ask the question that was already bedeviling the greater part of the town: "Is it *that?* The rabies? Must he die?"

"Rabies? Certainly not! Our young friend suffers from exhaustion — because of the wound, the shock, the loss of blood. There is, I assure you, no danger."

Correct diagnosis? How I wished I knew! For the hundredth time I racked my brain for the little I could remember about the dread disease. Once more, Aristotle was of no help: for in addition to believing that light things fell more slowly than heavy ones, that ancient had maintained that canine madness could not be transmitted from dog to man. *Dummkopf!* At the Medical College, Wellington had lectured on hydrophobia, but the only part of that lesson I could recall was that in human victims there was an incubation period — usually of weeks, sometimes of months, and rarely even of years — before the onset of symptoms. Surely that meant that at least for the moment, the poor boy was secure.

But was he? Most victims of rabies were wounded, as the other Yrekans had been, in the fatty tissue, or the extremities: a shinbone, finger, forearm, buttock, ham. The symptoms that came to mind from that long-ago lecture — the muscular spasms, the sensitivity to stimuli, the mental excitements and panic — all convinced me the malady was at root a nervous disorder. What, then, if the crazed dog, in sinking its jaws into Christie's neck, in ripping upward his nape, had penetrated with its fangs some part of the spinal canal — the dura mater or even the subdural space? Who could say then whether the symptoms would be delayed, or what form they might take? It would be as if the drops of rabid saliva had been injected directly into the brain.

While turning over these matters, I must have fallen asleep. In the afternoon the *Ingot* editor approached the armchair where I dozed and shook me awake. The patient's condition had dramatically changed. All the symptoms were reversed. The pulse rate, for example, was cut in half; and the temperature, which had been subnormal, rose to Fahrenheit 104. The cold, clammy skin broke into a heated sweat. The boy's father posed once again the fearful question: was this the onset of the canine disease?

"I do not know," I responded, keeping my worst fear — not of rabies but of lockjaw, whose virulence would also be intensified if the seat of infection were the spinal canal — to myself. This suspicion grew sharper when, during the night, the boy underwent the first of a series of convulsions. The icepacks I ordered failed to bring down the fever. The violent spasms continued through the next day, and if anything grew worse when, on the second night, the constant, dust-laden wind, the east wind, at last abated.

By then a true doctor, a large man with a high, freckled forehead and silvery hair, had arrived from Weaverville. Adolph, the amateur, was dismissed from the case. Nonetheless, Christie's fever, his intermittent convulsions, continued for another sixty hours. On the morning of the fifth day the crisis approached, then passed. Good news! The boy slept soundly until late afternoon. By evening he was sitting upright in bed, talking, laughing, and eating, with huge appetite, flapjacks and bacon.

The very next day the patient was out-of-doors, walking about on his own. The whole town turned out to see him. Everyone laughed at the hat he wore atop his turbanlike dressing. The other victims — you can imagine the agony of apprehension with which they had been following his progress — hugged him and slapped him on the back. The Chinaman, on crutches, kissed his coat. At noon everyone strolled to the depot to bid the doctor, Garvie by name, farewell. They tied his coach with festive ribbons. The physician, seated high on the box, would take no credit. He had held all along that his patient was suffering from nothing more than a poison of the bloodstream, brought on by inflammation of the original wound. "All the boy needed was rest," he called down from his perch. "And a square meal!"

The Yrekans, I along with the rest, laughed and cheered. We applauded the doctor's next words, which he shouted back from the rolling Kittle and Moffet express:

"Don't worry, boys! Not about that Indian dog. Looks like he never had the rabies to begin!"

The crowd took a good while to disperse. A number of us were still strolling the boardwalks, enjoying the fine turn in the weather, the gusts of fresh, cooling air, when Arch Osborne came riding bare-headed down Miner Street from the west. "Get to the stables," he shouted, already wheeling about, raking the flanks of his blowing stallion. "You got to see what I seen yourselves!" Then he was gone, stirring the same dust, we ruefully noted, as the departed Weaverville stage.

More than twenty Yrekans, with the dog-bite victims in the lead, assembled at the livery. We saw how the whole of Osborne's herd was crowded together at the near edge of the open corral, warily facing the stables. The horses were watching a plump brown mare. That animal's lips were retracted and her eyes bulged out. The tail incessantly switched. Suddenly she snapped her teeth, once, twice, a third time, at a spot in the air. Then all her muscles began to quiver, as if the swarm of horseflies, or perhaps stinging wasps, that she imagined to be circling above her had settled on her back.

"Oh, no," Simpson groaned, throwing both arms over his eyes. "No! No!"

The mare, hearing the barber's voice, catching the quick movement of his limbs, made for him, scattering the whinnying herd. At the fence she reared, turned, and flailed backward with her hind legs, her sharp hooves. Osborne had his rifle ready. But before he had cause to fire, the horse galloped back to the stable and disappeared inside.

Meek turned to the liveryman: "Is that one of the bit ones?"

Osborne nodded. "Bit on the belly. And under the throat."

The animal's hooves thudded now against the inside of the barn, knocking apart what remained of the wooden stalls. We all stood transfixed at the sound of destruction. I recalled, with exactness now, the words of Professor Wellington in that Fruit Street lecture hall:

> Each rabid animal, suffering from the furious form of the disease, experiences the irrepressible desire to attack with the weapons most natural to its species: the wolf with its teeth, the horse with its hooves, the bird with its beak, the bear with its claws. Even the timid sheep will rush forward in a frenzy to butt the antagonist with its horns.

"The horse," I murmured, repeating the words aloud. "The horse with its hooves."

One week after his fever had disappeared and he had strolled happily through the town, the younger Christie began to complain that his neck had gone numb, and that his wound, where I'd sewn it, was itching. "It feels," he said — and the long burst of rapid talk that followed became his regular manner of speaking — "like there's ants inside. Inside my head. Ants. What's the matter with me? Did that Jew put ants there? It's a nest. They're crawling. It wasn't no dog. No dog bit me. He came for me; but I tripped. My head got cut on a nail. That's where the ants got in. I would know. Wouldn't I know? Wasn't no dog. It was the nail. Go get the Jew. He put the ants in. He's the one to get them out."

This speech was interrupted by long, sudden sighs, a kind of sobbing sound, as if the sick child were at one and the same time attempting to catch his breath and bewailing his fate. What that fate was became clear to all, even to the boy himself, when after a sleepless night he demanded a glass of water to quench his thirst. At the last instant, however, the muscles of his throat, those for swallowing and breathing, went into spasm, and the fluid spilled from his mouth. For a moment it seemed he would suffocate from the paroxysm. Then the seizure ended, leaving him with a greater thirst than before. He begged for more water; when it was brought him, the fit of choking came on even before the tumbler reached his lips. What agony! Thirst tormented him, yet the presence of liquid filled him with dread. Soon the mere mention of the word *water,* even the silent thought of drinking, caused his throat to constrict with wrenching spasms.

"Save him, doctor! Dr. Pinto!" So cried the boy's mother, seizing with her strong red hands the shopkeeper — or schoolmaster, peddler, prospector even: but no doctor, never a doctor. A Hebrew, not a healer! But the woman would not release me.

"You see him! How he suffers! Help him! Cure him! Let him live!" Then she whirled round and ran from the sickroom, where her son was now spitting about him — onto the walls and onto the floor, in terror that he might swallow his own saliva.

Nor did the boy's mother return to the room for the two days that young Christie remained alive. Her absence was not caused by his fits of maniacal excitement, during which he would strike out at anyone near, barking doglike and showing, no less than a dog would, unmistakable signs of sexual arousal. It was in fact the doctor, not the patient, that the mother avoided: she dared not risk hearing me repeat Professor Wellington's warning that there was no instance in history, from the days of the Greeks to the present, in which a man who showed the symptoms was known to recover from the disease.

Then, early on the third evening, the boy grew tranquil; his muscles relaxed, and, strange to say, even the power of swallowing was restored. "I am sorry for the trouble," he said — perhaps to myself, hovering by him; or to his father, holding the guttering lamp; or to his mother, who sat rigid in the adjoining room. Then from sheer exhaustion he expired.

Voorsanger, the only one of those bitten to attend Christie's funeral, complained even at graveside of a tingling sensation on the crown of his head. By that same evening I had no choice but to diagnose the first, or melancholic, stage of the disease. "My pretty pony!" he sighed, with the same catch, or sob, in his voice that had marked young Christie's speech. "My little pony is shot!"

Professor Wellington had made no mistake: the greengrocer, suffering all the effects of hydrophobia — even the sound of water being poured into a glass brought on the paroxysm — succumbed fifty-two hours later, gagging in his own flow of mucus.

Next came a lull in the course of the plague. As the days went by, people began to hope the last victim had been claimed. Then a rumor spread through town that one of the two hotel patrons — he'd left almost at once for Weaverville, so as to put himself under Garvie's care — had perished. The arrival of the Kittle and Moffet express brought quick confirmation: the poor fellow, his leg entirely healed, had left for San Francisco, only to take ill while on the river, surrounded by the maddening waters. Someone thought then of the Chinaman. Imagine the horror that gripped the Yrekans upon learning that the co-religionists of the pigtailed elder had long since placed him in their hallowed ground.

Now the townfolk waited in anguish for the incubation periods to end. Inexorably, they did: first for Meek, and then for the barber, and three days after that for the second guest from the Metropolitan Hotel. The Yrekans, seeing the inevitable symptoms, became as restless, as irrational, as the actual sufferers. They recalled the most exotic remedies — crayfish eyes, for instance, mentioned by the great Galen himself; or bleeding the victims with leeches; or saltwater bathing. One faction began to talk of isolating the patients, in the Meek brothers' shaft or the empty stables, so that their breath would not infect healthy citizens. Another group began to complain of the Modocs. Whenever an Indian stirred from his shanty, he would invariably be driven back. Fear had become more contagious than the infection itself.

The case of the postmaster, whose seizure came on without warning, without so much as a headache or itch, caused a kind of panic. One moment he was standing at the bar of the Sazarac Saloon, drinking a glass of beer. The next instant that liquid flooded his windpipe and shot in a spray from his nose. Hours later, emerging from the sick man's room, I found that a crowd had gathered. "It was only a scratch on the finger!" they called in dismay. "His little finger!"

The summons I feared most came last of all, on a sunny midmorning. Gill, the hoistman, appeared at the slop-shop door, holding his infant daughter. His wife had shut herself into the windowless attic of their new brick house. A crowd, half crazed itself, full of brawlers, had gathered there. Many, it was clear, had been drinking. Their shouts were meant for me as I pushed my way through. They waved, in a menacing fashion, their fists. A firm wooden door had replaced the ripped entrance curtain. Gill turned there, facing the angry men.

"Be still. Your voices make her worse."

The hoistman, I soon discovered, was right. Noise it was that had driven the poor woman into the darkened room. The least sound, not only of running water, but a whisper, a step, the rustle of clothing, served to bring on the attack. So, too, did the weakest ray of light, or the lightest touch, even that of a breath of air. There was nothing for me to do but crouch outside the attic door until the period of calm.

It came at nightfall, almost as if the distracted patient could sense through the walls of the house the sinking of the sharp-rayed sun. She slid the latch, opening the room to the faint light that came from the stairway lamp. Sad sight within! The lady's hair was down, disheveled. Her clothing was shredded. The smooth skin of her throat, where her fingers, her nails, had attempted to force down the spasm, was scratched and bruised. Wordlessly she seized my frock coat and drew me into the dim, close space. She was, for the moment, tranquil. She smoothed, in a reflexive gesture of modesty, the bits of her bodice over her breast, and pushed back the loose strands of her hair. The only signs of the infection were the husky growl of her breathing and the peculiar pitch, when she spoke, of her voice.

"Please. My daughter." The words seemed muffled, as if forced through a gauze. "I want to see her."

Gill had been waiting, just beyond the door. He tiptoed forward. The infant was awake. She held her arms out to her mother, who, with a smile, raised her own arms to take her.

I was the one who, at such a moment, could hardly breathe. Was this not the reason I'd once sought a medical career? To heal suffering? To assist in creating just such a happy scene? Alas: before my eyes a terrible thing began to occur. Elizabeth Gill, yet smiling, with her arms outstretched, broke into tears. They were — there was no question of this — tears of joy. But they ran down her cheeks to her mouth. At once her face split into two, as if cut with a knife: half happiness, half horror. Then the muscles of her throat, responding independently to the sensation of wetness, convulsed. The poor woman fell back, gasping for breath.

"Help us! Oh, help us!" cried Gill, drawing away, removing the child from the grasp of her gagging mother.

It was not in my poor power to respond, nor did any higher force bend the fixed laws of nature — except, perhaps, to make the last agony a brief one: not days, mere hours.

That night, numb with weariness, I lay fully dressed upon my bed. No sooner had I fallen asleep than someone began a knocking. Surely, I thought, this sound was part of a dream. Who would call on a doctor now? The epidemic was over. The last possible patient had died. But below the steady *rap-rap* continued, against the slop-shop door. Suddenly my eyes flew wide. "The child!" I cried, with awful foreboding. "Ah! Ah! Little Miss Gill!"

But the figure at the door, once I'd flung it open, was the nut-skinned, plug-hatted Paracelsus Max.

"*Was ist das?*" I demanded. "We have here the middle of the night."

The little Modoc stood silent. His chest, beneath his stiff shirt, his formal lapels, was heaving. "Coom," he gasped at last. "Coom whilst there is time!"

Then another voice — it was that of Cavendish Sam — rang out of the shadows: "They want to kill them! To shed their innocent bluid!"

"What are you saying? Who wants to do this?"

"The villainous traitors! Policemen! And the damned white devils, too!"

"Calmness, friends. Kill what? Kill who?"

Parcelsus Max uttered a chilling wail: "Our darling dogs!"

Only then did I note the sound of gunfire to the north. Leaning from the doorframe, I made out the flash of powder from the Modoc quarter, along with a number of human, and perhaps non-human, cries. A third figure stepped out of the dark. It was Bacon Jack. The flathead broke into a bitter wail:

"Naebody would harm them! 'Twas a promise! A guarantee!"

Clearly something, in the Indian settlement, was amiss. Pausing only to snatch up my sombrero, I trotted after my pupils, toward the shanties of Modoc Town.

All was in chaos there. A crowd — white men, Yrekans — milled about the barracks, holding flaming bunches of tule. They were shooting their rifles and repeating pistols into the air. No Modocs, save for the force of policemen, could be seen. But their shouts, the ululations of the women, rose from the tin-topped huts. These cries, together with the whooping of the white men, the blasts of their weapons, and the baying of the beasts inside the closed building, made a deafening din.

Bacon Jack was the first of us four to arrive. He made directly for the door of the kennel. With the blunt edge of his knife, Scimitar Sal knocked him down. Another policeman, Hooker Jim, struck him with his stick.

"Halt! Halt! Heavens!" I cried, running at full speed to the spot.

A sharp yelp, a blood-curdling yowl, made everyone look round. Ben Piper had thrust the muzzle of his rifle through the barracks' high window, between the shutter slats, and fired. The next moment he took out a pistol and, without taking aim, fired again. There was a bright light — one could see, as in a lightning flash, the inner walls, the beams of the ceiling — and, simultaneously, another yelp of pain.

"That's it!" shouted the crowd, rushing forward. "Shoot 'em dead! Shoot 'em all!"

Everyone pushed as close as possible to the window. Each man wielded a weapon. Already Ben Piper had reloaded, ready to shoot.

"Nein!" That was the cry that rose from my lips. "The scourge is finished. There will be no more rabies. No further victims!"

One of the mob — it was Poland — responded: "You don't know what you're saying! You couldn't save a one."

Judge Steele: "Step back, Mr. Pinto. Your work is done."

"No, no! You do not understand! The incubation period has passed without symptoms. Therefore we may lift the quarantine. The animals are definitely disease-free. This is a medical fact."

No one was willing to listen to reason. On the instant there was an eruption of flame and smoke. Three marksmen had loosed a volley. Now they drew back, amidst the howls from within the building. Immediately a new squad formed, rifles at the ready. The smell of the animal blood, mingled with that of charcoal and sulfur, hung in the air.

Some person took my arm. It was Matt Cole. "Do not be foolish. It is dangerous to interfere."

Townsend had arrived on the scene as well. He leaned close to where I struggled to break Cole's grasp. "You, too, have ignored a medical fact. One of this pack had rabies. No one questions that.

The cur got it somewhere. If not from another dog, then in the wild: from a coyote, a badger, a squirrel. If these animals run loose, they're bound to contract it again. Killing them off is a kindness. Animals have to be shot to save men."

A wave of scorn rose within me. "Men?" I snorted. "You do not mean to say men. You mean workers."

These bitter words were lost in the crash of another salvo. Smoke poured from the building as if it were on fire. The pitiful wailing from within rose in volume, then faded; it was replaced by the fierce sound of scratching — the nails of the survivors against the hardened brick. Still the Yrekans were not done. Fresh gunmen crowded under the window. The sticks of their rifle barrels disappeared in the thick coils of smoke.

Before they could fire, a new sound broke out — this time behind us. I thought I recognized the washboard's clatter: true enough, the pockmarked chief was standing in front of a sagging shack. Beside him was Curly-Headed Doctor, horribly painted. His mouth was red. Lightning bolts zigged and zagged on his chest. He had a feathered stick in his hand, which he shook to the washboard's drone. Already, from the maze of shanties, the Modoc men were responding to the summons. They stepped into the open, into the square. In a group they advanced upon the barracks. Over and over the chief struck his washboard. What a noise it made! It was as if he were beating not only the corrugated tin of his instrument but that on the surrounding rooftops. It thundered. It roared.

Now from out of the line of marching men a rock came flying, followed by a second missile, and then a sudden fusillade. The stones thudded down upon the roof of the barracks, hit hard against the walls; dirt flew at our feet where we stood. In response the gunners made an about-face, leveling their weapons at the advancing crowd. The Modocs pressed on, stooping only to scoop up a new round of stones.

"Ah!" Townsend exclaimed. "This is what I feared."

Grinning, Ben Piper ordered the front line of Yrekans to drop to one knee. The second group leaned eagerly over the shoulders of their fellows. Into my mind flashed the similar scene on the Boston Common. All fifteen men of this firing squad peered down the barrels of their guns. Opposite them, however, were living Modocs, not a paper Pawnee. The Indians, startled, came to a halt. Behind them, in the doorway, the washboard roared on, louder than ever: it was as if the redskins were providing the drumroll for their own execution.

Glancing over my shoulder, I saw Cole slink toward the barracks, carrying what looked like loose papers in his arms.

"Get back," Piper commanded.

"Shooting's no good," Cole replied. "It's blind. It's uncertain. We can't allow a single dog to escape."

Piper hesitated. "Have you some better means?"

My former classmate did not answer. Instead he seized one of the nearby torches and touched it to his bundle. At once it began to sizzle. A fuse! "If the blast does not kill them outright," he declared, even as he heaved the cartridges in a sparkling arc up and through the smashed shutters, "the concussion in the enclosed space will."

"It's powder!" shouted the Yrekans. "A bomb!"

Cole walked quickly away. "That was a twenty-four-second rattail," he announced. "There will be no more than twenty seconds left."

In that brief time, however, much took place. The Yrekans, some of them actually throwing down their weapons, ran for safety. Scimitar Sal abandoned his post, leaping away from the bolted door toward the jumble of shacks. Inside my head I performed a number of arithmetical calculations: the number of seconds to reach the brick wall — five; to hoist myself through the smoking window — another six; to find, to quench, in that dark, hellish chamber, the charge — how many? Too many! The dogs were doomed!

Then, as if to protest that conclusion, came a familiar growl, the low rumble: *Rrrrrr!* Caesar! Still living!

Someone else had heard the note of the bulldog, too: Dumb George! From out of nowhere, the boy came tripping into the square. He headed directly toward the barracks. How many seconds left? Ten? Nine? This child had no more chance of rescuing his pet than I had of extinguishing the fuse.

"Stop! Halt at once, my dear!"

But the youngster did not pause for his foster father. The cuffs of his Academy pants unrolled behind him. His hat was tipping and turning upon his top-heavy head. Still the miniature Modoc made for the barracks — not for the window on the side of the building, but for the door at the front. Clever idea! Opening it was the most efficient way of decreasing the pressure of the blast.

For five precious ticks of the clock the little lad struggled with the heavy bolt. It would not budge. Two more seconds went by while he hauled and heaved.

"Attention!" I cried, darting forward. "Here is assistance!"

At that very instant the burning hemp reached the black powder. There was a flash, a loud thump, and the whole building seemed to rise an inch from the ground. Through the space where the door had been, dead dogs, and living ones too, went flying. The force of the blast lifted me off my feet and sent me hurtling through the air. Then bricks rained down about me. One of these, made of baked earth, landed square on the crown of my Mexican hat. I thought to rise. Instead I sank back. Everything for me became quiet, dark, still, save for two sounds: the roar of the tin board, which the pockmarked chief made thunder; and my own voice, which, in a last gasp, uttered a cry. "Aha! The answer! I have it! A definite cure!"

3

I thought, upon waking, I must be in Hades. The heat of the inferno was all about me. An eerie glow, green, phosphorescent, flickered through the shadows. And there, not ten feet away, with its wet tongue lolling sideways from its mouth, with slaver on its black lips and jaws, was the hideous head of Cerberus, the hell-hound. I blinked. I rose to my knees and looked again. Caesar! And not only that bulldog: more mutts, yellow bitches, Modoc curs, lay panting against all the walls. Sitting cross-legged in his banker's outfit, with his coarse hair sticking up atop his round, Buddha-like head, was Elbow Frank. Others were crowded near: Priestley Bill, Kepler Jim, and, with his eyeballs dancing, his head tipping off-center, General George. For a single mad moment I assumed the entire Academy, principal and pupils and pets, had been dispatched together to the nether world.

"My dear ones! My darlings! Are you ghosts? Killed? *Kaputt?*"

At these words there was a burst of laughter. Gleeful shouts rang off the low, jagged ceiling, the rocky walls. Even the Modoc dogs yipped and yapped with amusement.

Paracelsus Max: "We dinna be ghosts, Mister-r-r Pinto. The white men dinna smite us."

Cavendish Sam: "We hae escaped! With a' our bonnie beasties!"

"Dumb Indian smart!" said Boston Charlie. "Got lotta dog! Bring 'em here! Hide 'em! White men can't find 'em!"

"Here?" I inquired.

"To the mine! Number-one level! Naebody will think to look in this dungeon!"

"*Nein!* This is not possible. If I am not dead, then I am dreaming."

"Ha-ha-ha! 'Tisna a dream, Mister-r-r Pinto! You hae suffered a muckle knock to the head!"

Doubting, dumbfounded, I raised a hand to my brow. There was a bump, as large, it seemed, as any of the mushroomlike fungi that grew from the sides of the tree trunks that held up the earth above. Now I recalled all that had happened: the roaring sound of the washboard and the attack on the barracks; the sputtering fuse and the rain of bricks that had fallen about me. My students must have brought me, along with the surviving hounds, to this hiding place underground.

Yet no sooner had I grasped this explanation than I saw approaching, out of the gloom, a strange apparition: an old man, stooped over, with a candle in his hand. His face was as pitted as Washboard Bill's.

"*Gott im Himmel!*" I cried. "Who is this person?"

The Pioneers of Progress burst out in laughter again. Humboldt Johnny was the most gleeful of all. "Here is my father's father. Mister-r-r Steamboat Ed!"

I could not take my eyes from the old man's face, marked as it was by the scars of his disease. My own head, where the brick had struck it, began to throb. "His face!" I exclaimed.

The aged watchman drew closer. "Alla old Modoc," he said, displaying a toothless grin, "got plenty pock."

"*Ja!* I know it! The smallpox!" I practically screeched out these words. Everyone turned to look at where I sat, holding my aching head. It was throbbing still, swelling — but not from the bump on the surface so much as from the idea, half memory, half inspiration, that was blossoming within. In my ears was a roaring, like that of the washboard. Suddenly I heard my own voice shouting, just as I had when struck by the brick. "I have it! The answer! Sons of Galileo! Here is the cure!"

The Modocs scratched their heads. The bored canines yawned. Cavendish Sam said, "Cure for wha', Mister-r-r Pinto?"

"The rabies! Don't you see? Don't you hear? The washboard! That's how the chief got his name! Because of the pits, the same marks that we see on this gentleman's face."

"Pox," the old man volunteered.

"Ja! Smallpox! Smallpox! Scholars, a question: with what means did the great Jenner make his patients immune to this disease?"

Several voices — those of Kepler Jim, Newton Mike, Priestley Bill — rang out: "Vaccination!"

"Correct! Grade A!" I cried, beaming with pride at my audience of Modocs and mongrels. "What prevents one scourge must protect against another. What must we do? Discover the proper vaccine! Yes! Yes, friends! We shall work here, in this underground cavern. This secret spot shall be our laboratory. Here we shall perfect the cure for the dread disease!"

There was a pause while the young men, the boys, looked round at each other. Would they mock me? Jeer? Or might they grasp this glorious moment?

Kepler Jim broke the silence: "Wha' fame," he shouted, "for the Modoc tribe!"

Then all the rest cried out together: "A cure for the canine madness!"

" 'Tis joy to think of! A feeling of rosy pleasure!"

"A' mankind will thank us!"

On my feet now, but stooping, so that my Mexican hat scraped the crusty quartz of the ceiling, I raised an index finger: "Yes! From beneath the very feet of our neighbors there shall spread a blessing, a vaccine that will reach all men, in every nation of the earth!"

"Hurrah!" shouted the natural historians, loud enough, almost, for any person walking upon the surface to hear. "Hurrah! Hurrah!"

CHAPTER THREE

Underground

1

ORDER: INSECTIVORA. Family: Talpidae. *Scapanus latimanus.* The California mole. Little wonder that I, sleeping in the daylight hours, busily at work through the night, should know no more than that furry digger of the affairs of the earth. As well ask the nocturnal creature burrowing hungrily through the soil about the great question of slavery or the studies of Lister as question me, a pale-skinned Jew. In my brain there was room for but one thought: the cure for the disease of rabies. That goal would take unceasing labor: month after month, season after season of a relentless, single-minded search down mistaken avenues, blockaded passages, the collapsing culs-de-sac of science. In time the man, bent-backed, weak-eyed, with moustache bristles, would come to resemble the mole: the one chasing its grubs, its earthworms; the other, avidly, blindly, in darkness, pursuing his fixed idea.

The first of the many problems we scientists faced was the lack of a patient. As I had predicted, Elizabeth Gill was the last to suffer from the disease. Her daughter had escaped. The whole herd of infected horses had long since been buried. Without a victim, without venom, there was no way to begin our tests. After some weeks, however, a group of prospectors came across what proved to be the Meek brothers' horse, the old winch nag, at the side of an alkali spring. The infected carcass was half-eaten by coyotes.

"Excellent," said I to the Academicians. "This is good news. Those little wolves, *Canis latrans,* have surely contracted the malady from the victim. We have only to wait until the period of incubation is complete."

But more weeks went by without reports of a further outbreak. There were no attacks on local horses. The mules of the Neptune Mine remained untouched, as did the few flocks of sheep that had been introduced into the county. Naturally my team of researchers grew restless. Here they were, not in a classroom but in a laboratory at last; yet they had nothing to do but relearn their lessons from the dog-eared pages of Burns:

> "What signifies the life o' man,
> An' 'twere na for the lasses, O?"

Finally we decided to send the oldest Academicians out of the refuge, to search for the rabid coyotes in the wild. In the dark of night, Bacon Jack, Boston Charlie, and Kepler Jim crawled through the wind corridor at the rear of our chamber until they came to the ventilation shaft. Using the built-in steps of the chicken ladder, they climbed to the surface. There, by the sail, above the pond, they paused to listen. No signs of life came from our hidden abode. The dogs had been muzzled to prevent them from barking. The wind shutter had been propped open just enough to allow a stream of fresh air, without disclosing the light from our lamps, the smoke from our fire. The hideout was secure.

Throughout that autumn — the year was still 1857 — that trio of boys searched for the sick animals, half dogs, half wolves. As the weather grew cooler the plume of steam above the main shaft rose higher and higher, a measure of the winter to come. Down in the underground cavern, I noted another, more ominous sign of the passing time: the roof of the level was constantly sinking. The supports, thick tree trunks, already compressed to one third their original length, either cracked explosively under the enormous pressure or constantly ticked, like so many clocks. Each day, it seemed, I had to bend my six-foot frame lower, into a painful crouch.

Each day? Each night, rather, since it was only during the hours of darkness that I dwelled in the subterranean cavern. During the day I lived in the slop shop, sometimes selling, sometimes sleeping, always awaiting the moment when it was dark enough for me to return to the mine. How, you will wonder, did I enter, and regularly exit, the number-one level? There were three different ways to move vertically within that underground world. The first, of course, was in the lift that hurtled downward into the depths of the main shaft. Next, one could descend a hundred feet to the first level by means of the chicken ladder, that is, the handholds and footholds carved into the earthen walls of the ventilation column. These steps extended no further than the number-two level, which was twice as far as I — and Polly and Nan, on the nights when they joined us — needed to go.

Throughout the mine there was an intricate system of narrow chutes and drainage ditches through which one might squirm up or down from one horizontal level to another, though not clear up to grass. The levels were stacked at intervals of one hundred feet and ran south to north — from the wide, flat stations at the main shaft through a quarter-mile of drifts; then they narrowed down into the corridors, little more than crawl space, that emptied into the wind-tunnel doors. The entire mine was like a great building of unheard-of height, twenty stories and more, that had been planted upside down in the ground. Some floors were deserted and some teemed with men, yet each contained but a single room. This was the chamber that had been hollowed out of earth and stone in order to allow the hard-rock miners to get at the face of the ore. At the upper levels these caverns, already abandoned, had been compressed by the weight of the earth, and no less by the weight of the water in Etna Pond, to half their original dimensions, or less. Our own cavern, located directly beneath the reservoir, must have once stretched to a height of fifteen or even twenty feet. Now it lowered, it loomed, so that I had to stoop, hunched over, or scrape the crown of my sombrero against the jagged quartz.

Into this cavern the three scholar-scavengers at length returned. First back, in October, was Kepler Jim. A week later came Bacon Jack. Neither had found the least hint of the disease. Boston Charlie was the last to arrive. When he crawled through the corridor at the rear of the cavern, the mongrels shrank back, growling. Muffs of hair rose along their spines. "Boston Charlie got him!" cried the oldest of the Pioneers. He pointed upward. "Got sick sonabitch onna top!"

The two other hunters crawled back through the corridor and climbed the notched steps to the surface. Between them they lowered the bound beast, no larger than a collie, an Alsatian, to the level of the drift. At once the Modoc pets began to whimper, cowering at the far end of the cavern. One did not require a dog's sense of smell to pick up the reek, like an overripe banana, of *Canis latrans.* No question the animal was ill: its ribs bulged outward, the clear saliva dripped from its mouth, and its voice came out in a series of hoarse, high coughs that racked its frame, from hackles to hindquarters. More: it seemed to be trying, with its trussed forepaws, to claw at its open jaw, its furry throat.

"The rabies!" declared Newton Mike. "Scots! Nae doot 'tis the disease."

That diagnosis grew more certain over the course of the next days. Our water supply — either a leak from the pond above or an underground spring — dripped into the cave from a crack in the quartz. But when the coyote attempted to lap at it from the pan that Dumb George placed near, the liquid invariably caught in its windpipe and sprayed from the sharp black nose. Nor did the stricken animal eat. The Pioneers of Progress arranged a watch over the suffering beast, so as to obtain a sample of saliva at the very instant of death. As that moment drew near, I ceased my daily trips to the slop shop and began to sleep underground.

Thus it was that at mid-morning of the third day, both I and my pupils were slumbering within the cavern, with only Priestley Bill standing guard. The trouble was, that full-browed boy was dozing too, and so could not see that the coyote had chewed through the rope that bound its hind legs and had used the nails on those paws to claw off the tether on its front legs as well.

Ruhrrrrr! The growl of the bowlegged bulldog sounded the alarm.

"Take care, my dearies!" cried Priestley Bill, now wide awake.

All the sleepers opened their eyes. Think of the horror we felt at seeing, instead of the weak, prostrate creature, a fanged beast, eyes flashing, upon all fours.

"Hoot, mon!" exclaimed Paracelsus Max.

Said Boston Charlie, "Goddam!"

Then, before anyone could get to his feet, the crazed animal reared upward, like a colt; next, uttering its familiar hacking cough, it came down, hard on its forepaws. Immediately it stood again, head back, mouth open; an instant later, it threw itself a second time upon its stiffened forelegs — a jolting action that caused something shiny, solid, and ivory-colored to fly from its gaping jaws. Then, without a second's delay, it turned about and made for the dish of water, whose contents it began lapping as happily as any pup.

Steamboat Ed was the first to venture toward the shiny object. He picked it up and held it toward one of the candles that flickered in the rocky wall. "Bone, you betcher! Jackrabbit bone! Alla time stuck inna throat!"

What, after such disappointment, were we to do? What else but, like the great Harvey, who made his observations not once, not ten times, but ten thousand, try yet again? Hence we sent out the searchers. The days and weeks flew by. Our luck did not improve. Not only were there no infected coyotes, but in those wintry days of 1857–58, every wild animal was either hibernating beneath layers of frozen soil or had migrated to the south. Harvey at least had his wasps, his flies, his oysters, on which to perform his experiments. Yes, even, inside of eggshells, his unborn chicks. We, his heirs, could not find a single case of rabies in all of Siskiyou County.

Then, in the very depths of winter, in February, just such a victim — neither dog, coyote, nor horse, but a member of the primate order, species *Homo sapiens* — was found: a Christian convert, One-Eye Mose. That is to say, shortly before sundown — which in those winter days occurred as early as four in the afternoon — some person knocked upon the slop-shop door. Before I could answer, Ben Piper strode into the room.

"Come, Pinto. You're required at the mine. There's been an accident."

"Accident?"

"A miner's broken his leg."

"Broken leg? *Ein Indianer?* This is nothing. Bring him to me tomorrow. I shall make for him a splint."

"It's no common case," Piper insisted. "The man's on the fourth level. We can't move him at all. Look: I've brought a spare horse; we can ride back together."

I hesitated, glancing round toward where my adopted son sat in the corner, his spindly arm atop the bulldog's massive shoulders. The fact was, the tremendous heat below ground, the drenching humidity, had taken such a toll on the lad that I had been forced to bring him to grass a month before. Since then we had taken turns running the shop. When I slept he took the receipts, making change with his drumming fingers. Now he raised his head with a smile. The window light fell on him, illuminating the fluffy fringe of his hair, the pointed, papery ears.

"Well," called Piper, already on the walkway. "Are you coming?"

True: I had not taken my degree from the Harvard Medical College. Nonetheless, I felt bound by the doctor's oath. *"Ja!"* I responded. "Allow me only to fetch my hat."

The two of us, Piper and Pinto, arrived at the hoist works just as the sun, true to the Copernican system, cast the illusion of sinking in the west. We strode together toward the large plume of steam, three and four times a man's height, that revolved within the wooden girders of the gallows frame. The cage, larger than when I had seen it last, a double-decker, was waiting. Both platforms were loaded with empty ore skips standing on end. Gill, perched above the winding barrels, was at the controls. He lowered the upper deck to surface level. Piper and I walked aboard. For a moment we two hung motionless, while the rods of the Cornish pump clanged and clanked in their walled-off section of the shaft. Then, suddenly, the solid floor beneath us vanished, and down we fell.

On every side the timbering, the flat wood planks, flashed by. With my coattails flying, I stuck out my neck, craning upward to see the receding rectangle, still pink with the light of the setting sun. Ben Piper yanked me back. "You'll be killed!" he shouted. "Squashed like a melon!" Then, trembling and breathless, I withdrew, and half squatted beneath the illusory protection of an iron skip.

How rapid our plunge! How noisily the ore carts rattled and banged about us! The platform shook, tilting one way and another. To my senses it seemed that no braided cable attached us to the surface but that we were falling freely, at the same fantastic velocity as the metal weights dropped from the tower of Pisa. Is it any wonder that I, clutching my knees with one hand, my Mexican hat with the other, suffered from shortness of breath? For while we two travelers may not have been accelerating at the rate of thirty-two feet every second, our steady rate of fall was enough to send the hot winds whistling by, making it difficult to gulp the air into our lungs.

Down and down we continued to drop, with nothing below but a half-mile of empty space. Suddenly a light appeared, a single candle screwed into the wall of a gaping tunnel. "First level!" Piper shouted as we hurtled by. With a start I realized that well down this very drift, beneath the sinking roof of earth and stone, my class, my children, were now awaiting their professor's return. Cautiously, I twisted about to peer into the abandoned station. But as abruptly as the little light had appeared, so now it vanished, flickering precariously in our wake. The hot black breath of the mine blew by again.

Two more such beacons loomed from the darkness, at intervals — like my ward I counted upon my fingers — of fourteen seconds. The second level. The third. These, too, were deserted, since the ore in the upper vein had been mucked out long before. Onward we plummeted, rocking now not only from side to side but up and down as well, as the steel cord above us stretched and tightened, like a strand of India rubber. Then, without warning, we began to slow. Simultaneously, sounds of life rose toward us — clanging, pounding, a human shout, the bray of a mule. All at once the light from the fourth level flooded the shaft, as, bounding elastically, we came to a halt. The entire trip had taken no more than a minute.

A gang of Modocs had already set to work jerking the skips from the lower platform. Then the cage dropped a further six feet, bringing the upper compartment level with the station floor. At once Piper strode off into the maze of rails, mules, carts, the heaped-up piles of ore. As for me, I took one step on land and stood stock still. The world around swayed and rocked, as if, instead of standing on solid earth, I were still plunging downward at the end of our rubberized cable.

"This way! After me!" Piper called, even as he disappeared into the depths of the looming tunnel.

Dizzily I followed, stepping as best I could between the rails and the steaming, stagnant puddles of water. Now and again I was forced against the hot walls, so as to allow the bony, patchy-haired mules and their skips — filled not with ore but with ice — to pass by. Rats, I discovered, ran by my feet — not the giant rodents in Humboldt Johnny's tale, with three-foot whiskers, but ordinary brown rats, *Rattus norvegicus.* I knew that the stope at the end of this drift was the only one for several levels up or down that had continued to yield. But nothing prepared me for the sight that met my eyes when the rails beneath my feet bent leftward and I stepped into the fourth level's enormous cavern.

Here the roof, thirty feet high and more, was held up not by tree trunks but by pillars of uncut rock. Amazed, I halted, peering as best I could through this shadowy forest of stone. What I saw was not a vein but a sheer white wall of quartz, into which innumerable candles, in their black candleholders, had been stuck, like cloves in the fat of a ham. Three lines of men, unclothed save for clogs, mittens, and dangling clocks, were at labor. One row was crouched, one upright, while the third lay panting behind them, sprawled over melting boulders of ice. Still I stood, shielding my eyes against the wall's dazzling glare, watching the miners at work.

The kneeling Modocs held short steel shafts, which the upright miners behind them struck with heavy hammers. These drills were turned constantly in the face of the quartz, until the bit grew dull and a fresh one was inserted. Here and there, at some indecipherable signal, the man with the shaft would stand and seize the sledge, while the miner who had wielded that hammer collapsed upon the ice, taking the spot of the team's resting member, who had already risen to grasp the metal drill. It was all done in a single rippling motion, a wave that passed up the line, so that there was no break in the rhythm of blows, the movement of muscular bodies.

Here was a question: why did these sights, these sounds, which were like nothing I, a mere shopkeeper, had ever experienced, seem so familiar? I knew the answer: these toiling figures, half lit by flame, half lost in shadow; the clouds of dust rising from the points of the turning drills; the tremendous heat; the smell of sulfur that hung in the air from blasts of black powder; even the countless tons of earth that one could feel pressing down — what was all this but the vision shared by all men, city dweller and savage, Christian and Jew, of the underground existence that awaited every sinner?

"Pinto! Here!"

I whirled. Ben Piper beckoned from behind a tall pillar. I followed him away from the face of the stope and down to a low denlike chamber, where, piled on layers of sawdust, the jagged ice cakes were stored. Through the clammy mist that swirled through this burrow, I saw my new patient, spread-eagled on the glassy dust.

Cole was there, too, with a blanket over his shoulders. Frank Townsend paced with a lantern at the rear of the room. I knelt by the dozing flathead. "And what, please, is the gentleman's name?"

Townsend came closer, setting the lamp on the ground. "Don't you recognize him?"

I peered through the brighter light. Beneath his pulled-back lips, the Indian's breath whistled by his teeth. "Mr. One-Eye Mose!"

Immediately I began to press my hands along the dark flesh of the convert's left leg, then his right. Matt Cole leaned over the spot where I crouched.

"There's no need to touch him," he said.

"*Moment.* I am seeking the fracture."

"You won't find it," Cole responded, wrapping the blanket more tightly around his body.

I shuddered, though not from the temperature's sudden drop. "But Mr. Piper said the leg was broken."

Again Townsend came forward. "You were not the only one told that story. The entire shift thinks there was an accident. A fall down a narrow winze. But no fall occurred."

Piper spoke up. "Can't you see the man has a fever? He's flushed, for all the chill in the room."

"Sickness, then?" It was true: the flesh under my hands was hot. "But what sickness?"

In the lamplight I scrutinized my patient. At first it seemed the man had ceased breathing; indeed a full minute went by before One-Eye Mose drew a deep, sobbing inhalation. Then, at the exhalation, a bubble formed on the Modoc's lips, like one a boy might blow from a pipe of soap. I watched transfixed while the sphere expanded, gleaming gaily from the minute crystals of quartz it had picked from the air. Then the great gob burst, clinging in strands of spittle to the Indian's features.

"Our Fadder!" he cried, awaking. *"Our Fadder in de oven!"*

"Nein! Not possible! How can it be?"

"That is why I've asked you to come," said Townsend. "Is this the disease we suspect?"

"There is no wound. No sign of abrasion. Look: the feet, the abdomen, see here — the back: not even a scratch." I lifted the convert's hair. On the scalp underneath there was no mark. Indeed, nowhere on the body was there the puncture wound that might be left by the bite of a rat. "No. Not possible. This is not what you fear."

"Wait," said Piper. "I'll show you."

The anatomist, with the butt of his pistol, struck at a stack of ice. These were not the smooth, creamy slabs that Dandy Jack had once hauled from his secret source. The deeper the mine had gone, the more ice had been needed. Now relay teams, similar to those that had once hauled water, moved continuously into the Siskiyous, hacking this new ice, long, gleaming spikes, from the side of a huge mountain glacier. Ben Piper retrieved a fragment, opaque, aquamarine, which he offered to the smooth-skinned brave. The wide-awake Modoc at once opened his mouth. His tongue, long and pointed, flicked outward, eager to lick the frozen splinter, even as he reached to possess it.

Then the ice, which had been frozen for centuries, began to melt in the heat of the Indian's hands. At the sight of the drops One-Eye Mose was transformed. His face, one moment wreathed in smiles, was the next so contorted in terror — the lips turned down, the nostrils wide, the eyes all whites — that he might have donned one of his tribe's savage masks.

"Is it confirmed?" asked Cole. "Hydrophobia?"

I could only nod.

Townsend stepped near. "No hope of recovery. You confirm that as well?"

I nodded again. "*Ja.* No hope. But how did he contract the disease? There is nowhere upon him the sign of a bite."

"There isn't time to worry about the source," Piper declared. "We know what we have to: it's rabies. And mortal."

I turned back to One-Eye Mose. The convert was huddled toward the rear of the room, staring ahead, as if frightened by the coils of condensation. "You are correct: there is no treatment. Let us take him to the surface. He will be more comfortable in the infirmary there."

Cole waved his hand in dismissal. "Oh, no. The shift is about to end. The cage will soon be filled with men. You can leave with Piper and Townsend. I'll remain to trim the fuses. We'll bring him up during the night."

"No, no. This is now my patient. I cannot leave him."

Piper shook his dark locks. "This is nonsense. Did you sit with all the white men until the end? There's no more cause with a redskin."

I made no reply. There was little I could say to refute the anatomist's logic without revealing the real reason I wished to remain — and that was to secure a sample of the patient's mucus, or even, after the Modoc's demise, a portion of the nervous tissue itself.

Townsend moved toward the ramp that led back to the cavern and stope. "There is nothing further to discuss. This miner will not return to the surface, now or later. We all know the reason. The fourth level is different from the others. The vein here is richer than anywhere else. Do you expect us to abandon a fortune? If the Modocs learn of a new case of rabies, they'll panic. There are rumors enough as it is. They think the level is cursed: spells, spirits, a black eagle, a vulture. The men have been told a common enough story: a mucker fell through a winze and broke his leg. That tale must stand."

"*Nein!* I must make an objection. You asked me here as a physician. As a physician I tell you that before there is a second case, and a third, this level must be quarantined."

"Quarantined!" Cole exclaimed. "The assay values for the ore here are nine hundred dollars the ton!"

Piper: "Tell him the truth: there has already been a second case. And a third. And all on this level."

Townsend waved the others to silence. "I ask you to think of the wealth that remains below. Not merely in the working levels, but in the untapped vein. We do not know how far it goes. But if word of rabies spreads, the unrest will travel through the mine, to every level, every shift. Even the main shaft will be stopped."

"The shaft!" I burst out. "If you do not know the limit of the vein, you do know that of the men. You cannot continue. Even these strong Modoc miners are not fireproof. What will happen when the shaft strikes molten rock?"

"We're not yet at three thousand feet," Townsend replied. "The planet is eight thousand miles across. Molten rock, supposing any exists, is at the center."

"Mr. Frank Townsend: do you intend to go that far?"

Before the mine owner could answer — how startling to me that the Harvard man could actually ponder a question I'd meant only in jest — the Christian groaned. *"Hollow Ed your name,"* he muttered. *"The dumb king come."*

At these words, at the sight of the rheum that now poured from his mouth and nose, my heart stirred within me. "Poor fellow!

What torture to be surrounded by ice. Once more I insist: bring him to the surface. What does it matter if the miners learn the truth, if they must in any case abandon their work on the shaft? I have just seen how, after a few swings with the hammer, the Modocs collapse. And this is far from the hottest level! Even with ice on their backs the men can dig no deeper."

Here Townsend burst into his high, harsh laugh. "And what if I told you the Modocs will no longer have to swing hammers? Or twist the steel bits by hand? What if the very tool that drilled the rock should simultaneously, in the very act of boring, cool and refresh the drillers? What would the limits be then?"

Cole had also moved to the ramp. "Where once the problem of going deeper was solved by ice," he explained, "it shall now be solved by air. Gill has found a way to compress it at the surface — simply by letting the reservoir flow to deep tubular holes in the ground. From these cylinders we can direct the trapped air without loss of pressure through fixed and flexible hoses to any level. Thus the cool atmosphere of the surface will pour from our new mechanized drills — the same already at work in tunneling through the European Alps — in the form of exhaust. Right into the workers' faces!"

This speech was cut short by the sudden ringing of five, ten, a score of bells. The alarm clocks. It was the end of the daytime shift. Already, beyond our ice cave, the shadowy silhouettes of the miners were passing by.

Cole dropped the blanket from his shoulders and climbed to the exit. Fuse ends dangled from his pockets. He turned toward me. "Will you go up with the men?"

"No: I remain with Mr. One-Eye Mose."

Piper moved forward, to take my arm. Townsend waved him off.

"Let him be. He'll come up the next shift. What does it matter? The Indian cannot have more than a few hours of life left in him. After that, we'll spread the story that he fell down the shaft."

Cole moved out of the den, heading for the wall of the stope. Piper turned the opposite way, to the drift and the shaft. He paused for a final word. "It won't be a story. It will be the truth."

Before I could decipher that strange statement's meaning, Townsend stood before me. The light from the hooded lamp shone up from the ground, illuminating his teeth and the knot, the omega-shaped wen, that bulged at the center of his forehead.

"You asked," the mine owner began, "if I intended to go to the center of the earth. The answer, of course, is no — though I assure you, even that molten inferno will be preferable to what life shall soon be on the surface. Don't you know, Adolph, that a war is coming, that the nation is splitting apart? They are going to kill each other there. They are going to exhaust the last ounce of their treasure. But while that storm rages, we shall be beneath them, under their feet, under their graves. How deep, you wanted to know? I shall tell you. My plan is to take the Neptune Mine to a depth of one mile — and to do so before this decade is out. This is the only kind of achievement that lasts. Here is a project to rival the works of the pharaohs, or the Babylonian gardens, or the Colossus at Rhodes. This mine will be the eighth wonder, Adolph! The eighth wonder of the world!"

The last of those words — and what were they, I thought, but the ravings of a madman? — echoed from the cavern, from the drift. For Townsend had already begun his way back toward the station. I could still hear the far-off signal bells, calling the hoistman to bring the last cage of men to grass. Then all was silent on the level, save for the sound of the sick Indian, who had begun to belch, to hiccup, as his pharynx contracted against the passage of air from his lungs.

I turned toward my patient. The sufferer was on the verge of suffocation. His body worked to purge itself of liquids: sweat streamed over his chest, he urinated freely, and the thick mucus continued to pour from his mouth, eyes, nose. I stood, torn between pity and my desire to begin our great work. To do the latter I would need to collect a specimen from these very fluids. Grimly, ruthlessly even, I blew out the guttering lamp.

To my surprise, everything did not go dark. Behind me, in the great cavern, there was still a faint light. Quickly I moved up the ramp, into the enormous, hollowed-out room. Off to my right, by the stope, something was flickering. It was hissing, too, with a sinister sibilance. Was this the famed vulture? The taloned bird? I took another step forward and saw with horror that the entire face of the stope, where only moments before the Modocs had been at work, was covered by a diamond-shaped pattern of fuses. Some dangled limply. Others writhed, flopping against the wall as if alive. All sent out a sizzling spray of sparks.

Not a moment, not even a second, to lose. I dashed back to the darkened den and, feeling my way, inching forward, thrust the lantern globe, the still warm vessel, to the mouth of the moribund patient. It filled with his deadly drool. Then, while the rats fled left and right before me, I raced back to the safety of the drift. I was halfway to the station, clutching my glass container, when the charges, the pattern of relievers and edgers and lifters, went off in their predetermined sequence. I felt nothing more than a rush of hot air.

"Ho! Ho!" I laughed. And again, "Ho-ho-ho!"

What struck me as funny, as a kind of colossal joke, was not the puny effect of this single blast but the futility of all the explosions, the tremendous toil, that went into this and every other mine. The entire endeavor — the endless digging, the wagon trains to distant glaciers and far-off lakes, the underground work crews, and the pneumatic drills: all this effort was for nothing but a bauble, a trinket, a dull lump of gold. Compared to my own project, my own labors, how childish a prize! Someday the world would know that the *real* work of the Neptune Mine had occurred not on this fourth level, nor all the way down at the fifteenth, but just beneath the surface, on level number one. There, in my laboratory's tropical climate, would occur a discovery that all the treasure still locked in the earth could not buy. The mystery that confronted me was denser, more durable, than the rock that held the ore in its unyielding grasp. Yet I, the Hebrew, the Hungarian, would dig it out! Ahead, a light shone from the station. I halted. I held up my clear glass globe. Inside it the liquid foamed and bubbled, like a virulent witch's brew.

2

The two great ventures within the Etna butte differed in that one was secret, hidden just below the surface, and the other public, even celebrated, although carried out thousands of feet underground. But Frank Townsend and A. Pinto had this in common: we both were waging a battle not only against nature, the hardness of her stone, the inflexibility of her laws, but against the passage of time. For the mine owner the task was monumental. To reach his goal he had to accomplish as much in twenty-two months as he had in the previous seven years. Yet for all the Neptune's innovations — and this was the first mine in the hemisphere to use the mechanical drill, not to mention flexible piping, the flat-woven cable, the multideck cage — the main shaft descended at little better than three times the old rate of a half-inch an hour, one foot a day.

Nor did the project involve the main shaft alone. The ventilation column, with its connecting corridors and wind doors and shutters, had to be extended as well. How, when the strain on the Cornish pump had already caused the cast-iron rod to crack on three different occasions, would the crew disperse the steaming seepage? And what of the heat? Gill had recorded sump readings of 170 degrees, 129 in the air, with the temperature of the latter rising a further 2 degrees for every 140 additional feet. That meant, should the rate of increase hold constant, an ultimate working atmosphere of well over 160 degrees. If the relay teams hauled in the whole of the Siskiyou glacier, if they chopped off the snowcap on Shasta, an Antarctica of ice, they could never cool those infernal chambers.

All this was eagerly noted by the Yrekans, who were kept up through the nights by the boom of black powder and the whine of the new hydraulic bellows. Many in town, particularly those who favored the Sazarac Saloon, began to wager on Townsend's chances of making depth by the first day of 1860. Judge Steele, who offered ten to one against, had few takers — especially when rumors began to spread of how the forced air drills had twice punctured pockets of poisonous water, scalding the operators and filling the drift with a stinging, choking steam. People claimed to have heard how, at the lowest levels, plugs of rock would spontaneously shoot across the entire width of a tunnel, embedding themselves with the force of bullets in the wood of the supporting timber. The Modocs, gamblers themselves, would bet their fellow workers from the upper drifts that they could not cut across the resulting jet of water with an ax: invariably the metal blade, no matter how powerfully propelled, would whirl away in the stream.

But the greatest obstacle in the path of what the Yrekans mockingly called the miracle mile was the incidence of mortality among the miners. Naturally accidents were common enough in any hard-rock operation: cables snapped or cages, coming up, were overwound; cave-ins closed the drifts; a spark might set off a cartridge prematurely, or one of the mucking crew might drive his pick into an unexploded charge. A steady rain of objects — tools, buckets, wax candles, rocks, a loose timber, and on one occasion a full-grown mule — dropped down the shaft, more often than not striking through the mesh roof of the cage, killing or injuring anyone who might be inside. Worst of all, a Modoc on the bottom level might grow faint from the heat and tumble into the sump, up to the knees, up to the hips. No matter how quick his fellow tribesmen were to pull him out, even if they did so in seconds, the skin would slough from the doomed man's limbs.

Thus no one in town thought to wonder at the various mishaps as the shaft drove deeper and deeper — beneath the level of the sea, lower than any mine in California, or, for all we in Yreka knew, than any mine in the world. But the Modocs suspected that not all these accidents were routine. For one thing, many of the falls were from the same level, the fourth; and each of these occurred between shifts, when the drillers were supposed to have reached the surface and the muckers were not yet down. Even stranger, no one at work on the lower levels ever heard, echoing in the shaftway, a shout, a scream. It was as if the hearts of the falling men had stopped in the first instant from fright. Of course none of the corpses was recovered: no one, nothing, could drop freely the length of the shaft. Sooner or later any plunging body would strike the timbering at the walls and then, with ever-increasing force, begin to ricochet, breaking into pieces, turning to pulp. Steel brushes and lime were kept at every station to scrape the remains, which, with the boiled fragments skimmed from the sump, invariably fit into a single candle box.

More than once I had seen these tiny coffins as the Modoc mourners, starting off to the burial grounds at Wigwam, moved along Miner Street, past my shop. I alone, of all those in Yreka, knew they contained the remains of rabies victims. Ben Piper, or Cole, or Townsend himself, would throw the latest sufferer from the scourge over the lip of the fourth-floor station — almost as if these three had become doctors at the General Hospital after all. I was certain they had done as much with the corpse of the convert One-Eye Mose. Did they wait until these poor patients had expired? So I prayed — though I knew full well it would be an act of mercy to batter the Indians senseless against the sheer walls rather than allow them to suffer to the end of their incurable disease.

Incurable, indeed! When I, clutching the saliva sample from One-Eye Mose, made my way back to the number-one level, I understood that three tasks lay immediately ahead. First — and this was simple enough — we had to discover if the virulent serum would in fact cause rabies in our experimental subjects. Next, far more difficult, we had to determine the precise number of these germs that would make our test animals sick without proving mortal. Last, the crucial step, we had to prove that such survivors were immune to subsequent infection, as might occur from the bite of a maddened beast. Naturally I knew that the work before us would be time-consuming and filled with frustration and pain. Little did I imagine, however, that the first obstacle to be overcome lay not in nature but in the researchers themselves. For when, with needle, with syringe, I approached their frisking mongrels, the Academicians broke into revolt.

"Fie! Fie!" exclaimed Cavendish Sam. "Dinna ye touch e'en a hair o' their winsome heads!"

Said Paracelsus Max: "These bonnie beasties are friends. Mates. True-blue Scots!"

Then the rest of the children ran to their pets, snatching them out of reach. The animals themselves, apricot-colored, saffron-colored, began to cringe, to whine, as if they had grasped what fate lay ahead.

"Natural historians! Respected colleagues! We have long ago decided to allow our canine friends the honor of taking part in the great experiment. This means that, following the example of Jenner, we must inoculate each dog with the disease in order to cure him of it."

Priestley Bill's teeth had at last grown in. They flashed as he spoke in anger. "Do ye think the clan o' Modocs such fools as this? Will ye make a man well by bringing on sickness?"

"Take a helluva ignorant redskin," said Steamboat Ed, "gonna swallow that."

Resolute, I stood my ground. "We must fight fire with fire; that is the principle of vaccination!"

"Ha-ha-ha!" laughed Boston Charlie, from under his shiny top hat. "Next you gonna tell stinking Modoc he gonna get clean with a bath in the mud!"

Humboldt Johnny squeezed his arms round his pet's mangy muff. "How can we believe in such a wee winsome thing as a germ? Canna see him. Canna smell him. Canna clutch him wi' glee to the heart like a dog tha's a bonnie bold yellow!"

" 'Tis a trick!"

"A fantasy o' the mind!"

Here was more than revolt; it was heresy. The denial of the germ theory itself. The truth, however, was that in those days it was I who was the heretic, while my students maintained the orthodox view. Between the first half of the century, with its belief in spontaneous generation, its conviction, shared by white men and Indians alike, that mice might be bred from old rags and cheese; and the second half, during which knowledge of the existence of bacteria became commonplace, there stretched an abyss — a chasm that I, graduate of the *Technische Gymnasium,* summoned my eloquence to bridge:

"Pioneers of Progress! Sons of Galileo! Think, I beg you, of that great man of Pisa. Are we able to see the gravitational forces whose effects he described, and which we ourselves have demonstrated? We are not. Similarly, just because we cannot see the animacules of the virus does not mean they are not here. Alive. In this very syringe."

Now Kepler Jim came forward, with Hippocrates, his own precious pet, trembling in his arms. "Mister-r-r Pinto. I dinna doot the principle o' vaccination or the existence o' the wee germs. The tests must be done. But why upon our beasties? Wadna the fourth-level rodents serve as weel? The sad suffering of those whiskery creatures will na reach so deep in our hearts."

Of course! Addle-brained Adolph! Not to have thought of this solution myself! The brown-haired rat did not migrate south, nor did it sleep through the winter. Moreover, these warm-blooded mammals swarmed through the lower level in their hundreds, their thousands perhaps. I looked toward Kepler Jim. For all his flat head, his broken-style nose, a definite prize pupil. His hands, his fingers, long and delicate, struck me as those of a surgeon. "Congratulations, sir. You are a true Heir of Harvey. We begin our tests on the Norwegian rat!"

Securing these subjects proved a dangerous game. Our trappers would descend through the narrow winzes, the drainage adits, from level to level, until they came to a spot just above the fourth-level stope. Once there they would wait for the interval between shifts, during which they would drop through the chute to the chamber. Then they would throw their nets upon the packs of rodents that swarmed over the broken rock. The danger lay in this: no matter how careful the Academy members were, they could not avoid being raked by the nails and bitten by the teeth of the long-tailed creatures. Yet for all their scratches and scars, not one of the youths, nor a single member of *Rattus norvegicus,* displayed the least symptom. Whatever the source of rabies, it was not in this scurrying pack.

Had One-Eye Mose died from the disease? The only way to find out was to inject the victim's mucus into one of the rodents. The trouble was, the incubation period — that is, the time from inoculation to symptom — might be six weeks, or two months, or more. At that rate we youthful researchers would be old men before we could follow the course of the venom through a number of rat generations. It was then that I recalled how, of all the infected Yrekans, young Christie had been the first, and Gill's wife last, to succumb. Was that not because the boy's wounds were near the center of the nervous system, while the woman's were at an extremity? That meant the incubation period was nothing but a pause while the malady moved slowly from blood cells to nerve cells and then along those fibers to the very center of motion, thirst, thought, feeling. Question: what would happen if the virus were introduced not into the bloodstream but into the nervous tissue, the spinal cord, the brain itself?

The Disciples of Bacon set about discovering the answer. Paracelsus Max devised an airtight box, into which I placed a rat, together with a sponge soaked with $C_4H_{10}O$: the familiar compound of ether. Almost at once the subject fell into a deep and seemingly dream-free sleep. Next, with my little crown saw, I cut a neat plug from the skull of the anesthetized rodent and placed a drop of the viral broth directly upon the surface of the brain. Then the bone was replaced, the scalp sewn skillfully together, and — *Eins! Zwei! Drei!* — the rat woke, yawned, and began to frisk about. Two weeks later this animal developed the same unmistakable symptoms as One-Eye Mose. In forty-two hours it was dead of furious rabies.

Now the Highlanders faced their greatest task. We knew we possessed the virus of the disease. Now we must weaken it enough to cure, not kill. Through the winter of 1858–59 we attempted to exhaust the germs in every way imaginable: shrinking the dose, diluting it, boiling it — even freezing the venom in chunks of ice we filched from the number-four level. Yet sooner or later the altered potion had to be administered to a member of *Rattus norvegicus.* When it was, the rodent either died from the usual paralysis, with convulsions and final coma, or else — in those instances when, for example, we had heated the broth beyond the boiling point — developed no symptoms at all. Worse still, these survivors of the inert virus did not prove, upon reinoculation, the least resistant to potent venom: they began to drag themselves around their cages in even less than two weeks. Here was awful irony: by passing the virus from one generation to another, we had actually enhanced, not attenuated, its potency. Now our baleful broth could bring on the death of the underground rodents in just six days. Our months of work had ended in failure.

One cold dawn — though it was as hot as a tropical jungle in the underground cavern, and damp as a rain forest, too — I was preparing, as was my wont, to leave for the surface. All about me the demoralized scholars sat in a stupor. Some had already started to doze. Even the rats lay motionless in their cages. Only the Modoc mongrels — Hippocrates by name, and Galen, Euclid, the spotted Leeuwenhoek, orange-colored Warren — seemed wide awake, jumping about the figure of Nan as she prepared to fill their bowls with the milk she'd brought from her father's barn. Her twin, Polly, performed that task on alternate days, and sometimes Antoinette, the Panamanian, took the frightening trip down the chicken ladder, with the buckets slung over her shoulder. Now the mutts scattered: the sleek, tamed coyote trotted forward to drink its fill.

At the entrance to the wind corridor I halted, stooped like the figure of Atlas. The bones in my body, like the squat tree trunks, creaked — though less from the strain of supporting the rooftop, the countless tons of rock and earth, than from the weight of evidence piled up in my slop-shop ledger. Here was a mountain of data that crushed our high hopes. Where had we gone wrong? How miscalculated? Was there some flaw in the inductive method? Or had my protégés been correct in their skepticism, their doubts: was there not something mad in the idea of fighting fire with fire, the virus of rabies with rabies itself?

I looked to where the young Bosworth girl was pouring a fresh bowl for the young Pioneers. She might, with her long skirt, her golden tresses, have been one of the famed milkmaids of Jenner. What had the great doctor seen that I had missed? Certainly he had used inductive methods, moving from the examination of a single cowpox patient to note that the whole class of milkmaids, as if divinely protected, was immune to smallpox. The genius of the man lay in reasoning that these women were saved not by the heavens but by the disease they had already contracted from the animals they milked. And what was this cowpox? Nothing more than a case of the dread human scourge that some simple milkmaid had previously transmitted to the udder of her cow, and that the benign bovine in turn had transferred back to a different milker in a milder form.

Here I gave a start. My Adam's apple quivered like the plucked string of a guitar. An idea! Jenner had fought fire *not* with fire but with ashes — that is, with the cooled-off remains of the smallpox that had been created by the cow!

Stooped, bent, I dashed back among my weary pupils and seized one after the other by the silk of his lapels. "Mistake! Error! Definite miscalculation!" Then I went on to explain what my review of the origins of vaccination had revealed. Alas, the Sons of Galileo, long accustomed to failure, resisted.

"Are ye daft, mon?" asked Cavendish Sam. "We canna bring a heifer here."

"Ho-ho-ho! Certainly not! It is only the principle that we must follow. We shall alter the human virus, the germ that killed One-Eye Mose, by passing it through an animal species!"

"But we hae already spilled the bluid o' a hoondred rats! An' a' for nothing!"

"*Nein!* Not for nothing! The virus changed! Yes, true: in some creatures it will grow stronger, as with the rat population. In others it will weaken, just as the smallpox did within the body of the cow. From those exhausted specimens of the disease we shall make our vaccine!"

Paracelsus Max, who still greased his hair with fish oil, was the thinnest of the Pioneers. His black banker's suit hung on him the way the clothes of a scarecrow droop on crossed sticks. He raised a bony arm. "Na a cow. Na a rat. How will ye know which beastie to give death's dart?"

"That," I responded, "is what our next experiment must discover. Now in the upper world it is springtime. The animals wake from their winter sleep. They return from their journey south. You too must leave your lair and go forth over the earth. You must gather members of every species. Be brave! Be cheerful, friends! For just as old Noah filled his ark to save animals from the flood, so you shall fill this cave to save mankind from its age-old plague. Stout hearts, gentlemen! The goal is in sight! We shall not fail!"

All spring long, into the long days of summer, the band of Modocs spread outward, tracking east as far as the lava beds, south to the approaches of Shasta, and into the new free state of Oregon to the north. Every day new specimens — the order Rodentia mostly: meadow, brush, and harvest mice; muskrats, marmots, squirrels, a porcupine, even a skunk — were brought down the notched ladder into the underground cavern. The cave became a zoological garden, filled with small foxes, a bobcat, a doe. For the eager lads, what a bitter paradox: here were they, the Heirs of Harvey, modern men of science; yet they spent their days like the most primitive of their ancestors — hunting, trapping, even gathering roots, acorns, berries with which to feed their prey.

More bitter still, in not one of these animals did the virus become so weakened that it might be used as a vaccine. We operated on specimen after specimen. My young apprentices — especially Kepler Jim, who had the natural skills, as well as the delicate fingers, of a surgeon — reopened the skull of each new victim and removed the infected bulb, the medulla oblongata. This gray matter they would grind into a fresh soup, which in turn was used to inoculate the next group of subjects.

The trouble was, no matter what combinations the Academicians tried, a single drop of saliva from one species retained enough potency to kill a member of any other. All too soon the tropical forest became a charnel house. The animals, coughing, frothing, dragged their limbs about their cages, or threw themselves in fury against the hard stone of the cavern wall. An odor of decomposing flesh rose all the way from the bottom of the ventilation shaft, where the dead specimens were dropped; it mingled with the aroma, like creosote, of the rotting timbers.

By the summer of 1859 I realized I had no choice but to call the great search off. Polly and Nan, unable to bear the sight of the suffering creatures, no longer made the descent to the number-one level. That meant Antoinette, clumsily moving from foothold to handhold, had to bring the buckets of milk on her own. But it was no such practical matter that led to my decision. Nor was I swayed so much by the repeated failure of our experiments, as by the changes in the experimenters themselves.

No longer were my lads Children of the Enlightenment, their dear faces shining with the glow of the inductive method, with faith in the idea of progress. A callousness, a carelessness, had crept into all their actions. The same boys who had wept at the thought of their puppies undergoing a pinprick, who had winced at cutting the skin of even an etherized rat, laughed now when hurling the stiffened carcasses into the gloom. They were, toward the huddled rodents, the rabbits, as brutal as butchers. It was as if a virus had entered their bloodstreams, too. I feared that as it multiplied, as it grew stronger, it would force them to forget all their learning, making them as untutored, as uncivilized, as wolves in the wild.

So it was that once I'd come to a decision, I spent the entire day at the slop shop trying to think of a way to announce it to my fellow researchers. This was no easy task. How tell my students that the great experiment, their own spent youth, the pain and sacrifice of so many warm-blooded creatures, had ended in defeat? Where would I find the strength to lead them back to a world in which their foe, the most dread of all afflictions, had triumphed?

Hour after hour I sat at my desk and wrote out versions of what I must say that night. Then I trod through the rooms of the large brick building, trying out first one declaration, then another. Grimacing, smiling, I declaimed in front of my bedroom mirror. Finally, as the dark of night was gathering round, I descended to the cellar, where I had decided to make my speech to Dumb George and Caesar.

The boy sat against a crate of nankeen trousers, with his chin on his bony kneecaps and his fingers wrapped round the sticks of his shins. The dog, with his front legs bowed, his two sharp incisors pressed against his upper lip, squatted by his side.

"Friends," I began — only to have my voice box seize and fall silent. Out of my head flew each thought, every idea. Suddenly, an inspiration: if my own words failed me, I would use those of Burns.

"The best-laid schemes o' mice an' men," I pronounced, in the nasal twang of a Pressburg native, *"gang aft agley."*

I broke off. There was no doubt that my audience had grasped my meaning. Caesar gave a low growl. The hair on his muff began to rise. The face of Dumb George grew pale — that is, his skin turned from its light beige color to a kind of champagne. In his wide eyes the eyeballs began to swim through thickening tears. I continued:

> "An' lea'e us nought but grief an' pain,
> For promised joy!"

Now the boy jumped to his feet and stood quivering before me. The beast, the brute, blew a hot stream of air through his squashed-in nose. I swallowed once. Twice. Then I said, "*Ja!* You have guessed correctly the unhappy news. Our experiment has ended in failure. There is no cure for rabies."

Caesar gave a roar of rage; his master, shaking violently, so that the tears sprayed left and right, turned for the ladder. Nimble as a monkey, he dashed up the rungs, with the bulldog clambering behind him. I heard their six feet on the floorboards above me, followed by the tinkle of the slop-shop bell and the slam of the slop-shop door. They had, in their despair, fled from home.

And this was but the rehearsal for the task that still lay before me! I delayed until well beyond the hour of midnight and then made my way northward, to Mount Etna, and down the ventilation shaft. Even before I reached the one-hundred-foot level I sensed that something was wrong. I did not see, did not hear, anything amiss. But with my lengthy nose I picked up the scent of — what was this? Ammonia? Sulfur? No! The stink from one of our sickly subjects, the rabid *Mephitis mephitis:* a skunk!

I pushed through the shutter and crawled along the corridor. There, in the cavern itself, was a scene of chaos. The Modoc dogs, named for the world's great doctors, had run amok. They, no less than their human masters, had succumbed to the process of brutalization. All the animal cages had been overturned. The bodies of the little mammals, many of them in the last throes of hydrophobia, lay scattered about the chamber. The mongrels were chewing at their guts. At the cave's center the member of family Mustelidae, the skunk, lay stiff on its back. The froth of the disease that had killed it clung to its lips. Even as I watched, the coyote leaped upon the black-and-white carcass and sank its teeth into the fur and the flesh, and cracked the bones. Then *Canis latrans* — it was doomed now, as were all the Indian pets — wolfed down the poisoned meat of its meal.

Anguished, despairing, I looked about. The smell of hot blood was as strong as the stench of the skunk. Where were the Disciples of Bacon? For an awful instant I thought that they, too, had become the victims of their own enraged pets. Had the lads, to escape these fangs, these ripping claws, hurled themselves down one or the other of the bottomless holes? Just then I heard a faint thump, a repeated percussion, together with a murmur of voices. The noise came from down the drift, in the direction of the main shaft.

Ducking low, so that my high-stepping knees almost struck my chest and chin, I entered the drift. Old rails, along which mules had once pulled the iron skips, lay twisted at the bottom. From the gleaming chunks of quartz that protruded from the ceiling, water streamed, as if from the teeth of a swimming shark. I pressed onward, until I began to hear, from the distant shaftway, the noises of the working mine: drills and hammers; the hiss of the hoses; the clang of the various signal bells, followed by the whistle made by the displaced column of air as the cage moved up or down in response. Then, midway between the cavern behind me and the shaft ahead, the drift widened, opening into a semicircle that had been cut into the left-hand wall: a stable, once, for the half-blind mules.

From that spot, deep in darkness, came the sound of high-pitched voices. Moving closer, I made out a singsong chant, the burr of Burns:

> "Then gie the lass a fairin', lad,
> O gie the lass her fairin'
> And she'll gie you a hairy thing,
> An' of it be na sparin' —"

I knew well the voice of the speaker: Cavendish Sam. Then all the scholars sang out in unison:

> "Oh, hug our doxies in the hay!
> Hug our doxies in the hay, O!

I felt, in addition to the emotions of joy, of relief — for it was clear that the boys had not fled the animals; rather, the animals had taken advantage of the absence of the boys — a certain chagrin. Had I been wrong about their callousness, their cruelty, the coarseness of their feeling? Here was the proof of their gentler side. Clearly the poor children, plunged into a life underground, a dark, close existence, had secretly gathered in order to recapture in poesy the lost world of flowers, sunlight, and the high tumbling clouds.

"An' ken ye Leezie Lundie, O,
The godly Leezie Lundie, O—"

That, I knew, was the voice of Bacon Jack. It occurred to me, hearing these love lyrics, these fanciful flights, that science itself, with its facts, figures, numbers, was no less a gloomy grotto than our humid cave. Reason might flourish there, true, but at the expense of the finer emotions, the sentiments of the heart, the more tender feelings.

"She mowes like reek thro' a' the week,
But finger fucks on Sunday, O."

That verse brought me up short. So did an obvious smell, warm and familiar: the reek of gore. As the chorus rang out again—*"Hug our doxies in the hay, O!"*—I fumbled in my frock coat for a match and struck it against a jagged rock. The damp phosphorous flared. Instantly I released the stick, which fell, extinguished, upon the ground. But what I had seen in that second blazed yet before my eyes, as if illuminated by the gas lamps of a thousand stages: the naked Antoinette, like an animal, a quadruped, on elbows, on knees; with Boston Charlie behind her, stark naked too, his arms stretched forward and his hands on her hips. Nor was that all: Bacon Jack, old Steamboat Ed, and Cavendish Sam stood in line. Yet more. Yet worse. The little ones, my tots, my tads, the darling weanlings—Priestley Bill, Elbow Frank, Humboldt Johnny, the skinny Paracelsus Max, and even the sharp-witted Newton Mike: all these lay on the ground, their mouths gaping, groping toward the sacks of the woman's breasts. They were like a litter at the teats of a sow. No one spoke now, or chanted, or sang. The only sound came from the thud of the Panamanian's head as, moving to and fro, she struck against the wall of rock.

Naturally enough, I thought this a nightmare vision. Tremblingly I reached for another match. It was no dream. The sight that flickered in the little light was more horrible still. There was the thick purplish form of the woman, with her breasts hanging like breadfruit. The members of the Modoc tribe were behind her, beneath her, just as before. But what I saw now was that the faces turned toward me were covered cheek to chin with bright streaks of paint. The zigzag pattern flashed over their ribs. With the matchstick still in my hand, I stood rigid, as if each of those crimson spears, those lightning bolts, had pierced my own body.

But it wasn't paint. It was blood. A rabbit, one of our subjects, had been slaughtered on the stable floor.

The hot flame sizzled against the flesh of my fingers and went out. The last thing I saw was the worst thing: the mask on the face of Kepler Jim, his staring eyes, the red streaks on his cheekbones, the wicked flash of teeth in his mouth. "This cannot be!" I exclaimed. "Not our highly skilled surgeon!"

Laughter, cruel and inhuman, rang out of the dark. Then from that same blackness came a cry, a howl of anguish. Whose voice was it? My own.

"Savages! Savages! *Die Wilden!*"

Bad days for Adolph Pinto. For the first time schoolboys and schoolmaster were separated. The youths remained underground, amidst the ruins of their enterprise. I lived in my fireproof. How many such days? Four. Five. Six. Still I dared not think of returning to our former laboratory. I knew that the crazed coyote, having eaten rabid flesh, must now be entering its death throes. For that matter, all the mongrels that had taken part in the rampage surely suffered from the virus raging in their blood. Worse than that thought was the image — indelible, I knew — of the erstwhile Academicians, paint-covered, filled with lust, steeped in gore.

The pity was, I did not spend this time with General George. Neither the boy nor his dog had come back to the slop shop. Nor had they taken shelter at the Bosworth farm. I soon discovered that my ward was staying with his mother, Queen Mary, which was what the Yrekans called the new madam of the Sazarac Saloon. When I peeked over the bat-wing doors, I saw her on the dance floor, among her half-naked squaws. Dumb George sat on the lap of Jack-a-Dandy, at the pit for rouge-et-noir. The boy's head swiveled left and right, almost as if it were following the contrariwise motions of the spinning wheel, the bounding ball. I raised my hand in cheerful greeting. The bulldog, loose-lipped, tongue lolling between its upright fangs, saw me first: it raised its massive head. But my foster child, my firefly, would not respond. He turned his back upon me.

More days went by. I remained in Yreka, whose roads and boardwalks I had not freely trodden for years. Much had changed in the world of light and air. The only topic in town was the miracle mile, which Townsend had vowed to achieve at the stroke of midnight when the old decade ended and the new one began. At the winding drum the red arrow of the depth gauge stood at 4000 feet. That meant, with six months remaining, the main shaft would have to be extended at the unheard-of rate of seven feet every day. All the resources of the Neptune were already diverted to the task. One by one the drifts had been shut down, the vein abandoned. Every shift — the drillers and muckers, the station loaders — had been put to work on the main shaft. The extension of the ventilation column had ceased altogether. Instead, the pneumatic drills were disconnected, so that the air from the surface whistled downward, spraying like a shower over the upturned faces of the naked men who gasped beneath the metal-and-canvas pipes.

During this final push the greatest trouble came from the Cornish pump, which broke down repeatedly. The Modocs labored under the constant threat of being crushed by its tumbling iron rod, or scalded when the pieces struck the surface of the sump, throwing up water like molten metal. Gill, the engineer, had the idea of reversing the hydraulic pistons, so that instead of pumping air downward, he might, by sinking the ends of the pipes beneath the simmering water, draw the contents of the sump into the pneumatic system, the way blood from a vein is drawn into a syringe. In fact, for six minutes, with the compressors screeching and black smoke pouring from the boiler stacks, this siphon did manage to pull the liquid from level to level, a third of the way up the shaft; then, when the weight of the column of water proved more than the expanding steam in the engines could move, a cam cracked, the belts went slack, and a few seconds later the sump erupted in a boiling geyser.

Ten days after I'd arrived back in Yreka, the whole town was awakened by a large thump, a kind of shudder. A hissing came from the direction of the buttes. Outside, on Main Street, people were running by. "Accident!" they shouted. "Trouble at the mine!"

But there had been no mishap. When the next cage came to grass, we saw it was loaded not with wounded men or rock from the shaft but with what looked to be excrement, fresh and steaming.

"Mud!" Poland, the sheriff, exclaimed. "They've blown out the sump!"

Such indeed was the case. Matt Cole, the explosives expert, inspired by the sight of Gill's pipes submerged in the steaming water, had the idea of packing the same cylinders with black powder. The bottom of each section was sealed with waterproof wax, while a fuse poked through the top. Sixteen of these bombs were pushed into the water, so that only the rattails showed at the bubbling surface, like straws in a soda drink. Depending on where the powder was placed, the depth charges blew either downward, through rock, or upward, evaporating the sump. Hence with one blow the pumping problem was solved and the shaft extended not inches but five full feet directly down. The gamblers in the Sazarac Saloon, most of whom had bet against the shaft reaching depth, began to recalculate the odds. Judge Steele, who had staked what was left of his fortune at ten to one against the success of the venture, began to have plenty of takers.

Whatever the Yrekans thought of the chances of the miracle mile, word of the exploit was clearly spreading through the state and beyond. There was as much excitement now as during the gold strike of ten years before. Tourists began to pour in. There wasn't a room to be had at the Metropolitan, and a crew was at work rebuilding the old Hotel de France. At the Sazarac the hurdy-gurdies, the Modoc maidens, seemed never to sleep. They danced through the night, clinging to the necks of the white men who stood three deep at the zinc-covered bar. There was even a telegraph line, a series of cross-shaped masts, between which stretched taut double wires. One end came to rest against the roof of the building named for the *Ingot,* whose headlines were devoted exclusively to what it called

THE EIGHTH WONDER OF THE WORLD

SHAFT AT 4000 FEET
GOAL IN SIGHT

The far end of the line stretched off to the south — to the towns of Marysville, Stockton, San Jose, and finally to the Merchant's Exchange signal station on Telegraph Hill. The little town of Yreka was connected, at the speed of light, of electricity, to all of the civilized world.

My own thoughts, however, instead of expanding beyond the flat horizon, were once more shrinking to the dimensions of the underground cavern where I had spent virtually every night for the last two years. The truth was, I could no longer bear the separation from my youthful companions, who, whether in war-paint or waistcoats, were dear to me as nephews, as sons. Thus it was that some two weeks after I had arrived in Yreka, I threw one long leg over the back of Neptune the mule and — this was the dead of night — turned onto Main Street and moved off to the north.

For the first moments there was no sound save for the constant thud of the stamps, the plodding hooves of my mount. Then, at the outskirts of Modoc Town, Neptune slowed. From the direction of the shanties came a rasp, a rattle, as if a storm of hailstones were beating upon the tin roofs. In agitation I struck the heels of my bluchers against the mule's withered flanks. I knew the noise. It had begun shortly after the new air-driven drills had sent clouds of dust throughout the mine. This was the sound of the Modoc men, the veteran miners, coughing, sighing, spitting, because of the crystals of quartz caught in their lungs.

At the base of the butte I thought I could hear the same rasping sounds. I halted. The night was a dark one. The only light came from above, where the stars were burning like a thousand fuse ends in the blackened slab of the sky. Gradually I could make out the aged Indians, dressed only in loincloths, crawling about on the great mound of tailings. Up and down they moved on the expanse of the man-made hill. Now and then they stopped, stooped, and began crawling again. I shivered, in spite of the warmth of the night. Beneath me Neptune gave a shudder, too. I knew the old Modocs were sifting through the powder and pebbles for a rare gold nugget, the way the Hindoos of India were said to pick through a dung heap in search of a kernel of corn.

A half-hour later I descended the notches carved into the side of the ventilation column. Once more I swung through the shutter and crawled down the corridor that led to the cave. Little did I dream of the happy surprise that awaited me there. Even before I reached the half-open shutter, I heard the definite sound of — what was this? Could it be barking? The *yip-yap* of the Modoc dogs? I pushed through. What a sight met my eyes! The cavern was clean. The cages had been repaired. And all the Modoc children were present, going about their usual tasks. My heart leaped up. Was it possible that the spirit of the Enlightenment had triumphed over the power of instinct, the pull of the primitive past? So it seemed. The savages had turned once more into scholars!

Yet more amazing, and chilling too: here was the entire canine population, cavorting, panting, racing from spot to spot in the cave. Any person could see the yellow mutts were free of symptoms. But how had they survived the disease?

"Mister-r-r Pinto!"

That was Elbow Frank. The boy was grinning, waving his stump in the air. But his sound arm was around the corpse of — here I had to look twice — *Canis latrans,* the coyote! This was no cadaver. The animal, sitting upon its haunches, gave a wide, pink-mouthed yawn. Alive!

"Gentlemen! Dear youths! What does this mean?"

"Ha-ha!" laughed Priestley Bill. "Behold our noble beast! A true-blue Scot, like a' the rest!"

"But how can it be? I have seen him devour the sick *Stinktier,* the skunk, with my own eyes!"

Now Kepler Jim — in his striped pants again, his clawhammer coat, his topper — stepped forward. "Do ye recall t'ither coyotes? The ones that ate from the flesh o' the dead nag? Yet we cadna discover a single sick beastie. Here is a species wha' bears the charmed life!"

The sharp-featured Newton Mike was trembling head to toe from excitement. "Nae! Dinna speak o' charms! Listen, laddies! The germ ne'er reached the animal's brain. Why? Because of the eating. The eating! Dinna ye see? The eating!"

The others, the Pioneers of Progress, looked blank. But I could not help beaming upon this rude Indian boy. In my mind I made a note of the date: the seventeenth day of June, 1859. And what was the time? A quarter-hour to midnight. I knew that the idea of this rabbit-faced savage would be recorded in history's ledger.

"*Ja!* I comprehend! Question: why did our colleagues, the canines, not succumb upon eating the diseased flesh of the rodents?"

Again, only Newton Mike seemed to have the answer. "Because the virus didna reach the nerves!"

"Why did it not?"

Newton Mike grinned wide, displaying his large front teeth. "Because it ne'er entered the bluid!"

Breathlessly I persisted: "And? And, sir? Continue. Why did that not occur?"

"Because the virus was hurt. It was a' destroyed."

"Ho-ho-ho! Here is the question of questions: how damaged? How destroyed? Speak! Anyone! My bright Angus lads!"

But the Children of the Enlightenment, Boston Charlie and Bacon Jack, scratched in perplexity their flattened foreheads. Priestley Bill stood dumbstruck. Humboldt Johnny, and all the rest too, stared down at their patent-leather shoes.

I could in my excitement not wait another instant. *"Der Verdauungsprozess!"* I shouted in my native tongue.

Newton Mike put the same words in English: "Digestion! 'Tis the cure! The juices o' digestion!"

3

There is in science a long tradition of the accidental and unexpected: Isaac Newton and the not altogether apocryphal apple; Archimedes afloat in his bath; and Galileo himself, who discovered the principle of the pendulum upon seeing a lamp swing back and forth in the cathedral of Pisa. It was through just that sort of happenstance, then, that the quest for the cure of rabies continued.

The grand new hypothesis — that the viral broth should not be frozen or boiled or diluted, but in essence digested — had to be put to the test. The first difficulty for the Academy of Pinto was how to obtain the necessary ferments. We had neither the funds nor the equipment to purchase the acids in the commercial markets or to manufacture them on our own. The solution to the problem was elegant indeed. The researchers simply opened the belly of a full-grown rabbit, one of the thousands that were at that summer season hopping over the sage-strewn plain, and poured its gastric juices into a glass vial — more precisely, into an empty whiskey bottle from the Sazarac Saloon. This artificial stomach, with a portion of live virus added to the mix, was suspended just below the cavern's low ceiling, where the flow of air through the wind door kept it in constant motion, and where the temperature was almost identical to that within the body of the warm-blooded hare.

> 19 June: Inoculation by trepanation of *Sylvilagus nuttalli*, Mountain Cottontail, with virus subjected to twenty-four hours' digestive action.

So read the entry in my slop-shop ledger. Alas: six days later, that chart read as follows:

> 25 June: Subject expired.

Disappointment? Despair? I, the chief experimenter, did not allow my teammates such emotions. Already I held the amber bottle, where the viral sediment clouded the bottom like the dregs of a Moselle, to the candlelight. "No experiment, gentlemen, is a failure when a new fact is learned. And what," I added, returning always to the Socratic technique, "might that fact be?"

Elbow Frank waved his longer arm in the air. "One day. Four an' twenty hours. 'Tis na long enough!"

"Bravo! Prima! Score: one hundred!"

To the Heirs of Harvey, intent on their research, the holiday of the Fourth of July meant only that the virus had steeped for two full weeks in the digestive juices. That was when they spread the broth on the brain of a jackrabbit male. As a comparison, they also inoculated two other rabbits with untreated virus from the dead cottontail. Six days later, both controls were at their last gasp. One, doglike, circled its tail. The other, its limbs paralyzed, chewed at the wire mesh. But the furry brown buck hopped heedless about its cage.

> July 10: No symptoms.
> July 11: No symptoms.

Nor, most crucially, was there the least sign of disease on July the twelfth.

Just as there had been no dismay when the first subject had died, there were no cheers, no top hats thrown to the cavern ceiling, now that our latest subject had survived. All the Pioneers knew that this was merely step one. "Step two," I announced. "Inoculation of our black-tailed friend with fresh, potent virus. Let us hope this martyr of science has the strength to resist the force of the disease."

> July 18: Subject expired.

From this development the question was, what new fact had been learned? On the pages of my ledger I wrote the answer:

> The boundaries of digestive action. In one day, the virus is altogether undamaged. In two weeks, it is completely destroyed.

> Conclusion: to render virus strong enough to wound but too weak to kill, we must look between these limits.

No need to describe in detail the work that came next. There was no divine light of inspiration, no single moment of insight, no guiding genius: merely the slow, tedious effort, the drudgery of following the obvious line of inquiry, the way an old plow horse will plod in its furrow. Day after day, week after week, the rabbits were inoculated; they sickened and died. After each failure either Kepler Jim or myself would carve from the carcass the virulent spinal cord and squeeze a section of the rubbery, eel-like tissue into the mouth of a new whiskey bottle. Over time the ceiling of the cavern filled with these vessels, each containing, along with the gastric juices — pepsin, hydrochloric acid — the pestilent, germ-filled cords. There the amber bottles hung, shining, shimmering, like the stalactites of a cooler cave.

By the end of August, the first days of September, the results of the experiments had become all too clear. In brief: those animals inoculated with an emulsion made from cords that had remained in the digestive juices six days or less invariably died from the furious form of rabies, while those inoculated from cords a week old or more always survived — but without any resistance to subsequent attack by untreated virus.

No thought of surrender now. Feverish, unable to sleep, I vowed to determine the critical moment, between that sixth and seventh day, at which the rabies particles changed their disposition from malevolent to benign. If only we could arrest the process of amelioration at just that hour, snatch the cord from the acid when it was neither fully lethal nor altogether impotent, the vaccine might be able to ward off a new invasion of virus without dealing the mortal blow itself. But day after day the bodies of the victims, slick with saliva, rigid-limbed, caromed down the untimbered walls of the ventilator.

I cannot deny the force of the obsession that had seized me. Onward I went, making the inoculations, observing the symptoms, recording the grim results. I was like a miner who follows a subterranean drift, onward, downward, long after the vein of ore-bearing quartz has been pinched out. By the third week of the month I was attempting to determine the duration of digestive action not only to the day, hour, and minute, but to the very second. The brass alarm clocks tied to each bottle were constantly going on and off. The knife, the notebook, were always in my hand. Still the magic moment, when the virus would lose just the proper amount of toxicity, eluded my efforts. The data fell to one side, *no immunity*, or the other, *no symptoms*. At last, pale-skinned, with palpitations, I sank down against the wall of the dimly lit cavern.

For some hours I lay in this fit of exhaustion. Throughout these unending tests, the tedious trials, I had not once climbed to the surface. Like some early prospector, I had survived on beans and bacon; like any hard-rock miner, I had defecated carefully into an empty candle box. What was the weather? No way to know. The hands of the ticking brass clocks pointed to every hour. Finally, half dozing, breast heaving in the sultry air, I felt something strike the crown of my tasseled sombrero. I was, however, too weary to move. A second tap. I doffed the Mexican hat. Now a hot drop of water struck my skull, through the soft mat of hair. Only then did I realize I'd settled beneath the slow, steady dribble of water from which we Academicians drew our drinking supply.

Still I didn't budge. The minutes — were they of daylight? of darkness? — went by. Again and again the water struck my Semitic-type skull. I might as well have been made from stone, or been, like one of my many victims, paralyzed. I marveled how the dull drops, without force in themselves, shapeless, would over time cut through my scalp like one of my surgical saws, or wear away the solid bone. Long before that, I knew, the steady stream of this Chinese torture would have driven me mad. Even now I felt a force, a pressure, rising from the base of my skull. Suddenly I sat bolt upright. My Adam's apple hopped like a gymnast. *What if* — here was the idea swelling within me: *What if each weak dose of vaccine, like each feeble drop, protected not against the disease but only against the next dose, which might then be a little stronger?* I shook my damp locks, like a dachshund emerging from a pond. Here was a definite hypothesis! The effect of the dose was accumulative! The cure must come drop by drop, one inoculation after the other. The subject, guarded each day by the dose it had received the day before, would live until the protection became absolute — that is, until it could withstand the onslaught of pure virus. Even the bite of a wolf could not kill it then!

"Gentlemen!" cried I. "I have it! The process of Pintoization!"

There was no reply. Only then did I hear the slight snoring, the sighing, of the sleeping boys. The sole source of light, the eerie phosphorescence, came from the decaying timber. Meaning to light a candle, I struck a match. A young jackrabbit doe, startled, leaped from her hiding place and stood quaking at the center of the cavern. In three strides, I crossed the chamber and seized the hare by her long, limp ears. Naturally, given the number of doses that must be administered, there could be no question of trepanation. Still clutching the frightened doe, I filled a syringe from a bottle in which a virulent cord had been dissolving two full weeks. I injected the emulsion into the soft tissue of the animal's belly, then placed her with care inside a wire cage.

1 October: Inoculation by injection. Jackrabbit doe. Virus treated thirteen days.

Thus all the efforts of man and boys came down to one last experiment. On October second I inoculated the doe with vaccine that had been soaking in acid for twelve days; on the third the cord had been in the bottle for eleven. Each day we continued in similar fashion, injecting the doe with a batch of vaccine that was twenty-four hours fresher than the dose that had been administered before. Meanwhile, a number of cottontails were newly trepanned, so that a supply of infected spinal cords would be on hand throughout the two-week process. All went well until the morning of the sixth day, when Humboldt Johnny noted that our rabbit had begun running a fever. Her nose was hot and dry. A clear mucus drained from her eyes, and her translucent ears, which stretched nearly half the length of her body, drooped upon her back. I injected the nine-day-old potion nonetheless.

The inoculation of October eighth was the most difficult, for the liquid that filled the syringe on that date had been digested for only six days and might well — even for a healthy subject — prove lethal. Yet the doe seemed no worse off for having received the treatment. If anything, over the next few days, as the doses became more and more virulent, her fever abated.

12 October: Inoculation number twelve. Virus treated forty-eight hours. No symptoms.

13 October: Inoculation number thirteen. Virus treated twenty-four hours. No symptoms.

Everything remained as before. The hare continued to eat, drink, sleep, and wake. The humans, however, sat numb. Through the whole of that night into the following day, we remained sweating and sleepless, as if we were the ones with a fever. Then, on the morning of October fourteenth, all gathered round to bring the experiment to its conclusion. For this last inoculation, we resorted once more to trepanation. Five drops of raw virus were placed directly onto the exposed surface of the cortex. As a control, the same batch of mucus, seething with virus, was placed onto the dura mater of an adult cottontail doe.

15 October:
Cottontail: No symptoms.
Jackrabbit: No symptoms.

16 October:
No change.

17 October:
Cottontail: No symptoms.
Jackrabbit: No symptoms.

18 October:
Cottontail: No symptoms.
Jackrabbit: No symptoms.
Note: Subject has now survived ten days since receiving six-day-old virus.

19 October:
Cottontail: Body tremors. Restlessness. Lameness.
Jackrabbit: No symptoms.

20 October:
Cottontail: Expired. Furious rabies.
Jackrabbit: No symptoms.

The Heirs of Harvey, who had hardly slept or eaten for a week, lay about the floor of the cavern like Celestials in an opium den. None took his eyes from the jackrabbit doe. Another day went by. The animal frisked happily about her cage. The twenty-second of October arrived. Still the bunny bounded, clear-eyed, fever-free. Every soul in the cavern knew what this meant. Yet none said a word. All continued to stare, silent, unmoving, like people under the spell of Herr Mesmer. Then Priestley Bill giggled behind his hand.

"Ha-ha-ha!" That was, together, Boston Charlie and Bacon Jack.

The next instant all the lads broke into loud guffaws. Helplessly they clutched their chests, their bellies. They rolled about. I was as light-headed as the rest. I grasped full well the joke. It sprang from lack of proportion. On the one side, all our toil, our burdensome effort, the magnitude of what we had done — a cure for rabies, an effective vaccine, the eradication of dread and pain; and on the other, the creature at which all the youths were now pointing — a pink-nosed mammal, fluffy-haired, floppy-eared, with a powder-puff tail. A toy! A doll! "Ho! Ho! Ho!" My own hearty laugh rang out with that of my pupils.

The glee ceased when Antoinette approached the cage and thrust her fingers, clutching a wilted leaf of lettuce, through the wire mesh. Bare-handed! The medical Modocs gasped. The least scratch would prove fatal! But the sharp-toothed rabbit only nibbled at the scrap of leaf in the pink palm of her hand. Then the others, daredevils all, began to poke their fingers into the cage. What better testimony to the success of our project? The animal could not harm us. Nor, by the same token, could we now harm her. Of all the beings on earth, whether hare or human, this was the only one immune to the disease of rabies. The Modocs pressed their faces to the side of the mesh. Slack-mouthed, they stared at the charmed creature, the way any primitive people might before a powerful totem, or the way my own fellow tribesmen, the children of Israel, had gazed on the golden calf.

For all our hilarity, our euphoria, we knew that the experiment was far from done. No person contracted rabies from a rabbit. The virus entered the human population from its pets, its companions, its partners of the hunt. That meant in order to safeguard man it would be necessary to eradicate the disease in his best friend. How could such a thing be accomplished? Were we to inoculate every dog in the world? Absurd notion! More than a half-century after the work of Dr. Jenner, not one of these Modoc children was immune to the threat of smallpox. Why even I, A. Pinto, a physician, had not been vaccinated! How could our little band hope to inoculate tens of millions of canines, all the dogs of the planet, against rabies, when even the people who lived upon it had not been protected from a more widespread disease?

The only solution, I realized, was to determine if it was possible to apply the course of treatment, the full fourteen injections, *after* the bite, instead of before. No need then to vaccinate entire populations. I could attend to just those men and women who were in need of care. Here was the difference between prevention, which is all that the Englishman had been able to achieve, and a genuine cure. The smallpox vaccine was useless once the infection had begun. But the rabies vaccine, the process of Pinto-ization, might heal the sufferer before the incubation period had ended. What a discovery that would be! My head swam with the very thought. Before my eyes danced a vision of all the world's afflicted, the stream of sufferers, as they wended their way to my laboratory, the renowned Pinto Institute, where I would administer my treatments. *Ja!* I would become more famous than the great Jenner himself!

I woke from my reverie. All the young scholars had gathered about me where I stood stooped, the odd hair sprouting in the Mandarin manner from my chin. Definite tears were glistening in their eyes. Of joy? No: sorrow. In their busy brains they had come to the same conclusion that I had in mine. Horrible moment. The time had come to test the vaccine on their own dear dogs. Indeed, each of the lads stood beside the very animal that he had once protected from my needle and syringe. At the front Elbow Frank had brought up the coyote, which had been named for the great English doctor. " 'Tisna time for the faint-hearted!" declared the youth. "Here stands the mighty Jenner, brave as a sodger!"

Now Kepler Jim strode forward, dragging his favorite, the bitch Hippocrates, at his side. "Here, man! Take her. Take our darlin' wi' her undaunted heart!"

Others approached, sighing, sobbing, each with a grip on a wriggling mutt.

"Take mine!" all were shouting. "A giftie! For mankind!"

I could hardly see which lad stood before me, so filled were my eyes with sharp, stinging tears. How wrong I had been to think my dear ones could revert to the savage state, could backslide so far as to forget the methods of Bacon. For here stood the scholars, simple Indian boys, who for the sake of science were now sacrificing every one of their beloved pets.

> 23 October: Inoculation by injection of *Canis latrans.* Virus treated thirteen days.
>
> Inoculation by trepanation of mixed-breed bitch. Virus untreated.

In other words, Jenner, the coyote, and Hippocrates.

So virulent was the strain of rabies, so many victims had it passed through, that the long canine incubation period had shrunk to the standard six days. That is to say, on October 29 the bitch began to drag her hindquarters and foam at the mouth. In order to duplicate the conditions of an actual attack, the furious dog, chained at the neck, was put into a cage with her four lifetime companions: Galen, Leeuwenhoek, Euclid, and my own favorite, named for the deceased dean of the Harvard Medical College, Warren. At once Hippocrates attacked her fellow canines. She clamped her teeth on the withers of one, slashed another across the rib cage, and fell in a fury on the two remaining, snapping their leg bones in her jaws. Then poor Kepler Jim, using a section of flat lift cable, hauled the mad beast away.

The experiment that followed was clear-cut enough. One of the slashed mongrels, Galen, was inoculated immediately with the thirteen-day virus. The next day, October 30, he was given the twelve-day dose, while a second victim, the spotted Leeuwenhoek, began the cycle. On the third day, the procedure continued: Galen received the eleven-day dose, Leeuwenhoek the twelve-, and a third victim, Euclid, the curly-tailed pet of Cavendish Sam, started the series. Warren, the last of the mongrels, received his first injection on November 2.

The results at first were dispiriting. Hippocrates perished from furious rabies on the night she'd made her attack. On November 4, Warren, the last to begin the treatment, contracted the disease and died after just twenty hours. Then, on November 5, Euclid developed the unmistakable symptoms. As an additional experiment, Jenner, the coyote, who had just finished the entire two-week treatment, was dragged into the cage with the suffering favorite of Cavendish Sam. It was almost comical to see how the wild beast, twice the size of the crazed canine, cowered, whimpering, in the darkest corner. The mad dog went for its throat, sinking its teeth through the thick fur; it clung there until drenched by a bucket of water. The poor animal, our little Euclid, barking hoarsely, and red-eyed, died three hours later.

Two of the quartet were left. They continued to receive the Pinto treatment. On November 7, Leeuwenhoek developed a tremor in his hindquarters, together with a fever. Yet the next day, when he was inoculated with virus that had steeped for four days in gastric juices, the symptoms had not worsened, and no mucus spilled from his mouth. Meanwhile, Galen, the last of the victims, the first, in fact, to be treated, showed no effects at all, in spite of having been the most severely mauled. On November 11 that lucky creature was given the final dose of raw virus. Still, the next day, and the day after that, the animal displayed none of the typical symptoms: neither listlessness nor agitation; no clouding of the eye, no unquenchable thirst. Even the spotted dog, named for the discoverer of red corpuscles, continued to cling to life. And Jenner, the coyote, although bitten deep in the throat, remained completely free of rabies.

What did this experiment, so simple in design, so painful in execution, prove? First, that the vaccine had no power to affect the course of the disease once it had entered the nervous system; second, all-important, that the cycle of injections, if initiated shortly after the bite — within a day, and perhaps within forty-eight hours — could prevent the development of symptoms altogether. That meant — this was, for me, the undeniable conclusion — that if a victim came to a doctor immediately upon suffering a bite from a rabid dog, or even a rabid wolf, he might yet be saved. It was precisely that, the effect upon the human species, which was the only hypothesis yet to be tested.

Once more the Children of the Enlightenment had anticipated the thoughts of their teacher. Gloomy, trembling, they approached the spot where I stood.

"Now cooms," said the pale Humboldt Johnny, "many an anxious day."

Paracelsus Max: "We must venture where e'en the Devil would tremble to go."

"Aye," said Kepler Jim. " 'Tis time to treat that species in which the divine spark dwells."

Time, indeed. But doubts assailed me from every side. Did I dare inoculate a human being with the baleful broth? The virus at the end of the cycle, treated three days or less, was hardly less potent than that in the saliva of a maddened dog. Even the idea, the abstract thought of such an injection, set my knees into their regular woodpecker's knock. A man was not a rat, a dog, a rabbit. How could we know the cure would succeed on such a unique, two-legged creature? Yet without that knowledge, the demonstrated proof, all our effort would be for naught.

Surprisingly, the solution to this dilemma came from none

other than Boston Charlie. "We gotta test onna stinking Modoc! Gotta stick crazy sonabitch inna bum!"

On the instant the whole class, all the Academicians, took up the suggestion. They wanted to descend to the fourth level, to find a miner who had already been infected with the disease. "The poor wight," said Priestley Bill, wringing his hands. "Longing for a drap of water that he canna drink!"

Paracelsus Max: "Upon such a man, already doomed, we must make our test!"

The Heirs of Harvey gave a cheer. They began to move about, preparing for the three-hundred-foot journey to the deeper level. Just then I was struck by what seemed the ax of an idea. Immediately my head started to ache and I sank to the ground. What I had realized was this: there was no Modoc on level four, since every man had been put to work on bringing the main shaft to 5280 feet. The Academy members could not be blamed for not knowing that. What they should have deduced — and this is the thought that had struck me down — was, first, that even if a Modoc had been left behind in the level-four chamber, we could not know he had been infected by the virus of rabies until he showed symptoms; and, second, as our own experiments had just proved, it would then be too late to save him! There was no way round the fact that continued to hammer at my head with the force of an air-driven drill: *we could only cure a subject whom we had infected ourselves!*

I struggled to my knees. I looked around. Everything in this cavern, where I had dwelled so long, was familiar, yet somehow altered — as if I had been away on a journey and were seeing my surroundings for the first time in years. For one thing, the air about me felt hotter, more humid, than before. It seemed to me that my own body had sprung a hundred leaks, from each of which the sweat came pouring, soaking my clothing, my skin. And had not the cavern roof sunk further than ever? Were not the creaking tree trunks stouter, more compressed? I looked round for my scholars, who were standing ready at the winze, through which they wanted to squirm to levels two, three, four. The greatest change of all was in the Highland band. I realized now that the cavern had not shrunk about them, at least not as much as I'd supposed; rather they, seemingly overnight, in a single bound, had spurted upward. The tattered trousers, once worn up to the breastbone and rolled at the cuffs, now fit more than a few; just as the swallowtail jackets no longer dragged on the ground behind them or dangled at their ankles and calves. My children were growing into men.

"Coom, Mister-r-r Pinto," said Elbow Frank, waving his one good arm. "We must find our sufferin' subject."

Said Priestley Bill, "We canna wait the lee lang day!"

Then, with a mixture of sweat and salt tears stinging my eyes, I managed to rise. I lifted my throbbing head, with the half-dozen hairs of a beard affixed to the chin. "Academicians! An announcement! You are correct about our next test: it must be upon a human being."

The Sons of Galileo started to cheer. I cut them off. "But this is not the proper moment to do it. Our final test, the terrible inoculation, must take place at the stroke of midnight, at the start of the new year. Then, the next day, one January, the actual treatments will begin. Timing is everything, friends! I shall depart to secure our subject. When I am gone I count on you. On the morning of nineteen December you must place into the bottle of acids the cord we shall use for the number-one injection. Twenty-one December: into another bottle must go the cord for injection number two. And so on, my dears. And so forth. Just as we have done in the past. Is this clear? Is it understood?"

Boston Charlie folded his arms across his shirtfront. He turned the toothpick in his mouth. "You betcher!"

Bacon Jack: "Boot why wait more days? More weeks? Cadna we start at this very moment?"

Paracelsus Max: "Why the stroke o' midnight?"

"Good questions, youths! Already in Yreka the crowds have gathered to see the main shaft reach the one-mile record. When the moment occurs, reporters, newspapers, even a telegraph, will send the story to readers in every land. This is the joke we shall play upon them! Upon Mr. Frank Townsend! It is our miracle, not his, that will pass along those gleaming wires! The cure for rabies, the world's true eighth wonder — that is the message that will go at lightning speed to Rome and Paris and Vienna! To all the peoples of the earth! Fame, friends! And fortune! These are the things that await us, if only we have the courage, the patience, to wait until the moment is right!"

I did not pause for a reply. I whirled round, away from the winze and toward the corridor that led to the ventilation column. Behind me I could hear the shouts of the boys. I took a last look back. They were throwing their top hats, their gleaming stovepipes, high into the air — or so they would have, had not the hard rock of the cavern sent the headgear rattling downward, like so many black hailstones from the midst of a lowering cloud.

Moments later, as I began to climb the steps of the chicken ladder, the notches in the wall of the column, I could still hear their distant shouts. How innocent their voices! How untroubled their happy cries! I looked up, toward the patch of light at the sunlit surface. It was there, I knew, that I would find my human subject. And I knew one more thing that my gleeful children did not: precisely who that poor soul must be.

CHAPTER FOUR

The Vulture

1

ABOVE GROUND, winter had arrived early, and with unusual force. Alongside the sounds to which the Yrekans had long since grown accustomed — the unstoppable thud of the stamps, the cat's screech of air beneath the pistons of the compression tubes, the explosions at the bottom of the main shaft — came the steady howl of the hard, bitter wind. Balls of quartz dust blew before it, tumbling through the streets of town like clumps of sage. Then, early in the month of December, with a sound like a stretched wire breaking — indeed, at that sharp chord, we thought the cable must have snapped in the shaft — the entire surface of Etna Pond froze solid.

Within hours a team of mine mules, half blind, half hairless, were brought from the depths. Dragging a sharp plow behind them, they scored the reservoir into even squares. Then the Modocs sawed out the ice blocks and dragged them down the side of the butte to the level plain. This work continued as the pond froze and refroze. The mound of ice grew larger. The glacier cutters, returning from the northern mountains, added their aquamarine spikes to the pile. Then newcomers arrived — from the north, from Canada, ice trimmers, armed with broad axes and saws; and from the other direction, from Sacramento, teams of workers, carrying with them block and tackle and pulleys and tongs. These men attacked the great cubes, swinging them into the air, stacking them one atop the other. Then, from a huge steaming caldron, they poured boiling water onto the oversized bricks, cementing each to each.

Naturally we townsfolk came out to watch. None of us had any idea of what the construction, the night-and-day labor, might be for. All we knew was that hour after hour, before our very eyes, the glazed walls were growing higher, forming the arches and ramparts of a medieval fortress, like the Hradčany Castle in Prague. The clear ice from the lake alternated with the blue-tinted slabs from the mountains, gleaming with crystals that had been formed in the age of the mammoth. Later, toward the middle of the month, Two-Toes Tom, with his squad of Modoc policemen, went through the town, nailing leaflets to the porch posts and doors.

WORLD'S EIGHTH WONDER
— AT THE STROKE OF THE NEW YEAR —
Opening of the Palace of Ice
Coinciding with the attainment of a main shaft depth of
ONE MILE

It began to seem that Townsend might succeed with his miracle after all. The red arrow stood at over five thousand feet; only two hundred to go. Ironically, the greatest obstacle now was caused less by the heat than by the winter cold. None of the miners, laboring just above the kettle of the sump, could be brought to the surface without experiencing sharp spasms, sudden seizures, caused by the abrupt drop in temperature of 120 degrees. Thus the cage, which was fully capable of traveling the length of the shaft in two minutes flat, had to rise in stages that took close to an hour. Even at that pace the Indians emerged with their arms thrown over their aching eyes. For a time they staggered blindly, as if spun about by the cyclone of steam whirling over the pithead.

If that summer there had been much excitement about the prospect of reaching the near-mythical distance, the frenzy in December reached fever pitch. The streets were never empty, night or day. The Kittle and Moffet Company ran extra stages nonstop from Red Bluff, and rumor had it that the railway spur at Marysville was choked with private sleeping cars. Townsend brought in extra crews, to work not on the castle but on the appearance of the town. All of the false fronts on Main, on Miner, were whitewashed. Tubs of pine and fir were set out on the thoroughfare. Then all the Modocs — the hobbling invalids, the layabouts and drunkards, even the old squaws in their ragged blankets — were taken off the walkways and thrust into Modoc Town, which had itself been transformed. Gone were the stinking bullheads from the sloping tin roofs. The shanties were freshly painted, while gravel paths, with evergreen shrubs, had been set out along the alleys. Tourists peeking at the cooking fires, the women weaving baskets of tule, the old men sharpening arrows or curing leather, must have thought this was a model village, a workers' paradise.

December nineteenth. I did not rise that day from bed. All my thoughts were concentrated on the butte, on the underground cave. Were the Disciples of Bacon carrying out their instructions? If so, the first weak dose of the vaccine would be ready at the time of the test. If not, if the scholars had forgotten or there had been the least slip-up, the consequences were unthinkable. Better to remain beneath the quilt coverlet, atop my bed.

The twenty-first. Preparation of the second dose, less weak, more virulent, than the first. Still I lay unmoving, unthinking. A single emotion — fear — occupied every cell space in my brain. I quaked, I trembled, cold chills ran through my limbs — all for the sake of the first human victim.

Truth to tell, what filled me with anguish was not so much the thought of the disease itself, painful as it must be, as the means of its transmission. The world would never be convinced of a cure for rabies if the germ was delivered by an Indian pricking the skin of a Jew, or even by having the latter's skull opened up and the virus deposited within. No: the victim would have to be infected the way ordinary men and women and children were — by the bite of a maddened dog.

This, too, I might have accepted with lofty detachment, with grim scientific objectivity, had I not known that the only non-immune canine in the whole of Siskiyou County was my dread foe, the stout, bowlegged Caesar. Yet even that mental image — of my enemy clamping the vise of his jaw upon my own brittle bones; of that flat face, with its rubbery lips, upward-pointing incisors, cruel cuspids, grinning in triumph — was not the ultimate source of my fear. My real concern was for the dog's master, my own precious boy. General George! How could I rip the pet from that dear child's arms? How cause the tears to spring to those nervous, nystagmic eyes? Even the great Galileo, sentenced to exile, to silence, was not asked to sacrifice so much in the name of science.

December twenty-third. Far off, far down, the Heirs of Harvey were preparing the third, more potent dose. Impossible to delay another day. The first thing I did upon leaving the fireproof was make a pair of visits: first to the hoistman, Gill, and then to the publisher, Christie. Of all the men in Yreka — Yreka? perhaps in the world — these two most desired to find a cure for hydrophobia. That is why each agreed to my unusual requests: that on the night of December 31, when the dignitaries descended the shaft, Gill would halt the cage at the vacated number-one station; and that the *Ingot* publisher, with his telegraph man, would accompany me to the long-abandoned stope.

Next I returned to the slop shop. No sleeping now. No dawdling either. Through the twenty-fourth of December I prepared two tightly corked flasks — the one filled with sulfuric ether, the other with the virus of furious rabies that I had taken with me from the underground lab.

Christmas Eve. Once more out of my building, with both vessels hidden under my coat. Down Miner Street. Onto Main. I was moving steadily toward the loud laughter and lights that spilled from the Sazarac Saloon. Everything on the inside of the bat-wing doors was in motion. On the balcony Dick Rose sawed away at his fiddle. Cigar smoke boiled about the bare flames of the chandelier. On the dance floor countless couples moved round together. The teeth of the men flashed through their whiskers. The squaws leaned back, laughing, showing their calf muscles and the dark skin of their breasts. Blushing, eyes on my bluchers, I skirted this swirling mass until I came to the gambling pit.

There the scene was even more hectic. The keno cage tumbled, while the players waved their keno cards. At the faro table, people leaned forward to place their bets. The greatest activity was at the table for rouge-et-noir. Through the crowd, the haze of smoke, I made out the slick-haired Judge Steele playing against the elegant Gentleman Jack. Great stacks of coins rose before the Indian's place. On his lap sat his nephew, Dumb George.

"That's it," Steele was saying. "You busted the bank."

But the Indian wasn't done. He pointed to the white man's heart — rather, to the vest, brown wool with a design of gold horseshoes, that covered that vital organ. "Bet what-you-call-him?

Waistcoat, goddam! And gold clock, gold fob, too! Luck? You say luck? Jack ain't got luck! Jack got brains inna head! Smart feller! More smart than anyone! You watch out: he gonna be boss of the town!"

All about me the crowd pressed forward, in order to watch the two-colored wheel spin around. With my flasks clutched to my chest, I watched Dumb George. His head tipped and turned, while in his widened eyes the dancing pupils rolled high up under the blank white sockets. I knew what was occurring; indeed, I had seen it before. The same mind that had once calculated the velocity of a sphere speeding down an endless shaftway was now, in its trance, determining into what segment of the rotating ring another ball — ivory, not lead — would eventually fall. Gentleman Jack was correct: it was not a matter of luck. The sphere, in falling from outer to inner orbit, was describing the course of a fixed parabola. The fingers of General George, drumming on his uncle's shoulder, were spelling out the iron laws of probability and chance.

As the wheel slowed the Yrekans grew still. While all were engrossed in the game, I dropped down and peered beneath the table. At once I saw my ancient antagonist, beady eyes glinting in their pockets of wrinkled flesh, teeth all agleam in the gums. For an instant we stared at each other. Then with my own strong teeth I pulled the cork from the first of my bottles and shook the contents, $C_4H_{10}O$, over the black snout of the beast. The bulldog, instantly yawning, opened wide its black-and-pink mouth. Into that maw I poured more of the foaming distillation. One eye closed, then the other. The two front legs, as strong as andirons, gave way. The animal collapsed to the floor.

From above, at the gaming table, came a whoop, and, from Steele, a muffled curse. The sphere had fallen into the predicted slot. While everyone stood lost in wonder, I quickly slipped off my frock coat and threw the garment over the sleeping dog. I drew the ends of the bundle together. None of the crowd seemed to notice when I stood erect and began to back away, toward the stairs. Or if anyone did, he must have thought this was the figure of old Saint Nick, with, upon his back, his bag of toys, and, upon his chin, six noodlelike hairs, in lieu of the full, bushy beard.

The inoculation with rabies virus occurred within minutes — not in the slop shop, which was the first place my stepson would search, but upstairs, above the gamblers, in Antoinette's darkened room. Taking no chances, I twice emptied the contents of my syringe — once into the carotid artery, which carried the bloodstream directly to the brain; and then high into the animal's spinal column, at the base of the broad, blunt skull. Caesar did not wake until the following morning, Christmas Day, and remained alert only long enough to gobble the beefsteak that the Panamanian brought up from the kitchen of the saloon. Then the curtain of sleep, in the form of the black, ether-soaked frock coat, fell over his furrowed head, much as the robe of his namesake, the emperor of Rome, was said to have been drawn at the end around him, so that he might be spared the pain of seeing the act his former friends were about to perform.

No miner had visited this narrow room for a long time — not since the Modoc hurdy-gurdies had moved in. In any case, Antoinette spent the holidays on the dance floor, with the tourists. Thus we two old foes, Hebrew and hound, spent the incubation period sequestered together. Each new day passed much like the one before. Caesar, his four limbs tied, would wake just long enough to snatch down his piece of meat, to lap up his saucer of water, after which I'd put him to sleep again.

Then, on the fifth day, the thing I feared most occurred. The Indian boy came searching up the balcony stairs. The bulldog, deep in his stupor, heard him first: loose lips smacking, curved claws scraping the floorboards, he attempted to rise. The ear stumps twitched. The remnant of twisted tail straightened. A rumble rolled from his chest. A full minute went by before I could make out, at the upper level of human audibility, the high, piping sound:

Ceso! Ceso!

The animal, half awake, began to thrash. The air blew from its black, flaring nose. Snatching up the ether bottle, I poured a few drops on my coat's worsted fabric. From the staircase, the very hallway, came the cry:

Ceeeesooo!

I paused, paralyzed. Every fiber of my being yearned to throw open the door. How I missed the boy — his teetering, tottering head, the touch of his drumming fingers! If only now, at this instant, I could clasp him in my arms! But Caesar had opened his mouth, ready to howl. I fell on the beast, smothering its snout in the cloth. For a moment the dog fought back. I clung to the skin, which slipped about in my hands as if the animal had donned a fur made for a larger creature, a mastiff, a Dane. Then all the taut muscles relaxed and the great jaw fell slack. I gave a start: in that gaping mouth were the first signs of the disease — the swollen tongue, plump as a yam; the teeth, razor-sharp, rising like coral from the bubbling foam of saliva. Beneath the half-shuttered eyelids, the eyes of the bulldog had turned red.

Ce-eee-sooo!

At that cry, fading away, echoing now on the walkway, on the street, I threw my hands to my ears. I knew that if I heard the sound again, even a single wavering syllable, I'd have to leap up, to run after the child. Either that or I'd thrust my own head into the fume-filled folds of the garment, and so sleep away the few remaining hours of the 1850s.

2

December thirty-first. Night. How was I, with my burden, to reach Mount Etna in secret? Luckily the whole of Yreka, even the Modocs from Modoc Town, had gone out to the carnival at the palace of ice. Thus I rode with my bulging bundle through streets that were deserted. Soon enough we came to the edge of the celebration. Tule torches shone through the translucent bricks. They lit the way for the tourists, who ducked through the chill corridors of the castle. Above, at the bulwarks, children tobogganed over the ice. On a specially made pond men and women skated to Dick Rose's violin, to the player piano and the cornetist from the Blue Wing Saloon. From my shadowy spot, clinging to Neptune's neck, I could see that all the townsfolk were dressed in their best. Most splendid of all was Gentleman Jack, with rings on his fingers and pearls at his ears. The gold tooth glittered in his smiling mouth. I could see the watch and watch fob glowing against his horseshoe vest.

Suddenly, at precisely half past the hour of eleven, the festivities came to a halt. That was when the clutch at the Neptune Mine disengaged from the giant flywheel and the cloth belts fell away from the camshafts. That is to say, the metal-clad stamps came to a halt. The newcomers went on with their singing, their sport. But at this silence the Yrekans stood stunned. It was as if the beat of their hearts had stopped.

Moments later I was on the deck of the lift, plunging toward level one. All I could hear was the ringing of the bell and our cable's elastic twang. My two companions stepped onto the station before me. One was Sid Christie, bald-headed, bullet-headed, his clothes already soaked through with sweat; the other was young Ray Moffet, grandson of the express company owner, who operated the telegraph key at the *Ingot.* With my bundle over my back, I followed both men through the drift, toward the underground cavern.

Moffet was the first to reach our lab. He halted at the entrance and turned back toward where I was still struggling along with my sack. The young man was dressed like an easterner, with his red hair parted and a cane over his arm. "Why," he exclaimed, "they're only children!"

He meant, of course, the Sons of Galileo. With Steamboat Ed they had drawn themselves into a line, standing shoulder to shoulder. They looked, beneath their crushed stovepipes, like a row of pillars propping the heavy roof. But these timbers, upon seeing us, came to life. Some ran to my heavy sack, and pulled the drugged dog out of the frock coat. Others moved to the thirty-foot section of cable that lay coiled on the ground. One end of the flat, braided wire was already tied round the thick trunk of what had once been a Siskiyou fir; the other was shaped into a loop, a kind of collar, which Steamboat Ed slipped over the bulldog's head. I noted that the clever device was fashioned so that the more the animal thrust against it, the tighter — like the paroxysm of its own throat muscles — the cinch would become. With that task accomplished, the Academy members gathered before their teacher.

With a quavering voice I asked the crucial question: "The virus, gentlemen? Is it prepared?"

Bacon Jack pointed to the cavern roof, where the bottles, like a kind of wind chime, were hanging. One could see, through the amber glass, the cloudy liquid, the shape of the half-dissolved cords.

"Prima!"

Little Elbow Frank was staring behind me, toward the strangers. "Where are the witnesses? The writers? I thought a' the wide world would be here."

Christie blinked away the sweat that continued to pour down his egg-smooth brow. "There are such reporters. From the *New*

York Herald. From the *Tribune* of Chicago. From every large city. But they've gone down to the last station. A futile journey! Did you know the muckers collapsed on the last load? And there are fifty or sixty feet remaining before the mark of a mile. Fifty feet of solid rock. Even the chances of curing rabies are better than blasting through that."

Moffet, the redhead, gave a laugh. He twirled his cane. "Our trip is no less foolish than theirs. A cure for hydrophobia? Mr. Christie here says that some fellow is going to allow himself to be bitten. Deliberately bitten. By a dog that's rabid."

"You betcher," said Boston Charlie. "Jew feller here."

Moffet looked about. "And the mad dog? The wild beast?"

Paracelsus Max pointed to the tan-and-white bulldog, with its lopped-off ears, its truncated tail. The loose cheeks of the animal flapped as it drew in each breath.

"Ha-ha!" laughed the telegraph man. "Asleep! Taking a catnap! I thought to see a wolf!"

"Error, sir," I exclaimed. "Not sleeping. This is the work of anesthetic. Soon the subject will wake."

Christie, however, was looking at his watch. "We don't have the time, Dr. Pinto. The hour approaches."

"*Ja!* So. We now are beginning!"

Between myself and the sickened Caesar stood the line of children. I stared into their faces. "My colleagues," I said. "My dears. I regret the time our work has taken. All the years of your youth."

Newton Mike: "Dinna speak of that. How the raptured moments hae flown!"

Priestley Bill: "We would do the thing a' o'er again!"

I was, for the moment, overcome. To hide the tears that had sprung to my eyes, I opened the slop-shop ledger. For the last time I wrote on its pages:

> 31 December 59 / 1 January 60: Inoculation by rabid canine of subject: *Homo sapiens.* Six foot. 149 pounds. Mosaic persuasion. Black hair. Brown eyes. Definite moustache.

Christie interrupted the scratch of my pen. "By my watch," he said, "the new year is only minutes away."

I closed the ledger. The scholars stepped aside. Beneath my black-and-silver sombrero I strode to within the ten-yard radius of the taut steel rope: in other words, to within reach of the curved, slick fangs.

Nothing occurred. I looked about. To the right, far off, was the arch, the dark tunnel of the drift. To the left, nearby, the wind corrider that led to the shutter, the ventilation shaft. Straight ahead, perhaps twenty feet off, the snoring Caesar. I turned to the two other members of the Caucasian race.

"Gentlemen of the press," I began. "You are about to witness the fruits of our experiments, the harvest of the inductive method. Before your eyes a living person will be infected with a deadly dose of rabies. This will happen in precisely the way our species has always contracted the scourge — from the bite of a suffering hound. After receiving his wounds, the human will undergo a series of injections. There, over your heads, you see the vaccine. Here is a liquor beyond compare! An elixir no sum could buy! The only such nectar on earth! Once this treatment, the process of Pintoization, is complete, the subject will be the first man in history to survive the dread disease."

Still the bulldog had not stirred. Had it, I wondered, been given too large a dose of the ether? I took a gliding step closer. Then I resumed my speech, but in louder tones, as if the sound of my voice might rouse the beast. "But only the first! Others will be bitten, and will also survive. No man, or woman, or child, whether in the teeming cities or attacked by wolves in the forests of Russia: no such person need ever more succumb!"

"Too late for my lad," said the *Ingot* editor, with a shake of his head.

"Ha-ha!" laughed young Mr. Moffet. Then, to the horror of all, he walked briskly to where Caesar lay in his coma. "This is a farce! The dog is not sleeping. Look here! The animal is dead!" By way of proof the telegraph operator raised his cane and once, twice, three times, poked it into what did seem the lifeless fur, the soft, yielding flesh.

"Nein! Achtung! Verboten!"

But Moffet only laughed and raised the tip of his cane yet again. The effect it produced upon coming down was the same as that made by a miner's bit that enters a drill hole where a charge of black powder remains. With a roar the animal exploded. The whole body sprang upright. Then the foam-flecked jaws opened just wide enough to clamp the shaft of the cane, which snapped in two. Horribly, the dog chewed the splinters and gobbled them down.

Moffet, terror-stricken, uttered a shriek. "Help! Mad dog!"

The sound of his voice seemed to infuriate the beast. It gave a shake, so that strands of spittle flew to every side. Then it turned to Moffet, whose hair, standing visibly on end, acted as a red flag might to a bull. The jaws dropped open. Beneath the wrinkled brow, the eyes gleamed with scarlet light. Under this gaze Moffet stood as rigid as his cane. The dog gathered itself to strike.

"Herr Caesar! Here, sir!"

Slowly the massive head of the beast turned toward where I stood, only five yards away. At the sight of its age-old enemy, an unmistakable grin spread across the animal's flattened features. The lips drew back, revealing every one of the slime-covered teeth. The swollen tongue dangled from the jaw. A low growl, a kind of purring, came from deep in the powerful chest. This was, for the bulldog, bliss.

"Look! Caesar! See!" Turning my back on the savage creature, I dropped my checked gabardine trousers, along with my silken drawers. Exposed thus I stooped, my bony buttocks thrust toward my four-footed foe. "Come, sir! The nates!"

There was an answering howl, and the maddened canine launched itself forward. To me, viewing the scene upside down, from between shaking knees, the attacker seemed to rush with the speed of a locomotive. The red eyes, deep in their sockets, glowed as bright as lamps, while the foam, the froth, blew backward like steam. On came Caesar, teeth clacking, closer and closer, until with a last mighty roar he gathered his four legs beneath him and sprang toward his target's twin orbs.

"So," I said, with uncanny calm, "the test commences."

The next instant I found myself hurled to the ground, unbitten. Indeed, all the others in the cave, red men and white men, were sent sprawling as well. Not only that, but the very earth shook, it heaved beneath us. While the humans lay stunned, there came through the crosscut, into the cavern, a blast of hot air, followed by a thick cloud of dust. Then, from the other direction, up the ventilation column, a similar tornado of dust, of hot gases, came whirling across the first level.

"Goddam!" said Boston Charlie. "Buggers set mine on fire!"

"Wha' folly!" cried Humboldt Johnny.

Slowly I lifted my head. Above, about, the dust cloud hung thick in the atmosphere. The rock floor under my body quaked and trembled. Deep in the earth the dull roar of the explosion continued to echo, now loud, now muted, as if a huge metal ball were rolling unchecked through all the corridors of the mine. Next, closer to hand, a series of mournful groans began to rend the air. At first I thought my wounded colleagues were uttering these pitiful sounds. Then, with a feeling of terror, I realized that the humanlike cries came from the tree trunks, which were splintering between the pressure from below and above. In particular, the stout fir to which the bulldog had been tethered cracked now quite in two. Even as I noted the wood's exposed and rotted core, the unsupported section of ceiling fell by the ton to the ground. The passage to the ventilation shaft was blocked completely.

"Trapped! Trapped, laddies!"

"Coom, Scots! We must fly t'ither way!"

The Academicians, who had started to crawl toward the wind corridor, now halted. But when they started in the opposite direction, toward the archway, they had to halt once more. The flow of hot dust and gases boiled thick from the drift.

"I know!" shouted Elbow Frank. "Let us fly down the winze! To the number-two level! Fra' there we can reach the column for air!"

Alas! Just as that hellhound, Cerberus, stood guard at the gates of Hades, preventing the sinners from ascending to the sweet air of the upper earth, so now at the portal to freedom sat Caesar. Muff raised, jowls awash in slobber, the animal never shifted its bloodshot eyes from the sight of my prostrate form. Alack for A. Pinto! I lay, with my trousers about my ankles, within a single strong bound of the monster. Once more the animal's lips stretched wide, to reveal the venom-dripping fangs. The brute gathered its strength to attack.

But Caesar sprang not. Instead, he shifted his head, cocking it to the left, to the right. Was this the rabies symptom? Did this victim see the swarm of nonexistent flies? Or hear their imaginary buzz?

Ceso! Ceso!

It was no hallucination. This was the piping call, the whistling wail, of my adopted aborigine. Where had it come from? Caesar knew! With a roar he leaped, dove, disappeared down the winding winze. The sound of his claws echoed behind him, as did the length of the slithering chain. I was only a few seconds behind. I threw myself down at the entrance to the hole. Horrible sight! After the concussion, the pressure, the passage had grown too narrow for even a slim Semite to fit.

"Dumb George! Dear fellow! Darling chap!"

I leaned into the chute to listen. The channel, with its twists, its turns, amplified sound like a hearing tube, or like the coils of the ear itself. At once I heard the low rumble of the bulldog's growl, followed by the cry of the little lad.

Ceso! Ceeeesooo!

Before I could utter a sound in reply, another tree trunk collapsed. Immediately a chunk of stone, now unsupported, thundered to the floor of the cavern. Through the dust came an awful shriek, and then another. All the old firs, as if witches had been trapped inside them, set up a howl. We had no choice: one by one the supports were collapsing. The whole of the roof was sure to cave in. All the Modocs, and the white men too, dashed toward the entrance to the drift. Christie, his face blackened, reached the archway first. I staggered along in the rear. At the last moment I looked back, over my shoulder. A great stone slab broke from the ceiling and fell with tremendous concussion. The two sides of the vise were closing about us. Already the scholars were moving away, down the dark drift. Hot cinders flew about them. Smoke seared their lungs. I lingered a moment more.

"Coom, Mister-r-r Pinto," cried Cavendish Sam, from within the sooty tunnel. "We must bid this grim dungeon adieu."

"No! No! *Nein!*"

I stared in anguish at the top of the cavern, where the whiskey bottles were shaking, shattering, spilling to the ground. I took a step back, in an attempt to save the final flask. But another fall of rock dropped just before me, practically upon my high-top shoes. Then the last of the bottles smashed to smithereens. The vaccine for rabies no longer existed.

Soon our whole party emerged from the gloomy corridor and huddled at the edge of the number-one station. It was only too clear that the timbering at the bottom levels was ablaze. Smoke and ashes boiled upward, through the light of our little lamp, toward the black window of sky above. Every surface, including our clothing, our skin, was covered with a film of grease and soot. The shaft was burning like an enormous candle turned upside down.

Humboldt Johnny shook his head. "Every ray o' hope destroyed."

As if to confirm these words, yet another explosion caused the ground to shudder, so that all the loose stones, the quartz pieces about us, rattled like so many dice. The flames below had touched off a cache of explosives, or a pocket of gas. Soon a black ball of smoke, medusa-shaped, with tentacles of dust hanging beneath it, silently rose past our station, even as wood scraps and pebbles rained down from above.

The natural historians, half blind from smoke, and coughing like veteran miners, turned to their teacher. "Tell us," demanded Bacon Jack. "Wha' is the signal for the bell?"

I did not reply. My thoughts were concentrated less on how to go up than on some means of dropping downward. If only we could descend a hundred feet, we might yet reach the ventilation column, and on the way search level two — and, if need be, three and four — for General George.

"Coom, man!" shouted Priestley Bill. "Dinna stand like one bewitched! Do ye na see the peril?"

I snapped from my trance. "Three long: that to send up the cage at once. One short: to indicate the level. Mr. Gill knows we are here."

Steamboat Ed, standing at the signal cord, gave the four tugs. Moffet leaned out into the shaft, craning his neck upward, as if he hoped somehow to see the very clapper vibrating upon the bell.

"Do you hear it?" he asked.

The others shook their heads. Their aching, Asiatic eyes were focused at the center of the shaft, where, now obscured by the haze of smoke, now glinting in the weak rays of the lantern, the flat, braided cable hung motionless and taut. The cage remained deep in the earth.

"Sonabitch!" exclaimed Boston Charlie. "How come that sonabitch don't wanna move?"

"Once more! Anither pull!"

Again the bell ringer hauled on the cord. But the only sound in response came from a mile below, where the heated air roared through the tunnels and drifts like the blast through the bellows of a forge. From somewhere in the shaft itself came a pounding, a series of hammer blows, together with the echo of what must have been human shouts. Rising for thousands of feet, reverberating, these voices had become unintelligible, a kind of gibberish — as if the depth charges had unexpectedly broken through to the far side of the planet, where the inhabitants spoke an outlandish tongue.

Upon hearing those sounds, at the sight of the cable that hung straight as a plumb line, fixed, unmoving, the Pioneers of Progress gave way to a fit of anger. Gagging, they gathered at the rim of the shaft.

Bacon Jack extended the lantern recklessly over the gaping hole. "I feel the breath o' the Devil himself, wi' a' his brimstone squadrons!"

"O horror-breathing night!" lamented Priestley Bill.

"O burning hell!"

Elbow Frank shook his one good fist over the verge. "We Scots defy grim danger's loudest roar!"

Then, exhausted, breathless, the scholars dropped to the floor of the station. Steamboat Ed gave a last perfunctory pull on the signal cord. Then he collapsed as well.

Said Boston Charlie, "Ain't gotta Chinaman's chance."

The others were not breathing now so much as gasping. Hot tears spilled from their eyes.

Humboldt Johnny: "Without one wee hope to gild the gloom!"

Said the panting Kepler Jim, "This weary mortal round is done."

Newton Mike plucked the handkerchief from the pocket of his cutaway coat and dipped it in the trickle of water that had started to run down the grade of the tunnel, over the station floor. That wet mask he tied over his toothy mouth, his sharp, pointed nose. In a muffled voice he said, simply, "Finis."

Then the silent Modocs stretched out on the ground where they lay. They put their hands on their chests, preparing for an endless sleep.

Nor were we of the white race unaffected. For a moment Christie stood swaying. Then he fell to his knees. So did young Moffet. The faces of both men had turned cobalt-colored. Only then did I note that the skin of the natural historians, as if they had suddenly reverted back to the savage condition, looked as if it had been painted blue. Any physician would know what that meant: lack of oxygen. Cyanosis. Sentence of doom. My own face surely bore the same tint. Not only that: my chest burned, my throat felt seared, as if with each breath I were swallowing a fiery schnapps. How drowsy I had become. How pleasant to take a brief nap. But I knew it would be a sleep from which I'd never wake. Hence I roused myself. I reasoned.

Two facts must be explained. First, why did the lift not respond to our signal? The answer, of course, was that it could not. And why was that? Undoubtedly because the force of the explosions had caused parts of the shaft to bulge, to buckle. Hence the sound of hammering, as those trapped below attempted to bring the walls back to rectangular trim. Second, what was the source of the water that, with increasing velocity, flowed from the crosscut and over the edge of the shaft? Had one of the rockbound pockets been breached? Squatting low, I thrust a finger into the swift, shallow stream. Cold. Almost freezing. That meant the source had to be at the surface. Most likely the crews, in their efforts to put out the underground fire, were sending water into the ventilation column. Some of that downpour must be splashing into the first level. But if the water was being admitted, then the wind shutter and the cavern must be open, or have been reopened from above. The survivors might yet have a means of escape.

Quietly, for fear of raising false hopes in my comrades, I crawled back to the fume-filled drift. Bent double, I splashed through the current. Then, some thirty yards into the tunnel, in the pitch darkness, I felt the hard, heavy drops fall onto the crown of my Mexican hat. A spray washed over my body. I reached up, feeling for the origin of the flow. What I found chilled me far more than the icy shower itself. The water was gushing through a crack in the ceiling — a fissure, I realized, that must continue upward to some point near the man-made pond. This was Tule Lake water! Soon the whole of the reservoir would drain into, would fill up, the mine!

Down I sank, without strength or desire. How many ways there were to die! By being buried alive, by suffocation, by burning, and now by the flood. Earth, air, fire, water: the very elements of nature had turned against those who had dared expose their secrets. I heaved a sigh. My heavy eyelids fell over my eyes. What did I see on the instant but, in a vision, a miracle, Dumb George: Dumb George in his bath! Bubbles of soap rolled over his tiny shoulders. They clung to his downy hair. About him the air was all ashimmer. Ah, the rose perfume! On every glistening sphere was an iridescent spectrum, from the color violet to the color red. Principle of refraction. Discovery of W. Snell. Dutch citizen. 1621. That was my last earthly thought: for my spirit had escaped. It soared upward to where light was bent — first by invisible vapors, then by innumerable atoms — to create the blueness of the sky.

Then an alarm bell rang; some person shook my shoulder. "Go. Leave me," I murmured. "Allow me to sleep."

"Nay! I wadna do a thing such as that!"

The speaker was the hook-nosed Kepler Jim. The alarm bell rang once more. No: the signal bell! Again my protégé squeezed the flesh of my shoulder. "Ye hae made a surgeon from the reeking savage. I canna let my master remain alone!"

Even as the Modoc spoke, I felt a rush of hot air. It had soot in it, and cinders, but also oxygen. Oxygen! Down the length of the tunnel, from the direction of the shaft, came a weak cheer. I understood: the cage, pushing the hot air before it, was rising! It had answered the call!

Stumbling, crawling, we two, doctor and disciple, reached the station. There the Indian boys had revived. Sid Christie, seeing us emerge from the drift, pointed toward the main shaft. He said, "We are saved."

Elbow Frank ran forward. "Mister-r-r Pinto. The sight of ye enchants my soul!"

The others, their flesh no longer the color of dahlias, or Druids, were dancing about.

"The cage is aboot to come!"

"Let's give them a Highland welcome!"

"Hurrah!"

It took only a glance to confirm that what the lads said was true. The taut cable was whipping along almost faster than the eye could register. With its signal bell sounding, the cage moved upward, pushing before it a neat column of air. This whistling wind blew through the Modocs' hair. It scattered the tears from their eyes. Joyously they leaned into the gale. To the ice-cold torrent that rushed over their ankles they paid no mind. By now the water covered most of the station floor, before narrowing again at the rim of the shaft to form a bubbling cascade. But the flood, the waterfall, did not impede the ascent of the lift. Onward it came, upward it flew. Then that daredevil, Bacon Jack, leaned with his lamp over the chasm:

"I see! 'Tis a mere five hoondred feet down!"

"Three hoondred!" Newton Mike shouted.

"One hoondred fifty!" said Cavendish Sam.

"Goddam!" yelled Boston Charlie. "O goddam! You think that sonabitch gonna stop?"

Everyone fell silent. They listened to the rush of the wind, the roar of it, as the cage, not slackening, not slowing, rose like a rocket from the lower to the upper earth.

Said Humboldt Johnny, "I hae me doots."

"Curse them!" cried Christie, running toward the rim. "They must stop!"

And stop — suddenly, lurchingly, with a high humming whine from the straining cable — the vehicle did. The lower floor of the cage came to rest even with the station. All those marooned rushed forward.

"Help! My God, help us!" That was Moffet. He pushed the rest of us aside, and stumbled to safety aboard the bottom deck.

The Modoc miners, their skin smooth, naked, black as the blackest Negroes', squeezed backward, so as to make room. I stared into the crowded cage, looking from face to face. Where was Dumb George? Had they picked up my beloved boy? All around me the members of the Highland band were pressing forward, attempting to force their way into the narrow space. Then one of the passengers stepped into the gap, barring the way.

"White men only!" he ordered. "All the rest back!"

I was now at the rear of my surging comrades. In astonishment, I gaped. These were not workers! Not Indians! They were white men, their clothes torn away, and covered from head to toe with mud. General George, with his brittle bones, his wobbly head, was not among them.

Boston Charlie took a step forward. The man at the gate — it was Ben Piper — struck him on the side of the head with the barrel of a gun. The Indian collapsed. Piper leveled the weapon at the others. "Don't think of boarding. I'll shoot the one who tries. There's no room for niggers."

A groan rose from the castaways. They clutched each other. On the upper deck, a mud-covered man leaned down. His pale eyes showed in the smooth black shell of his mask. Matt Cole! "Do not give up!" he shouted. "The miners are still alive at the bottom. We shall send the cage back for them. It will stop for you!"

With those words the once-blond engineer reached for the signal cord.

"Wait! Don't go! Wait!" Sid Christie pushed through the Indian boys. Piper stood aside. The editor of the *Ingot* threw himself into the mass of men on the cage.

Cole said, "Is there anyone else? Do we have you all?"

No one responded. No one, it seemed, dared breathe. Even the roaring winds below seemed briefly to abate. Again Cole reached for the cord. Then, from behind their backs, the Sons of Galileo heard the following words:

"Pardon. Excuse, please. *Entschuldigung.* Begging your pardon."

The crowd parted once more. Through the ranks of my partners in science, I, Pinto of Pressburg, made my way. Looking neither left nor right, I stepped onto the few inches of space that remained on the deck of the rocking platform. No one said a word. I shut tight my eyes and gripped my gay sombrero. With a jolt, a lurch, the cage rose through the tunnel of space that led to the top of the world.

3

Everyone on the surface knew there had been a disaster at the Neptune Mine. New Year's revelers as far away as Etna Mills, Happy Camp, even Weaverville, had felt the tremors. The Yrekans, however, close as they were to the blast, were at first misled. When the tongue of flame, with pinwheeling sparks, shot from the top of the shaft, they thought the pyrotechnics a part of the carnival. But their cheering stopped when the draft reversed and the wind sail caught fire. It flared up in seconds; the burning boom toppled into the lake. For a brief moment the crowd held its breath, as if in instinctive sympathy with those underground, who at each inhalation drew in the poisoned air. Then the whole population swarmed up the hillside toward the shaft.

Thus a thousand people, white-skinned and red-, were milling about the hoist works when the last of the cable coiled onto the winding drum and the cage came to grass. How strange to them the figures on board must have seemed: dwellers on another planet, black-bodied, with heads smooth, featureless, and dark as ebony eggs.

None stranger, more alien, than I, who was the last on board to step onto solid earth. If only these citizens could have glimpsed the inner man — a deserter, betrayer, murderer even — they would have recoiled from me the way healthy folk do from a leper. Yet none in that crowd gave me so much as a glance. And when, a half-hour later, back at the fireproof, I saw myself in my own looking glass, I was amazed to see the same sad face, though a trifle more turquoise, and soot-smeared, with which I had lived the whole of my life.

But Neptune the mule knew better. She woke to find herself confronted by precisely the monster I felt myself to be. What she saw was a creature that stood upright, like a human being, but with skin that was wrinkled, rubbery, like that of an elephant; and it had, coming out of the bulging ball of its skull, a trunk longer than that of any pachyderm. More horrible still was the great eye, like the unwinking orb of a Cyclops, fixed at the center of its face. Naturally Neptune snorted. She turned about and let fly with her hooves. Then she whirled again and, with her yellowed teeth, attempted to bite through the mammoth's tough skin. Nothing availed. The two-legged animal mounted the four-legged mule.

"Quick, you darling! Back to the butte!" The voice, pinched and spectral, seemed to come from the forty-foot nose.

The aged mule resisted. She reared. Like a youthful bronco she bucked. At that her rider dropped the reins and with a single sickening gesture removed its head from its shoulders.

"Ho! Ho! It is I, sweetheart! A. Pinto! Inside the De Groot diving suit!"

Hee-haw! bellowed the hybrid, as the headless horseman spurred her in the direction of the mine.

At the hoist works all was confusion. People ran aimlessly every which way. Black smoke rose first from one shaft and then, as the draft reversed yet again, from the other. Thick, greasy cinders swirled on the wind. The great Cornish pump was once more in action, the cast-iron rod bobbing upward and down over its boxed-in section of the shaft. A sweet smell, almost fruity, hung about the gallows frame. Dismounting, high-stepping in my cumbersome galoshes, I sniffed the air.

"Flesh," said Matt Cole, who was squatting near the pump's evacuation spout.

"Mule flesh?"

Cole said, "Perhaps."

A wail broke out at the shaft. Alarming to see there a group of squaws: in their grief they seemed to wish to hurl themselves over the edge. Indeed, they might have done so had not the empty cage, hanging at the pithead, blocked their way. Clumsily I strode — in this heavy garb I might just as well have been moving beneath seven fathoms — toward Gill at the winding drum. I waved my rubber mitt toward the mourning Modocs.

"Mr. Gill: what is the significance of these women? Where are their menfolk? Have you not in this hour transported the miners inside the lift?"

"No. Not yet. The timbering is loose. Rocks keep breaking away. We're trying to make a shield for the roof." The hoistman gestured toward where a crew was hammering out of sheet metal a kind of giant conical cap that would fit over the top of the cage.

"What of the number-one level? Where are my children? Rescued? Saved? They were only one hundred feet down."

Gill shook his head. His own face was blackened by the exhaust, and his hair had been singed away. "We've tried. There's an obstruction. At fifty-five feet. But we can't send anyone to remove it until we've got protection from the slough. Another half-hour."

"A half-hour! But they have not fresh air to breathe! Listen: no bell! No ringing! Perhaps they have been swept over the brink! By the flood!"

Before the hoistman could respond, Cole began to shout from his spot by the pump. "Pinto! Gill! What do you make of this?"

With slow, undersea steps, I moved toward the ex-Harvard man. Cole held his torch over the curved pipe, from the end of which the effluent emerged in periodic bursts. "Do you see?" he asked.

I leaned over, so that my head stuck from the stiff garment like a tortoise's from its shell. The water from the far-off sump came streaming forth. It was a pale red. A pink. Then it grew darker, close to the color of blood.

Filled now with horror, I reeled away. With air hose looped over one arm, helmet under the other, I began the trek to the crest of the butte. Impossible to wait until the skip had been fitted with its cap. Instead I would take the same route down as had General George. But once I'd gone round the lake and arrived at the mouth of the ventilation shaft, I found that the updraft, filled with smoke, with noxious gases, was pouring out. Undaunted, I placed the helmet over my head and locked it onto the collar. Through the thick lens of the porthole I peered into the murky depths. Then, feeling in my cloglike boots for footholds below, gripping with my vulcanized mittens the notches above, I descended the hollow column.

The difficulty was that while the indentations of the chicken ladder went down two levels, that is, for some two hundred feet, my air hose, stretching above like a reed in a pond, would allow me to travel only one quarter the distance at best. When I reached the end of that tether I halted. Pearl divers, I knew, weighed down by stones, could remain submerged for two and three minutes. Thus I took a last deep inhalation of the upper air and resumed the desperate plunge. Alas, I exhaled even before I had reached the clogged number-one level. What now to do? The free end of the rubber tube had long since tumbled by, dangling in the darkness below. It would take longer to ascend than to make the dash to the second level. The only option was to continue.

Awful moments! As I plodded downward the interior of my suit, the hemisphere of my helmet, filled with a fog: part carbon dioxide, part lethal gas. I grew dizzy, light-headed. A ringing began in my ears. Then of a sudden I missed a step. My hand slipped on a notch. I swung out, teetering over the blackened void. Then, well below, at what must have been the number-two level, a pinprick of light glittered and danced. Foundering, waving my padded limbs, I groped to regain the ladder. Hanging there I had a thought: a light meant a flame. A flame meant oxygen. The element isolated by Priestley! With my last gasp I fumbled at the porthole. The glass circle swung open. *Ja!* The current had shifted! The downdraft, cold and wintry, blew by. I sucked in breath after breath. Thus refreshed, I moved swiftly downward, not stopping until I reached the last notch, the final foothold.

The light had indeed come from the second level. The trouble was the source: the whole of the wind shutter was on fire. The flames blocked my way. Before I could begin to think, I heard, from deep in the mine, the voice of my stepson:

Ceso! Ceeesooo!

Then, as the fierce Bengal tiger will hurl itself through the circus master's burning hoop, so did I leap across the abyss and through the fiery wooden slats. There was a brief sound of sizzling, a smell of burnt rubber, and then I found myself crawling on all fours through the narrow artery to the abandoned stope.

The surprising thing was, nothing on the second level seemed to have been touched by the disaster. A current of air flowed softly by my open mask. The tree trunks were all in place, emitting a dim phosphorescence. By that glow I crawled to where the drainage ditch angled down toward the next level. Open. Unblocked. I called down, into the open mouth of the chute:

"Hola! General George! Have courage! Comes now Papa Pinto!"

Already I was transforming words into action, and had begun to wriggle along the course of the twisted channel. Strange to say, my fondest hope was that I should find, awaiting me at the exit, the sharp-toothed hound. To meet that threat I had something even sharper, the curved blade of the De Groot oyster knife. And my greatest fear? That the dog would *not* be waiting — that is, that my innocent child would find the crazed animal first. But when I dropped to the floor of the third-level cavern, all was dark, quiet, still. Was anyone there? My first thought was to warn the boy — *Achtung!* Mad dog! — that his pet was rabid. But the instant I drew breath to shout, my chest began to burn, as if a plaster of mustard had been laid upon it. The third level was filled with poison gas!

In a flash I slammed shut my mask. Inside the hose that trailed snakelike behind me there could not be more than six shallow breaths of life-sustaining air. Here was another difficult choice: to attempt the climb back to the second level, where there was oxygen aplenty; or to take the gamble of descending to the fourth, where there might be nothing to breathe but more deadly fumes. There was, inside my helmeted head, no debate. Dumb George was not above me. Ergo, he must be below. Down, then!

Even before I had arrived at the four-hundred-foot level, I realized my wager was lost. The lower reaches of the winze were lined not with stones but with strange, soft objects, the size, the consistency of bread loaves: rats, rats by the dozen, and asphyxiated, every one. More of the poor creatures lay on the floor of the drift, onto which I now despairingly dropped. Already the invisible fumes were filling my airtight casket. I was like a mummy, the dark-skinned Paddy, wrapped in a permanent shroud.

What now? I looked around. There was nothing to see in the coal-black air. Then I reached upward, feeling along the ceiling for the thick, canvas-covered hose of the pneumatic system. Everything depended on one factor: had the compressors, like the pump, been restarted? Or had the crews on the surface shut down the network for fear of feeding the underground flames? Frantically I slashed at the pipe with the knife blade, sawed at it, stabbed at it, until with a hiss audible even inside my sturdy helmet the canvas ruptured and the air, under the pressure of many atmospheres, came rushing out.

In three quick seconds I had inserted the end of my narrow air hose into the severed line. At once the welcome wind shot through the one-way valves into the rubber suit, and exited with a rude noise through the exhaust cock at the hip. Inhaling the delicious draft, I started forward. As it happened, the forty feet of my hose were just enough to bring me within the confines of the familiar vaulted chamber. The stone pillars there gave off no phosphorescence. Yet I saw, off to the right, a faint gleam of light. A pocket of breathable air seemed to have been trapped in the old icehouse; it circulated through the vast space of the cavern as well. Cautiously, haltingly, a step at a time, a breath at a time, I moved toward the low-ceilinged den.

Here my journey came to an end. Dumb George and Caesar were both inside the little room. On the ground a lantern flared and flickered, as if lapping whatever oxygen was left in the air. By that guttering flame I saw how the boy, sitting cross-legged, held the animal on his lap. The hindquarters of the dog were clearly paralyzed. The venom-filled mucus poured from its open jaws, onto the little lad's shirt and his buttoned banker's vest. The beast's loose jowls were slick with the poison, its teeth wet and shining. The eyes, deep in the furrowed folds of skin, glittered with red motes of light. Rooted at the entrance ramp, I squeezed my weapon. My thought was to slit the veins, and perhaps sever the windpipe, in the hound's thickened throat.

Still I stood, not moving, not breathing, not blinking an eye. General George had gathered the great blunt head in his arms. He pressed the fierce face to his chest. The lips of the boy moved. He was speaking. Something, water droplets, a hot steam, made a mist within my mask. With care I swung it wide on its hinges. The condensation was not on the glass. Salty tears blurred my vision. I listened to how, in a warbling, peep-peeping voice, the dumb youth addressed his pet:

"Ceso. Sweetheart-you. Darling-you. *Liebchen.*"

Lost in wonder, I stared. That a mute should speak was not so startling as the way all rules of instinct, the powers of nature, were here overthrown. It was as if, contrary to the laws of Newton, of Galileo, the very earth should come to a stop. The beast was *bound* to attack — as surely as a thrown rock must fall, or a gas lighter than air must rise. The least sound, the slightest motion, the smell of flesh, must drive it into a fury. Yet the bulldog lay calm in its master's arms, while, slowly, the boy's head drooped on the weak stem of his neck and came to rest on the animal's furrowed brow.

A moment went by. Two moments. Perhaps a third. Then from the corner of my eye I caught a movement, a fleeting shadow.

Turning, I saw a mud-covered man, his clothes in tatters. Townsend! Frank Townsend! With his Voigtlander under his arm!

"Is that a lamp? A lantern? Hopeless! A joke! Listen. I'll give you the mathematical rule: if the intensity of light is diminished by any given factor, and the time of exposure is increased by the same factor, the useful energy expended is reduced by half. What? Confused? You, the brightest among us —?" Townsend strode forward, toward the lamp. "Look here. I am now just two feet from the lantern. Can you hold still for ten seconds? *Without that damned knocking of the knees?* Now I back up. You see? Here I am, at sixteen feet. The lamplight on my lens is now only one sixty-fourth of what it was before, and you and your half-breed must remain motionless — motionless! — for 640 seconds. Over ten minutes!"

With a shudder I recoiled. Had the mine owner taken leave of his senses? Why else would he be talking of mathematical ratios, of figures for time and distance, at such a moment? When all his great venture had been destroyed? Did he really mean to take a portrait? Warily I watched as he bent toward his camera. He held a stick, a cross of sticks, in the air.

"Numbers don't help. Nor all your science. The only way to learn is through pain. The nigger: remember? *Come to my arms, my Katie.* Oh, the stink of that foot! But from him I conceived the idea of a light box. Of phosphor in a bottle. Instantaneous light! And our ship, in the storm. Ha! Ha-ha! How they all cowered below decks. Done for! That's what they thought. But nothing is accomplished without danger. I *used* the lightning! To illuminate my plates. Only one task remained: how to put these sparks into a bottle? Like Thor: to hold the bolts in my hand!"

No doubt now. These were the ravings of a madman. But when I turned back toward General George, Townsend barked out a command:

"Don't move! Not an inch! You're about to see my discovery. Conceived in the greatest pain. You remember when: sewing up the white men, the Chinaman, the Christie boy. Cauterizing the wounds. From that suffering, an idea! Sulfur! Saltpeter! Here is more light than pours through a glass dome. No more darkness! A miracle: turning night into day!"

On the instant, lightning struck. The forked bolt flashed through the den. It illuminated the cavern, all the way to the crags, the cracks, in the high vaulted ceiling. Dumb George, blinded, fell backward. The bulldog, on its bowlegged front limbs, hauled itself to the den door. Now was the moment: I raised the curved blade of the oyster knife. But Caesar did not attack. Instead, he dragged himself from the icehouse and into the giant chamber, whose stope and stone pillars and high walls were enveloped in darkness once more. The dog was listening to something. To the right, to the left, he twisted his head. The ear stumps were twitching. Yet there was nothing to hear, unless it was the buzzing in his fevered brain.

"Ceso!"

Dumb George stumbled forward, holding the kerosene lamp. I seized the boy and wrested the lantern from him. I held it high. The yellow rays of light shone up and out, disclosing a sight that made me wonder whether my own mind had become infected with the germs of disease. A patch of pure darkness, of utter blackness, was floating at the top of the cavern. With each second it grew larger, like the cloud of a coming storm. Particles of the murk, the mist, were sifting downward from above. I strained backward to see. High up in the vault was a crack in the rock, a ragged rift. Darkness poured from it, mixing with the air of the cavern like black ink filtered into a flask of clear liquid. Suddenly my disordered thoughts, like the particles of the cloud, came swooping together.

"Der Blutsauger!" I cried. "The vulture!"

No sooner did that shout echo throughout the chamber than the great bird darted downward upon its prey: the bulldog, Caesar. The next instant, as if prodded by the touch of the talons, the poor canine hobbled with surprising speed over the ground into the tunnel. The wings of the cloud beat around it. From within the dark drift the animal uttered a single hoarse howl.

"Frank Townsend!" I cried. "It is true! No myth! No legend!" But the crazed daguerrian, when I turned to find him, was gone.

What happened next was so much like a frightening dream that I, seeing it all, attempted to pinch myself through my vulcanized hide. With a shriek General George wrenched free from my grasp and began tottering away after his pet. He got halfway to the tunnel entrance. Then the black bird, suddenly returning, swooped onto the boy. It covered him, too, with its wings.

Instantly I snapped shut my helmet. Waving my burning lantern, I dashed to the scene. The scavenger was fluttering about the head of its victim, clutching at his bare skin. With an oath I jumped into the fray. The cloud wheeled to attack. A thousand pairs of wings beat upon me. Tiny teeth and sharp claws ripped at my rubber armor. A fuzzy face, then two fuzzy faces, each with pointed ears, with beady eyes, stared from the other side of the porthole glass. Truth dawned: this was no bird, no vulture. These were bats! Order: Chiroptera. Family: Vespertilionidae. Plainnose bats!

With what fury did I fight them! I beat my way through the swooping, swarming mammals and picked up the child in my swollen arms. Dumb George was limp. His mouth hung slack. From loss of blood, from lack of oxygen, or perhaps from sheer terror, the boy had fainted. Stooped, drawing my own breath in pain, I stumbled to the tunnel and ran down the endless passage. The bats came swooping after, crazed by the taste of blood. Twice I stopped, whirling with the lantern, knocking eight and ten and twelve of the quick creatures to the ground. Then, with the living cloud still about me, I lumbered on, toward the distant shaft.

Strange the nature of the human brain! Even as I fled, there took place in its thinking portion a rapid cerebration. Here, at last, was the reason the Pioneers of Progress had been unable to find a rabid animal on the surface. Here, too, was why the cases always seemed to originate at the fourth level, and why the victims showed no wounds. The bats were the source of the disease! The whole pack was infected with rabies! One beast alone, with its near-invisible bite, could inoculate an unwary miner, or an unlucky mule. "Aha!" I exclaimed, as my unconscious stepson and I arrived at the number-four station. "Mystery solved!"

The senseless boy could not hear this exultant cry; even if he had wakened, the words, issuing from the dangling end of the air hose, would have been lost in the roar of the cataract that came pouring down the shaft from the upper levels. The silvery curtain of water seemed to confuse the flying mammals. They looped erratically in the chill spray. Then, wet-winged, with ruffled fur, they darted into the tunnel, back to their high, hidden nest.

I dropped to my knees and lay my beloved burden on the station floor. I lifted my helmet from its collar. Once again the draft had reversed direction. A current of air blew by my face. It revived the guttering lantern, but not the flame of consciousness in General George. The boy's eyes remained shut. His breath, oddly sweet-smelling, came in gasps from his open mouth. Every inch of skin was covered with scratches from bat claws, with puncture marks from bat teeth. Ruby-red blood welled in the wounds.

Meaning to wash the lacerations, I crawled to the edge of the station and held the helmet like a bowl under the deluge. Through the shifting layers of water, I saw a series of sudden shadows: rocks hurtling downward, splinters of wood tumbling by. Then, dimly, obscurely, I noted what had to be a trick of the eye. Just as when a nearby sailing ship slips silently from its berth, or the parallel train leaves the station, one's own craft, or carriage, seems to be the one that is moving; so now the steady fall of the flume, the rain of rocks, made the taut tether at the center of the shaft, the lift cable, appear to rise. "Illusion of optics," I declared.

But it was no illusion. Crashing sounds, thumps and bangs, came from below. Now I realized that the loosened rocks were striking the tin top, the conical roof, of the cage. The lift was ascending from the depths! I crawled well to the right, to the part of the station where the waterfall did not reach. Gingerly, lying prone, I peeked over the edge. The cage, moving slowly, shakily, was only one level down! I could see the dents in its shield, together with a layer of rocks and debris. At the top, flattened, like the skin of an animal that has been turned into a rug, was the motionless carcass of Caesar.

The stones, the earth clods, whizzed close by my unhelmeted head. With all my strength I called to the rescue party:

"Hola! Humans here!"

A shout, confused, unintelligible, rose in response. I leaped to my feet. There was hardly time to gather the feather-light form of the child into my arms. With a pang I noted how the boy's hair had been pulled out in patches. The tip of one ear, through which the lantern light shone, was torn. We two, father and foundling, remained at the verge of the shaft. Through the wavering wall, the strands of streaming liquid, the dark shape of the lift hovered into view. On board, the mud-covered wraiths gestured weakly. An arm was raised; a head nodded; a mouth fell wide. Then, shuddering from the force of the blows that rained down from above, straining from the weight of the cargo within, the shadowy rectangle rose past us out of sight.

I stood thunderstruck. A numbness spread through my body. My limbs felt mineralized. Suddenly the bell on the lift started ringing. Cautiously, I leaned over the dry section of chasm. The cage had halted a few hundred yards overhead. It dawned on me now why it had not stopped for us. They were going to rescue the Angus lads instead! My heart swelled joyfully within my gum-rubber breast. Over the crash of the cataract I shouted:

"Wake up! Wake up, my dear! Good news! Our comrades are saved!"

Had I, however, spoken too soon? For some reason the bell continued ringing, over and over. Even as I watched, the cage lurched upward and halted. Then the process was repeated: a sudden lurch, a sudden halt. Now the bell rang wildly, in a desperate call for assistance. The cage only shook in place, quivering beneath the impact of the various missiles falling upon it. The hundreds of rocks piled on the disk of the shield were weighing it down. Then, above the sound of the thudding rocks, the clanging pump rods, the ringing alarm, there came a shrill creak, as if a thick metal door, like the door of a rusted vault, were being forced askew.

"Was ist das?" I inquired.

But I knew. The great iron hook, the link between cage and cable, was starting to straighten. Then the lift came loose. In a shower of sparks the cage struck the wall of the shaft. Its bars bent and crumpled: the living people spilled out. In a reflex, I jerked the head of my son to my chest, so that even in his sleep he would not have to risk seeing either the fragments of the cage or the bodies of his fellow tribesmen — Boston Charlie, for instance, or perhaps Elbow Frank or the intelligent Newton Mike — as they fell freely by.

4

What most threatened the lives of Indian and Israelite? Not, for the moment, the soot-filled air. Not the deep explosions that continued to shake the ground beneath our feet. Nor was it the deluge, the flood. The most imminent danger was the despair that had seized me. Indeed, my first impulse was to follow my close associates, my trusted pupils, to their doom. Had it not been for the slight pressure, a flea's weight, a feather's force, of my adoptee's arm about my neck, I might well have stepped into the long vertical coffin of space.

But the weight of that flesh and blood, the mere ounces, moved me to consider a means of escape. The cage, of course, lay smashed in the sump. What remained of the cable must be inextricably snarled. No hope of aid from above. Pointless, too, to think of retreating to the ventilation shaft. Behind us, on our own fourth level, were the plainnose bats. On the third — even if I had room enough, and strength enough, to carry Dumb George up the winze — there wasn't a breath of sweet air. In any case, we'd have to climb to the second, since the ladder notches extended only two hundred feet. Impossible task! What burst from my lips was a bitter laugh: "Ho-ho." Was I to ride to the surface in a hot-air balloon? Chew my way like a mole through the earth, the rock? Or should I hammer the timbering into a wooden boat and float to the top as the flood filled the shaft?

Suddenly my mad musings ceased. Not so mad! The contents of the sump, the waters of the deluge, *were* arriving at the surface! Hundreds of gallons every minute, brought up by the Cornish pump! Across the shaft, boxed in their own section, the long lines of iron rods were constantly clanking. I tried to picture the scene within the partition boards. The staggered pipes were set in two parallel rows, so that with each stroke one length moved downward while a second, matching it, moved up. The water was hauled from section to section, from a tank in one line to a tank in the other, all the way to the top. No solid object could be pumped along with it. But the ends of the rods were massive, a foot and a half in diameter, with room enough for a man to stand erect. In theory, a skillful person ought to be able to step from the top of one pipe at the conclusion of its upward motion onto the top of a parallel pipe just as it was completing its downward stroke. Then that person could ride the upward thrust once more, and transfer again to the parallel plunger the instant it came to rest. It would be, in its balance, its timing, its leaps and its rhythm, a kind of dance.

Fine theory! Dare I put it into practice? Dare I not? Both arms, I knew, had to be free. Therefore I wrenched the air hose from the helmet and wrapped the makeshift rope round and round my body until General George was securely bound to my torso. Unconsciously, in a reflex, the boy clung to me the way an unweaned monkey, a little lemur, will cling to its mother's breast. Crouching, with the lantern hooked over a forearm, I moved to the lip of the shaft. To the left, dousing us with its spray, the water thundered downward. Boulders like asteroids tumbled by in the black chamber. The scaffolding that separated the pumping compartment from the shaft proper was opposite, some eight feet away. The timbering of the adjoining walls had sprung enough planks to provide handholds. No longer hesitating, like a mountaineer, or a marmoset, I swung into the void.

This was, perhaps, our most dangerous moment. The wood was slick with spray. Rocks banged around us. At any time one of the loose planks might give way. Nonetheless, we adventurers, like alpinists, slowly advanced toward the X-shaped boards, behind which moved, piston-fashion, the rods of the Cornish pump. As I had already noted, the spaces in the strapping were too narrow to allow entrance. I would have to kick through one of the narrow slats. This was easier said than, in gumshoes, done. Still, under repeated blows, the wooden board gave way with a snap.

There, just ahead, two long lines of iron rods, the ends of each link bolted together to make a staggered row, were rising and falling. Each section of pipe moved through a stroke equal to its own length. Since the rod directly before me loomed twice as high as I could stand, our journey would take place in a series of twelve-foot steps. That meant I must make the perilous transfer from rod end to rod end more than thirty times! Without room for a single error! Whose heart would not shrink at the prospect?

The long cylinder plunged by, its dull round top stopping only a foot below the spot where I stood. It paused — how briefly, for less time than it took to draw a breath — before lumbering upward again. A few seconds later, ten seconds, twelve, the rod completed its cycle: the end, round and taut as a drum skin, halted beneath me once more. Without thinking, eyes shut, I sprang. I landed, half crouching, at the center of the target. Both arms clutched Dumb George tight. Upward we rode, a passage that seemed even faster than it was because of the companion rod swiftly descending only inches from my nose. Abruptly, so that my Adam's apple felt as if it would be thrown from my throat like a stone from a sling, we stopped. So did the top of the parallel pipe. I stood undecided. The two sections reversed direction. We passengers found ourselves back where we had begun.

In this fashion a minute went by. The cycle repeated itself again and again. With each rise and fall my intestines heaved. It was time, before dizziness overcame me, to act. But what, I wondered, if I slipped? The two pipes, moving in opposite directions, would grind my flesh to jelly. And if I did not move? Then the very blood in my veins would be churned to butter.

"Houp-là!" I cried, and with a little hop, a jump, I leaped from the motionless tip of my own rod to the trembling top of the other. Immediately I felt myself rising again. Now the stone of my Adam's apple sank, seemingly to my knees. All at once we came once more to a halt, as did the next descending section from our original row. This time we travelers were ready. With one long stride, as if I were stepping over nothing more challenging than a puddle in a roadway, I crossed to the rod that hung two full lengths above the piece of pipe on which this perilous journey had begun.

Three minutes later our ascent came to an end. By then I, a non-skater, was gliding back and forth from one line of rods to the other with the ease of a performer on ice. I did not, however, think to look up. Thus the walking beam to which both lines of pipes were attached bobbed downward in its normal arc and struck me a glancing blow on the unprotected crown of my head. I tumbled sideways, onto the apron of the shaft. Dizzily I sprawled on hands and knees. Then I felt the cold, clear breeze pouring down from the hilltop and saw the pink sunbeams that heralded the birth of a new day. "Look, my dear," I said to my stepson. "We have come from hell to heaven."

There came, in response, a voice I knew well: "Goddam! Slop-shop feller. Got a helluva bump onna head."

It was the old Indian, Steamboat Ed. My initial thought was that the blow I'd sustained had knocked me senseless. What was this sight, this savage, but an hallucination? What were these words but a voice from the dead?

"Are you flesh, sir? Breathing? Not a ghost?"

"Ha-ha! Breathing! You betcher! Same as Humboldt Johnny! Same as Kepler Jim!" So saying, the grinning grandfather turned. Behind him, in the tatters of their banker's outfits, their ripped cutaways and ragged trousers, stood all the members of the Highland band.

I gasped. I gaped. I sat upright, holding General George. With enthusiasm I shook the thin shoulders of the half-conscious child. "Did I not say it? We are in heaven! Such a place definitely exists! What happiness now lies before us: to spend our days with these angels! With such celestial colleagues we shall look down on earth from the clouds. We shall observe the progress of mankind. All the new discoveries! The advances in metallurgy and transportation! The conquest of every disease!"

Boston Charlie stepped forward to interrupt his former instructor. "Ain't spirits! Ain't angels! We stink like Modoc stink! Walk like Modoc walk alla time onna ground!"

"But this is not possible. With my own eyes I saw the cage halt at the first level. To allow the Pioneers to board. Alas, the weight was too great! Terrible vision! The bodies flew through the air. No person could survive the fall to the steaming sump."

The caretaker, Steamboat Ed, responded. "Not Steamboat Ed. Not Cavendish Sam. Not Priestley Bill. Alla dumb Modoc ride that cage onna first trip. Go up easy. No trouble. You seen trip number two!"

It was true: all my colleagues were saved! This was a miracle! If this were not heaven, it was heaven's plan. Surely we had been plucked from death for some noble purpose. I got to my feet. I lifted my arms in greeting. I strode toward old Steamboat Ed. "What joy to see you alive, sir. Now our great work will continue."

But the senior pupil, Boston Charlie, stepped between us. He pulled the aged Modoc aside. "You don't talk to a bloody Jew!"

I reeled, as if from a palpable blow. The others stood huddled, not ten feet away. "Attention! Pioneers! We must not delay. General George, our co-worker, has been bitten. It is he who must become our first human subject. Yes! Our own sweet boy!"

The others stonily stared. Bacon Jack crossed his arms over his chest. "A curse on thy barbarous art!"

Priestley Bill: "Ye canna be a true-blue Scot, Mister-r-r Pinto!"

"What can you mean?" I protested. "What are you saying?"

"Avaunt, traitor!" cried Humboldt Johnny. "Turncoat! How dare ye abandon a' your wee laddies to the dungeon's grim confine!"

Now I understood! The youths thought that in order to save myself, I had left them to their fate. It was a misunderstanding. "*Nein!* Here is falsehood! I went up for the diving suit. Then I returned for General George. To save him! Kepler Jim! My pupil! Protégé! You believe me. Speak to the others!"

The young surgeon started to speak, stammered, stopped: without a word he turned his back on his mentor. One by one Newton Mike, Paracelsus Max, and the others did the same. Elbow Frank was the last in line. With his single sleeve he wiped the tears from his cheeks, his lips, his chin. "Och, Mister-r-r Pinto! We loved ye like a very brother! Why must ye prove the faint-hearted knave?" Then he turned from his teacher, too.

What more could I say? What more could I do? With the wounded child in my arms, I stepped from under the hoist works; then I made my way past the excited Yrekans, the mourning Modocs, and down the slope of the hill.

CHAPTER FIVE

Paradox of Zeno

1

THE FIRE AT THE NEPTUNE proved to be the most serious mining disaster of gold-rush California. No one could prove what had caused the conflagration. One theory was that Cole, in attempting to blast through the remaining barrier of stone, had planted too massive a charge. Another was that Townsend's gunpowder, meant to illuminate the daguerreotype of the great event, had somehow touched off a pocket of gas, that is, the quartz dust and marsh gas released by the decomposing timbers. What the newspapers wrote was that the mine owner, buried now in the bowels of the earth, had literally dug his own grave.

Whatever the cause, the calamity did not end with the start of the new year. The underground forest fire — thousands of board feet of timber, acres of the Siskiyou firs — continued to burn day and night. Finally, at the end of the first week in January, Matt Cole decided to seal off both the main and the ventilation shaft. With no oxygen entering from above, and with the reservoir still draining to the lowest levels, it would be only a matter of time before the flames were extinguished. How much time? Days? Weeks? Months? This much was certain: the interval would be too long for those trapped in that oven to survive. Even if the refugees found a cool layer of air, they must starve long before the newly plugged shafts could be reopened.

And was there a soul left alive? No one knew. Save for the mine owner himself, all of the white men — Cole, Piper, Steele, Poland, as well as the reporters and a handful of tourists — had escaped unscathed. Of the Modoc miners, half had been killed outright in the crash of the cage. Dozens of others, including the chief of the tribe, Washboard Bill, were missing. It was on their behalf that Two-Toes Tom led his policemen to what was left of the hoist works. They were armed with axes. Scimitar Sal had his curved knife. Hooker Jim had gotten hold of a musket-type gun. They refused to allow Cole to set off his charges. Another three days went by. During that time Gill agreed to lower a number of veteran miners into the shaft. Those Modocs tied themselves at fifteen-foot intervals to a rope attached to the winding drum. Hallooing, waving their torches, they disappeared into the smoke-filled shaft like a living chandelier. There was no response, no reply, nothing to see. That night the Indian police withdrew. Then Cole exploded his black powder on ninety-foot fuses. The fate of anyone below was literally sealed.

Thus it was that from the underground inferno, only a single casualty had been brought to grass: General George. From the beginning, however, I numbered my ward among the dead. The reason, of course, was that there was no longer any vaccine to protect him from the virus already circulating in his blood. All the digested cords, every acid-filled bottle, had been destroyed. Nor did I place any hope in the manufacture of a fresh batch. Our animal tests had shown that the patient must be inoculated with the weakest dose immediately after having been bitten, with a delay of no more than thirty hours. It would take one week to produce a rabid subject, and another two before its spinal cord was ready to use. I knew only too well that young Christie, who had been bitten no more severely than the Modoc boy, had come down with symptoms in just twelve days. Mathematics told against my fragile friend: he must succumb to the disease before I could begin to treat it.

Must? Issue decided? No hope of appeal? General George, after all, was no rodent, and of a different race, even, from poor Christie with his tray of type. Who could say whether the same rules, the same timing, would apply? In any case, there was nothing to lose in making even a quixotic attempt. Thus, in the slop-shop cellar, amid heaped-up dry goods, I began my final test. The rabies virus came from the same batch with which, only one week before, I had inoculated the now deceased Caesar. The spinal cord was provided by one of the Bosworth family cats. The blond-haired twins held the new subject, petting it, caressing it, while I pressed down the ether-soaked rag. They continued to stroke that plump tabby even while I opened a section of skull and dripped the contents of my syringe directly onto the surface of the animal's brain.

That trepanation took place just before dawn of January 2, 1860. Six days later, the fat feline began to limp, to hump its back, to spit, viper-like, strands of venom. That was the sign for Antoinette to lead in the same goat, old now, and gray-whiskered, that she had brought to the slop shop years before. In the style of my ancestors, I slit the animal's throat, then cut through the four chambers of the stomach in search of the juices that might — just as the milk from her udder had in the past — save the sickened boy.

The cat died on the afternoon of January eighth. Minutes afterward, I placed a cross section of its spinal cord, the size of a slice of spring carrot, into a frothing whiskey bottle. Two days later, January tenth, at four o'clock in the afternoon, I deposited a second such disk in a similar manmade stomach; and two days after that the third wafer, a thin round of rubbery tissue, began steeping in its acid bath. By then I could no longer avoid posing one of the most difficult of all my many queries. "Question —" Polly was with me, and so was Nan: but I was doing no more than thinking aloud. "On what date must we begin the process of Pintoization?"

The answer, seen one way, was simple enough. January twenty-second. That was when the attenuation of the virus would be complete. From another perspective, however, this response, conservative and correct, bore the greatest risk of all. For each passing day meant that the germs of infection were moving nearer the seat of the nervous system. In animals the virus could be allowed no more than a day and half's head start on the vaccine. Our sole hope was that the allowable gap between infection and inoculation might be wider in the highest of species. It was folly, however, to assume the treatment could succeed after a delay of three full weeks. Prudence dictated haste, not hesitation. Was it not possible that in a human, as opposed to a hound, a hare, the potency of dose might be increased — perhaps by a third, perhaps even a half? Could I not strike a compromise between the two incompatible needs — to shorten the time, to weaken the virus? Thus I might begin the treatment on 15 January, when the first dose would be one week old. In just three days!

But when those days passed the debate was not done. There sat Dumb George, hale and hearty. The bite marks on his skin, the myriad wounds and scratches, had healed with hardly a trace. Even the hair pulled from his scalp was being replaced by a fuzz of new growth. How could I inject such a healthy fellow with a virus that was, at seven days, half alive? I put off the inoculation. On the fourteenth day, when the virus had turned entirely to vaccine, I found myself wrestling with a new, yet more vexing question:

What if the bats had not been rabid?

In other words, what if the inductive method, the teachings of Sir Francis Bacon, had failed us? There was no denying that in reasoning from the particular — the various deaths from hydrophobia on the fourth level, the absence of visible wounds on the victims, the rumors of a black bird, a vulture — to the general, the assumption of an animal carrier of the virus, we were taking a calculated risk. If, in fact, the order Chiroptera, family Vespertilionidae, proved as innocent as *Rattus norvegicus,* then the dread situation I had found myself in just three weeks before would be reversed. Instead of being confronted by a case of rabies and no means to cure it, I would possess a vaccine without a disease.

On the cold, clear morning of January 22 I set out for Mount Etna. My goal, insofar as I had one at all, was to find a plainnose bat, living if possible, dead if not. Even old Neptune, plodding along beneath me, must have known the odds against finding such a creature. The shafts were closed and the workings flooded. But was it beyond the realm of possibility that one or more of the flying mammals had made its way from the poisoned atmosphere of the cavern to the upper air? Perhaps — such was my hope — its black corpse lay shriveled and frozen somewhere about the surface of the mine.

We searched, Neptune and I, the greater part of the day. The tailings lay white, drifting, swirling in the wind, like sand from a dune. The hoist works were deserted. The shaft beneath was completely clogged, as was the ventilation column on the far side of the reservoir rim. The reservoir itself had drained away. The bottom, still frozen solid, was covered by hoarfrost and, here and there, the jagged chunks of ice that had remained from the surface of Etna Pond. We walked slowly among these white boulders, which seemed to thrust up like iceberg tips. No sign, anywhere, of the rabid bats. Near the center of the lakebed was a five-foot-wide crevasse that extended to within forty yards of the northern rim. I dismounted. This was the crack through which the waters had drained. I stared downward. The sun, overhead, lit up the yawning walls. Far down, dozens of yards, perhaps hundreds of feet, I could just make out the hard granite that covered one of the underground caverns. I shuddered. It was like a stone slab rolled over the top of a tomb.

I returned to the slop shop in mid-afternoon. There was General George, at play with Polly and Nan. The lad was staring at a giant apothecary jar that had been filled to the brim with buttons. His bulging brow was wrinkled, but from concentration, not worry or pain. Already his eyes had begun to roll, trancelike, up into their sockets. His hands, his long, thin fingers, were beating on the cellar floor. Polly, all eyes, all ears, followed the course of the drumming.

"Three thousand!" she cried. "Three thousand and seven hundred and —"

Nan leaned forward. She had also decoded the message: "And forty-nine!"

With a laugh the twins jumped up and seized the fat jar. It weighed as much as either of them. General George rose to help. The three children poured the glistening buttons like a stream of minnows from the bowl. In a pearly puddle they spread over the floor.

From my spot in the doorway, I watched this playful scene. I did not move a muscle. In the presence of my flesh-and-blood boy, so healthy, so happy, all thoughts of bats and caverns and rabies seemed nothing more than the broodings of an evil dream. How could I think of injections? Inoculations? Of puncturing that smooth, delicate, unmarked skin?

"It's a miracle!" Nan shouted in glee. "He knew! He made the calculation!"

All three of the children were throwing the buttons about them. Polly cried out as well:

"What a wizard he is! We counted last night! He guessed the right number!"

The next thing I knew the bony arms of the boy were clasped about me, about my waist, and then, when I knelt, about my neck.

The child's thin lips pressed to my flesh. Again and again, on my cheeks, my chin, my forehead, I felt the feathery touch, as if General George meant to shower me with as many kisses as he had proved, through geometry, through triangulation, there were mother-of-pearl buttons in the transparent jar.

Yet all the while I knew that, with proof or without, the time had come to act. I waited until nightfall. I waited longer still. Then, in nightcap and nightdress, taper in hand, I descended the stairs to the floor of the shop. I walked to the trap. I climbed down to the cellar. Anyone looking on would have thought that I, all atremble, sweat-covered, was the feverish patient. My heart, like the pendulum of Galileo, swung against the walls of my chest. There General George lay, on his back. His chest rose and fell in calm, peaceful sleep.

Lined up on the crate of nankeen trousers was the row of whiskey bottles. I chose the first, aged fourteen days: hence harmless. I drew the contents directly through the airtight cork into the barrel of my syringe. Next, on tiptoe, I moved to the sleeper and leaned over the still, frail form. The abdomen was half covered by a cotton blanket. The skin of his chest, like the membrane that had once covered his skull, trembled from the pulse beneath it. The child's mouth hung slack. If only — this was the terrible thought I now entertained: if only mucus were pouring over those lips and a bubbling foam covered the tongue. How easy, how free from doubt my task would be then! Monstrous notion! Horrid wish! But is there a person alive who would blame me? True, the first injection held no risk. And perhaps not the second. But what of the third — and even more, the fourth, the fifth? Above all, what of those yet to follow, which would contain more living virus than dead? Here was a dilemma: if I carried out the treatment, *I might well cause, not cure, the disease!* But if I failed to act and the virus was in fact boiling in the Modoc's bloodstream, *I would be no less the killer!*

The boy's eyes, I saw, had opened. They were not those of a maddened dog, red, clouded, squinting. Under the long curling lashes these pupils, so dark and deep, so limpid, reflected the candle flame.

"Ho! Ho? Awake? Non-sleeper?"

Dumb George nodded.

"You understand why I have come?"

Slowly, gravely, the boy nodded again.

"Correct! I wish to offer congratulations. Three thousand, seven hundred, forty-five. Astounding achievement, sir! Gold star! Well done!"

The sleepy youth smiled. He reached up to embrace me. Drowsily he drummed against my cervical vertebrae. I felt the pads of his fingers playing upon my neck. Forty-nine. Not forty-five. And again, lightly, sleepily, the correction: *forty-nine!*

I put down the unused syringe. I climbed the same steps I'd just come down.

Here was my coward's compromise: at all times we would maintain a full complement of treated cords, beginning with one that had been steeped in stomach acids fourteen days; should General George display the least symptom, we would begin the series of injections. So it was that my subterranean cellar came to resemble our underground lab. Each week we killed one cat, even as we opened the skull of another. The bottles, all carefully labeled, were lined up against the walls. Whenever a specimen was held for more than two weeks, it was destroyed and a fresh section of cord inserted and corked.

Thus did the winter of 1859–60 go slowly by. The cold days, the cold weeks, passed, one after the other. There was never a cloud in the sky. But just as the sunshine of one day does not preclude a storm the next, so the continued healthiness of our patient could not help us predict whether he was indeed free of the scourge, or whether this robust spell was only the period of incubation.

Meanwhile the Modocs spent the cold weather inside their shanties. They ate what food they had dried before the mine collapsed. Only a few slim threads of smoke rose from their quarter. There was no wood, no charcoal to burn. Once, at night, the Modoc police set a huge blaze. The fuel was the mining tools, the picks and shovels and axes that the tribe would not need again.

Nonetheless, Cole had not abandoned hope of reopening the mine. He was only waiting for spring to pump out the drifts. He encouraged Gentleman Jack to persuade his people to return to work. The new chief tried. Again and again he exhorted the mourning Modocs, telling them of the new village that would be built over the old, with solid buildings, glass windows, and a school for the children. "We gonna have progress. We gonna be same as white feller here. We gonna have a herd of horses. Make a sum of money like what I got. Everybody gonna have horseshoe vest. Ain't alla men equal? Gonna work in the mine and make a what-you-call-him: *investment!*" But the Modocs remained in their tin-topped shacks, huddled about their fitful fires. None of the miners would agree to return to what had become, for the whole of the tribe, a giant sarcophagus.

Then, at the thaw, in the middle of March, two things occurred, both on the same day. It seems that Matt Cole had been walking along the muddy bed of the old Etna Pond, near the north end of the jagged crevasse. He'd heard, from the depths of that abyss, a crack, a knocking. At first he assumed this was caused by the drip of melting ice on the top of the underground rock, which still radiated heat from the fire. Yet these sounds, the pattern they made, came from no natural source. Immediately he called up the white men from the town. Lying flat on the half-dried lakebed, the Yrekans, myself among them, could hear the rhythm: three raps, a pause, three more.

"A code!" Poland exclaimed.

Judge Steele said, "A signal!"

Everyone shouted, "Survivors!"

Immediately Gill dropped a plumb line. The cable struck rock at 282 feet. The fissure extended to the top of the third level. The north end was almost over that cavern's abandoned stope. Gill made a further calculation. The volume of the lost water would indeed fill the hollow, honeycombed excavation to approximately that height. It was not inconceivable that a group of miners, retreating before the rising tide, could have found themselves in the cavern one hundred yards below where we now stood. With both shafts obstructed, with the waters still climbing, they would have had no choice but to haul themselves yet higher, scaling the pillars, chopping handholds in the sheer face of rock. Of course the atmosphere, with whatever lethal gases were in it, would be forced upward as well. If the men reached the very top of the chamber, where any pocket of oxygen would be trapped under high pressure, they might be able to breathe.

"But for ten weeks?" asked Arch Osborne. "In the pitch dark? In the heat and the damp?"

"*Ja*," said I, adding a question of my own. "And what would they eat?"

Gill came forward, with the hoisting cable looped under his

armpits. "I'll go down. If there are miners alive, we've got to let them know they've been heard."

The Yrekans lowered him over the side. He carried a lantern and three heavy wrenches. At the two-hundred-foot level he began to bellow, to shout. No response. The tapping went on as before. He descended another fifty feet. The rock beneath him glowed like charcoal. He dropped, one after the other, the three metal tools. When the clanging echo died away there were a few seconds of silence. Then the tapping—only it was a pounding now, a frantic beating and banging—resumed. When Gill came up the skin of his face was as red as a lobster that has been plunged in a pot. "Did you hear? They answered! My God! Seventy-four days! Alive!"

The only question now, we realized, was whether these victims could remain alive for seventy-five days, or seventy-six, or for however much time it would take to bring them out. There were only two ways to save them. The first was to blast open the ventilation shaft and pump out enough water to allow access to the level on a three-hundred-foot line. The trouble was, the pumps alone would take a week or more to do the job. Worse, more dangerous, if the men were just above the flood line, the debris from the explosion might force the waters high enough to dislodge and drown them.

The other approach would involve tunneling through the roof of the cavern, directly above the spot where the miners had taken refuge. The problem facing the rescuers, of course, would be the same one that had plagued all drilling operations at the Neptune Mine: heat. No man could work at the temperature generated by the rock, which was actually glowing, incandescent, and no explosive could be brought near its convex surface. If the problem was familiar, so was the solution. The Modocs. Already the long-silent mine whistle had started to blow—not the long blast that called the men to work, but a repeated howl, a hooting. And the Indians, as if they had instinctively understood the meaning of the alarm, responded. By the time I made my way to the foot of the butte, the first of the tribe, the spectral, emaciated veterans, were already starting upward. Neptune and I rode toward town, against the stream of miners. I strained for some sign of my pupils, the scholars, the Academicians. But there was not a single top hat, or a half-squashed stovepipe, in that gaunt and haggard crowd.

The second event occurred that very night. In the early evening a warm rain started to fall. Needle-thin at first, it swelled as the night went on. Finally it came thundering down. Sitting at my slop-shop accounts, I listened to the rattle of the storm against the tin roofs of the walkways. Suddenly I leaped upward. A thunderclap had sounded. I waited. Almost at once a second bang, a clatter, broke out. Now I ran toward the trapdoor. To my ears, these thunderclaps, the boom of them, the echo, seemed to come from the depths of my building and not the clouds. I rushed down the steep ladder steps. There, undressed, stood General George. He was beating upon the same tin tub in which he had bathed as an infant.

"Was ist das hier?"

Alack! What we had was all too clear. With this roaring the child was attempting to drown out the constant drumroll of the rain, beating — or so he imagined — directly upon his boiling brain. Poor boy! Dear fellow! There were too many raindrops to count.

No time to think now. Already I was moving to the crate on which the bottles of vaccine stood. I filled my syringe from the fourteen-day vessel. On my face, beneath the thin lines of my moustache, was — I felt it, I practically saw it — a bitter smile. My wish, my perverse prayer, had been granted. All doubt was indeed removed. The bats had been rabid, every one.

I turned about. My fear was that the sight of the syringe, or of the liquid within it, would bring on a fit. But General George — he had upended the washtub over his head, like an oversized helmet — stood stock still. From under the tin rim of his hat his eyes peered, unblinking. Then the tub fell with a clatter. It rolled, on its side, away. For a moment the sick boy stood, rubbing his ears with his wrists. Then he lay down; he placed his hands upon his chest.

I approached him. I knelt. I could feel the heat rise from the flesh of his belly. I could see his eyes, with their dancing pupils, follow the course of the needle and syringe. I paused, with one finger aloft.

"Ho! Ho! The method of Sir Francis Bacon has not failed us after all. Does this mean we may be certain of what is to come? Are we justified in continuing this experiment? Let us consider the interesting issue of doubt in science. Of course you remember what I have told you about the great day in the city of Boston, the day when Dr. Warren decided to operate upon —"

Now the lad raised a finger, too. He placed it upon his lips, in the worldwide symbol for silence. Then, with his other hand, he reached out and gripped my wrist. He drew the needle to him, guiding it under epidermis and dermis. His eyes grew wide. The hair on his head was matted.

"My chick!" I cried. Then I pushed down the plunger. The vaccine entered the bloodstream of my son.

2

All the questions I had asked in my life came down to a single one: would General George live or would he die? There was little I could do to determine the answer, save, each night, repeat the cellar scene. On March 15 I gave the second dose; on March 16 the third. One week plus four days to go. Would my patient endure till then? Would I? To my dismay I found the treatments harder, not easier, to administer: not only because it was increasingly difficult to find, on the bruised and bloated flesh of the abdomen, a spot to place the needle, but because I knew that each new dose was more virulent than the one that had come before. March 17: dose number four. March 18: number five. How much longer, I wondered, could I go on pouring this pus, the poison, into the patient's swollen and tender belly?

What could not be denied was that each day the patient was growing more ill. Hiccups wracked him, as if his body were being lashed by an unseen whip. The classical indicator, the abhorrence of water, the spasms at the very sight or sound, became manifest, too. The boy's larynx twisted in visible knots. There was danger of suffocation. And a greater threat still: dehydration. As these symptoms steadily worsened, I never left my foster child's side. On the night of the nineteenth, when I had to deliver the sixth dose, aged hardly more than a week, I slept in the cellar, on a thin layer of cotton. All the next day I could hear above, in the shop, Polly and Nan and Antoinette moving about. They were not the only ones keeping a vigil. The Yrekans, all the regulars from the Sazarac Saloon, dropped by to ask about the child they had named. Nor was the case a secret from the Modocs, who lingered in groups of four and five on the Miner Street promenades.

The night of the twentieth marked the crisis. In the dark I could hear Dumb George on the far side of the cellar. A clicking sound came from his dried-out throat. His fingernails, and his toenails too, clawed continuously at the skin of his body, as if the poor sufferer felt himself under insect attack. Fearfully I rose to administer the dread seventh dose, which contained more lethal, living virus than dead and digested cord. I approached with my candle, my syringe. The light, which usually made the patient shy back, or even go into spasm, had no effect. His enormous eyes stared upward, black and unblinking, like the blank button eyes of a doll. Quickly, so that my own tears would not fall upon him, I gave the injection.

An hour, a second hour, went by. In my sleep I could hear, just above me, the heavy boots of the Yrekans. Strange my sensations: I knew I was having a dream, yet my heart turned to ice within my chest. I rose and, in my nightgown, my curled slippers, climbed the ladder to the floor of my shop. Here were the Yrekans, indeed. A mob from the Sazarac Saloon. They whirled upon me. They threatened. They accused. They wanted to put me under arrest.

"Arrest, friends? And what is the charge?"

The crowd closed around.

"Murder!"

"We know you grow those germs!"

"You tested on a human! A living person! A boy!"

My head was spinning. My heart pounded. A thought, dark and bitter, came into my mind. Someone had betrayed me! Then a contrary thought, defiant, proud: what of it? Was that not the fate of every man who sought to advance the cause of science? The great Harvey had been persecuted, his library burned. Galileo himself had been tried by the court of the Inquisition. "Ho! Ho! And who has sought to inform against me? I will defy him!"

Then the white men pointed to where, in striped pants, in starched shirts, the Pioneers of Progress were standing. Joyfully I strode forward to embrace them. To my persecuters I cried, "Excellent! Here are my colleagues! They will tell you: I used the germs of rabies to produce a vaccine. Like the famed figure of Jenner!"

Imagine my horror then when the dearest of my pupils, and the most talented too, scowled like a Pawnee and pointed a finger at my chest. "Wicked man!" said Kepler Jim. "Ye hae given the foul brew to our bonnie babe!"

Now the mob surged forward. A dozen hands reached to seize

me. They tore my nightshirt. They twisted my limbs. All were shouting at once:

"He did it!"

"He poisoned the Indian boy!"

"Killed young Christie, too!"

"That's how the plague got here! He brought it!"

"He'll poison the town!"

I dropped to the ground. The Yrekans surged over my form, kicking, spitting, beating. It was as if all of us, the group of men, their immigrant victim, had been picked up by the winds of a sudden storm from our town in modern America, from this thirty-first state of the Union, and whirled backward in time and space to an ancient village in Spain, in Germany, in France, where the population believed it was the habit of Jews to poison the wells and use the bones and blood of children in unspeakable rites.

Suddenly the crowd drew back, and I opened my eyes. I was, of course, in the cellar. It was still the middle of the night. Before me, as naked as the day he was born, stood General George. The light, the single candle, fell on his skin, his delicate bones. I dared not move. The boy, teetering, tipping, took a step toward me. What held him up? What moved his limbs? His translucent ears jutted from the sides of his top-heavy head as if they were balancing it, the way wings steady a hawk, or sails an unstable ship. Then he raised his arm, thin as a pencil, and pointed to the wooden crate, atop which sat my cold mug of coffee.

"What is it? What do you desire?"

Even if the boy had not been a mute, his dry throat, the desiccation of his vocal cords, would have made it impossible for him to answer.

"Ein Kaffee?"

The boy slowly nodded. This was stranger, far, than any dream. Instead of fleeing from the liquid, flinching at its sight, this rabies patient was actually requesting that I bring it near. I rose to do so. My fingers trembled more than his when I handed him the brimming cup. To my amazement, he raised it toward his lips. His hand remained steady, even though, as I could see, the bands of muscle in his throat contracted, like twisted leather straps. Then the spasm relaxed, and slowly, with deliberation, Dumb George drank the liquid down. So thin was his body, so frail his frame, that I thought I could see the dark fluid pass like a shadow through his throat and esophagus, pooling at last in his belly.

"*Mein Gott!*" I whispered. "Cured!"

My patient heard me. He nodded. He smiled. Then he crossed to his pallet, lay down upon it, and fell into an easy sleep.

No sleep for A. Pinto! In mere seconds I was up the ladder and out the slop-shop door. The crisis had passed! The strong doses had taken! The remaining injections would make him well! The world must hear of it! Even an hour's delay, a minute's, meant unnecessary suffering for other, unknown victims. In my slippers I loped down Miner Street to the intersection. I dashed onto the boardwalk in front of the *Ingot* building and began to pound on the bolted door. No one responded. I pounded again. Then a voice sounded from overhead. Sid Christie's. I backed into the street, and stared up to where the editor leaned from his upper-floor window.

"Who is it?" he asked. "What do you want?"

"A message, sir! For your telegraph operator. To the *New York Herald,* the *Chicago Tribune*! Also the *Prager Tagblatt*! Where is young Moffet? Attention! This is what he must send: *Miracle in Yreka! Cure for rabies found! Test on human successful!*"

The window above me slammed shut. Had Christie heard me? Did he believe me? Was he sending the word? I cried out once more:

"This is a scientific fact! The first person to survive in the history of the world!"

No reply. Only stillness. And darkness. It must have been three in the morning. The peat lamps were out. Even the Sazarac was shut for the night. The only sounds came from the north, on the breeze. There, on Mount Etna, the miners were working around the clock. The top of the vault, the glowing stone, had not cooled enough to use explosives. Nor had anyone been willing to take the risk of blasting open the shaft. What I now heard was the rescuers digging into the ventilation column by hand.

No! There was another sound. Closer by. A buzzing. I looked around. Nothing to see in the darkened streets. Still the hum came. I glanced upward. Above my head a moonbeam seemed to glitter in thin air. It was the telegraph wire! The buzzing, the humming, came from the twin strands that, starting at the *Ingot* building, looped away southward from pole to pole. Moffet! He was sending my message! Eagerly I ran to the first of the stout oak masts and placed my ear against it. The wires were singing right through the wood. They reverberated with the dots, the dashes of the earthshaking news. I ran to the second pole, and then off to the third. Still the ringing, the buzzing, the whine of the wires. I staggered off further, while my mind raced far ahead of where my legs could take me. I imagined the scene of astonishment at the end of these moonlit lines. Even now the people of Marysville, of Stockton, of San Francisco must be dancing in the streets. Soon whole populations would be making merry in all the capitals of the world!

Onward, southward I stumbled, following the sagging, silvery strands. Soon I found I had left the town completely behind me. Yet the further I went, the louder the hum became. Finally, in open country, among the sage, the bitterbrush, it seemed to me that the lines sighed with the sounds of syllables, of whispered words, as if the magical instrument were capable of sending actual human voices:

Our Fadder . . .

Heart pounding, I ran full speed toward where the next pole reared from the ground. Round that firm base, with their hands clasped under their chins, knelt the pious Christians: Shacknasty Jim and Shacknasty Jake, Big Ike and Humpy Joe.

"Our Fadder . . ." Shacknasty Jim began again. Once more he halted, looking around.

Humpy Joe nudged his companion with his elbow. "Pssst! *In de oven!"*

Shacknasty Jake: *"Hollow Ed your name!"*

I saw then how the raised eyes of every convert were fixed upon the great looming pole. At once I understood. These simple folk believed that the mast, with its horizontal bar, was the cross on which their Savior had suffered, and that along its wires they could hear the whisperings of the Holy Ghost. Seeing the tears in their eyes, the way they rocked back and forth in fervent supplication, I could not help but smile.

"Attention, gentlemen," I called. "This is of course a primitive superstition."

Big Ike, with his ears sticking out, his jaw hanging down, turned round. "Gotta pray for General George!"

Humpy Joe: "Make him fit like a fiddle!"

Shacknasty Jim: "Put him inna pink!"

"Aha! Do you not know the news? Your prayers have been already answered! But not by the supernatural, not by heavenly powers. *Nein, nein!* It is man himself, through the experimental method, who has performed this wonder. Here we see at work the principles of Galileo, not the powers of the Galilean!"

"Goddam!" said Shacknasty Jake. "Dumb George ain't gonna die lika dog?"

"Do you doubt me? Look! There are the lines. Listen! That is the code of S. F. B. Morse."

All the Indians burst out laughing. Humpy Joe said, "Crazy feller, you betcher! Ain't nothing but wind!"

I looked up. Could it be? Had the message been merely the hum of the wires in the blowing breeze? If so, what was this clicking? For now, plain to all, the lines had begun clacking away, much like the noise from a telegraph key.

Big Ike stood, cocking his head to listen. The sounds, a regular clatter, grew louder. They seemed to be coming from the direction of town, the way I'd just come. The converts rose, staring into the gloom.

Shacknasty Jim: "I see him! Some kinda bird maybe."

Shacknasty Jake: "Damn fool brudder. Got to be maybe some kinda horse."

The sound drew closer. A hazy shape, with feathers, but four-footed, galloped out of the night. Then Big Ike started to laugh. "Ha-ha! Porcupine, you betcher!"

Humpy Joe: "Pincushion maybe!"

Now the beast came within reach. It was bucking, rearing, and shaking its head.

"Hee-hee-hee," laughed the Modocs.

Hee! whinnied the stricken creature in response. *HAW!*

Neptune the mule! Covered with arrows! They stuck in her ribs, in her croup, in her flanks. The shafts shook in the air.

"My dear!" cried I, dashing to her side.

The old nag turned toward the familiar voice. I saw at once that her halter had snapped: she had bolted. But who had pursued her? Who had shot the barbed missiles into her flesh? The answer, the only one possible, chilled me through. Redskins! Modocs! My building was under attack! Instantly, with a surgeon's skill, I plucked a handful of arrows from Neptune's back, and leaped upon her. Then I dug my hands into the coarse hair of her mane and struck my slippered heels into her flanks.

"Onward, you sweetheart!" I shouted. "Faster, you darling!"

The steed leaped forward. The feathered sticks still at her sides might have been Pegasus's wings, so lightly did her hairy hooves skim over the ground. The converts fell back, and were left behind. The night parted ahead. How we raced along! The tassel of my cap, the black brush of Neptune's tail, streamed backward. The stout oak poles flashed by. Not even the copper wires, which rose and dipped and once more rose between them, could have carried a message more swiftly.

The town, into which man and mount galloped, was still dark and deserted. We pulled up in front of the slop shop. I dashed across the walkway and through the door. The interior of the store was empty. A single light shone up from the cellar below. With another bound I was at, I was through, the gap in the floor.

Two Modocs were in the cellar room. One of them, Scarface Charlie, was near-naked, his body painted in swirls of red and black. The claws of an animal were braided round his arms. Sharp teeth hung in a necklace at his throat. The other redskin was Two-Toes Tom. The old man seized my arms. With surprising strength he pinned them behind my back.

"Where is he? My sweet boy!"

Neither savage uttered a word. But a choking sound, a gagging, came from the far side of the room. I strained to see. The child's body lay in the shadows, stretched on its back. For an instant, a nightmare moment, I thought that his corpse was being devoured by a wolf. A furry form was crouched there, with its long snout buried in the skin of the boy's swollen belly. Then the animal snorted and lifted its head. It was an Indian! Curly-Headed Doctor! He was wearing, stretched over his scalp, his shoulders, the pelt of a coyote. Spellbound, stunned, I watched the medicine man. Once more he made the gagging sound, while clawing at his throat. Next he shook his double heads. Were those his own ears or those of the animal that were twitching? The howl that now rose: did it come from the man's throat or out of the stiff, whiskered mouth of the hide?

"Stop, sir!" I shouted. "What have you done?"

But the ceremony was not yet complete. The medicine man fell once more on his victim. Snarling, growling, he attacked. It seemed he wanted to gnaw the entrails beneath the skin.

"Are you mad? Are you a monster?"

With that cry I broke free of the old Indian's grasp. I started forward, only to halt, frozen in fear by the sight that met my eyes. Beneath his furry hood, the lips of Curly-Headed Doctor were bright red, smeared with a ring of blood. Then they spread wide, and out of the mouth's dark cavern there spewed bright gobs of vomit. Next the medicine man reached into his own throat and withdrew some small squirming creature: a tiny toad, it looked like, or a salamander, or newt. The Modoc, grinning, held it up in his hand.

"Goddam! Goddam!" That was Two-Toes Tom. The old man was pointing at the evil amphibian. "Sucked out the bastard! Goddam Modoc doctor! Best doctor! Ain't gonna be rabies now!"

Curly-Headed Doctor gave a howl of triumph. He set the poor little creature on the cellar floor. Then, before it could hop, he stamped on it with his foot. Tom rushed forward. He joined in. The two of them danced in a frenzy on what remained of the source of contagion.

By then I had already arrived at Dumb George's side. The boy wasn't dead. He was living. Nor was there so much as a scratch on his body. For a half of a second I thought the primitive cure had been achieved. Then the boy raised his head. His wide black eyes were open. He stretched his arms toward me, his foster father.

"*Nein. Nein. Kein Problem.* Do not worry. It is only a trick. Here is a charlatan, a humbug, as in the carnival show. We have here not true science."

But the boy's eyes stared past me. They grew even wider with alarm. Turning, I saw the reason why. Scarface Charlie had moved to the crate of nankeen trousers which supported the seven remaining bottles. His upper lip, because of his scar, was raised in a smile, or a sneer. "This stinking *Indian* boy! This goddam *Modoc* feller. No Jew doctor gonna put white man medicine inna Dumb George!"

"No! No! No! No!"

Over and over I howled out this word. Scarface Charlie seized the corked bottles. Before I could take a single step forward, he began to hurl them — the eighth dose, the ninth, and then the five yet remaining — against the walls. The last of the vaccine spilled down the fireproof brick; away it foamed, onto the cellar floor.

3

Hope! What a thing it is! Like a worm! Cut it and cut it and still it will grow. Principle of regeneration. The suffering of General George, each new seizure and symptom, only confirmed what I already knew: my lambkin, by *Liebchen,* was doomed. At the end of each fit, however, during every fresh period of calm, I thought that my patient might yet be cured. After all, no other rabies victim had lived more than fifty hours after the appearance of symptoms. The Modoc, smiling, nodding, with his heavy head propped against my bedroom wall, had already survived more than a week. What else could this mean but that the series of doses I'd managed to inject had proved sufficient to retard the spread of the disease?

Yet no sooner had I persuaded myself that the painful spasms were not going to recur than the child would once more jerk his head left and right, and claw at his itching skin. Down I plunged, into the black pit of despair: for there was no denying that each new attack was more acute, more frightening, than any that had gone before. In the midst of one such fit the boy chewed at the meat of his hands. After another he tore every stitch of clothing from his body and began to rub his little male member, which had sprung erect, first against the bookshelves and then like a dog against the leg of A. Pinto, myself, his horrified mentor.

That last attack, unlike the others, did not entirely pass. General George remained in my bedroom, atop my bed. Instead of sleeping, he rocked for hours, his fingers pressed to his ears — either to steady his lopsided head or to muffle the myriad sounds of the outside world, where the least whisper seemed like the whirling blade of a buzz saw. The next seizure was even worse: the throat muscles clamped tight; each breath creaked deep in his chest; saliva ran from his mouth and off his pointed chin. The patient, too weak to stand, crawled on the floor, moving about the furniture like an infant who had not yet learned to walk.

It was then that I had a providential thought: the child's trail through the room was not as aimless as it seemed. I looked close at the sweat-covered brow, furrowed with thought, and at the eyes, whose pupils were rolled up in their sockets. I heard the rap of the knuckles against the planks of the floor. Why, the lad was counting! Counting what? I watched him crawl from spot to spot, object to object. Legs! The legs of the bed, four; the legs of the table, four again; and the chair legs — knock, knock, knock, knock, times two — eight altogether. What followed? The legs of the rolltop desk and its three-pronged swivel chair. Then the boy clasped my own two limbs and, after that, squeezed the two thin sticks of his shins. There was a pause. Then Dumb George rapped out the final sum: *twenty-seven!* The fit ended. Counting, the old preoccupation with numbers, had been the cure.

Minutes later, with my patient tucked back in bed, I stole downstairs to prepare a pudding of rice. My idea was to recreate the game two of us, infant and Israelite, had played long ago: counting the raisins in our delicious dessert. Perhaps by this means I could trick the boy into having something to eat. The fact was, day by day, even moment by moment, Dumb George seemed to be wasting away. In the course of the last week his features — the thin-lipped mouth and paperlike ears, the chin jutting further and further toward the bulging forehead — had come to resemble those of a sideshow Punch, or the profile of the man in the moon. My fear was that the patient, unwilling to swallow, unable to bear the thought of water, might die of starvation before he could recover from rabies.

After some time I marched back upstairs with the steaming, Vienna-style pudding. The dark specks of fruit floated on top.

"Question: how many currants are there within the bowl?"

The patient lifted his pale, pinched face; he draped one of his matchstick arms over my shoulder. I felt the distinct pressure of a finger pressing nine separate times against my skin. "Nine? Nine? Shall we see? So. *Eins* and *zwei* and *drei* . . ." With each new figure I spooned up a single raisin and placed it in the boy's gaping mouth. The ninth was the last. "*Wunderbar! Prima!* What a smart chap!"

Alas! There was a sudden clatter from the boy's chest, as if each of the raisins were a stone rattling down a drainpipe. Then he grimaced, pulling his lips back from his foaming gums. A new fit was coming on.

"Next question!" I hastily interposed. "Let us suppose we take a single grain of rice. This one. Here. In the spoon. And then suppose we place it in your mouth. So. Good. Capital! And swallow it! Ah! Ah! Gold star! Then with the second bite we double the amount. How many will we have? Easy! You see? *Zwei!* And after that, doubling once more, the third spoon will have how many grains? Eh? *Vier!* Too easy for you! Let us skip to the seventh bite: how many grains then? Too many, do you think, to fit into the spoon? So? Silence? No answer? Are you a Modoc? Or moron? Can it be you do not know?"

Stung in his pride, the boy forced his fingers — the ring finger for units, the middle for tens — to drum out the answer upon my neck, at the base of the skull.

"*Vierundsechzig!* Head of the class! And now, how many rice grains to fill up the spoon for the bite that comes next?"

The trouble with this game, with its simple equations, was that the meal was done all too soon. Then the smooth bowl, reflecting the lamplight, and the spoon, jangling against the side of the dish, seemed to attack his eyes and ears. The muscles in his tiny neck rippled. He seemed to gag on his thickening tongue. Another seizure.

"Oh, poor Neptune! Such sore feet she has! What cracks in her hooves! Solution: new shoes. But I cannot afford to pay for the nails. What? Cannot pay? For just four shoes? With only eight nails required for each? Making — come, come, you know this, answer me: how many in all?"

The boy, recovering, tapped his fingers lightly at my nape.

"Correct: *Zweiunddreissig!* But here is the difficulty. Mr. Arch Osborne wishes to charge for the first of these nails a single penny. But for the second nail he demands two pennies, four pennies for the third, and so on and so forth, up to the last nail of all. Question —"

But there was no need to ask the sum. Already the boy was massaging the back of my neck with all five fingers: in only a minute I discovered that I was in debt to the liveryman for more than forty million dollars.

By then I had grasped that a new problem had to be set the instant the old one was solved. "Question," I began, already breathless at the magnitude of the sum I was requesting. "How many pennies must I give the blacksmith if I order nails for an extra set of shoes?"

The happy boy flung both arms around his parent. It felt to me, while Dumb George raised the number two to the sixty-fourth power, as if my cervical vertebrae were a kind of keyboard on whose bumps the musician was playing a wild fantasia, a Hungarian rhapsody. Minute followed minute. The mathematical Modoc kneaded and drummed. At last, feeling, fumbling, as if he were reading from the system of the Frenchman L. Braille, the lad delivered the total in twenty digits. Then, drained, he collapsed on my chest. I, the Old World native, could feel the Indian's heart surging against my own. That fitful pulse gave me a new idea.

"So. Attend, please. Let us assume that the heart beats once each second. Let us also assume that a certain gentleman lives out his allotted three score and ten. More precision: seventy years, seventeen days, twelve hours, and two minutes. Question: how many times did this gentleman's heart beat during his lifetime?"

It took the distracted boy the better part of an hour to find the answer, which he calculated to be 2,210,500,920. As soon as I received that sum I jumped up and began to dance crazily upon the floorboards. "Error! False total! Ho! Ho! Ho! Too much by millions, hundreds of millions! Dunce cap for you!"

General George, his face now as ashen as mine, crookedly smiled. He beckoned me to the side of the bed. Leaning close, I saw, with dismay, the reddish glint in his eyes. A saliva strand ran from the side of his mouth. With two bony fingers the boy signaled seventeen. I grasped then my mistake. "Ho! Ho! Apologies! Pardon! I have the leap years foolishly forgotten!"

In this manner more days went by. I hardly slept. I hardly ate. Neither did my charge. The two of us lived in a haze of roots and powers and logarithmic tables. I had long since concluded that in order to avoid another seizure, not only did one question have to follow immediately upon another, but each succeeding problem had to be more difficult than the one previously set. Thus, after determining how many days a balloon moving at 3878 feet a minute would require to go round the planet, General George calculated how long it would take light, which traveled from the sun to the earth in eight minutes, to arrive from the nearest fixed star. Yet the minute he gave that figure — it was six years plus four months — the mathematician again bent to his task, reckoning the dimensions of a cubical bin that would hold eight bushels of malt.

All too clearly we two, man and boy, were caught in a vicious circle: the more complex the question, the less strength available to work it out. Obviously we could not continue. Just as obviously, we could not stop. Even the least pause threatened to bring on the fatal fit. Indeed, during the few seconds it had taken these very thoughts to pass through my mind, the Modoc had begun to thrash restlessly about. Two tears, one from each eye, ran down the cheeks of the lightning calculator. When they touched his lips the cords in his throat contracted in a painful spasm. His eyes bulged. He gagged. He was choking to death! Aghast, in anguish, I stumbled to the bed and took the child in my arms. Then I began to speak, pouring the words, as if this were a kind of trepanation, directly into the Indian's ear: "So. My *Liebchen.* My Leibnitz. Imagine now a clock. Yes: one of our brass alarms. Do you see it? Yes? Look: the hands are straight up. One is atop the other. Ho-ho! Hour of twelve! Twelve o'clock! Question: when will these hands next be so exactly aligned?"

A wrinkle of concentration appeared on the brow of the poor wasted child. His eyes, with the eyeballs rolled up, turned marble white. I shuddered. It seemed to me that I could make out every bone in my patient's body, along with the dark lines of the arteries, the tangled, twisted veins. While the wan wizard performed his calculations, I crossed the darkened room to the shuttered window. I had no idea of the solution to the puzzle I'd set my student. I brought my pocket watch toward the dim lines of light that came through the slats, so that I might, through this mechanical means, discover the answer. The timepiece had stopped. No movement. No ticking. The hands of the watch read a moment past three. Three in the morning? Three in the afternoon? I knew neither the time nor the date, nor whether it was now day or night. All at once, as if a spring in the instrument of my own body had snapped, exhaustion overcame me. My mind went blank. I leaned against the closed window, unable, in my weariness, to do the sum of two plus two.

How long did I remain in that swoonlike state? Impossible to say. Gradually I became aware of a warm, gentle touch. Sunbeams, much like the boy's fumbling fingers, were pushing through the slats and falling weightlessly upon my skin. I turned. I drew the shutter aside. The sun was rising. Here was the dawn of a day I wished would never arrive. If only the sun could be stopped in its tracks, so that time, like my watch, might stand still! Suddenly my mind went back to a similar moment of weariness, of despair. It was when I had tried to convince old Lewis that we would never reach the shores of Europe. How could we succeed in crossing the whole sea, I had asked him, when we must first cross the half, and then the half of that, and then the third half, *ad infinitum*? On that occasion, outside our basement room, the sun had been high in the sky. My partner had said it was the start of a bright day.

With fresh vigor, I whirled about. I called to my patient, my pupil. "Hola! Look here, sir! I have a new problem! The last I shall set you! The last you must solve. Paradox of Zeno!"

Across the room, at the center of the mattress, the stricken boy was frantically signaling the solution to the riddle of the clock: *One hour, five and five-elevenths minutes.* I was struck dumb to see how, from hiccups now, the frail body was shaking. With each of these tremors there was a rattling gasp, a sharp inhalation, and the membrane of skin covering the breastbone bulged outward, as if the heart within were hurling itself against that bolted door. I knelt beside the bed. How cruel was this unnatural picture we made: the pupil more aged than the teacher, the shriveled child beside the youthful sire. I gathered my strength to speak:

"Let us say that here, in the town of Yreka, during the next Independence Day celebrations, a great race is held between a tortoise and the fleet Achilles, bravest of all the Greeks. So. The tortoise will begin just here, outside our window. Achilles comes to the line at the eastern end of Miner Street, in front of the Hotel de France. Thus the tortoise, family Testudinidae, has a lead of one thousand feet. So? Understood? All is clear?"

General George nodded his top-shaped head.

I resumed. "Now Zeno, disciple of Parmenides, wishes to gamble on the outcome. He maintains that even if the swift-footed Greek should race at ten times the animal's rate, he will not catch him. Not only that, he will never reach even the starting line of the tortoise, opposite our fireproof building. Question: do you wish to accept Zeno's challenge?"

Gleefully General George nodded again.

"So! Let us see what occurs! The haughty Achilles takes his position. Is this not the conqueror of Hector? Has he not been dipped in the River Styx? The poor old tortoise also toes the line. On your marks, gentlemen! Ho! Ho! The pistol shot! They are off!"

The little lad, red-eyed and trembling, was panting from excitement, as if he, too, were running the race. I leaned from the window, as one might from one's seat at the course.

"So! So! The tortoise begins: he stretches his neck; he lifts his leathery leg. But what is that light? The leaping flame? It is the golden-haired Greek! He flies like the wind! Like the arrow from the bow! Already, in fifteen seconds, he covers a third of the distance between them. But remember: this is a mortal, not a god. Thus he begins to tire. In the next fifteen seconds he covers only a sixth of the ground, and in the fifteen seconds after that but a twelfth—and so on, my dear, and so forth, a twenty-fourth, a forty-eighth, until either the race or the runner is done. First question: who wins the bet? The philosopher or General George?"

A pause. I prodded. "Come, come, my darling, my *Dummkopf*. Has Zeno won?"

With great effort the boy shook his head. He lifted his arm, pointing to himself.

"Aha! So you are the winner! That means you must answer question two: how many seconds will it take the runner to reach the starting line of the reptile?"

Another pause. Slowly, clumsily, the ailing Indian began to work his fingers — pulling one digit, another, a third, then using all ten at once to make a rapid beating motion, a drumming sound. Now my thick, cracked lips broke into a triumphant smile. *I* had won the wager! The vicious circle was broken! For here was a problem with no solution at all. Zeno was correct. As long as the first, and fastest, fraction of the course was less than half the total distance, Achilles could not finish. Even if he ran for as many years as it took to destroy the city of Troy, he could never quite come two thirds of the way to his goal.

Neither, therefore, could General George! The two of them were on a perpetual treadmill, the Greek unable to plant the final foot, the Modoc the last decimal point: *.66666*. With a sigh of relief I looked back toward the bed, where the boy was merrily cracking his abacus of knuckles and thumbs. It was he, the Indian, who was the real winner — not Zeno of Elea or Pinto of Pressburg. As long as he was preoccupied with the infinite figure, the disease would not seize him. Thus, as Achilles had found his Homer and would live forever in legend, so Dumb George had his Hebrew, who, in making him the first man to survive the scourge of rabies, had given him a kind of immortality as well.

Suddenly, from afar, there came a dull clang, a single thud. At the same time, as if an unseen spirit had seized them, all the items on the open desktop — the pens in their holders and the cap on the inkwell — began to rattle, while the crescent-shaped blotter rolled back and forth, as if drying an invisible message. From the north came a second crash. Now the whole room became animated: the unoccupied chair swiveled on its hinge, the shutter slats clacked, and the porcelain plate, the tin cutlery, danced on top of the square pine table. Indeed, the only still object in the room was the unmoving form of General George. The boy lay abed, his old man's mouth slack, his black eyes unblinking. Impossible, under this assault of sound, the deafening thuds, to keep the tally.

"Was ist das?"

Again I ran to the window and leaned well out. But I knew what this was, had known from the fall of the very first stamp. The Neptune Mine was once more at work. The batteries were crushing the stockpile of rock, of ore. Why, then, did I look off to the north with such horror? Because I never dreamed, after the mine had been sealed, that I would hear those sounds again. It was as if the dark smoke should pour from the shiplike smoke-stack, and the great wheel turn round, long after the ship itself had run aground. Nor was there life aboard — only, in the hold, below the water line, a heap of corpses.

"Ein Geisterschiff," I said to myself: a ghost ship. With a shiver I turned from the bright glaring light of the morning sun. I walked to the bed. Bending, I took the shrunken body of the child — question: what has shape, volume, mass, but is weightless, as light as air? — into my arms, I hugged the boy, drawing the sharp-featured face against my own. Then I began to pace, aimlessly, in a random motion, from corner to corner, from wall to wall. *"Eins,"* I whispered. *"Zwei, drei . . ."*

What do you suppose I was counting? The time, in seconds, that Achilles must spend in the race? The repeated thud of my heartbeats, or that of the iron-clad stamps? Perhaps I was merely adding the number of months, June 1850–February 1851, between the time I had lain with Queen Mary and the birth of — here was simple arithmetic, a sum for nine fingers — my son. Or I might have been performing a feat of higher mathematics, excelling Euclid himself. No matter. Not important. Allow me to pace up and down until long after the morning light turns to plum-colored shadows, and then to the dark of night; let me square the circle, find the last digit of pi, or discover the proof of Fermat's final theorem, $X^n + Y^n = Z^n$: still I could not answer the riddle of General George, the coldness of his body, and why his fingers, so quick, so clever, so nimble, were now clamped together in a stiff and inextricable knot.

4

On Mount Etna the rescue workers, unable to open the ventilation shaft, had turned their attention to the stone vault at the bottom of the crevasse. While the rock remained too hot to attack directly, Gill thought to work it with machines. It had been his idea to dismantle the frame of one of the stamps and then reassemble the battery directly over the curved surface of the buried stone. Of course no camshaft could be made to work at such length. Neither could any of the flexible belts stretch the distance. But one of the flat lift cables was welded together in an enormous loop, which hung down to the gears. This vertical band was turned by a second battery which had been hauled to the edge of the fissure and was itself activated by a series of horizontal belts. The fall of these five-hundred-pound stamps, driving onto the underground granite, was what I, and Dumb George, had heard the moment he died.

Nor did the sound abate. Thudding and pounding, shaking the slop shop from basement to bedroom, the stamps continued for two days more. I did not, in that time, venture outside. Nor did I bury the boy. South of town, I knew, near Hardscrabble Creek, was a cemetery. But before I could bring myself to make that short journey, the Modocs — Scarface Charlie, with Two-Toes Tom and his men — returned. They wanted to take General George to Wigwam, to the sacred ground where the ancestors continued to dwell. I was too numb with grief to protest. What did it matter where the shell of the child was buried?

It was only after the Indians had departed, bearing their tiny burden, that I stretched out to rest. For all my weariness, I did not fall asleep. Hour after hour I lay, while the springs of my bed, and the bedstead itself, yes, and the very floor and walls and ceiling, shook and trembled — in part from the distant fall of the iron weights, in part from the sobs that wracked and wrenched and twisted my earthly frame.

Yet I must have dozed off after all, since I woke with a start to the sound of a whistle, a wail. The mine! The alarm! One blast followed another, a howling, a hooting. Something had happened. One thought, a mad one, filled my brain: there had been a mistake! General George was alive! He had only been in a coma. Now he had awakened: to smile, to walk, to make his lightning calculations on the back of my neck. A mad thought? Not at all! Was this resurrection any more far-fetched than the idea that miners could survive in a tomb, without light, without air, without sustenance, since the first of the year? I leaped to the window. In the dark streets men were running about. Could that mean that the Indians were bringing him back? I threw on my frock coat. I donned my Mexican hat. I raced downstairs to join them.

The minute I opened the door, Ruggles, the Sazarac barkeep, came running along the walkway. "Pinto!" he shouted. "They need a doctor! They're about to take the miners out of the rock!"

A great crowd, white men and Modocs, had collected atop Mount Etna. I pushed through, to the bed of the pond, to the very edge of the crevasse. Below, on the domed rock, the stamps had fallen silent. By the light of tule torches I could see that a kind of station, a horizontal ledge, had been carved out of the soft fissure wall. There, some fifteen feet over the arch of rock, a number of rescuers, Indians all, squatted. They were waiting for the iron bucket that would haul them to the surface, two at a time. I looked about. All of Yreka seemed to be gathered on the reservoir rim. The Modocs stood nearer, on the far side of the crack. In the light of the flickering torches I saw Elbow Frank, Paracelsus Max, and then the whole group of my Angus lads. Before I could call out across the gap, Cole took my arm.

"The tapping has stopped," he announced. "No sound for over ten hours. We don't dare waste a moment more. There are medicines and bandages down on that ledge. Water as well. That's where we'll bring the wounded. Are you willing to go?"

"*Ja!*" I declared. "Willing!"

The two of us, Cole and I, went down in the same bucket that had just brought up the last of the workers. From our perch on the ledge I could see that the stamps had sunk a diamond-shaped pattern of holes, each a foot and a half deep, in the exposed patch of rock. They were like the holes of a trepanation bored into the hard bone of a skull. Far above me, I could see the black sky, and the featureless faces of the watching crowd. Heat radiated up from the smooth granite — too much heat, surely, to think of inserting a charge in the bore holes. But how, without powder, with no saltpeter or sulfur or charcoal, could the stone be shattered?

Just then Cole pointed upward. Between the two walls of the crevasse the iron bucket was descending. It was filled not with men, or medicines, but with chunks of ice. For a full minute it hung over the rounded dome of rock — long enough, at such temperatures, to turn the frozen element to liquid form. Then, from his spot a hundred yards higher, the invisible hoistman drew taut the cord that was attached to the bottom of the giant pail. Slowly it tipped. The cold water poured directly onto the center of the diamond pattern. Recklessly I leaned from the ledge, watching the way the icy sheet spread over the convex granite surface, streaming into each of the deep, angled holes.

"Watch out! Get back!"

With that shout Cole pulled me aside. Simultaneously there was a tremendous clap, a sharp report. For an instant I feared both halves of our narrow canyon had come crashing together. But no: there was now a loud sound of wind, an eruption, and a blast of foul air swept both Cole and myself against the inner wall of our earthen shelf. I knew what had happened: the freezing water had cracked the hot stone. The trapped air, all the underground gases, had thus escaped through the passage. Indeed, so great was the pressure that the gale still whistled by.

Now I drew myself upright. Out of the gap in the granite, objects came flying. They hurled overhead, against the canyon walls. For a single mad moment I feared that the bats had been released from their secret nest. Then this hurtling matter began, like a sack of tumbling sticks, to rain downward — into the iron bucket, against the rock, onto the ledge. I picked up the nearest thing. A bone! An ulna! Bones were coming out of the earth!

Then something larger, darker, whirled by, landing with a thump just to one side. I shuddered. I hardly dared look. This was black, wrinkled, leathery, the size of a human head. Could such a thing be? At the front something glinted, like the pupil of a single eye. But nothing, after the last few days, could daunt me. I seized the charred specimen. It was the Voigtlander! Its box, its bellows, its lens! At that very moment the rush of air abruptly ceased and a human person — with hollowed face, with scrawny neck and spare, bony shoulders — appeared in the ruptured rock. Frank Townsend! His eyes were shut. His mouth hung open. But he lived: his sunken chest rose and fell, and his skinny arms beat up and down, up and down, as if he had not grasped that there was no longer a need to continue signaling for help.

For a full moment my old comrade remained trapped, half in and half out of his stony grave. What was the obstruction? Why did he not climb into the empty bucket? I could not help but imagine a chain of Indians, each desperate for light, for air, clinging to the feet of the daguerrian. Then, with a sucking sound, the trapped man pulled himself free. The obstacle, all too clearly, had been his own belly, which hung grotesquely distended upon his otherwise shrunken frame. No victims came with him. Nor did any appear in the rock's gap. At the surface, the Modocs began to call down to their missing comrades. They shouted. They hallooed. No response, only a fading echo, came from that empty tomb. Silence, then. The only sound in the whole of the narrow canyon came from the creaking caldron, which, with the potbellied white man inside it, rose slowly upward through the stale, stinking air.

A half-hour later I too reached the top. I saw that the whole of the tribe had gathered at the center of the pond. Standing before them, in the glow of the torches, was Townsend's white, unclothed body. At the distance, in the leaping light, he looked — with the sticks of his arms still striking up and down over the stretched, swollen skin of his belly — like a man beating a drum. To the Modocs, however, he must have seemed an indestructible force, a terrible spirit, the devourer of their people. Before this god the savages and scholars fell to their knees.

END OF BOOK TWO

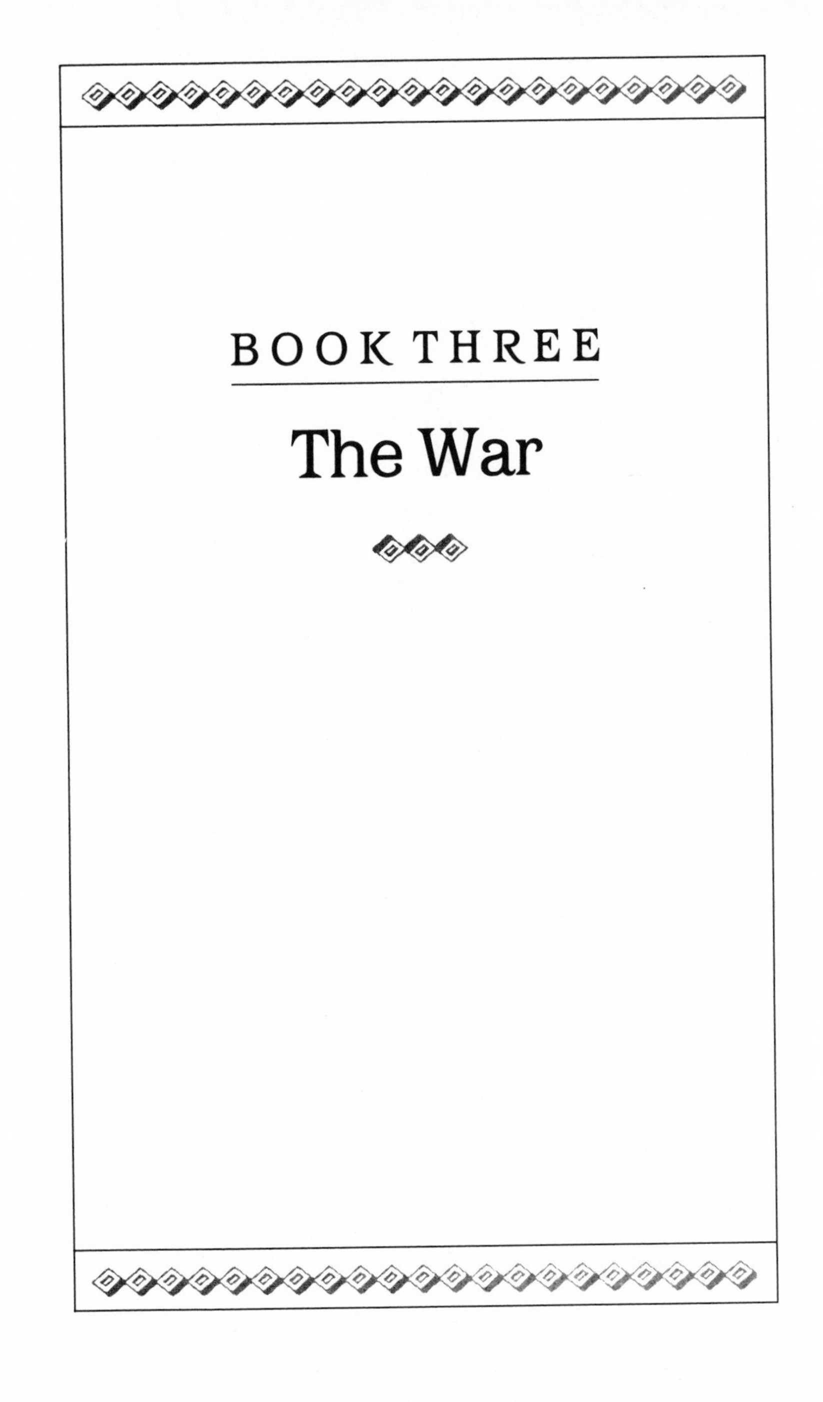

BOOK THREE

The War

BOOK THREE: THE WAR

CHAPTER ONE

Ghosts

1

MANKIND HAS ALWAYS BELIEVED that great events, such as battles, or cataclysms, will be preceded by telltale signs. That is why in ancient times the sages marked the path of every comet; and why, too, during eclipses the Indians of America shoot flaming arrows at the darkened sun. Primitive peoples are not alone in these superstitions. Christians, for example, maintain that a new star appeared at the time their Savior was born. Even in modern California, grown men swear that animals can sense a coming earthquake, and that before such shocks foxes and coyotes and even mountain lions will descend from the foothills to stalk the streets of the towns.

What portents did we in Yreka possess to warn of the coming war? The only visible signs were the columns of smoke, three altogether, that hung in the sky through that spring, into the summer. The first, of course, was familiar: the thin, hazy line, the faint smudge, that rose from the top of Wigwam. That was far off, on the eastern horizon. Then, to the south, snowy Shasta vented a plume of steam that stretched to the upper realm of the atmosphere. Last, close to hand, a cloud of dust, a mist, billowed over the top of the long-extinct mound of Mount Etna. Unlike the pulverized quartz to which we townsfolk had grown accustomed, this powder boiled up from what had become, by mid-May, the hard-packed bed of Etna Pond. When the Modocs danced there, shuffling around in a constant circle, the dust rose from under their feet, as finely ground as the ore beneath the iron stamps.

The Yrekans, however, needed no heavenly signs. By the summer of 1860 there wasn't a man among us who was not thoroughly alarmed by the actions of the natives on earth. The first disturbing thing was what they did *not* do — that is, move back to Modoc Town. Instead, the whole tribe remained in the cracked crater of Etna Pond. They put up shelters there. They built fires for cooking, for warmth. Food was brought in by my former students, the Pioneers, who, as in the days of old, scavenged for field mice and ground squirrels and brown-furred cottontails. Clearly the Indians wished to be close to where so many of their comrades were entombed.

Most of the white men might have been content to let them remain had it not been for the dancing. This unnerved them. It was like nothing they had seen or heard before. There was no music. There were no drums. The dancers wore no special costumes, nor did they paint their faces. Strangest of all was the silence: no one sang; no one chanted. The first indication that the dance was under way would occur sometime after noon, when the churned-up dust rose over the rim of Mount Etna. Some people claimed they could hear the thud of the dance steps, the crash of the left foot, the drag of the right. They said the pounding rhythm troubled their sleep as the fall of the stamps never had. The ritual went on all night and into the following day. Sometimes it would last into the second night as well. Only when the dance had stopped, and the last puffs of powder had blown clear, could we hear the far-off wail of the squaws. It was a song in an unintelligible tongue.

Naturally, people wanted to see the performance for themselves. Gentleman Jack agreed to lead a group of us to the reservoir rim. From there we saw the entire tribe — the braves, the squaws, the broken-down veteran miners — moving, with that peculiar left-footed thrust, the right-footed drag, in a clockwise circle. To my dismay, I saw the Disciples of Bacon in the midst of the dance. More startling still was the figure in the center: Townsend, seated, a blanket over his shoulders. His thin arms still jerked up and down, as if he were beating the rhythm on the stretched skin of his belly. I ground my teeth and put my hand over my mouth to stop myself from calling out to my former partner. Was he a captive of the natives who danced around him, or was he the conductor of the dance?

On and on, for hours, the mute, staring Modocs continued their slow revolutions — until they at last began to drop. Whenever that happened those still in the circle closed the gap, reducing the radius, until only a handful remained on their feet. These, the hardiest, clustered about the seated shaman. Then they too collapsed to the ground, and the long ritual came to an end. Imagine the horror among those of us spying from above when the women, lying face down on the soil, began to writhe and wail. Their voices, deep, unearthly, filled us with fear. It was as if they were speaking to those beneath them.

Odd as it sounds, this notion was not far from the truth. Once we had returned to town, Gentleman Jack explained that the squaws only seemed to be lying on the bottom of Etna Pond. Their souls, or so the Modocs believed, had traveled more swiftly than a skip cage to the underground drifts and caverns. They were not speaking to the dead: rather, the words they chanted, the very voices in their throats, belonged to those fathers, husbands, brothers, sons, who lay crushed within the Neptune Mine.

And what was the message these oracles sang? The young chief could translate the glad tidings. The dead miners were returning. Families would be reunited. Everything would be as it had been once before. The tribe would return to Tule Lake, where the braves would fish and hunt. The gold they found, all the pretty nuggets, would be worn round their necks or their ankles or in their hair. When would the dead be raised? Soon. On the big day. The Fourth of July.

"Ha-ha-ha!" laughed Gentleman Jack. "Goddam Modoc are a helluva ignorant people. They mix up day of independence from jolly King George! Mix him up with day of what-you-call-him: *judgment!* How-you-say-it: *resurrection,* you betcher! You smart white fellers gonna laugh at fool ideas!"

What Jack, with his flashing gold tooth, the gold horseshoe vest, neglected to tell us about the new religion was our own fate. For not only would the dance restore the miners to life, but all the intruders on their land, on both sides of the Oregon-California line, from Happy Camp on the west to the lava beds in the east, would disappear. There would be an earthquake, a volcano, a flood. Then a great tide of mud would sweep over the land, the way, in washing — and here the Modocs would make the appropriate gesture — one hand slides over the other. Only the white man's property, his horses, his tins of food and bottles of whiskey, the very bullion locked in the mine, would be left behind for the people to enjoy.

All of this we heard from the Indians themselves, who now began to act as if these goods were already theirs for the taking. Toward the end of May the Modocs began to leave their camp on a series of raids. They rustled sheep and cattle and brought them back to the bed of the pond. Arch Osborne found a mare, still alive, though an arrow had been driven with such force through her flanks that she was pinned to the post by which she'd been standing. Then the Kittle and Moffet stage was surrounded by members of the old Indian police — Rock Dave, Split-Lip Sam, Scimitar Sal. They forced down the passengers and the driver. Sardine Frank climbed up to the box. "Ha-ha!" he laughed, as he gathered the reins. "Alla you white feller gonna sink inna mud. Make you black like nigger!"

The ranchers, indeed the whole town of Yreka, sought retribution. After each incident, Cole made good the loss. He knew he needed the Modocs if he hoped to reopen the mine. What he bought with his money was time. "We have only to wait out the month. The Fourth will come. Nothing will happen. Then the tribe will move off and we'll seal the crack with black powder."

The question was whether the Yrekans could wait until July. Each day the Indians grew bolder. After every dance they would saunter into town, usually in broad daylight, and seize whatever struck their fancy. In the Sazarac, and the Blue Wing, too, the former beggars climbed over the crowded bars and poured out tumblers of liquor. They would depart with full bottles under their shirts or in their arms. At the slop shop the coughing miners helped themselves to velvet waistcoats and cotton caps, while the squaws wrapped up in calico. A number of Modocs made for the restaurant at the Metropolitan Hotel. Two braves — these were the Shacknasty brothers, Jake and Jim — walked up to the square table where a couple were having dinner, sat down in the two empty chairs, and ate up the three-course meal. An even stranger incident occurred at Professor Bosworth's, where Polly and Nan woke one morning to find old Steamboat Ed fast asleep in their bed.

To these developments the Yrekans were too stunned to respond. The behavior of the tribe was worse, more brazen, than in those far-off days when Jack-a-Dandy had supplied them with alcohol. But these Modocs were not drunk: they were enchanted. They thought the ritual dance at Etna Pond had given them the powers of the dead. Thus they could move among the citizens as invisibly as ghosts, and — this was more ominous than any tales of erupting lava, whirlwinds, floods — as invulnerably, too. No wonder the Modoc police swaggered down the promenades, three abreast. They held their hands up to shade their eyes, as if blinded by the light of their vision: an army of miners, in the white armor of their bones, streaming up through the dark crevasse. By these shining warriors the Modocs were protected. It was the white men, mere flesh and blood, who had to scatter from the shaded walkways, into the choking dust of the road.

As the Fourth approached, the tension reached a crisis. On the butte the dancing never ended. The Modoc women and men remained in a constant stupor, a trance. All day long the dust cloud hovered over the top of Mount Etna, like the unmelting snowcap on Shasta. Down in Yreka the white men were no less frenzied. The bars never closed on the night before the big celebration. Most of the men were drunk, or near drunk, before Independence Day dawned. That is part of the reason why the festivities — the parade, the brass band, the demonstration by the fire brigade — had more than the usual amount of patriotic fervor.

All the excitement of the day, together with the pent-up emotions of the last several weeks, came to a head with the Cornish wrestling. Here Ruggles, the Sazarac giant, was pitted against Poland, with the Free-Soilers and Abolitionists supporting the former, while those with Southern sympathies rallied behind the husky sheriff. The white-maned Bosworth was supposed to serve as umpire for the bout. When he gave the signal each wrestler gripped the other by the forearm and the cuff of his linen coat. In less than a minute the Cornish rules disintegrated into catch-as-catch-can. The two men rolled in the dust of the street, kicking and clawing. One bit the other. Each gouged at his opponent's cheeks, his eyes. Then the adherents of both men joined the fray. They swung their fists and hurled bottles at the heads of those in the opposing camp. The brawl spilled down Main Street and onto the promenades. A window shattered. A porch support snapped in two. A streamer of bunting billowed down onto the backs of the fighting men.

No telling how long the donnybrook might have lasted, and what the casualties might have been, had not, at that moment, from the east end of Miner Street, a gunshot rung out. Was this a squib? A rocket? The start of the fireworks display? Not at all. In the fading light of the afternoon, Ben Piper stepped from the walkway in front of the Hotel de France. The barrel of his rifle was smoking. Back at the intersection, the citizens froze. They watched while the sharpshooter crossed the street to the sheriff's office and knelt over his victim's body. Then everyone ran to where Piper had shot Scarface Charlie through the lungs.

"Pinto! Pinto!"

Once again it was I who had to answer the call for a physician. By the time I reached the scene the wrestling match seemed to have resumed — only this time the crowd was pummeling the Modoc's prostrate form.

"Nein! Do not touch him! You will kill him!"

With those words, I pushed my way through the mob. Kneeling, I used my fist, wrapped in a handkerchief, to plug the wound. But the blood boiled from the poor fellow's mouth and nose. He was drowning in the liquid.

"Look at that!" someone shouted. It was Kane, the faro dealer. "Look what the redskin stole!"

All turned to the Modoc's plunder. The thief had not taken, as he had years before, meat from the butcher, a brace of quail.

"Guns!"

"Those are guns!"

True enough. The Indian's spoils — two rifles, a short-barreled carbine — lay beside him.

Piper leaned on his own smoking weapon. "I thought this would happen. I knew it. That's why I watched Poland's office."

"Listen!" Jeff Ruggles held up his hand. The crowd of Yrekans drew in a collective breath. From the north, from the butte, we could hear, we could feel, the stamp and thud of the Modoc dance.

"My God!" said Osborne. "We been fools!"

"That ain't no religion!"

"No dance for ghosts!"

Sadly almost, the publisher, Christie, shook his hairless head. "It is no rain dance, either."

Judge Steele spoke now for us all. "It's a war dance! It's been a war dance all along! Tonight's when they mean to attack!"

There was, from the crowd, a convulsive movement. They all closed on Scarface Charlie, kicking at him, pounding him with the butts of their guns.

The sheriff called them off. "Leave him be, boys! It's the rest of the tribe we got to worry about. This one's a dead man already."

Accurate diagnosis. When the Yrekans pulled back, no breath remained in the body of Scarface Charlie. The Indian's head was twisted downward, so that his chin touched his chest, which shone with dried blood, like the peel of a candied apple.

What frightened me about the Yrekans was not their drunkenness, their rage, but, on the contrary, their coldness, quietness, sobriety even. Not that they were no longer drinking. The men, more than a hundred now, closer to one hundred and fifty, had crowded onto the floor of the Sazarac Saloon. When they drank it was without a word. Sullenly, determinedly, they waited for darkness to fall.

It was I, the teetotaler, who was reeling with vertigo. I knew my fellow townsmen intended to force the Modocs out of the basin. But what if the natives resisted? There would be shooting. Even if the tribe remained docile, these men—I looked round at the blank faces of the Yrekans, at the wet lips and bright teeth that showed in their beards: they were likely to start the fight on their own. The Indians, caught on the bed of the pond, would be targets that even the tipsiest gunman could not miss. And my children were there! My chicks!

How warn them? Spread the alarm? Impossible to leave through the saloon's guarded doors. Impracticable to send a message. There was nothing for me to do but accompany the column as, less than one hour later, it marched north on Main Street, under the moon and the first half-dozen stars.

The vigilantes did not continue directly to the top of the butte, but drew up first at the site of the charcoal fields. That soil, while no longer glowing, remained warm to the touch. A foot deep, at the bottom of the furrows, the coals remained live. This ash the Yrekans smeared on their necks and throats and faces, as if they had become the painted natives. They even covered their wrists and the barrels of their guns.

Above our huddled army, behind the walls of the natural basin, the Modocs were still at their dance. We could feel the rhythm of their steps through the hard-baked earth. There must have been a fire on the lakebed, because the dust that boiled up over the rim was lit, volcano-like, from below. Now a movement went through our ranks. The citizens started to rise.

Someone, anonymous, in blackface, hissed a protest. "Down. Stay down. The redskins ain't near to finished."

But Arch Osborne countermanded the order. "We got no choice. It'll be broad daylight before that dance is done."

Then the large, dark shape of Poland rose before the posse. "You know what to do. Keep quiet. I'm starting for the far side."

With that everyone began to move off, splitting into smaller groups so as to deploy completely about the reservoir rim. My band moved up the familiar southern slope, past the stamp batteries and the rubble of the gallows frame. At the top we stopped in amazement. There, below us, was a whole Modoc village, with twig huts and cattle and a small herd of stolen horses. The dancers were at the center, moving clockwise around the squatting, blanketed form of Frank Townsend. A bright bonfire burned nearby. In the leaping light the rest of the tribe, the braves, the many squaws, could be seen spread out along the circumference of whatever circle they had been on when they collapsed to the ground. To my eye they seemed like the planted objects in some ancient sundial, or calendar, or vast horoscope: there one read the time, or the year, or the events yet to come.

Would that I could determine what would happen in the next five minutes! I lifted my gaze to the rim above the opposite bank. I knew the militiamen were lying there, as they were about the entire edge of the pond; but, squinting, staring, I could not make out the least telltale glimmer — not the spark of a match, the shine of a button, even the white of an eye. Could the Indians, with their sharper senses, see that they were caught in a closing net, the springing jaws of a trap? Seemingly not: one of the dancers threw up his arms and dropped in a heap to the ground. The others, closing ranks, shuffled closer to the idol at the center. Only he was aware that something was amiss. His arms, poking through his blanket folds, stopped drumming. His head was up, alert.

What he had seen was the advance of the Yrekans. Slowly, like a ripple in black water, the line of men had begun their descent along the inner curve of the bowl. They made hardly a sound.

Weaponless, witless, I moved with them. Now the horses, picketed across the lakebed, started to stir. They tossed their heads. They snorted. The shadowy army was advancing through the herd. Everywhere the armed men had reached the floor of the lake. Some had even begun to march round, or step over, the fallen forms of the dancers.

But the dance went on. The converted Christians were the last to remain on their feet. They moved in a tight, agitated circle about the obscured figure of Townsend. Nor did their movements stop when the ring of vigilantes advanced into the light of the bonfire to surround the shuffling Modocs. Instead it was the white men who came to a halt. They stood, rifles forgotten, mouths agape. They had been frozen by the spine-chilling shriek, the warbling ululation that came from the scores of squaws. All these women became animated at once. They writhed like snakes over the ground. While the Yrekans stared, the Modocs seemed oblivious of the intruders. They crawled by them, right by their boot tops, in their motion toward the center. There the converts, in a frenzy now, jerking spasmodically, suddenly fell away, revealing the straining god at the center.

The militiamen could not help but gasp at the sight. Townsend seemed to be on fire. A light, from which we had to shield our eyes, darted from him. His sweating head was thrown back. His legs, under the blankets, were spread wide. Now the first of the squaws came wriggling to the spot where he sat. She stretched forward, reaching under the half-open blanket, between his parted legs. Then, with a long, low wail, she withdrew what appeared to be the head and shoulders and then the torso of a human figure. It was as if the man had given birth.

A shout went up, a cry of triumph. The prophecy had come true. Here was one of the long-buried miners! The dead were returning to life! Already a second squaw approached the tentlike folds of the blanket. A new light gleamed in the cavern between Townsend's open thighs. He trembled. He groaned. And then, with a shimmer of light, another wraith, the shade of a suffocated miner, appeared. Both these specters now joined the circle of dancers. Each shuffled round and round, clutched to the bosom of a convert.

From the far side of the posse, opposite where I stood, the sheriff's voice rang out. "This dance must stop. Seize them. Arrest the dancers!"

But the Yrekans stood rooted. They stared in horror as a third phantom, and then a fourth and a fifth, seemed to rise from the earth itself and, glimmering, shining, half-transparent, join the circle of the dance. It was I who broke the spell:

"Here are not demons! Here are daguerreotypes!"

Of this I had not the least doubt. These figures of the lost miners, victims of catastrophe, were nothing more than images etched onto metal plates. That, the burnished copper, was what flickered and gleamed in the light of the flames. Townsend, the sole survivor, must have taken the portraits when trapped underground. The whole religion, the dream of reincarnation, the rising of an army of the dead, was nothing more than a trick.

At my shout the dancers, the half-dozen converts, came to a halt. They held the shining metal tight to their chests, like medieval armor, or medieval shields. The sheen on the metal plates was already fading, as the bonfire started to dim.

Just then I noticed, stepping out of the shadows, a new group of Modocs. The Disciples of Bacon! They were still in their stovepipes. The tatters of their striped pants and cutaways clung to their dark, dusky limbs. This was our first encounter since the collapse of the mine. I trembled to hear how they would address the traitor.

"Mister-r-r Pinto!" That was the sharp-faced Newton Mike. "Wha' dunces we be!"

Priestley Bill let out a wail. "They swore the dead would coom back to life!"

Kepler Jim, my protégé, took me by the sleeve. There were creases like a much older person's on his flattened forehead. "They promised fair," he softly said, "and performed but ill."

Then, with tears in his eyes, and on his cheeks too, Paracelsus Max made a query. "Mister-r-r Pinto. Is there, in the system o' Sir Francis Bacon, such a thing as a ghost? A hope o' life after the grim avenger?"

I gave, of course, the only possible answer. "No. No, my dears. Such heavenly hopes are contrary to the laws of nature. That is why we seek, in the realm of science, to build a paradise on earth."

"Bloody hell!" cried Boston Charlie. With his big, bare fist he struck his own slanting head. The others heaved a piteous sigh.

"My sweet sons," I began. "Why so sad? Did you truly expect that all the dead miners would return to life?"

"A fig for the miners!"

" 'Tis na for those men we lament."

"Ah, pardon," said I, suddenly stricken myself. "You have been thinking of our dear colleague . . ." Here, at the thought of the child, of even his name, my Adam's apple began to throb with simultaneous sensations: heat and cold, hardness and softness, as if an ice cube were melting in my throat. "Our colleague, General George."

Bacon Jack shook his head. "The tricklin' tear is na for the sweet silent lad."

Elbow Frank: " 'Tis Hippocrates we weep for!"

Newton Mike: "An' Jenner we mourn!"

"We thought that a' of the lovely litter would be wi' us, waggin' their tails and lolling their tongues as in days o' yore."

"Our bonnie wee pups!"

"Our darling dogs!"

Even as pupils and pedagogue stood thus engaged, a small band of Modocs, led by Curly-Headed Doctor, had edged its way toward where, tepee fashion, a pile of fresh kindling was stacked. From the corner of my eye I saw these natives seize armfuls of wood and run back toward the blaze.

Arch Osborne had seen them, too. "Watch out!" the liveryman cried. "Those are rifles! The devils! They're taking to arms!"

The stable owner was right. More braves jumped up. They seized the guns from their comrades. Others were running for the cache. All were yelling, whooping, shaking their fists in defiance.

Poland, on the north, shouted his orders. "Prepare to shoot! Take aim!"

From all round the ring of vigilantes there was a rattling, a clanking, as the militiamen raised their guns to their shoulders. It was a terrible moment. The white men stood with their cheeks upon the wooden stocks of their rifles. They sighted down the barrels. Surrounded, some fifteen Modoc warriors did the same. The two forces — the one standing in a ring, aiming inward; the other crouched at the center like a bristling beast — confronted each other. Neither side flinched. Neither side moved. Then in clear English came the dread command:

"Fire!"

How long was the pause that followed? A second? A half-second, perhaps? Long enough at any rate for me to recognize the voice: Gentleman Jack! Chief of the Modocs! His people heard him, too. Distracted, they turned their heads to where, atop the southern rim, resplendent in his reversed silk smoker, he stood. In that instant the guns of the Yrekans erupted in flame and thunder.

The roar of the volley echoed about the basin. The smell of powder, like that of a damp, dirty dog, filled my nostrils. From the thick cloud of smoke rose the groans, the cries of wounded men. From far off, at Poland's position, came the frantic call, "Reload! Reload!"

There was, however, no clatter of ramrods, nor the powder horn's snap. As the smoke dispersed, the citizen soldiers stared wide-eyed, bug-eyed, at the center of the field of fire. There stood the Modoc braves, holding their rifles. Not a hair on their heads had been touched. Was it a miracle? Were the Modocs invulnerable after all? No question the militia were mortal. Here and there on the perimeter of the battleground lay a wounded Yrekan. The men, aiming high, had shot each other in the salvo.

Suddenly, simultaneously, it dawned on white man and Indian alike that their situations were now reversed. The vigilantes, for all their great number, were helpless. The Modocs, whose rifles were loaded with bullets, held the balance of power. Once more, from atop the southern rim, came the terrible command:

"Fire! Fire!"

Only then did the Yrekans understand that the order had been meant not for them but for the tribe. I stood frozen, uncertain. Was Gentleman Jack a traitor, as much a turncoat as the garment he wore? But which side was he betraying? His own people? Or the white men, whose very smell he preferred to his own? I stared up toward his silhouette. Nothing to see but the gleam, the glint of gold: from his tooth, from his watch fob, from his rings and jewels. Once more the dread word came echoing down:

"Fire! Goddam! The town! It's what-you-call-him? *Conflagration!* Town of Yreka on fire!"

It was true. How could I have failed to see the glow, like a rosy dawn, in the sky? Not to the east, however. To the south!

Matt Cole called out, "It's the Modocs! The Indian police! They've put a torch to the town!"

Suddenly an awful fact became clear: not one of the followers of Two-Toes Tom was on the bed of Etna Pond. That meant that instead of the citizens surrounding the village, the villagers had taken the town! *We* were the ones who had been surprised!

"My God!" That was the voice of Judge Steele. "Yreka is not defended! There's not a man with a gun left behind!"

At that the whole volunteer army broke formation and ran pell-mell for the reservoir's southern wall. The Modocs ran too, but in other directions. They mounted their horses. They gathered their cattle and drove them up the sides of the crater. The squaws snatched their goods from the huts and dragged their bundles behind them toward the slopes. The tribe was in headlong flight.

I stood stock still at the center. Which way was I to go? With my scholars? I looked round to where the men and women and animals on the walls of the pond seemed like nothing so much as tea leaves washed to the sides of a cup. Or should I dash back to town? The slop shop, a fireproof, was in no danger, but every man would be needed to fight the blaze. Just then, nearby, one of the wounded men let out a sigh, a groan. I peered through the shadows. It was Moffet, shot through the soft flesh of the shoulder. The voices of the other men sounded about me, two, three, four in all. My dilemma was solved. The teacher and shopkeeper must for the moment give way to the healer, the physician.

It was dawn by the time I made my weary way back to Yreka. By then the flames had damaged every third building in town. On Main Street I saw that the porch and gallery that enclosed the two sides of the *Ingot* building had been destroyed, and that the facade was blistered from bottom to top. Further off, I made out the scorched paint of the post office and, across the street, the remains of the row of shops. A group of men were chopping away at the upper floor of the Metropolitan Hotel. Smoke billowed up over what was left of the Sazarac Saloon. Down Miner Street live flames were still leaping. The exhausted fire fighters let them burn.

I sank in the roadway. I could have fallen asleep on the spot. Would that I had! And never wakened! For just as my eyelids, heavy as asbestos curtains, fell over my eyes, some person shook me awake. It was Gill, the hoistman. "Come, Pinto!" he shouted, pulling me to my feet by my frock coat collar. "Stand up, man! It's Goody Bosworth—and the minister, too. We've found them. They've been dragged nearly to death!"

At those words I leaped fully upright and began to run down

Miner Street toward the rear of my shop. Everyone, it seemed, had heard the news. The whole town was running against me, heading west, to where Miner Street turned toward the cut-off that led to the Bosworth land. Suspended above that spot was a smear of smoke.

In seconds I had darted round the brick building to where Neptune was tied. Without a saddle, without reins even, I jumped on the elderly mule. "Go, sweetheart!" I shouted. "That way! Oh, my poor Polly! Poor Miss Nan!"

With a snort, a whinny, the mule galloped off, through the intersection, toward the ominous plume of smoke. As I feared, the minister's chapel had been burned to the ground. Of the adjacent living quarters, only the stone chimney still stood. A score of townsfolk were gathered in its shadow. Gill, mounted himself, was a good way off. He motioned for me to follow, then rode to the south. The trail was marked all too clearly: wagon wheels to either side, occasional hoof marks, and two deep furrows where — it took no keen woodsman or scout to make this deduction — the minister and his wife had been dragged behind. The grim path went on and on, a quarter-mile and more. At some points the twin ditches narrowed to a single groove, as if the trailing victims had managed briefly to cling to each other.

The torture had ended abruptly, at the bottom of Greenhorn Creek. My steed and I, racing headlong, heedless, might have plunged down ourselves had we not been warned by the sound of a single shot. Below, on the creekbed, Osborne stood with a pistol in his hand, having just put one of the two runaway horses out of its pain. The other, its neck broken, was dead already. The buckboard lay shattered. One axle, like a thrown javelin, was stuck upright in the ground. Hard to see how any passengers, much less the victims towed behind, could have survived. I looked left and right, where two separate groups of Yrekans were crouched. The couple, clearly, had been hurled apart by the impact of the fall. Gill was running to the group on the left. I dismounted and stumbled down the embankment to join him.

Here was the former Goody Peacock. Every stitch of clothing had been rubbed away; much of her skin, and one of her breasts, had been worn off as well. I knelt by the raw body. Nothing could be done. There was no more hope than there would be for a person covered with third-degree burns. Indeed, no sooner had this thought passed through my head than the old Harvard servant, with a single sigh, gave up the ghost.

"Too late," Arch Osborne declared.

Some ten yards off there was a disturbance. The Yrekans stood. They backed away. Professor Bosworth had somehow gotten to his feet. His clothes had been ripped off as well, but his skin, though a web of cuts and scratches, was intact.

"Where is she?" he demanded, staggering off in the opposite direction from where the corpse lay.

The others came after. Poland, in a near whisper, asked, "What happened? Was it Hooker Jim? Two-Toes Tom?"

Bosworth suddenly halted, as if he had reached the end of an invisible rope that tied him to his wife. "Dead?"

The bystanders nodded. The minister clutched the white wings of his hair.

Poland persisted: "Rock Dave? Was he the one? What about Sardine Frank?"

Bosworth didn't reply. He remained motionless, his fists tugging at the wild wispy locks that flowed out from above his ears and around the base of his skull. It was as if he thought that by pulling hard enough, he could yet scalp himself.

"We got to know," the sheriff continued. "Otherwise we got to hunt them all."

Someone — it was Gill — came up with a blanket. He draped it over the minister's round, thick-matted shoulders. Suddenly, at the touch of the wool, Bosworth started. He ran three steps. "The children!" he howled. "My girls!"

"Mein Gott!" Before my eyes I saw the gutted chapel, the ruined house, the score of — yes, surely they were mourners: *"Die Kinder!"*

At once Neptune and I galloped back to the burned-down buildings. Among those in the crowd at the chimney I saw my former colleague Matt Cole. The Harvard man came toward me as I slid from the back of the mule.

"We found them last night, while it was still dark. They were in the open, not in the fire. They were not abused. They did not suffer. Pickering's done his work already."

I nodded. Pickering, I knew, was the undertaker. *Pickling* was the joke in town. Cole led me through the crowd to where the girls lay side by side on the ground. A man's sheepskin coat was large enough to cover them both, from collarbone to round, knobby knees. Their hair had been combed and tied with bows. Their lips were pulled back from the gap in their square, bucked teeth. They might have been sleeping, except — and I, a former surgical student, was quick to see this — for the row of sutures that crisscrossed the throat of each. Not just the throat: crouching down, I saw that the neat line of *X*'s went clear round to the back of the neck. At the sight the blood drained from my own head, as if it, too, had been severed by Scimitar Sal's sharp, curved sword.

From far off, it seemed, I heard Cole's voice: "It was quick. Painless. Like a guillotine."

"Such cruelty!" I exclaimed. "Such heartlessness! Here were premier pupils. Top of the class!"

Another of the mourners uttered a shrill shriek of sorrow. It was Neptune. The grief-stricken mule snorted and stamped. With open arms I ran to embrace her. But the quadruped, her dangerous teeth snapping, her sharp hooves flailing backward, was not to be consoled. Trembling, twitching, the poor beast fixed her brown eyes upon the identical shapes, the yellow bows, the flaxen hair, of the girls. Suddenly, as if the thought in her head had been transferred to my own, I knew what was the matter. For a moment I thought I must go mad. I, too, wished to wail, to whinny, to snap my teeth and stamp on the ground. Neptune, sensing my sorrow, trotted forward and draped her hairy head over the shoulder of her two-footed friend. Together we stared at where the undertaker, in error, had sewn the head of one twin onto the body of the other.

Just then, horribly, Gill led the white-haired minister to the scene. The old fellow strode through the mourners to the side of the lifelike Polly, the realistic Nan.

The Yrekans, of course, grew silent at the sight of the old fellow and his daughters. More than one man wiped his tears. Not I, however. No. We two, Hebrew and hybrid, stood at the fringe of the crowd. I strained upward to whisper to the long-eared offspring of the horse and the ass:

"Look, darling. He is nearsighted. A myopia sufferer. All to him is *Dunst,* a haze. Thus can affliction be the gift of the gods. He does not see what we do. Shhh. Silence, sweetheart. It is our secret. No, no, no, no: not a word!"

So saying, I led the beast apart from the spectacle of the minister and his tangled twins.

2

The first battle of the Modoc War was fought at mid-morning of the following day. That's when the Indian fighters, comprising virtually the whole of Yreka, caught up with the fleeing tribe. Since the fugitives had such a head start, the pursuers had had to push through the night. There was no question as to where the Modocs were going: to the lava beds at Tule Lake. The only issue was whether we could catch them in time. Everyone knew that once in those stone passages, the ditches and air holes and cooled-off bubbles and caves, the Indians would disappear, as Charlie Kane put it, "like a hundred ants in a sponge."

When dawn broke after our long night's ride, we could see that the tribe, driving their cattle before them, dragging their goods behind, had not yet reached the eastern edge of the plateau. Their position was marked by a great cloud of alkali dust. Here was the fourth — or, if one counted the black plume of Yreka behind us, the fifth — of the war's portents.

Poland, at the head of our column, pointed out the enemy's position. "At the gallop!" he shouted. "We'll catch them all!"

Our whole troop sprang forward. In less than an hour we could see the actual figures at the bottom of the swirling dust cloud, and in a half-hour more could distinguish the humans from the herd and the warriors from the squaws. The women, leading the rest, were already disappearing over the edge of the embankment. It was clear that if we could but keep our pace, we would catch the whole of the tribe between the plateau and the lava. We would descend upon them, fall upon them, from above. It would be a bloodbath.

What amazed me most was that the prospect of such slaughter caused me not the least anguish. If anything, I felt a certain giddiness, such as a young lady might feel on the eve of her first midnight ball. Was this the well-known follower of the inductive method, the child of the Enlightenment, who now called out to the white men around him, "Hola! Mr. Ben Piper! Mr. Osborne! Matt Cole! No quarter! No prisoners! No mercy!"? Perhaps the voice was at a higher, shriller pitch than normal. Perhaps, too, because of the bone-bruising vibrations caused by the mule, it emerged with a tremolo. Make no mistake. This was I, A. Pinto, who called out the next spine-chilling words:

"Onward! Onward, friends! We shall turn Tule Lake from blue to red!"

Suddenly, as the last of the tribe vanished over the edge of the escarpment, a force of defenders appeared on the lip of the same plateau. It was the converts! Their bright shields, their gun barrels, glittered in the morning light. Poland, at the head of our force, held up his hand, bringing the pursuit to a halt. "Hold on," he ordered. "Watch for a trick."

But one, at least, of the vigilantes would entertain no thought of delay: the fierce Hungarian. How account for my vengefulness? It may be that under the pressure of grief, some small vessel had burst in my brain. Indeed, I could actually taste, on my tongue tip, on my liverish lips, the saltiness of human blood. The reek of gore was in my nostrils. My eyes were covered by a scarlet film. Maddened thus, I beat my bluchers into the soft belly of my mule. "*Houp-là!* Away!"

Thus in my own cloud of dust, like a uhlan, I trotted forward, over the last few yards of the plain. Ahead, through the tossing tufts of my sombrero brim, I saw the foe: Shacknasty Jake and Jim, Humpy Joe, Big Ike. At their chests were the shining daguerreotype plates, at their shoulders the rifled guns. Neptune saw this the same moment as I. She must have recalled that in my own hands there was no weapon at all. She slowed. She halted.

"Remember Miss Nan!" I cried, whipping my reins. "Remember Miss Polly!" But Neptune would not budge.

No matter. All around me the ground was shaking. The air rang with bloodcurdling shouts. My comrades were coming! With Poland in the lead, and Cole, and Piper, they swept by my stationary mount and closed the distance between themselves and the Modoc rear guard. Just then, as if in submission, the converts threw down their metal shields and lay prone on the ground. It was no surrender! For behind them, at cliff's edge, the cruel flattened faces of the Modoc police had suddenly appeared. An ambush! Before I could give the warning there was a tremendous roar, followed by screams, shouts, and the pitiful neighing of horses. A circle of smoke, like the enlarged ring from Judge Steele's cigar, rose unsteadily into the air. The Yrekans, a score at least, were down!

For some seconds all was chaos. Horses plunged and reared, trampling upon their riders. The Yrekans did not know whether to retreat or attack, or which way to level their guns. But the confusion soon ended. Another volley, this time unleashed by the row of converts, crashed into the milling crowd. More of my fellow townsmen fell to the ground. The rest retreated, turning their mounts, whipping them westward, the way they had come. The line of Modoc police had run off. The band of converts, their weapons discharged, had plunged down the precipice as well. Thus did Neptune and I remain alone, amidst the scene of the carnage.

The next instant I slid from the back of my mule and ran toward the wounded and dying. Jeff Ruggles and Charlie Kane, I saw, were done for. And Christie, the *Ingot* editor, had been shot through the foot. I heard a groan. Cole, my old classmate, lay bleeding horribly from a wound at the head. Before I could help him, however, a third line of Modocs rose up over the edge of the plateau. But the foreheads of these natives were unflattened. The Pioneers of Progress! The Heirs of Harvey! At the sight I was overwhelmed by the emotions of relief, gratitude, joy!

"Come, gentlemen! Assistance! Bring bandages, tourniquets! This way! Yoo-hoo!"

But the cry that rose from their ranks was fierce and chilling:

"For Bruce and loyal Wallace!"

Impossible, even at the distance, not to see the scowl on the young faces, or the weapons they held in their arms. These they now lowered. But to shoot at whom? I was the only person upright upon the field. My mouth, in an involuntary reflex, fell open. I wanted to utter a shout: *I am your teacher! Your father!* But my Adam's apple clogged my throat, like a lead ball in a musket barrel.

At the end of the firing line the youngest, the littlest Modoc was aiming his weapon. One eye was closed. The other was staring straight at my chest, where my heart muscle was wildly contracting.

"Herr Elbow Frank!"

Those were the only words that escaped my mouth. There came from behind me, and rapidly approaching, a kind of blackness, a blur; while from straight ahead came a flash, a loud report, and the whistle of a flying bullet. Then something struck me, not from in front but from the rear, throwing me forward. There was a single shriek, and Neptune the mule fell lifeless at my side. The ball meant for my heart had pierced her own. Noble beast! Heroine! Still on my knees, I embraced her hairy head, and pressed her whiskered muzzle to my clean-shaven cheek. Her lips, I saw, were pulled back in a smile from her long yellow teeth. "Darling!" I cried, broken-hearted. And I repeated the sorrowful wail: "You darling!"

And still this first battle of the Modoc War was not done. Battle? Massacre, rather. Slaughter perhaps. But no battle — not when one side loses the greater part of its number, both killed and wounded, and the other side not a single man. Within half an hour all the remaining Yrekans had gathered at the scene of the ambuscade. Only a few of the wounded could stand the trek back to town. We'd have to set up a hospital on the spot for the rest. The question was, when? Of course time was of the essence. Cole, in particular, needed immediate attention. Nonetheless, many of the citizens wanted to take out after the Modocs, though every last member of that tribe had found refuge within the vast expanse of plutonic rock.

Our force stood, stymied, on the verge of the steep plateau. To our left, at the north, the lake stretched away, with its beard-like fringe of tules. There was not, on that July day, the slightest breeze. The effect of motion, of waves, was made by the swarms of flies that darted by the million from angle to angle across the shining surface, like a tic in the muscles of a flat, broad face. To our right was Wigwam, much as I'd seen it a full decade before. Nor was the ancestor, the old grandfather, missing: there was the smoke, a thin strand of it, rising from the crater, curling in the atmosphere. Between lake and cone, directly before us, was the lava, frozen into fantastic forms. Thin fingers of pumice, knobby and knuckled, stretched outward along the circumference, providing a kind of natural palisade. The whole bed, with it crannies, its crevices, seemed an impregnable fortress.

Then, even as we watched, a lone figure came riding out of those crags. Jauntily he cantered this way and that before the backdrop of black and gray stone. It was, in all his finery, his glittering jewels, Gentleman Jack.

"Damn the bastard!" cried Poland.

"There's the general," said Piper, "who planned the sneak attack."

There was a sharp report from our rifles. Three men, four

men, were shooting at once. But the prancing Indian was well out of range.

"What do you say?" asked Steele. "Do we go after?"

Poland shook his head. "When they can shoot freely at us? From a thousand, ten thousand loopholes? And we unable to reply?"

Steele's cheeks, with their ginger muttonchops, seemed to darken from frustration. He yanked at his collar to free his throat. "Now look," he said.

Down at lake level, some half-dozen Modocs came trotting out of the gnarled canyons. They began to jump and dance. They shook their fists to taunt us.

Said Gill, "It's the criminals! The worst of the devils!"

Pickering added, "The Modoc police!"

Now the red curtain seemed to drop once more before my eyes. My throat, mouth, palate, went desert dry. O, would that I had wings, like the underground bats, so that I might dart from this precipice and sink my fangs in the necks of the murdering Modocs. Beneath my clothing, I could feel my body begin to grow, to swell, as if it were that of a leech, a tick, family Hippoboscidae, slaking its thirst on the mere thought of its enemies' blood.

"Villains!" I cried, and, half striding, half tumbling, I began to bound down the sheer face of the bluff, toward the waiting foe.

Whether my unthinking reflex inspired my comrades or shamed them to action, the whole mounted troop poured over the edge of the plateau. Even before I had reached the bottom they were passing me by, galloping across the flats toward the lava. Gasping, breathless, I raced after; but in no time the whole force had left me behind.

Up ahead, the criminal band — Hooker Jim, Scimitar Sal, and the rest — seemed undismayed at our charge. Even when the first of the horsemen drew within rifle range, the Indians sauntered slowly back toward the narrow gullies, the webbing between the twisted fingers of stone. It was almost as if they were daring us to overtake them. Well behind now, gagging on the dust cloud kicked up by the horse hooves, I clutched my Mexican hat to my head. I knew, every man in our posse knew, that at any instant, from those volcanic ramparts, there must erupt a deadly fusillade.

And now it came, lighting up the gray fissures like fifty struck matches. Spent balls went whining over my head. Others found their targets. Horses went down. Yrekans tumbled from the saddle. I saw Arch Osborne, the liveryman, crushed by his own crippled mount. Rose, the fiddler, was struck — not by a ball, by an arrow. The shaft went clear through his chest. But the charge was not broken. The enraged horsemen thundered on to the very tips of the rocky spurs. Here the defenders put up fiercest fire. From where I lay, behind the corpse of a speckled stallion, with the bullets as thick about me as the black, buzzing flies, I saw how the vanguard went down. Poland, from the force of the volley, was turned completely round in his saddle. His face was black with powder. Gill, the first to reach the lava, had taken the balls at near point-blank range. The back of his shirt was smoking, as if about to burst into flame.

Suddenly the salvo ceased. Were the Modocs out of ammunition? Had they paused to reload? Or was this, too, a feint? The Yrekans sensed victory. A cheer went up from their ranks. Then to a man they plunged forward, into the dark twisting gullies of stone. All was still. After some minutes, I lifted my head over the flanks of the stiffening stallion. Smoke hung over the lava. Dust swirled above the field. In this haze a dozen men lay dead and dying. Some person was weeping like a child. I had just made up my mind to make the dash toward the wounded Yrekans when a terrible scream reduced my limbs to jelly.

This cry, I knew, came from no human throat. It was like a trumpet's blare. It was the shriek of horses. What I saw next made my eyes start from their sockets. From every opening in the lava wall, like flotsam cast up by a combing wave, the men and their mounts came tumbling, dashing, hurtling. The fearsome thing was the way in which the Yrekans, as if by some terrible storm, had been stripped not only of their uniforms but, so it seemed, of their very skins. Their bodies had been sheared and the horses flayed. Ribbons of flesh waved behind them. Bloody perspiration sprayed in the air.

Out of this jumble of sights my mind sorted the explanation. The horsemen had dashed full speed into the narrowing canyons. The rock there, basalt, obsidian, was as sharp as cavalry swords. The stones to either side, the rocks underfoot, were literally made from glass. The steeds, charging forward, might just as well have exposed themselves to ten thousand arrows, or impaled their breasts, like the French mounts at Agincourt, upon the sharpened stakes of the foe. Then the animals, in swinging about, had thrust their riders against the keen-edged stone. Awful! Terrible! Still the remnants poured from the canyons in a reddened tide, like a fresh stream of molten lava.

Long after the survivors of the charge had regained the safety of the upper plateau I remained in hiding behind what rapidly became my stinking stallion. I had, in fact, little choice. The sharpshooters, from lava loopholes, continued to shoot anything that moved, whether beast or man. My one hope was to steal off when darkness fell. What horrors filled the rest of that long, dread day! The men soon enough grew still on their own. Their heartrending cries, for assistance, for water, gradually ceased. At the end many begged for the Modoc marksmen to put them out of their pain. The stench from the dead filled my nostrils.

At dusk, well before I could think of escape, the Modocs came from the lava. These were the squaws. Barefoot, paying no more heed to the sharp stones than had the braves to the mine's subterranean heat, they ran toward where the Yrekans lay. The hurdy-gurdies, still wearing scraps of their Sazarac lace, moved among the men, seizing rifles, scooping up ammunition, and looting the corpses. Each one had a knife. Though there was still light to see, I shut my eyes. I could not bear the sight of how they wielded their weapons. Impossible, however, to block out the sucking sound made by the skin of the scalps as they came away from the skull. Nor was this the worst of the mutilations. The scene that followed might have taken place in the city of Sodom, or of Gomorrah: and I, frozen in fear, might have been the sole witness, turned to a pillar of salt.

An hour later, in deeper darkness, I began to creep away. I stopped short at the sound of my name:

"Mister-r-r Pinto! Why do ye flee?"

It was one of the Highland band! Cavendish Sam! The next voice belonged to Priestley Bill:

"Do ye think we canna spy your lanky form, plain as in the light of day?"

I turned, but there was nothing to see. Even the black crags had been swallowed up in the night. "My boys! Dear pupils! Are you going to shoot me?"

"Ha-ha-ha!" laughed Elbow Frank. "If that were our purpose you'd hae been a moldy corpse ere now!"

At these words the tears sprang to my eyes. "What a calamity, chaps, has fallen upon us. Elbow Frank has pointed a gun at my breast; I have led the attack upon your rocks. To think we might have harmed each other!"

There was a pause. Did I hear, out of the darkness, a sigh, a sniffle? The next to speak was my protégé, Kepler Jim. "A' too true, Mister-r-r Pinto. Turn about, mon! Walk this way. Why would you bide wi' that band o' perfidious men?"

At that all the Pioneers chimed in together. Boston Charlie said, "Goddam! Gonna be friends again!"

Newton Mike: "We shall hae need of a doctor in the dark days ahead."

"Coom, mon! Join us!" said Paracelsus Max. "Take ten wee steps to our arms!"

For one mad moment, I hesitated. More: I took a half-step toward the frozen lava. After all, the Academicians had backslid before, even to a state of near savagery. But they had never failed to right themselves, and pursue the path of progress. I was certain that once I could speak with them, calmly, in the plain light of day, I would make them see reason. But before I could take a second step I heard, from behind me, a cry, a moan, carried on the western wind. It must have issued all the way from the high plateau. Cole! Or if not my classmate, one of the other wounded Yrekans. They needed me more than my own dear lads.

"Mr. Kepler Jim! Boston Charlie! I must return. Now I must be a physician. Please, I ask you: join me! Come back to civilization! You have committed no crime. These poor men were killed in the heat of battle. You will be forgiven. Come. I am holding toward you my arms. We shall continue our experiments. Who knows, perhaps we may yet find the cure for the dread hydrophobia. Or for some other, no less terrible disease. We will study together. We will work. In the safety of our home!"

From the Pioneers there erupted an outcry:

"*This* is our homeland!"

Kepler Jim: "Our nation! Our republic! Our state!"

Bacon Jack: "Here is brave Caledonia! Home to the true-blue Scot!"

I had already begun my retreat. As I moved off to the west I continued to hear, echoing through the rocky redoubt, the voices of my children raised in song:

> "Thus bold, independent, unconquer'd and free,
> Her bright course of glory for ever shall run.
> For brave Caledonia immortal must be."

CHAPTER TWO

D-A-N-G-E-R

1

THE NEXT MAJOR BATTLE of the Modoc War was not fought until after the November elections. There were any number of reasons for the delay. First and foremost, every small engagement, each skirmish, demonstrated anew that the Indians could not be dislodged without a full-scale invasion — that is, without the commitment of regular infantry regiments with artillery support. Such forces could not be assembled overnight, or even, given the tensions throughout the country, within the two or three remaining summer months. In the meantime, the task of containing the Modocs fell to the Oregon and California Volunteers. These units were led by Judge Steele, who had also been appointed Indian agent for the duration.

Understandably enough, Steele was a man possessed. He did not limit his mission to preventing Gentleman Jack from making forays beyond the bed of lava. Again and again he sent his raiding parties against the stronghold. The men were eager enough, though none could get within a hundred yards of the outermost spurs. At night the Volunteers would creep as close as they dared to the lava and then, under cover of darkness, dig trenches from which they might direct their fire by day. The trouble was, there was no one to shoot at. From our far-off vantage atop the plateau, we could see the smoke from the enemy cooking fires and the cattle in their natural corral. We could hear the Indians' voices, laughing, chanting, and the thunder of the washboard at night. But of the Modocs themselves, the warriors in the flesh, there was not even a fleeting glimpse.

Another reason for putting off the confrontation of infantry and Indians was the sentiment in the country at large. Though there was a good deal of outrage at the burning and killing in Yreka, there was also a natural feeling of admiration for the Modocs' fighting skills, together with a certain furtive sympathy for a foe outnumbered by ten and fifteen and finally twenty to one. In the eastern cities people began to argue that the natives — exploited in the mine, penned up in their shanties, and decimated by the Neptune disaster — had cause enough to rebel. The newspapers pointed out the need to distinguish between the murder of the Bosworth girls and the mutilation of the posse, which, if not justified by the heat of battle, was nonetheless consistent with the Modocs' own rules of war.

But the crucial factor in prolonging the truce was undoubtedly General Webb, the head of the gathering army. When the population of the Northwest learned that the commander was a Virginian, they accused him of supporting the Modocs on states' rights, or secessionist, grounds. Indeed, several Southern representatives in Washington had asked that the encircling troops be withdrawn and the matter of recognition for the enclave studied. Webb, of course, had no patience for such ideas. His policy was shaped by temperament more than anything else. His instructions were to settle the rebellion by any means necessary. While the local citizenry, and perhaps the War Department as well, interpreted this to mean the rapid application of force, Webb believed he had a mandate, first, for negotiations.

But the Modocs would not agree to talk: rather, the only terms they would consider were those not for their surrender but for the army's retreat. Time after time the brigadier general would send his representatives to the perimeter trenches, even to the outstretched fingers of rock. At great risk he ventured to the lava himself. All he heard, echoing from the redoubt, were taunts and curses, and snatches from the works of Burns.

About these arguments, and the various tactics, I knew nothing at the time. Even during the long lull between battles I — no longer a mere immigrant but brevetted to the rank of acting assistant surgeon — had more than enough to do. The casualties, most of them victims of the Modoc snipers, arrived in our hospital tent day by day. The most serious cases, however, were left over from the original battle in the month of July. Naturally it was Matt Cole who caused me the greatest concern. He had long since come out of the coma brought on by his gunshot wound, but the ball was still lodged in his head. At first I thought the brain might heal of itself; but soon a number of symptoms — weakness in the limbs, and a slurring of speech — made that hope seem forlorn. The question before me was not whether I should intervene but when.

One night, while I stood deliberating that very issue, the door flap rose and the brigadier general, alone, without an aide, stepped into the bell-shaped hospital tent. This was the first time I'd seen the man close. He was, as always, hatless, his dark hair close-cropped on his head. His beard, square-cut and white, left his upper lip free and hung to his collar like a napkin. A black cloak was wrapped about his shoulders. Before I could come to attention, Webb had begun to move among the various patients. At this late hour most of the men were sleeping. Cole was not. He swung both feet from his cot to the ground. Though the officer made to dissuade him, he unsteadily rose. Through the dim light of our coal-oil lamp, I noted the disturbing symptom: my old classmate could no longer raise his arm for the salute.

Webb came round to where I stood. "I have been told," he addressed me, and his voice came out slowly, in a drawl, "that you are the surgeon in charge?"

"Ja!" I responded, clicking my blucher heels together. "Acting Assistant Surgeon A. Pinto!"

The general stepped closer. He covered his eyes, as if even the weak light from the lamp caused them pain. "I do not wish to take you from your patients. I've come for a sleeping draft. I have been wakeful these nights."

"Moment!" I replied. "We have here excellent soporifics." I strode to the cabinets and chose an elixir of paregoric flavored with aniseed. The general, however, waved me off.

"Oh, opium has no effect on me. A little of your ether will do."

"But are you in pain? That is the correct purpose: for use during operations."

"Even so. I would like the compound. A single dose. What I have seen here tonight will not make it easier to sleep."

I picked a can of ether from the shelves. I noted, as I handed it over, that the general, for all his stiff white beard, was in fact a young man — not yet fifty. Webb paused at the leather flap. "If you don't mind, doctor, I expect I shall have to return."

And return he did, not only the next night but each of those that followed. He always took his slow, sorrowful tour of the patients, at the end of which he would find me standing with a fresh tin of ether. The pressures upon him — above all the constant calls for action by the governors, the local press, his own army captains — were immense, and took their toll. There were dark circles under his eyes, and his fingers had begun a constant shaking, a twitching, as if even they were eager to pull a trigger.

Against the push for war the commander could pit only the slim hope of negotiations. With the first signs of cool weather he at last opened communications with the tribe. That is, he would set up a chair just before the westernmost spur of lava, and, with his cloak wrapped around him and a squad of riflemen at the ready in the closest ditch, listen to the disembodied voices that floated out of the rugged crags. The first set of Modoc demands were easily met.

"They are thinking of winter," Webb explained, on one of his tours of my tent. "They have no trouble now, fishing in secret from the reeds. But they want guaranteed access to the lake when it freezes, so they can spear through the ice. I granted it to them on the spot. Can you guess what else they wanted? That chief? Gentleman Jack? My long knife! My sword! Look here, Surgeon Pinto. My scabbard is empty. I left the fellow my blade. If it were my choice, he could have every saber in the army! What's a scrap of metal compared to the suffering in this tent now, and the greater pain that would follow an invasion? If Gentleman Jack thinks I've surrendered, so be it. I'm pleased to allow him to think he's won the war!"

As the weeks wore on, however, the Indians began to ask for more than the general could grant on his own. These demands, clearly enough, reflected divisions within the Modoc ranks. One faction — could this be the Angus lads? — wanted the territory they now controlled, from Wigwam on the south to the northern edge of Tule Lake, recognized as a republic on its own. Webb, arguing that the whole nation might well go to war over just that issue, immediately turned down the demand. Then the Modocs asked that their traditional lands — the lakefront where they'd had their village, the expanse of useless lava, the waters of the lake itself — be made into a reservation, or else leased to them with exclusive hunting and fishing rights. Moreover, the Indians wanted the freedom to engage in all tribal customs, including the ghost religion. Webb explained that while he thought these requests reasonable and would give them a favorable recommendation, he could not incorporate them into a formal treaty without explicit authorization from the War and Interior departments. And that, as the Indians knew well, would surely entail a long delay.

Meanwhile, another faction began to insist on quite different conditions. Some of these — a base pay of $3 a day; no searches; no shifts at depth for more than four hours; and removal of the remains of the buried miners to the sacred burial grounds in the lava — envisioned a return to the Neptune Mine. And there was more, from the Academicians: a brick schoolhouse and a paid teacher. To the latter demand Webb immediately acquiesced. And he promised to take Gentleman Jack to the capital to meet whoever should be elected president. As for the mine, he promised to do his best to persuade Cole to come to terms.

The pity was, Cole's condition had grown so critical that there was no way the general could approach him. The crisis was brought on not by my friend's paralysis, though that now involved the entire right side of his body, but by his sharp, sudden fever and the convulsions that worsened by day and night. I hadn't the least doubt these symptoms, too, were the result of the bullet lodged in Cole's brain. But where, exactly? The Modoc who shot him had aimed upward, from the lip of the plateau to the angle of the white man on his horse. Cole's head must have been turned, because the ball had traveled from the occiput to some spot near the top of the left hemisphere.

The morning after Cole had been shot, while he still lay unconscious, I had plucked out the bone fragments and pushed a makeshift probe, tipped with a porcelain button, up through the course of the wound. But when I withdrew it the white surface was unmarked by lead. Impossible now to attempt the search with a true instrument. The channel had long since closed; the probe would cause as much damage to the gray matter as the track of the missile itself.

I had, however, another idea. If the weapon that had caused the damage had been a captured Sharps rifle, with its new ammunition — and the velocity of the bullet, together with the lack of lead tracing, suggested it had been — then the steel content of the ball might be high enough to affect a magnet. I had no choice but to try, and quickly too. Thus, when my patients and stewards were asleep, I put Cole deep under the influence of ether and shaved his golden locks. Then I went over the bare skull with a horseshoe magnet. I hoped to feel in my fingertips the least shift from the plumb. No luck. No deviation.

I next recalled one of the experiments from my own school days, and which I had often used in the Academy of Pinto: the demarcation of polarity by iron filings scattered over a field of force. Here was an amazing fact: no matter how finely one cut a lodestone, a magnet, and cut it again, even to the width of a hair, the molecules it was made of still arranged themselves to north and south. Thus, unless the bullet were molded or pure lead, or lay so deep in the cortex that it could not be reached in any case by surgical means, I thought I might be able to repeat our demonstration — except in reverse. The bullet would act as the bar, and the filings would come from the polarized horseshoe. Success! As soon as I spread the shavings onto the taut skin of Cole's scalp, the dust lined up in two symmetrical semicircles. "Ah! Ah!" I exclaimed, though there was no one near but the sleeping patients. "Like the wings of *der Schmetterling,* the butterfly!"

I paused now for breath. And no wonder. I felt oddly like a shaman, a medicine man, who with magical eyes could see the bullet through the wall of bone. But where was the witch doctor who was prepared to operate within the confines of the human brain? Old Warren himself had never dared such a feat.

I began by carefully drawing the outline of the bullet in India ink. Then I reached for my surgical tools. In theory this trepanation did not differ from hundreds I'd performed underground. In practice, this was no animal; it was a man. I had to will the tremor from my fingers, my hands. Yet all went as hoped. With the saw I cut through the scalp and skull. The cranial fluids came bubbling out under pressure. The bullet, which had been flattened to a disk on the underside of the skull, fell onto my foot when I removed the piece of bone. Inside the cavity the blood slowly welled. Grasping the torn meninges with tweezers, I squeezed them dry, then tied off the tissue with silken suture. Would not Warren have approved, I thought, of such nimbleness, such neatness?

The first light of dawn was arching over the crown of the tent when I replaced, much like a bung in a barrel, the plug of bone. I sewed the scalp in place over the wound. Then, struggling to remain awake myself, I studied my sleeping patient. Within moments, it seemed, his fever began to abate. His eyebrows, also blond, were knit, as if, beneath the effects of the ether, he realized he was in pain. But his lips were moving, mumbling, murmuring, without any sign of paralysis. By leaning close, I made out the words.

"Will I live?"

I nodded.

He smiled. "You were always the best in class."

At Tule Lake, General Webb could delay no longer. Even those most disposed toward the Modoc cause understood that as the entire country approached civil war, the last thing the federal government could tolerate was a general Indian uprising on its western flank. And a general uprising was precisely what those in the Northwest most feared. Ominously, other tribes, in Oregon, in the neighboring territories, had picked up the ghost religion. They too had begun dancing behind invulnerable shirtfronts or daguerreotype shields. If the Modocs could hold off the United States infantry — such seemed to be their reasoning — why couldn't they?

Webb put his forces on alert. He marched one regiment through the narrow gap between lakefront and lava and deployed it as the Army of the East. The second regiment, the Army of the West, moved in ranks to the flat land at the bottom of the cliff. Atop the plateau, the artillery batteries — brass Napoleons and mountain howitzers — moved into position. Still the general would not give the final command. Instead, he decided to make one final attempt to secure the peace treaty. He would risk approving, and on his own authority, the perpetual lease of the Tule Lake district. But in return the Modocs would have to grant what had been until then the government's two unspoken conditions.

It seemed initially that the tribe would agree. That is, when Webb told them of the first of the demands, which was that they surrender their stock of captured arms, Gentleman Jack called out that they would do so. Not only that, the Modocs would turn over their old weapons, muskets mostly, and flintlocks, as well. All they asked was that they be allowed to retain their bows and arrows, so they might fish for bullheads as they had in the past. To this the commander gave his assent.

The trouble occurred when Webb stated the second, and final, requirement. Even if he had wanted to waive it, or subject it to negotiation, he could not: the governors of California and Oregon, as well as the secretary of the interior, had made it an irreducible condition of any settlement. Thus the tribe would have to hand over to the army Hooker Jim and Scimitar Sal and Rock Dave — indeed, all those in the Indian police who had set fire to Yreka and murdered the Bosworth twins.

The instant the general announced these terms, he and the infantrymen in the nearby trench saw their first Modoc. It was Two-Toes Tom. The old man leaped like a youth, an athlete, atop the knuckled spur of lava. "You wanna kill Modoc," he shouted, waving what was all too clearly the gleaming blade of a captured bayonet. "Modoc kill you!"

The shots that rang out next — they were made by the infantrymen firing into the air — could be heard inside my distant hospital tent. So could the shouts, the notes on the bugle, and the tramp of the horses' hooves. As it turned out, there was no cause for alarm. Webb stood his ground, then wrapped his cloak about him and walked slowly back to the bluff. The negotiations were over. He gave the order for the invasion, the pincer movement from east and west, to begin at dawn.

2

Do you remember that bloodthirsty avenger, the vampire who had ridden at the head of the posse of vigilantes? The one who had wanted to turn the Tule Lake waters from blue to red? That person had not, as it happened, vanished. That is to say, I had not forgotten poor Polly, poor Nan, nor the unfortunate Neptune — not to mention the dozen, and more, fellow Yrekans who had fallen in the fight. Indeed, I remembered them most vividly when, on the night before the invasion, the howitzer section, the twelve- and twenty-four-pounders, began their mighty barrage. At the very first round my Adam's apple — in legend a piece of the forbidden fruit that had lodged in the progenitor's throat, but in fact merely a part of the thyroid cartilage — leaped up against my frock coat collar. There was a loud, rolling boom, a bang, and the ground shuddered beneath the soles of my high-topped shoes. Then, far off, over the lava, there was a series of explosions, each white at the center, with tendrils of fire radiating outward. They lit up the crags and ragged boulders below. I strained forward for a more perfect view. I did not give a thought to the redskins as, hour after hour, the thunderbolts fell upon where they were huddled in their narrow crannies and pumice caves.

"Es ist schön. Wie Blumen." The bomb bursts — or so I, or the demon in me, supposed — were like flowers.

With the dawn, everything changed. There was a sudden silence. The blackness of night gave way to a band of light, the color of tincture of iodine, in the east. All my eagerness, my bloodthirstiness too, turned to deep foreboding. We could see that the gray surface of the lava bed, cracked and rutted as old elephant hide, was just as it had been before. The barrage had caused no damage. Clearly visible at the center of the bed was a collapsed crater, an ancient fumarole. Into this the Modocs had easily retreated, so that the shells, on their low trajectory, had skipped harmlessly off the pumice like stones on a lake. It would take mortars to penetrate that fortress within a fortress, the secure redoubt.

Nor was the failed barrage the only ill omen. This was the first really cold day of winter. In the sky, low clouds gathered; the sun shone weakly behind them, like a worn spot on worsted. On the ground, at lake level, a mist blew off the waters. The hundreds of troops stood knee-deep in the fog, as if their legs had been wrapped in puttees. Webb, surveying the scene from cliff-edge, shook his head.

"No reason for worry," cheerily said I, though the sight of the thickening haze made me uneasy as well. "Coldness of air. Warmness of water. Principle of condensation!"

But the general had fixed his gaze upon the outcroppings of lava, where four or five natives had climbed onto the rock. I recognized them by their copper shields. The converts. I shuddered. It was almost as if the Indians had conjured these clouds and were now coming to greet them: their allies, their ancestors, the great pale army of the Modoc dead.

Silently the invasion began. The men, or the torsos of men, advanced through the mist toward the lava. The rows of their bayonets sliced through the cloud bank, cutting like fins the white-capped waves. There was no gunfire from either side. No shout of command, no curse or cry, reached our high plateau. In the damp air every sound — whether tramp of feet or clang of metal — was muffled, as if the men were trodding upon a vast mat of feathers, or the down of swan.

One after the other the battalions disappeared into the dark bed of lava. Only then did I begin to hear a faint click, a clicking, for all the world like pairs of rattling dice. Soon the noise was multiplied a hundred times, echoing along the rocky ledges, as if all the gamblers in the state of California were shaking their hollow cups. I knew the source of the sounds. To protect their feet from the pointed rocks, the cutting obsidian, the soldiers had donned wooden clogs. It was these that struck against the hardened lava as the troops marched, like an army of Dutchmen, into the shrouded stones.

Another quarter-hour passed. Finally, distantly, I saw how, first on the eastern front, then the west, the fog bank began feebly to flicker, like the frosted globe of an expiring lamp. The sound of the gunshots was weak, and not unpleasant, like popping kernels of corn. Then, almost simultaneously, the first carts of wounded soldiers emerged from the mist. As the acting assistant surgeon, I repaired to my hospital tent.

That was the last I observed of the day-long battle. Yet for a time I could follow its course from what I saw, and heard, under our crowded canvas. Even from the start the injuries I had to treat were far from routine. Massed in the ravines and gullies, in close quarters, the infantry could not fire their weapons; either that, or, in the blaze of the fog, dazzled by the light, they could see nothing to shoot at. Indeed, the men swore that the Modocs must have chalked their bodies, so as to become all but invisible. But their foes had an easy target. A single Indian at the head of a such a gulch could keep a whole company at bay.

As time passed the situation worsened. When the soldiers abandoned the trap of the gullies, they had to make their way over a landscape of basalt boulders, twisted knobs of pumice, and tall ridges of frozen lava. Now it was they, the white men, who were the ants crawling over the sponge — except, as the infantry ruefully noted, an ant had six legs to climb with.

By noon, the high layer of clouds burned away. That meant the rays of the sun beat all the more fiercely upon the bank of mist on the ground. The men within it were stunned by the light. Everything about them grew white; even the dark stones, the jet-black obsidian, was bleached in the glare. All across the battlefield the soldiers stumbled and groped, as if caught in a sudden blizzard. The patients I treated were suffering from amaurosis — that is, from the inflamed membranes brought on by snow blindness.

A little later, at two in the afternoon, a company of the California Volunteers, led by Ben Piper, became the next invalids. His men had come to the muddy corral, made from windblown dirt, in which the Modocs kept their herds. The men removed their clogs. They fixed bayonets. Piper, with his mint sprig dangling from his mouth, led the charge through the fog-covered meadow. Minutes later he and his men came staggering back the way they had come. Their breath was ragged. For all the chill of the day, the sweat poured from their skin. Many had begun to vomit.

"Gas!" That was the cry that went up from the ranks. "It ain't fog! It's poisoned gas!"

By the time the stricken company had made its way out of the lava, the rumors of gas had spread across the front. The offensive on the west ground to a halt. Many of the men seemed about to throw down their weapons. Hard to blame the soldiers for their panic: they had seen with their own eyes how the limbs of the victims had swelled with liquid. When they brought Piper to my tent, his legs were bulging below the knees to twice their normal size, and had split the seams of his pants. Not only that: the men were gasping. Their faces, twitching, with drooping eyelids, were contorted. One of the Volunteers was paralyzed. Who could say that the thick white air they had breathed was not the source of infection?

As it happened, I could. Immediately I fell to my knees and began to suck at the bare soles of Ben Piper's feet. Then I spat the stream of liquid, like juice from the cheeks of a tobacco chewer, onto the ground. "Genus, *Crotalus!* Species, *scutulatus!*" I cried. "Poison of rattlesnake!" Correct diagnosis. That genius Gentleman Jack had directed the Modocs to bury their arrowheads upright, first smearing them with toxic venom. The California Volunteers had stumbled one and all into the trap.

For the rest of that terrible day our hospital tent was the scene of misery and despair. The wounded, the dead and dying, came in far faster than our team of surgeons could treat them. The casualties lay in pools of the previous victims' blood. I was far too busy to follow the course of battle. Some of the wounded had three or four bullets in their flesh; or, a still greater challenge, an arrowhead barb might be cunningly hooked behind a section of bone. I tripped over a pile of amputated limbs. Remember, too, that I had had no sleep the night before. Hence more than once I caught myself dozing off on my feet, even before the soldier to whom I had just administered a dose of ether had passed out. Horrible sights: one surgeon, finding a wounded soldier too cold, too stiff to dismount from his horse, simply shot the animal out from under the patient. Another did not observe that the cupfuls of water he gave a thirst-ridden corporal were spilling through the perforations in the doomed man's belly. Our most pitiful case, or such was my opinion, was that of Pickering, the undertaker, who had been struck in the head by one of the first volleys of the engagement. The bullet had passed through both temples, forcing the eyeballs from their sockets. He fell dazed, disoriented, unaware even that he had been shot. No one had the heart to tell the Yrekan he was blind. That was why he spent the battle striding about the hospital tent, cursing the pea-soup fog.

Finally, at about dusk, I realized that the sound of shooting had stopped. Who, I wondered, had won the battle, and who had lost? Though our tent was filled with wounded, and more were still coming in, I slipped outside and made my way to the edge of the plateau, where Webb and Steele were standing. I saw in an instant that the white men had been defeated. The long lines of casualties making their painful passage out of the lava, toward our bluff, had not a single Modoc among them. The day's great fight had ended not with a climactic battle, a single fierce engagement, but with yet another Modoc trick.

What happened was this. Late in the afternoon, the Modoc fire slackened. The Indians began to withdraw. It appeared they were about to run out of ammunition. The regiments on the east and west gave a cheer. With the bulk of Wigwam looming before them, the enemy could not retreat to the south. The waters of Tule Lake lay to the north. Thus the troops launched themselves forward to close the pincers. Their only problem now was to avoid, in the mist, the confusion, firing upon each other.

But as the Indians drew back, the terrain at the center of the bed grew steeper, more treacherous. Great blocks and slabs of stone leaned helter-skelter, in ten-ton chunks of basalt. It was like a dense city of lava. The infantry, however, was committed. There was nothing the men could do but charge on at full strength.

This proved an impossible task. It was as if the soldiers had been ordered to seize a town by fighting from street to street, alley to alley, house to house. The trouble was, these streets formed a maze, the alleys were blind, and each lane ended in a cul-de-sac. Which way to go? The troops saw a hundred intersections, a thousand corners, an infinite number of directions to take. Thus, as some went one way, some another, the invading army began to break up. At each new corner, every turn, a similar division of forces occurred. Lost in this labyrinth, the battalions became companies, the companies platoons, and the platoons squads of five and four and three men. The Indians, crouched within, waited until the torrent that had threatened to engulf them shrank to rivulets, mere trickles, and at last single drops. Then, at leisure, a Modoc with a musket shot down the stragglers one by one.

General Webb had remained atop the plateau until the last survivors of this rout had come in. Upon hearing their story he turned as white as the few lingering wisps of fog below. Judge Steele, also on the cliff edge, exclaimed, "The devil!"

He pointed to where the longest spur of lava jutted outward, toward the west. At the tip stood Gentleman Jack. Even with the naked eye I could see that his appearance had changed. First, he waved Webb's sword above his head, back and forth, in a glittering arc. His chest, too, was ablaze with light. The general, with shaking hands, passed me his admiral's aid. Then I saw the chief plain. He wore the jacket of a U.S. Infantry captain, with crossed swords on his collar and a line of decorations across his breast. Other medals, ribbons and service badges, were pinned between the two rows of brass buttons that shone upon the dark blue cloth. Even his trousers had a cavalry stripe down each leg, and all his accouterments — boots, hat, gloves — were, or had been, the property of officers of the army.

Then Captain Jack, as he was henceforth to be called, disappeared. The last of our long line of wounded came out of the lava. With that the sun went down — or so, for the moment, I thought. Then I realized that the darkness that swallowed the scene had another cause. Out beyond the tules, over the water, a black cloud had formed. It moved rapidly toward the southern shore. Beneath it the lake was rippling, dimpling. Even at our distance we could hear the hiss of a thousand, ten thousand splashes.

"Rain," said I, feeling for the brim of my silver sombrero. "Or hail."

"No," Webb replied. He peered out toward where the thick, swirling cloud had already flattened the fringe of rushes and was starting to move toward us, over the lava and land. "It's the flies. They're dying. Killed by the cold."

In only seconds this black snowfall reached the plateau. The first of the insects were dropping about us, onto the general's bare head, onto our hats, our clothes. Their wings beat feebly as they lay spent on the ground. Then the remnants of the swarm passed on. But the earth around was black with their bodies, as if the nearby crater had once more erupted, scattering a blanket of ash.

3

Two months and more went by. The lake froze over. More troops arrived, and more of the citizen militia; but no offensive was mounted. On the northern edge of the lake, on the Oregon line, the Army of the Pacific began work on a new fort, with a stockade and docks for barges. Steele's Volunteers continued to dig their trenches on either side of the lava, and to man them, too, so that by the first of the year the Modocs were virtually surrounded. Still, for all Steele's raging, the infantry did no more than drill. The truce at Tule Lake more or less reflected the situation in the country at large: not yet at war, no longer at peace. A new president had been elected, but the old one held office. And as Buchanan vacillated, so, it seemed, did General Webb.

Finally, with the first signs of early spring, Judge Steele decided to force the hands of both his commanding officer and the newly inaugurated Lincoln. He sent out, by night, Ben Piper's company with kerosene and torches. The men doused the fringe of tules for a quarter-mile in either direction, and set them ablaze. By morning the whole southern edge of the lake was on fire. The column of black smoke could be seen, we learned, as far off as Whiskeytown and Redding. Even before the flames died out, the Volunteers moved in with scythes made from their bayonets. They cleared the stubble from the southern shore of the lake. In the muddy ground they began work on new trenches. The Indians, coming out of the northern edge of the lava, exposed on the smooth black plate of obsidian, would be unable to reach the water. Steele sank a second row of trenches behind the first. No need for an invasion now. The Modocs were under siege.

At first nothing happened. Two more weeks went by. Then, at the end of March, the ice on the lake broke into puzzle pieces, and quickly dissolved. It was like a signal. The next day, at mid-morning, two Modocs, the Shacknasty brothers, strolled onto the puddinglike stretch of black stone. They held a white flag, made from a fancy shirtfront. Webb rode from the plateau and approached them on foot.

"You gotta cigar?" asked the first of the brothers.

"Gotta coffee?" asked the other.

Then they declared together: "Don't wanna fight!"

For a moment the general stared at the two negotiators. Then he said, "I am very glad to hear this." Those were the only words he spoke. He turned on his heel and walked away.

The next morning Shacknasty Jake and Shacknasty Jim returned to the spot on the smooth tongue of lava. But no white man went to meet them. The same thing happened on the next day, and the day after that. Meanwhile, the sun was growing constantly hotter — and the Modocs thirstier. One night a group of braves tried to sneak past the line of trenches manned by the Oregon Volunteers. They were driven back, leaving one brave, by name Bogus Ed, behind. He had been shot through his flattened forehead. The Volunteers — indeed, the whole army — rejoiced. If you didn't count Scarface Charlie, this was the first dead Indian of the Modoc War.

Why did Webb refuse to meet with the enemy? In part he may have wished to increase the pressure upon them. In large measure, however, he was waiting for instructions from the War Department. They came by Pony Express, and were signed by Lincoln himself. The president had taken the hardest possible line. There was nothing further to negotiate. He had accepted the Modoc terms; now they must agree to his. That meant the wanted men must be handed over. Then and only then could a peace treaty be signed. Meanwhile, Webb must prepare for a second invasion. Along with the president's order came a memorandum from the secretary of the interior, in which the composition of the peace commission, should one be formed, was made explicit: Webb himself; Steele, as Indian agent; Professor Bosworth, for the town of Yreka; and Cole, if sufficiently recovered, to sign for the Neptune Mine.

The general, as instructed, put his troops on alert, and brought the artillery back to the lip of the plateau. It took no more than these simple maneuvers for the Shacknasty brothers suddenly, surprisingly, to agree to all terms. Immediately Webb made arrangements for the signing of the peace. This had to be done at a secure and neutral site. Both sides agreed to the lake. A barge was fitted out at the Oregon docks and hauled by a little steam launch to a spot just off the southern shore. Two small dories were put over the side to ferry the signatories for the government and the tribe. Within the week all was in readiness. Yet the date for the signing had to be — not once, but two and three times — postponed. The reason, of course, was that the Indians failed to produce the Modoc police. Two days running, Webb, with an armed escort, had waited upon the glassy surface of stone. Instead of the criminals, the chief of the tribe had appeared to plead his case.

"Mr. Webb a gentleman for sure, like Captain Jack a gentleman too. We are what-you-call-him: *diplomats!* One chief ain't got no business making another chief turn in his people. Ain't no gentleman gonna do that! Listen, mister! It's a big problem. Can't ask a terrible thing like that! Mister, you tell President Polk, ain't possible! Not hand over people. You asking Captain Jack to tear himself into two!"

The turning point came three days after that. The Indians had made another attempt to break through to the water and had again been repulsed. The next morning, the commander met the two brothers. "Where is Rock Dave?" he asked them. "And Scimitar Sal? And Split-Lip Sam?"

"Make treaty first!" said Shacknasty Jake.

Said Jim, "Then you gonna get him!"

This was, for the brigadier general, a dilemma. His orders were explicit: the Modocs had to be in custody before negotiations could resume. Nor could he ignore the element of personal risk. *You wanna kill Modoc* — those had been Two-Toes Tom's words at hearing that he must surrender — *Modoc kill you!* But Webb did not dare send for further instructions — not because of the inevitable delay, but because he knew the order would be to attack. The last chance for peace would be lost. What he said next was therefore on his own responsibility:

"Very well. We shall meet tomorrow at dawn upon the barge.

All must be unarmed. Without any escort. There will be no negotiations. We shall sign the treaty. Immediately afterward, the Indian police must be surrendered. If they are not . . ."

Here Webb paused. He looked back, toward the west. At the edge of the bluff the muzzles of the brass Napoleons were shining, as were the tips of uncountable bayonets. "If not," the general resumed, "then there shall be a bitter and bloody war."

Atop the plateau the commissioners spent a restless night. And not just the commissioners. Matt Cole had not yet fully recovered from his operation. He was unable to stand for more than a minute at a time; even sitting upright was a chore. He could not be allowed to make the difficult move to the barge unless accompanied by his old colleague, the acting assistant surgeon. To this condition of mine General Webb agreed. That is why I, like the others, paced nervously about, listening to the sounds that rose from the distant lava: shouts, the roar of the washboard, laughter, even gunshots.

Judge Steele did not like what he heard. From the start he had resisted the idea of a treaty of peace. The siege alone, he argued, would bring the Modocs to their knees. Before midnight he approached General Webb in the hospital tent. "I know this tribe through and through," he announced. "Why should they betray their brothers when they can betray their enemies instead? You, Webb. Myself. Our good friend Bosworth. Cole. Let me tell you how the savage mind works: they think that when the leaders of the army are gone, the men in the ranks will simply run off. They're bound to shoot us in cold blood!"

Webb remained in his chair, wrapped in his cloak. "I do not believe," he said, "that you have considered the meaning of your words. The last engagement cost us one quarter of our attacking force. The next battle will be worse. The Modocs will not give up until their last man, their last woman, the last child, is dead. Do you put fear for yourself before the attempt to avoid such bloodshed?"

What could Steele do but withdraw? Nonetheless, the reasons for alarm only multiplied as the night went on. Ben Piper reported that his scouts had penetrated the lava. From their vantage they'd been able to make out a number of small fires where the Modocs were molding bullets. More worrisome still, the captain of the squad patrolling the obsidian plate reported that his men had stumbled on a band of six Modocs, all painted black and armed to the teeth. They were in rifle range of the dories. Once discovered, they'd jumped up and fled southward, into the rocks. Webb was unperturbed. He merely remarked that after all, the infantrymen had sharpened their own bayonets, and that the captain's patrol had been as close to the Modocs as the Modocs to the soldiers.

I was as uneasy as any of the others. At the darkest hour of the night I slipped from the hospital tent. The very moon in the sky, a new one, seemed to hang over my head like the blade of Scimitar Sal. The far-off drumbeats were like a funeral march. I could see, amidst the basalt crags, the reddish glow of the Modoc fires. Perhaps at that very moment a brave was pouring molten lead into a mold, shaping the bullet that one of his comrades would fire into my heart. Nonsense! Foolishness! Girlish fears!

Then I saw, or thought I saw, another light, a mere pinprick, among the hollows of the distant rock. At once my heart turned over in my chest, like a miner's pancake in his pan. This light was winking, blinking. A long glow and two short flashes. Then a quick flash and a steady glow. After that the sequence was reversed: first the steady gleam, then the glimmer. It was almost — this was my thought — as if someone were sending a message in code. Someone! It had to be members of the Highland band! Long ago, in the early days of the Academy, we had studied the system of Mr. S. F. B. Morse.

I stared ahead, looking for the signal lights. There they were! Two gleams and a brief glint: that was the letter *G.* And here, with a single flash, was the letter *E,* followed by another gleam, a glow, a glint: the letter *R!* What could it mean? *G-E-R?* Was it *DANGER?* Dear boys! Stout fellows! Were they sending their teacher a warning? I racked my brain for the pattern of the earlier letters. All I could recall was a pinwheel of dots and dashes. I stared unblinking for the rest of the code. An hour went by. Two. Nothing. Only darkness. Had I imagined the event? Dreamed it? Dare I report the message — less than a word, a mere syllable — to the commissioners, my colleagues and friends?

Too late! While I sat debating the question the dread dawn arrived. When I approached the commission, its members, dressed now, and shaved, were already sitting down to a breakfast of steak and eggs. "Ho-ho!" laughed the acting assistant surgeon. "Last meal of the condemned!"

* * *

An hour later our party started down the zigzag trail. Cole rode backward on a mule-born stretcher, so that his torso was at the same forty-five-degree angle as the animal's neck. The rest of us had the rising sun in our eyes. I stood at the verge, next to the last in line. A California Volunteer — it was the sightless Pickering — fumbled for my frock coat.

"Take this," he said, holding out a Colt's navy revolver. "Hide it. Under your belt."

I paused. I looked down the path, where Bosworth and Webb inched ahead at the slow pace of the ambulance mule. Unthinkable that either of them would accept such an offer. Judge Steele was behind me, waiting to begin the decline. He stared. Then, unmistakably, he nodded. At the same time he drew a tiny gun, a one-shot derringer, from the top of his leather boot. What to do? I recalled the flashing lights: *D-A-N-G-E-R*. Quickly I seized the weapon and, with a gulp, almost a sob, stuffed it into the waistband of my gabardines.

Near the lakeshore, at the edge of the rock plate, we halted. Steele called us near. "None of us can know what lies ahead. We would be fools not to take precautions. If trouble should arise, if the criminals should not be surrendered, let us consent to whatever the Modocs ask. We'll sign our names to paper and get back to our lines."

The general turned his cold gaze onto the Indian agent. "We cannot have that sort of double-dealing. I have dealt with Indians before and not once have I broken my word. I shall not make any promise I know the government unlikely to keep. Nor will I allow such behavior from any of you. There is the shore, and there our boat. If you wish to turn back, do so now."

Bosworth, the minister, looked about. There was actually a smile on his round, wrinkled face. "Surprising, is it not, how much less frightening the world looks by day. Especially when the fresh breeze is blowing and the sky is clear. Our fears have been exaggerated. Brave soldiers patrol the shore. The Lord watches from above. If our purpose is just, no harm shall befall us. The hand of the savage will be stayed. Come, my friends: let us continue our good work on this good day."

The orderlies carried Cole's wooden stretcher ahead to the lake, while we walked behind. It struck me that what the former Harvard professor had said was true: in the daylight one's fears evaporated, like perspiration. How blue these lake waters! And blue the sky! In this bright sunshine the cold touch of metal against my skin brought a flush of shame. I cast about for a place to throw the revolver. Before I could do so, however, the general called from ahead. "Will the surgeon make haste? Your boat is waiting."

There were two skiffs at the shore. My patient and I rode in one, which had a number of parcels — gifts of clothing, coffee, cigars — heaped in the bow. The commissioners took the other. Both vessels tacked back and forth in the stiffening breeze, until we reached the side of the anchored barge. The men clambered up the rope-and-wood ladder. Cole, still in his stretcher-saddle, was hauled up on lines.

Once on board I saw that a makeshift table had been formed from a cable drum, and was surrounded by straight-backed chairs. A piece of canvas was stretched over what might be the stern, to make a high awning. We placed Cole in its shade.

A full hour went by, during which no one spoke. Now and then one or another of the commissioners would lean over the side to see if the Modocs were on their way. But the sails remained furled on the masts of the two little tenders. I went to the opposite, or lake, side of our craft. I was surprised to see that close up, the water was not a transparent blue but cottony white, as if reflecting the overhead clouds. I glanced up: the sky was still perfectly clear. I leaned over the gunwale. Directly below a few reeds broke the surface. Around them the creamy stain spread through the waves. Suddenly I realized that the shapeless cloud in the water was alive. Here was a multitude of tiny wriggling forms. The summer flies! The larvae! The barge was floating on a sea of worms.

"Gentlemen," old Bosworth announced, "I believe the Indians are approaching."

The commissioners crowded the rail. One of the skiffs was indeed heading toward us, with a group of Modocs inside. They soon drew up beneath our three-step ladder.

"Have these fellows been searched?" Judge Steele called to the soldier who manned the tiller.

The corporal nodded. "Yes, sir. There's no gun with them. No knife either, that's certain."

Webb said, "We'll have them on board."

Curly-Headed Doctor was the first up the ladder. Steamboat Ed was second. Next came two of the wanted men, Two-Toes Tom and the short, powerful Rock Dave. They were followed by

Humpy Joe. All were dressed in odd pieces of army apparel. The last man to board, however, was in tatters — the torn trousers striped, the jacket a swallowtail. At once I strode toward this eldest of the Angus lads. "My dear friend! What happiness I feel to see you!"

Boston Charlie stood scowling. The furrows deepened on his angled brow. I leaned close enough to whisper confidentially into his ear. "Did you send the message? Last night? With a mirror? What was the first letter? A dash, eh? Double dots? Ho-ho: letter *D*? Are we in danger?"

Instead of replying, the ex-Academician turned his back and marched to mid-deck, where his fellow tribesmen were standing. The Modocs were silent and grim. So, for that matter, was the small knot of white men. I turned now to the former professor of materia medica. "Problem?" I inquired.

"We may, it seems, have failed after all. The chief of the tribe has not appeared."

Yet no sooner had Bosworth uttered those words than Steele gave a shout. "A boat! Coming straight on!"

The breeze had shifted. The second skiff sailed on a line. Seated in the stern, with his medals flashing, his buttons burnished, was Captain Jack. The Modocs, seeing him, began to laugh and talk animatedly among themselves. As soon as the chief came aboard, the Indians moved about, shaking hands with the commission members, and with myself. They went over to Cole and shook his hand, too. At the approach of the two policemen, I hesitated. But I had seen how Bosworth greeted them both. Who was I, then, to withhold my hand?

Next, the representatives of both sides drew their chairs about the wide cable drum, while I squatted by the side of my patient, under the awning's shade. From there I watched the general pass out expensive cigars. The men puffed on these, in lieu of a peace pipe. Steele, however, kept his cold cigar in his mouth, as if he did not wish a smoke cloud to screen his view. His pale, popping eyes shifted from one of the savages to another, but always returned to Captain Jack — not to the Indian himself, but to the curved blade, the steel saber, that Webb had rashly, without a search, allowed the chief to bring on board.

The hour was approaching eleven. The fitful breeze had nearly died. The sun beat on the awning, heating the air beneath. At the table the commander removed his cloak. Bosworth hung his jacket on the back of his chair. Steele put his hat on the table. The slick strands of his hair were stuck to his scalp. One after the other the Indians finished their cigars. Before Webb on the table were a bottle of ink, a quill pen, a leather tablet. This last he opened, revealing the parchment inside.

Now the general rose. There was sweat on his upper lip. Even his white beard looked damp. "The time has come, gentlemen, to sign the treaty between our nations. There is no need for speech-making. Each of us knows the importance of the moment. Many lives depend on what we do. There has been —"

Webb broke off. I saw how his hands and, beneath the table, his knees were shaking. It was not from fear. It was from the emotion of the moment. He resumed: "I have seen much suffering, in this war and others. Each day I have visited the wounded men. I did so in order to strengthen my determination to secure this treaty. Now we stand on the brink of success. For the United States Army, and for the president, I congratulate each one of you; and I thank you myself, from the bottom of my heart."

Once more the head of the peace commission paused. Two-Toes Tom reached into the cigar box and bit off the end of a cigar. Humpy Joe did the same. Steamboat Ed also took a second smoke; he slipped the band from the leaf. Then, in a quick, deft movement, he leaned to the side and snatched up the sword from Captain Jack's lap. The white men froze. Next to me Matt Cole gave a low groan. Then the Indian brought the sword edge down through the blunt tip of his cigar. He put the cheroot in his mouth. I heard the commissioners sigh. I saw Judge Steele lift his hand from his boot top. Now Rock Dave took a cigar. Like Two-Toes Tom, he bit off the end. Why did the gesture seem full of menace? Because the brave's teeth were bared and the head jerked sideways, as if biting a powder cartridge. Matches flared. Smoke boiled up over the table. The commander continued:

"We are not here to negotiate. That work has been done. Whatever the Modoc people have requested has been granted. The government guarantees you your tribal lands, your tribal customs, together with a schoolhouse and a schoolmaster for those who wish to learn new ways. In the mine there will be short hours and fair rates of labor. Mr. Cole is here to sign his name to that. Captain Jack will be my guest in the capital. I believe I might arrange a meeting between him and the president, as one chief of state with another. In return, we have but two conditions. To the first — the surrender of all firearms — you have agreed. You know the second. Modocs have killed and wounded many soldiers. For these acts of war we do not hold them responsible. But before the hostilities began, there was a terrible crime: the cruel murder of two young girls and their mother. That deed cannot go unpunished."

This was, of course, the crisis. The commander had reached the point at which the Modocs had always balked. Webb did not flinch. "The tribe must surrender those who committed the crime."

No one leaped up. There was no outcry. Even Two-Toes Tom continued to suck at the end of his cigar. Hastily, Webb turned the treaty paper around, so that it faced the Modocs. "The terms I have just spoken have been written down. If you like, Boston Charlie can read them aloud. But if you trust my words as to the contents, both sides are now free to sign."

Curly-Headed Doctor reached for the general's pen. Then he stopped. "What gonna happen to Hooker Jim? To Scimitar Sal?"

The general said, "They will be tried in a court of law."

"After," said Steamboat Ed. "After goddam law."

"They will be punished," said Steele.

Bosworth: "If found guilty. If not, they will be freed."

Rock Dave leaned through the smoke of his own cigar. "Who gonna find 'em? Dumb Modoc fellers?"

"No," answered Bosworth. "The people of California."

"Ha! White sonabitch!"

Steele: "The murdered women were white. They were citizens of the state."

"Lemme say the idea I got," put in Boston Charlie. "What about that feller Scarface Charlie? Feller got killed. Not by soldier. Not in war. By bloody Ben Piper."

"Inna cold blood!" Humpy Joe exclaimed.

Boston Charlie went on: "Question is, will that bad man get found by Modocs?"

Bosworth answered: "I am sorry. No. He would have to be tried by his own people."

"When? When found guilty? When punished? Same time as Hooker Jim?"

"You must," said Bosworth, sighing, "accept the truth. No jury will convict a white man for killing an Indian. With all my heart I wish that were not so."

Steamboat Ed: "Give feller to Indians! Then we give you Scimitar Sal! Ain't that fair? Ain't that right?"

Webb said, "I have no authority to do such a thing, and would not if I had. You may speak of this killing, and offer any other evidence you wish, at the trial. I give you my word as an officer of the army that it shall be conducted fairly. The decision will be reviewed by the governor of the state and then by the president. Mr. Lincoln is just. He will not permit an unfair verdict to stand."

"Lincoln! Mr. Lincoln! Ha! Can't fool dumb Modoc! He president of North!"

"Got another chief inna South!"

"Gonna be big fight!"

"South gonna win!"

"Gonna give Mr. Lincoln fair trial!"

The Modocs laughed. They thumped the table in delight. The two seated commissioners looked uneasily about. Steamboat Ed grinned at the pale men. "You think ignorant Modoc don't know nothing. We know! Gonna be war!"

Curly-Headed Doctor ripped open the front of his army tunic, revealing his painted chest. He began to rock in his chair. "White man gonna kill white man. Seen it! Heard it! Know it good inna head! Gonna shoot each other with guns! Blond hair shoot black hair. Brown eyes shoot blue eyes. Hairy skin shoot smooth skin. Shoot inna head! Shoot inna belly! Shoot inna heart! Shoot last white feller dead. Watch out! Look out! Ain't gonna be one left alive!"

Humpy Joe: "No more Mr. Lincoln."

Rock Dave leaned clear across the table and seized Judge Steele by his silk lapels. "No more Judge Steele."

At this, the judge and the minister jumped to their feet. Captain Jack, who had not yet said a word, rose as well. He turned to General Webb. "Listen! Modocs talk alla last night. Make a big decision! You don't gotta give us such a helluva lot in your treaty. Don't need no schoolhouse. Don't need no teacher. Now we gonna give back alla jobs in the mine. You listen to this: we gonna say to beautiful idea about living with white man in America like brothers how-you-say-it: *farewell*. Farewell! Ain't gonna be no goddam progress! Now Modocs gonna live here: inna rocks. Fish for fish inna lake. Mighty fine idea: whites not gonna see stinking

Indians, stinking Indians not gonna see whites. Mister! You see? You gotta comprehension? Captain Jack poor feller not gonna admire beautiful city of Washington! Not gonna have head-of-state conversations. Now he gonna take off alla shiny medals! Tear up alla ribbons onna chest! You gotta humble Indian here. Therefore. Right? *Therefore* you call alla soldier away. Therefore you move alla big guns. Just a bunch of ignorant people live inna rocks make no trouble gonna have peace!"

Webb put one boot on the seat of his chair. He leaned forward, elbow on knee. "I want to make certain I understand. You no longer make any demands except to live in the lava beds and fish at Tule Lake?"

"Yes! Goddam!"

"You: Humpy Joe. Rock Dave. Everyone. Do you agree?"

The Modocs nodded, one and all.

Two-Toes Tom turned to the head of the peace commission. "Now you gonna sign him. Ain't that right?"

"Gladly," Webb responded. "If we consented to the greater terms, we can hardly object to the less."

There was a pause. It dawned on them all, the men on both sides, that there was nothing further to say or do. Boston Charlie lunged forward, across the surface of the cable drum, and plucked up the pen. He dipped it into the inkwell and pulled the treaty papers to his chest. Concentrating, so that the furrows deepened on his slanted forehead and the eyebrows gathered into a single dark line over his eyes, he began to write.

"Ha-ha!" he laughed. "One smart Indian! Letter *B!* Now I make letter *O!* Look: this is letter *S!*"

Just then Humpy Joe interrupted. "Sardine Frank. Hooker Jim. Gonna live inna lava, too?"

General Webb said, "The change in your conditions does not alter ours. Those men must be surrendered."

Again, at those fateful words, there was no clamor. The only sound was the scratch of the pen as Boston Charlie, his tongue plastered to his upper lip, crossed the vertical line of the letter *T*.

Almost politely Two-Toes Tom asked the next question: "You gonna shoot Sardine Frank? Shoot Hooker Jim? Shoot poor old Two-Toes Tom?"

"You mean after the trial?" asked Webb. "Should the verdict be guilty?"

The Indian nodded. "Guilty."

Judge Steele: "In California the penalty for murder is death by hanging."

There was a sudden crack, as loud in that silent boat, on that calm lake, as the report of a twelve-pound cannon. The pen in the writer's hand had snapped in two. There was a dark blot on the paper. All the Indians were on their feet. Their mouths hung slack. They gaped. Their skin took on a darker patina, as if the smoke from their cigars had made them ill.

I understood their emotion. To their minds, the tight noose would prevent the victim's spirit from escaping to the ancestors, to the land of the dead.

Two-Toes Tom was the first to recover. He leaned forward, glaring at Bosworth's head. "Good hat," he said, menacingly. "Fit good."

Bosworth, alarmed, plucked the hat from his head and held it out to Two-Toes Tom. But the old Indian knocked it aside. "Don't wanna hat. Want goddam silk coat." He tugged at the sleeve of that garment.

Bosworth took his jacket from the back of his chair. "Here, Tom. Take it."

Steamboat Ed: "No. Give here. You look. Fit fine." He put the coat on over his army tunic and did the buttons to the chin. He waved his arms. "Modoc the minister now!"

Bosworth forced a laugh. "So you want to look like me? Ha-ha! Here. Take my spectacles, too!"

"Don't worry, old man," said Curly-Headed Doctor. "We will."

Now Webb turned to his counterpart in the Modoc delegation. "Jack, what does this mean?"

Captain Jack was on the far side of the table, with the saber in his hands. He strode to the commander, who reflexively drew back. But the Indian dropped to his knees. He held the weapon up, offering it to the general in his outstretched hands. "Big mistake. Big mix-up. Mighty army not surrender to Modoc; Modoc surrender to army. Here you got mighty fine excellent sword. It sharp! It shiny! Take it, master! Now you gotta have mercy on humble foe! See these tears? Captain Jack, he not weeping because he gotta say farewell to fine steel sword. No! No! He weeping tears for that bad Hooker Jim and bad Scimitar Sal. You gotta be a Christian feller and forgive those what-you-call-him-inna-Noah-Webster: *uncivilized chaps!* Gotta have mercy! Believe me what I say. You promise you won't hang them fellers. I promise they gonna live inna rocks and not hurt a fly. Gotta give word quick! Don't be damned fool! Please, sir! Just say what I beg you to say. Speak what I tell you to these damned stinking Modocs. Your highness! Hurry! Gonna be Christian and let 'em go! Say what you got to! Goddam fool: *say!*"

The head of the peace commission stood dumbstruck, tongue-tied at this outburst. Yet even if he had been able to bring himself to utter the words, it was too late. Rock Dave sprang past the general and snatched up the cloak from the back of his chair. He whirled it once in the air and brought it down where Captain Jack squatted upon the deck.

"Ain't no Modoc chief! Modoc squaw!"

The rest of the Indians came near. Curly-Headed Doctor threw himself onto the black cape and ripped a hole in the garment. The head of Captain Jack, with his gold tooth and his earring, showed through, as if through the top of a gown.

"Squaw dress!"

"Woman's clothes!"

"Clothes for coward!"

The men stood about him, pointing, jeering. Humpy Joe ripped off his shirt and tied it, shawl-like, under Captain Jack's chin. The rest hooted with glee.

"Humpy Joe's gal!" said Steamboat Ed.

"Pretty squaw!" said Rock Dave.

"Smooth-face woman!"

Curly-Headed Doctor leaned close to the chief. "You kiss. Kiss onna mouth!" And while the savages roared with laughter, he did touch his lips to those of Captain Jack.

Rock Dave played the part of the jealous lover. "My squaw! My miss! She don't have sweet kiss for you!" He threw the shaman aside, seized Jack by the head, and kissed him three times, with loud, smacking sounds, on the mouth. The excited Modocs howled.

I could stand this sight no longer. I moved out of the shade of the awning. "Gentlemen!" I cried. "This is not proper behavior. Please stop at once."

Judge Steele seized me. "Let them fight with each other. It is our chance."

But the Indians seemed to heed my words. They drew back. Then Rock Dave pointed to where a pool of liquid foamed under Captain Jack's haunches. In his fear, his humiliation, he had released the contents of his bladder.

"Ha-ha!" laughed Curly-Headed Doctor. "Damned fool piss like woman, too!"

Captain Jack remained squatting, clasping his knees beneath the cape. Tears dropped from his eyes. His whole body trembled. There was from the Modocs a last burst of laughter. Then, in the silence, I saw that the lips of the chief, or ex-chief, were moving. But the sounds that came from his mouth, to white man and Indian alike, made no sense.

"Has he gone mad?" exclaimed Bosworth in horror.

I knew he had not. In that moaning, the muttering, I made out five familiar words:

Wee, sleekit, cowrin', tim'rous beastie —

For a brief moment I, the teacher, and he, the pupil, exchanged a glance. Then I saw a light, like a candlelight, go out in the black irises of my first student's eyes. Captain Jack shuddered. Slowly he rose. He removed the cape and dropped it behind him. Equally slowly he undid the brass buttons of his officer's tunic. Then, while everyone watched, he reached inside the garment.

"Watch out!" cried Steele. "He's hidden a gun!"

Such proved the case. Captain Jack now held a pistol, old and rusted, in his hand. General Webb took a step forward, to wrest the weapon away. Just then Cole gave a strangled cry. "Look! My God! We're doomed!"

According to the great Harvey, blood is pumped from the heart at the same rate it returns. False theory. At that instant the entire contents of my veins rushed back to that organ with a single sickening thud. For I had seen, peeking over the gunwale, not five feet from where I stood, the mean face of Hooker Jim! With a knife clutched in his teeth! Next to him, the water streaming from his hair, was Scimitar Sal!

"Attention!" I cried, while in my mind I formed a picture of how these criminals, these killers, had floated beneath us, breathing through the hollow pipes of the nearby reeds. "Ambuscade!"

But the members of the peace commission already knew what their fate was to be. General Webb stood stock still, turning aside from the gun that was aimed at his head. Curly-Headed Doctor had picked up the saber, which he held at the throat of old Bosworth. There was a splash at the gunwale. The head and arms and torso of Sardine Frank came over the rail.

"Are you going to kill us, Jack?" asked Steele.

The Modocs seemed to have the same question. They too

looked at the chief. Captain Jack let out a chilling wail. "Got to! Oh sonabitch! Got to kill all!" With that the Indian took a step toward the commander and at point-blank range pulled the trigger of his gun. Nothing happened. The weapon misfired.

Steele for some reason declared, "Mark the time. It is twelve minutes before the hour of noon."

Then Jack cocked his pistol again and fired a bullet into Webb's cheek, just below the eye. The general went down. With blood pouring from his head, he began to crawl across the deck. Two-Toes Tom picked up a chair and brought it down upon the officer's back. The thin wood splintered. The old Indian used one of the legs to beat the prostrate man over the head.

There was a strangled cry. Bosworth staggered backward, blood oozing from his shirtfront. Curly-Headed Doctor sprang after and raised the saber again. "Don't stab me," Bosworth said. "I am already dying."

But the medicine man thrust the point of the blade directly into the old man's heart.

Like pirates, the rest of the Modoc police sprang aboard. They went for their victims with knives. Hooker Jim and Scimitar Sal fell on Cole, who was crawling across the deck. They stabbed him in the back and between the ribs.

In less than a minute three men had been killed. Two of us were left alive. Judge Steele was scrambling up the prow of the craft, with Sardine Frank but a step behind. At the top, by the rail, the judge turned. He had his derringer in his hand. "Stop there! I am armed!" The gun went off and the bullet whizzed away in the air. Steele leaped over the prow. Wildly thrashing, he made for the distant shore.

All my life I had been a non-swimmer. Hence I retreated in the other direction, toward the awning, where Hooker Jim was trying to get a grip on the stubble growing upon Matt Cole's scalp. Only then did I recall, tucked into my waistband, the Colt's revolver. Here was a problem: there were, in the revolving breech, six bullets. But on board the boat were nearly twice as many Modocs, eleven in all. One of these, Rock Dave, came trotting toward me now. "Kill Jew feller," he said. The others moved closer as well.

I drew my weapon. After all, I knew some mathematical tricks. With one shot I could solve the equation. Thus did I turn the gun round, so that the muzzle pressed against the side of my temple.

The Modocs halted, hesitating. Far off, at the southern shore, I heard the crack of rifles and saw a puff of smoke. Rescuers? Liberators? No: the Indians were shooting from the lava, so as to distract the army from the treachery at the barge. They distracted me no less. In that split second, while hope surged through me, a hand reached out and snatched the pistol away. Aghast, I whirled.

"You too, Boston?" I inquired. "An Academician?"

Then did the eldest of the Highland band bring the pistol butt crashing through the crown of my Mexican sombrero and onto the shell of bone that enclosed all of my memories and feelings and thoughts.

CHAPTER THREE

The Siege

IF THE MODOCS had thought that by severing the head of the white man's army they would cause the multitude who made up its body to flee, their strategy failed. The murder of the three commissioners created a shudder of revulsion down the length of California, and throughout the land. In particular the shooting of Webb — the highest officer ever lost to the Indian wars, a general struck down by a savage — caused a paroxysm of sorrow and rage. Great crowds met his sealed casket at every town along the Sacramento, from Red Bluff through Trinidad City, Colusa, and the capital itself. At San Francisco, where the lead-covered box was hoisted from the deck of the river steamer to an ocean-going vessel, the throng surged forward, crying for revenge, demanding an immediate attack.

At Tule Lake, Judge Steele, now the acting commander of the combined infantry and militia, put off the invasion until fresh artillery support should arrive. But he knew the Modoc War would be over long before mortars could be assembled and floated across the lake from what was already known as Fort Webb. In the days following the treachery aboard the barge, the Indians had made repeated nighttime thrusts toward the lake. Each one had been repulsed. Now, from well up in the lava, there came a terrible wailing. It was an unbroken moan. The enemy had started to die of thirst.

Of all those who, in state and nation, called for revenge, few longed for the attack, the rattle of musket and rifle, more than I. I? Pinto of Pressburg? Alive? Correct: if it can be said that a prisoner, a slave, a hostage, is truly living. The butt of the Colt's revolver, falling upon the juncture of coronal and sagittal sutures, that is, upon the strongest part of the skull, had merely knocked me unconscious. I awoke some hours later within the bed of lava — within, to be more specific, the fumarole, the great collapsed bubble of gas at the center of the barbarians' redoubt. Immediately I realized I could not move in any direction — neither upward, where clouds and sky showed over the rim of the cone, nor down, to where, eons ago, the crust of this crater had collapsed in a jumble of shadow and stone. My immobility was caused not by guards or chains but by an even more effective restraint: the Modocs had removed my bluchers. If I took five steps in any direction, my feet would be cut to ribbons.

Thus did I remain day after day on my rocky ledge, halfway up the fumarole slope. During this time I hardly noticed the various members of the tribe. Before my eyes there was room for nothing but the horrible image of what had occurred aboard the peace craft: the shot to the general's cheekbone; poor Cole attempting to crawl away from the flashing blades; and, worst of all, Bosworth calling for mercy, *Don't stab me!*, while the blood spread on the front of his shirt. But it was not the recollection of that butchery that made me pray for the army to launch its attack. Rather, I preferred to face bullets, to be caught in a crossfire, to be crushed by the bombs' jarring concussion — anything, any fate, so long as I no longer had to endure this constant, unquenchable thirst.

Truth to tell, I did not suffer from the lack of water any more than the Modocs. The portion they gave me — one silt-filled cup each morning, a half-cup at night — was the same they shared among themselves. Clearly they had not thought to create a reserve before being cut off from the lake. Their source now seemed to be captured infantry canteens, and the muddy meadow that served as a corral. It was from the direction of that enclosure that I heard the same moans as had Judge Steele down at the trenches. I knew the sound came not from the Modocs but from their parched and piteous cattle.

The lowing went on for two full nights and days. Then the Indians set about slaughtering their herd. At dawn I was awakened by the sound of gunshots, by the bellowing and bleating that came over the fumarole rim. The crater itself was deserted. Not only that, my high-topped shoes had been left within reach. Could I not, while the tribe was occupied with its grisly task, make my escape? I hesitated. It wasn't only that the soldiers were shooting anyone, anything, that attempted to move from the lava. More telling was my own dry throat, my swollen lips: the meadow, with its water, was only minutes away.

By the time I arrived on the scene the slaughter was done. A small group of squaws had already begun to butcher the carcasses and spread the meat in the sun. Most of the tribe had moved to the edge of the shallow pool, whose banks were trampled to a sodden swamp. There, a single animal was left alive. A tan-colored ox. It stood, its legs spread, noisily sucking the dirty water. None of the Indians moved to stop it. At the sight, at the sound, I was overcome by unbearable thirst. I could have bellowed myself from the craving. I glanced toward the Modocs. They, too, were licking their lips. They sucked on their cheeks, as they might the flesh of plums. Still the humans stood, silent, motionless, as if they were the dumbfounded ox and the ox, busily satisfying its needs, were the rational being.

At last Boston Charlie stepped forward and put the muzzle of the navy Colt's against the animal's head. At the report the legs of the ox buckled, and it dropped heavily into the wallow. There was no rush from the tribe. The Indians did not hurl themselves down at the bank. Nor did anyone thrust his head into the turbid water. Instead, with great discipline, each person came forward in his or her turn and dipped a hand under the surface. They sipped the few teaspoons of water out of their palms.

From somewhere, it must have been earliest childhood, I remembered the story of how the Lord had formed his army by choosing, from among thousands of thirsty soldiers, the three hundred Israelites who had paused to cup the water in their hands. For all my cracked lips I smiled at the notion that these people, mustard-yellow, with flattened foreheads and paint on their ribs, could be the Hebrews' lost tribe.

Here I shall make a confession: I felt at the moment a pang of pity for my bitter foe. How could the Modocs withstand the siege? This pond, no more than a puddle, could not last longer than a single week, even without the herd of thirsty cattle. The sun, beating down from above, would lap it up faster than the most ravenous beast. Indeed, as I knelt to take my turn, I felt its rays strike the bare skin of my neck. It seemed to lick me dry with its hot, rough tongue. And this was only springtime! The mild month of May!

In fact, the meager water hole lasted until the first days of June. Through those weeks — though one of Two-Toes Tom's men was never far off — I was left free to move about wherever I wished. Slowly, day by day, first one and then another of the Highland band would seek me out. In time, and in our common plight, we came to sit together beneath whatever shade we could find. The sun was now like a burning tong. My broad Mexican hat provided little protection. The bright rays struck through the crown with palpable force, like needles; while below the brim the reflection of the lake, smooth as metal, sharp as an ax blade, blinded my dry, drooping eyes. The only relief came at night, not because it was cooler — indeed, the volcanic stone radiated back after dark the heat it had collected during the day — but because then, while asleep, I invariably dreamed about water: the springs and spas of my youth; the linden-lined Danube; and even the Charles, the Chagres, the Sacramento. One night, the sweetest of all, I dreamed of — no, no, I actually saw, I smelled, I even heard — the infant Dumb George paddling about in his galvanized tub. Such splashing spray! Smell the rose perfume! See the glistening bubbles! And there, in the center, the shiny shoulders, the wet hair, the toothless grin of the boy.

"My dear!" cried I. "Are you alive?"

I woke to yet another blistering dawn, and, what was worse, the cruel sight, maddening, mesmerizing, of the Tule Lake waves. Impossible to avoid that glittering, mirrorlike surface. Even when I turned away I saw its glinting sparks, like spear tips, dancing before my eyes.

Finally, in June, we were reduced to little more than two thimbles of water, thick as Turkish-type coffee. Once again, during the night, I thought I heard the lowing of cattle. The sound, however, came from no throat, whether animal or human. To its grinding, its groaning, the Modocs, the braves and squaws, had started their shuffling dance.

" 'Tis the abode of the idol," said little Elbow Frank, pointing all the way down to the heap of toppled rock, out of which the eerie sounds continued to rise.

Priestley Bill: "The voice of the banshee!"

"The call of the hoary sire!"

They meant, of course, Frank Townsend. It was he, with the tribe's washboard, who was making the infernal sound. No: the noise did not come from the reverberation of tin. This rumble, the roar, was louder and deeper. It came from the rubber rollers, the mangle drums, that were attached to the very wringer I'd seen at the John Harvard wagons. The mine owner, like some mad washerwoman, was endlessly turning the crank.

And what of my old colleague, my prospecting partner? More than once in the course of my month's captivity I had descended the fumarole slopes in the hope of seeking him out. Each time I had been turned back without a glimpse of my friend. Indeed, I had not laid eyes upon him since that night when, in the midst of the dancers, he had pretended to give birth to the army of the dead. Was he in truth the idol of the tribe? Or was he as much a prisoner as I? Perhaps this roaring was meant to be not Modoc music so much as a cry for assistance. I peered down to where the crumpled crust of our crater lay in gigantic blocks. I decided that once the thunder had ceased, I would make my way to the bottom and seek out my companion once again.

But the dance went on all night. In the morning we saw that the braves had painted their bodies for war. Unable to penetrate Steele's defenses by night, they had decided upon an open assault on the enemy lines. Such an attack, I knew, was reckless, even suicidal, yet there was nothing I could do but watch as the ragged army moved down the northern ravines and onto the smooth, shiny, licorice-like slab of stone.

The strategy of General Jack — for he had abandoned his captain's clothing for Webb's tunic, Webb's cloak — was clear enough. The first to step out into the open were the former converts — Humpy Joe, Big Ike, the Shacknasty brothers, and a handful of others. Each held one of the shining plates, the metal shields, before him. If the images of the ancestors did not stop the soldiers' bullets, then the copper itself surely would. Next came the squaws, the hurdy-gurdies, in their scraps of silk and lace. Last of all, crouched low, using the women as living, not copper, shields, came the male fighters. They carried their army Springfields, their Sharps rifles in one hand, and in the other, great sacks sewn together from animal hide. They knew that the soldiers, unwilling to fire on unarmed females, would withdraw in panic.

Then the warriors would dash forward, fill their leather canteens from the lake, and return to the stronghold.

The skirmish, once it began, lasted less than two minutes. The daguerreotypes had lost their magic. Up stood the infantry in the first of the ditches. They fired. The lead balls of the volley went through the thin sheets of metal as easily as they might through paper. The converts, stunned, wounded, reeled away, back toward the fingers of lava. Humpy Joe remained, face down on the adamantine rock.

Now the squaws were exposed. For an instant the troops held their fire, watching as the hurdy-gurdies, with the men behind them, advanced. Then, as had been expected, the blue-shirted soldiers leaped from their trenches. Instead of fleeing, however, they ran to the flanks, so as to fire on the crouching braves from east and west. General Jack had prepared for that threat. The ends of the line of squaws fell back, forming a hollow square. This might have been a company from Wellington's army, or that of Frederick the Great, except that the perimeter of the classic formation was made up of the weaker sex.

Thus were the tables turned. The braves, the Modoc marksmen, were the ones who were protected, while the infantrymen, out of their ditches, were exposed. Would the white men withdraw? How could they fire? Looking on from above, I saw Judge Steele canter up on a horse. He was shouting an order. Impossible at the distance to hear what it might be. But I was amazed to find myself hoping that it was a call for retreat. More astounding still, the sight of the crumpled form of Humpy Joe, cruelest of the converts, filled me not with glee but with woe. The next instant I discovered the nature of Steele's command: the infantry leveled their guns and opened fire.

On either side of the formation the squaws tumbled down. In the center the Modoc men milled. A second group of soldiers came out of the trenches and prepared to shoot. At that the women rushed screaming for the lava, and the braves, unable to get off a single shot, went running after, for the safety of the crags. But two squaws and a brave refused to take cover. Crazed by thirst, they broke in the other direction, for the lake. The whole of the second volley stopped them in their tracks, spun them about, brought them down.

Above the fray, I stood sickened. Already I could hear, wafting up from the lower reaches of lava, the shouts of the wounded:

Water, water! they cried, in the Modoc tongue. I might have been a prisoner, but I was acting assistant surgeon still. Immediately I turned and, in my laced-up bluchers, strode toward the meadow. To my horror I saw that of that swamp, not a drop of water remained. The ground was as baked, as cracked as my own swollen lips.

General Jack was on the spot, sifting the soil through his ringed fingers. Seeing me, the chief stood up, then motioned that I follow. I did so, stumbling southward, over the trenches of lava. Suddenly General Jack disappeared. One moment he had been there, in plain daylight; the next moment he'd vanished. Then I saw, seemingly from underground, a light. The head of the tribe stood at the entrance to a cave, holding a match in his hand. By the time it burned out, I was at his side. Then the Indian struck another match, and the two of us proceeded inward, downward, along a narrow path. Already, I noted, the temperature had dropped. A cool breeze ruffled the cuffs of my gabardine pants. The further we went, the colder it got. I could not help but recall how a decade before I had followed a similar trail to where the bones of an animal — a goat, had it been? A deer? Gazelle? — lay by a liquid pool. Now it was I, with a mouth that felt as if it were stuffed with dry crackers, who wanted something to drink. I pressed forward, outracing the Modoc, to the furthest reaches of the underground cavern. There was no liquid here. No pond. No pool. Instead I made out, like a taut sheet stretched on a bed, a flat white panel of frozen water.

"Das Eis!" I exclaimed. *"Phantastisch!"*

There were two reasons for my joy. First, here was the solution to the long-standing mystery of where Gentleman Jack, the old Jack-a-Dandy, had found the ice blocks he'd brought to the Neptune Mine. Second, this same cave represented the tribe's hidden reserve. I knew that the frozen water had not formed from an underground stream; rather, it had been distilled over centuries from the very air we were breathing. The two of us were within a kind of natural refrigerator, which wrung the moisture from the hot current of air that passed by my sombrero and made the cool breeze that blew by my knees. Here was hope: this cave, and there might be, must be, many more like it, was nothing other than a machine for the manufacture of ice!

High summer arrived. Africa could not have been hotter. The sun burned as fiercely upon rising as it did at noon. The poor

Indians prayed for a breeze; but when the wind sprang up, like a blast from a furnace, they yearned again for the calm. The papooses, the infants, who never cried, never complained, whimpered now for their mothers, whose flat breasts held no more milk. Even Two-Toes Tom, who had walked barefoot on charcoal, shied from the burning basalt. Day by day the Modocs were being baked alive: already their skin was darker, browner, the color of gingerbread in an oven.

I had been incorrect about the number of cooling caves. There were only four altogether, and two had been hacked to bare rock long before to supply the Neptune Mine. Now, as we entered the month of July, the Modocs chipped the last frozen slivers from the cavern revealed by General Jack. He cut our rations. Then, three days later, cut them again. Impossible, it seemed, for the tribe to hold out for more than another week.

What to do? The Highland band called a meeting. We gathered outside, as had the Academy of old, only now the scholars lay dark, broken, motionless, like scattered pieces of pumice. The cruel surface of the lake glittered below us, like pewter.

"Ah," said Cavendish Sam. "For a wee dram that's cold and wet!"

My favorite, Kepler Jim, raised his hoarse voice. "Do ye ken what drives a man truly daft?"

Priestley Bill: "Surely 'tis the many drops o' water in that cursed lake, with none for us to drink."

Humboldt Johnny: " 'Tis the torture of Tantalus!"

But Kepler Jim, hollow of cheek, flat-headed, frowned. He gestured to where, all about us, the piles of captured weapons, with heaps of ammunition, lay upon the ground. "So many guns. The thousands o' deadly bullets. But hardly a Modoc to shoot them!"

"We need," said Elbow Frank, "to use our wits to make a death-dealing machine."

"Tut, tut," I interrupted. "This is poor science. The inductive method is for the good of mankind. Think of the discovery of ether. The cure for rabies."

"A pox," cried Cavendish Sam, "upon the inductive method!"

"It didna cure our winsome George!"

Now the near-black face of Newton Mike brightened. "Wait! Mister-r-r Pinto! Wha' did ye tell us about the great Archimedes? Did he not, when his homeland was threatened, turn to the engines o' war?"

" 'Tis so!" cried Bacon Jack. "He saved his Syracuse from the fleet o' mighty Rome!"

Humboldt Johnny exclaimed, "I remember! He lifted the ships from the boiling torrents. He shook the vessels in the air till a' the sodgers fell out!"

"He fired upon 'em wi' ten thousand darts!"

"He burned up the galleys wi' a resistless beam o' light. From the center of a polished mirror!"

The Academicians laughed aloud at the rout of the besieging Romans: "Ha-ha-ha!" Their stretched lips broke open; eagerly they licked off the blood.

Kepler Jim, in whom dwelled a surgeon's soul, was now on his feet. "Are we, Sons of Scotia, less brave than the hoary Greek? We are no more Academicians. Archimedeans, now!"

"We must be bold as Hector!"

"Aye," wistfully sighed the stout Cavendish Sam. "But how?"

First there was a silence. Then, of a sudden, a shout:

"Principle of the lever!"

That was the sharp-witted Newton Mike. He continued: "Canna we use that instrument to send muckle boulders upon the heads o' the foe?"

"Gae me boot a place to stand," shouted Elbow Frank, *"an' I will move the world!"*

I shook my head. Not only were the infantrymen too deeply entrenched, but the same wall of rock with which the lads hoped to crush their enemies would block their own access to the shore.

But the Archimedeans were far from daunted. "Principle of the screw!" cried Priestley Bill. "If we canna approach the water, we might wi' this machine draw up the liquid to us!"

This suggestion was no more practical than the last. There was not time, nor had they the tools, to fashion such an apparatus. And even if they had, it would take months to blast through the lava and dig a tunnel to the level of the lake.

Next to speak was Paracelsus Max. "I ha'e it! The mirror! Look at the bright glass all about us! Obsidian! Let us make a glaizie light. We will blind 'em in the eye! We will fry the skin frae off their bums!"

"Ha-ha-ha!" laughed the lads. "A mirror!"

Had Archimedes really made such a weapon? According to legend, he had set fire to the Roman fleet while it lay more than a bowshot away. Certainly the rays of the sun, if properly focused, possessed the strength to cause such a conflagration. The Indians had more than enough sunlight. They had acres of glass. What they lacked, again, was time. There was no way to cut and polish the rock in the few days that remained — nor had they a solid target, a ship, a battery, a fortress, on which to direct a burning beam. With a certain sadness I shook my head. "*Nein.* A pity. Here we have a non-practical scheme."

The Pioneers hardly heard my words. Their minds were ranging far beyond anything dreamed of by even the fertile genius of the Greek. Cavendish Sam wanted to make a catapult. Bacon Jack insisted they tunnel beneath the trench and set off a black-powder bomb. The plan of Newton Mike was to sew a balloon from the leather hides and inflate it with heated air. Then the airborne Indians could attack from directly over the soldiers, pouring fire and brimstone upon them; or else float like a swift-winged cloud over the lake and with bucket and line scoop up the contents — as, in the young scholar's words, the rude farmer draws water from the mossy well.

At that very moment, high noon, a terrible hum arose from the north, from the surface of the lake. I whirled about. What I saw made me gasp. A black spear, a wedge-shaped blade, was rising off the water and heading upward, southward, toward the bed of lava. For a moment I could only stand and gape. It was as if, while the Archimedeans had been dreaming up weapons to use against the soldiers, the soldiers had forged some dread machine to use against them! The horrible humming grew louder, the dark cloud nearer. "Attention!" I cried. "Run, my dears!"

But my pupils were already running. So was the rest of the tribe. As quick as they could, they set a series of fires. For all the heat of the day they ducked close, under the smoke. But I was caught in the open. Thus the cloud of flies, order Diptera, fell upon me, pinching, biting, stinging every spot where the skin was exposed. They clustered, furlike, on my shins, on my neck, on the hands with which I tried to slap them away. Thus did I at last, after so many difficult years of living, grow upon my cheeks and chin a full, thick, shining black beard.

The infestation was no surprise to the Modocs, who had witnessed the behavior of the black-winged flies ever since their ancestors had arrived at Tule Lake. That is, for hundreds of years. They knew this swarming would last for only a week or ten days, after which the whole population would resume its zigzag formation over the water. Alas! By then the Indians themselves, whose life cycle was more ephemeral even than that of the members of family Muscidae, would be extinct — killed or disbanded or dead in the stronghold from thirst.

To me, the attack by these leechlike insects, the black, buzzing plague, was the worst of all imaginable sorrows. Not because of the pain: the bites were mere pinpricks compared to the torture I felt in my mind. This suffering was brought on in part by the memory of how other winged creatures had attacked my silent son. In greater part, however, what galled me, what filled me with bitter fury, was the way Heaven mocked both me and the tribe. Not content with denying us all hope of water, the gods, if such they be, now wished to suck from our bodies the last drops of blood.

Error. The worst had not arrived. That occurred some days later, when the last of the caves began to run out of ice. On that dread dawn General Jack appeared with his bucket of shavings. I was forbidden the least lick. Here was the act I had feared. How long could the Modocs go on providing the precious slivers to their captive, when they had little enough for themselves? Still, when the moment came, I leaped to my feet to protest. But my throat, from dryness, from terror, had gone into spasm, so that my Adam's apple protruded from it like a rabbit from the belly of a snake. There was not room for a word, or a solitary syllable, to come out. General Jack spoke instead:

"Modoc tribe got ice for maybe four, maybe five days. But only for what-you-call-him: *combatants.* Ain't got no ice for no Jew."

At these awful words — a death sentence, really — my head started to spin. Once more sparks, the sharp little lights, swam in front of my eyes. But General Jack was not done:

"Same for women. No ice. Same for papoose. No ice. Same for what-you-call-him-inna-Noah-Webster: *octogenarian!* No ice! Finish! Finish! All done! You look down there: alla old people, alla women and children. They gonna ask for mercy. They gonna beg onna ground."

I turned to where the head of the tribe was pointing. Sure enough, a large group of Modocs had gathered in a crevice below. Queen Mary was there, with all the other squaws. Many had papooses in their cradle boards or in their arms. The oldest of the men, those too weak to fight, were with them.

Now General Jack unhooked from his belt Webb's blood-stained sword. "Sword of surrender. Kindly take it. So soldier according to rule of war ain't gonna shoot. Last chance for Modoc. Old friend, our fate gonna be up to you."

Finally I managed to swallow. *"Me?"* I croaked.

"Soldier ain't gonna shoot white man gonna give up sword. You gotta take alla weak Modocs to Judge Steele. Make a surrender. With alla squaws, alla old men, we gonna perish in maybe two days. Without, maybe we last a week. You make surrender for Modoc. Then you gonna be goddam free man!"

Mechanically I reached for the saber. I wasn't thinking of freedom. I wasn't thinking of surrender. The women, the babes, the elders, could have been at that moment upon the moon. What I did think of was the lake, with its uncountable cubic feet of water.

General Jack smiled. His gold tooth flashed. "I say with the heart farewell to fond friend. Gave education to stinking Indian. Gave hope for future, too."

Those words might just as well have been spoken in a foreign tongue. I heard nothing but the pulse beating in my ears. The ground about me lurched up and sank down. The familiar sparks seemed to be leaping out of the flinty stones, as if someone were striking them together. I knew the symptoms: sunstroke; acute dehydration. I stumbled across the lava to where my flock was waiting.

They were in even worse straits than I. A number had fainted, so that those with strength remaining had to hold them upright. All swayed on their feet. An old man, his head back, his mouth open, made a dry, rattling sound in his throat. There was not, I realized, a moment to lose. With my own head spinning, and squeaking sounds coming from the unlubricated joints of my limbs, I waved to my thirst-crazed companions and moved into the narrow ravines.

Our party emerged a few minutes later, staggering to a halt on the smooth slab of stone where a number of lives had already been lost. We were clearly in the sights of the white men's rifles. Yet no one fired. Queen Mary started forward. Still no gunshots. Thus encouraged, the women, the aged men, began to hobble across the black strip of obsidian. For all their weakness, their weariness, they broke into a trot. Each of them smelled the water of the lake. They could hear the wavelets break. I swore that I could taste the very spray upon my tongue.

Suddenly, all was confusion. Sparks, splinters of light, shot in front of my dazzled eyes. Not splinters, not sparks: bayonets! The soldiers had lined up before us, their weapons leveled. I groaned. Above the troops, atop a horse, sat Judge Steele. He gave a sharp command. I gave it no heed, but continued to move ahead. Let them shoot: I awaited, I welcomed, the bullet that would enter my steaming brain. Still no one fired. No soldier restrained me. The sky above had broken into prism pieces. The ground below moved like quicksilver. I leaped one trench. I hurdled another. Then my legs gave out. Tripping, tumbling, I came to rest where the soft ripples of the lake lapped against the soil of the shore.

Mouth wide, tongue extended, I drank my fill. A tremor almost of ecstasy passed through my body. I gulped faster, mouthful after mouthful. I might have been an infant, a newborn babe, sucking at his mother's inexhaustible breast. How much could I swallow? More! Still more! My stomach expanded, my chest swelled up. The veins in my body seemed to stretch with fluid. I was like one of those paper blossoms that open their petals inside a glass of water.

"Friends! *Indianer!*" I cried. "An excellent sensation, *nicht wahr?*"

But there were no Modocs about me — not an infant, not a squaw. I looked round. The entire band was still confined behind the line of soldiers. They stared down at me with wide, woeful eyes. Quickly I upended my hat and filled it with Tule Lake water. Then I got to my feet and unsteadily, as if my ballast were shifting, strode back to where the soldiers had leveled their guns at my companions.

The instant they saw the dripping sombrero, the poor prisoners surged forward. Those in front almost impaled themselves on the points of the bayonets. The rest stretched out their hands, trying to reach the water that streamed through the cloth bucket to the ground.

"Captain Piper!"

That was Steele, upon his speckled mare. "Seize that hat. Spill the contents."

An officer, Ben Piper indeed, stepped from formation and yanked the half-full vessel from my hands. He tipped it over and wrung it out like a rag. A pitiful groan rose from the redskins. Again they pushed forward, stretching their arms over the human barricade. I was the one they were after. They wanted to touch my moist skin and my waterlogged clothes. But the infantrymen pushed them back.

"No. Please," I said, while retrieving my soggy sombrero. "Here is a misunderstanding. The folk wish to surrender. It is not a ruse. I give a guarantee."

Steele yanked his horse about to face me. "We are pleased to have you once more in our ranks. We feared you had come to harm. But there is no misunderstanding. These Modocs cannot be allowed in camp."

"Not allowed? These are prisoners. What of the rules of war?"

The Indian agent smiled, so that his gingery muttonchops spread on his cheeks. "There is nothing in the rules of war, Surgeon Pinto, that requires an investing army to feed and clothe the enemy it hopes to starve into submission."

"But here are women. Here are children. *Die Kinder.* They throw themselves on your mercy."

"We *are* being merciful. Would you prefer us to use bullets and bombs rather than hunger and thirst? The fewer mouths to feed, the longer the siege, with all its suffering, must last. It is only humane to return these people to the rocks from which they came."

Judge Steele nodded toward the captain. Piper took his place among the line of troops. The Modocs did not withdraw. Instead the old men reached out, grasping the bayonets in their bare hands. All along the line the Volunteers, the infantrymen, drew back the hammers of their guns.

It was Queen Mary who resolved the crisis. She raised her hand and, in her own tongue, gave what must have been the order to withdraw. Without a sound, without so much as a whimper from the children, the woebegone band turned about and began to drag themselves across the hot glass that lay between them and the deposits of lava. Queen Mary herself hesitated. She spat at the feet of the soldiers. Rather, she attempted thus to show her contempt. But the glands in her cheeks were dry as husks. The fierce squaw only spluttered. At this the soldiers burst into laughter. They roared. It was as if, like their cocked weapons, they had been held back by a spring.

These guffaws grew steadily fainter — not because the militia grew less merry, but because I, loping quickly across the dark stone, was drawing further away. What did this mean? Simply this: I had thrown in my lot with the Modocs! At this act, no one could have been more surprised than the actor. It was less a moral decision than a physical reaction: the laughter, the loud haw-haws, had made my body recoil, as if I, too, had been pricked by the points of the bayonets. Thus did I flee the white men and approach the natives, who had come to a standstill, just before entering the first crags of lava.

Now I saw the reason for the halt. The sight made me disgorge, almost, my full belly of water. A number of braves, the entire force of Indian police, stood at the ravines. They were armed with breech-loading rifles. These were aimed not at the distant foe but at the derelicts, the castoffs from the tribe. Now it was the Indians who would not allow their people to pass!

A terrible wail rose from the throats of these refugees. None howled louder than I. Imagine my anguish: I could not remain with my own race, because they had refused to take in the Modocs. But how could I join the Modocs when they would not accept their own mothers, sisters, grandfathers, wives? Ah, A. Pinto! Pariah! Loneliest man on the face of the earth! Must I now sink down, even as my flock was doing, and so await my fate? No! Never! If Queen Mary, if the hurdy-gurdies, would not resist, I would. I marched, therefore, to Two-Toes Tom.

"I demand to see Mr. General Jack. He must explain this outrage! We are here human beings!"

But there was no confrontation. The old man only grinned, as did Hooker Jim and Split-Lip Sam. Rock Dave dropped the muzzle of his Sharps rifle. The others did the same, clearing the path all the way to the keen-edged ravine. It was only after I had entered the gully and was squeezing gingerly between its flinty furrows that I became filled with sudden terror. Why had those killers allowed me to pass? What did those grins, those horrible smiles, portend? Suddenly I began to shake. The cruel savages were admitting not me, A. Pinto, but what was inside me! I trembled at the thought of how they would slit my abdomen for the quart of fresh water that even now churned within its rubbery walls.

But when I emerged from the gulch, there were no threatening natives in view. Indeed, the first of the tribe I encountered were my own Academy members. Even Boston Charlie was with them. He was smiling. In his hand he held my captured Colt's, the navy revolver. With it he waved a greeting. "Goddam! Mighty happy to see you!"

The rest of the lads chimed in as well:

"Mister-r-r Pinto!"

"Coom hither!"

"A Highland greeting, mon!"

My thick, crusted lips broke into a grin. A cloud lifted. A weight, a burden, dropped away. How could I have thought of myself as abandoned, homeless, a leper, when my own dear lads provided such a welcome? "Hola!" I responded, staggering toward them.

The Disciples of Bacon drew round their mentor. Newton Mike seized my hand and began to stroke it, again and again, with his own. Humboldt Johnny clasped me about the knees. Little Elbow Frank grasped the hem of my frock coat and brought it to his lips.

"Sweet sir!" said Kepler Jim. The others, too, murmured endearments:

"Such a gallant!"

"Wha' bliss to lay my eyes upon thee!"

"Ho-ho," I chuckled, pinching the cheek of Priestley Bill. "Did you think I had left you? Never, friends! Never!"

"Ye have come i' the nick o' time," announced Bacon Jack.

"Our one last hope!" cried Cavendish Sam.

"Solution to our puzzle!"

"What puzzle," I asked, "is that?"

Kepler Jim provided the explanation. "After we have all one by one killed each other, who will kill the last?"

I felt as if I had been plunged in a bath of ice. "Kill?" I echoed.

"Goddam!" cried Boston Charlie, holding up the Colt's revolver. "Shoot 'em between the eyes!"

"Can this be? Am I now dreaming? Do I hear such words?"

Elbow Frank continued to tug on my frock coat hem. "Dinna be fainthearted," he pleaded. "Stand forth like the savage Turk!"

Still I shivered, violently, as if I had been transported to an arctic zone from this desert clime. "Do not think such thoughts. Have hope, friends! While there is breath in our bodies, anything may happen. Why, in the next hour the skies may darken with clouds. It might start to rain!"

"I hae me doots," said Humboldt Johnny.

Added Bacon Jack, "We shall ne'er taste anither drop o' water, whether fresh or salt."

"Listen!" exclaimed the spindly Paracelsus Max, putting a hand to his ear. "The grannies, the graybeards, the darlin' babes! All wretched an' destroyed!"

The young scholars turned to the north. They strained to hear.

From below, on the obsidian, as hot and black as the surface of an iron pan, came the pitiful cries of the outcast Indians. In the direct glare of the sun they must have been roasting alive.

Now I understood why my students, like noble Romans, were offering themselves to the sword. It was not so much that they had abandoned hope of victory, of survival. No. The Angus lads reasoned thusly: if they did not drink the last of the water, or lick the dwindling ice, then the luckless lepers, the tribe's untouchables, might. They were sacrificing themselves. The darlings! The lambs!

Now from among the midst of the scholars came a clacking sound. For a moment I thought this must be the children's teeth chattering with fear. Then I saw it was the cylinder of the repeating pistol, which Boston Charlie was spinning around. It was the summons.

Bacon Jack got to his feet and moved toward the gunman. He ambled easily, with a spring in his step. His voice, addressed to Boston Charlie, was without a quaver. "A steady hand, old cronie! Make me dead as a herring, sure!"

One after the other, each smiling, insouciant even, the Heirs of Harvey arranged themselves in a semicircle. They tipped back their top hats, to uncover — flattened for the three eldest lads, full for the rest — their foreheads. Each youth embraced whichever companion was to do him the final favor. Hence Newton Mike hugged Humboldt Johnny. "Ace o' hearts!" he exclaimed. "I'm yours for aye."

Likewise, a grinning Cavendish Sam put his arm about Elbow Frank. "Am I na devil-may-care?"

Last of all, of course, the pedagogue was approached by his protégé. "Coom, coom, Mister-r-r Pinto," cajoled Kepler Jim. "Think o' bright wines and bonnie lasses. Join wi' Scotia's sons: one, two, three gleesome huzzas!"

"Huzza!" shouted the Academy members. And again:

"Huzza! Huzza!"

One last time Boston Charlie spun the deadly chambers. He placed the muzzle against the temple of Bacon Jack. That victim cast a final, furtive glance toward the founder of the Pioneers. So did all the Academicians. As one, they gasped. What they saw was that their schoolmaster had indeed taken Kepler Jim's words to heart. That is to say, I was merry. I danced. I frolicked. I slapped at the worn gabardine that covered my knees. At the same time, with my long legs, I jumped in the air, as high as a frog, order Anura, family Ranidae.

The Modocs stood amazed, watching my mad mazurka. How could they know that I had been struck, as if by a lightning bolt, by the force of a sudden idea? But I had. Indeed, the instant I'd seen the Colt's chambers, the way they had spun round and round, I grasped that I might yet save us all. I would make a weapon, like that of old Archimedes, which would shoot ten thousand darts. I would hurl not a cloud of boulders, but a storm of bullets instead. Naturally the lads could not see my thoughts. Nor could they hear my unspoken words. All they knew was that the head of the Academy of Archimedes was leaping about like a frog and hoarsely crying, croaking, the very words of the great Greek himself:

Eureka! Eureka! Eureka!

CHAPTER FOUR

The Peacemaker

1

FAR TOO OFTEN had I, in my still youthful life, been forced to dwell beneath the surface of the ground. In Boston, at my harborfront cellar. At level one in the Neptune Mine. Now I found myself once more in a subterranean abode, engaged in a great work of science. On this occasion, however, the Children of the Enlightenment and I were not one hundred feet down but merely within one of the basalt dens that had been stripped of its ice. Nor did we have years to complete our project; only days, only hours. Yet the issue now, no less than during the search for the cure for rabies, was one of life and death. Our lives: Elbow Frank's, Cavendish Sam's, Priestley Bill's, my own. Our deaths as well.

It took my smart scholars only minutes to grasp my idea: if revolving chambers allowed a pistol to shoot many times without being reloaded, why could a similarly equipped musket or rifle not do the same? I did not mean a long-barreled weapon with a Colt's-type cylinder. Even if every Modoc should be thus multiplied by six, the tribe would still face impossible odds. But why stop at six shots? A six-shooter? Why not eight? Why not twenty? A hundred, even? A thousand-shooter and more! What had come into my head was a vision of a single barrel behind which a wheel of breeches would revolve. The same chamber from which a bullet had just been fired could be reloaded while on its journey to fire again. "Remember, my dears," I concluded, pointing with my index finger to the low ceiling of our new cave. "A circle is *endlos.* Infinite. Without beginning. Without end. In theory our gun could shoot forever!"

" 'Tis a bewitching fancy," said Paracelsus Max. "But how will the death-dealin' balls be loaded into the infernal machine?"

"That is for you — and you, and you" — I pointed to Priestley Bill and Cavendish Sam — "to determine. We have no lathes, no drills, no tools. You must devise a loading hopper from ready-made parts."

Next I turned to the three eldest Archimedeans. "And you gentlemen: your task is to find the chassis upon which the breeches will revolve. Hurry! Hop to it, lads! We have only as much time as there is ice: forty-eight hours!"

Immediately the two teams dashed away on their treasure hunt. As for the inventor, I remained behind to choose, from the array of muskets, rifles, carbines that my team — Humboldt Johnny, Newton Mike, Elbow Frank — spread out before me, the one weapon that would serve as the heart, the center, of the Pinto gun. I saw at once that the older muskets, the blunderbusses and flintlocks, were worse than useless. Even the new army Springfields, because they loaded at the muzzle, could not serve. We needed a breechloader, and one with a percussion lock. That left the latest Sharps carbines, of which the Modocs had captured just nine in working condition. Each of these guns had an automatic priming system. Tiny tablets, each filled with fulminate of mercury, were spaced along a roll of tape, which advanced every time the hammer was cocked. There were fifty such caps to each roll. If six of these locks, each fitted with its own roll of tape, could be made to revolve behind a single barrel, then the rifle machine could fire some three hundred shots without being reloaded — three hundred a minute, three thousand by the time an enemy could get off more than a handful of volleys. Here it was! Victory!

With a will my team went to work, dismantling six of the rifles so that each of the locks could be fixed to the revolving drum of the chassis. As they separated the pieces I closed my eyes. The half-dozen chambers turned in my mind like the hands of a backward clock — open and accepting the charge at the twelve-o'clock position; down to ten and eight, where the breech closed and the hammer cocked; at six, the bottom of the cycle, the muzzle shot flame; and, rising, at four and two, the breech opened again and the debris from powder and cap blew away.

How clearly I saw it all! It was as if Galileo, before inventing the telescope, had envisioned each of Jupiter's moons.

"Mister-r-r Pinto!"

"Mister-r-r Pinto, mon!"

The team of Priestley Bill, Cavendish Sam, and Paracelsus Max were calling me from where they had drawn up at one side of the torchlit cave. Each had a smile on his face.

"Coom, sir! Join us!"

"You must have a wee drop!"

Bitter jest. There was, I knew well, nothing for the Archimedeans to drink. Indeed, General Jack had allotted to the invention, and the inventors, the tribe's last block of ice. Staring into the shadowy nooks, I could make out where it sat, its edges licked smooth by the Highland band. It looked like the head of a man. With a shudder I turned back to my pupils. "Ho! Ho! And what is it you are drinking? A hot cup of tea? *Mit* lemon? *Mit* cream?"

The trio, in their tattered top hats, the strips of their swallowtails, grinned. "Nae, nae!" they shouted. "Coffee! Java coffee!"

Then the youths separated, to reveal the old green coffee mill, a Netherlands product, that I had once sold the tribe. I shrugged. I sighed. There was no value in a mill without water to boil the beans. "This is not, friends, a time for humor. Return please to your work."

Paracelsus Max: "Dinna think we have been idle."

"Look," cried Priestley Bill, "at our black brew!"

The team of youngsters busied themselves about the battered grinder. Cavendish Sam upended a sack, causing a stream of beans to rattle into the top of the hopper; and when Priestley Bill tripped the levers, out they came at the bottom.

In three long strides I covered the space between myself and my co-workers. I thrust my hand into the bouncing beans. Not coffee! Balls of metal! Ammunition!

The Modocs laughed at their joke. The coffee beans were .52 caliber balls, in diameter just over half an inch. The grounds were in fact black powder, packed into linen sacks just behind. The three lads had turned the mill into a magazine!

Now Priestley Bill took one of the disassembled locks and moved it, counterclockwise, round an imaginary drum, from the shooting position at the nadir to the loading position at high noon. Instantly the hammer tripped the lever: the ball and its sack fell neatly into the breech.

A cheer went up from the front of the den. "Hooray for our spunkie Scots!"

This was the third team — Boston Charlie, Kepler Jim, Bacon Jack, who were dragging behind them what was meant to be our chassis. I was thunderstruck to see the big clothes wringer, with its mangle, its gears and cogwork, and its large galvanized tub.

"Ha-ha!" laughed Boston Charlie, even while he licked at the dwindling oval of ice. "Stole the sonabitch! Took it from that bloody idol!"

Kepler Jim: "Mister-r-r Frank Townsend!"

Now our real work began. Already long hours, the whole of a day, had gone by. But we could not sleep. The melting ice was dripping away like hourglass sand. We dared not think of those outside the cavern, who had no water at all. Instead we worked through the night. With the mangle and tub we had the chassis for our death-dealing device. Even the crank, the camshaft, and the revolving drum came ready-made. The tub was upended so that it turned on a vertical, not horizontal, axis, and the hard-rubber rollers, instead of sitting atop the machine, became the central shaft. Next we built a fire and melted down hundreds of bullets; the lead solder we used to fix the six locks to the circumference of the galvanized drum.

Finally, at dawn, the Apostles of Archimedes were ready to join the three parts of our invention — the fixed barrel, the chassis, and the magazine — together. Only then did we realize that three men would be required to operate the gun machine: one, lying flat, to aim the barrel; the second, crouching, to turn the crank; and the upright third to load and reload the erstwhile mill. Not only that: so heavy was the assembled weapon, and so tipsy on its improvised frame, that the same three men would be needed to move it from one spot on the battlefield to another.

The time to test the Pinto gun had arrived. At the rear of our den the scholars had constructed a barricade of oilcloth stuffed with pumice dust. To the front of this, as a target, they hung a brass clock. We carried the invention well off, to near the cave's entrance. The three gunners — Elbow Frank, flat on the ground; above him, Paracelsus Max; and behind him, Bacon Jack — took up their stations. The rest of the Highlanders moved back, to either side of the cavern. Squinting, I made out the hands on the distant target: eight minutes after eight. Before the hopper and priming magazines were loaded, Paracelsus Max took the mechanism through a last dry run. The crank turned the crankshaft, which set in motion the metal drum. There were a series of sharp, precise clicks as, like water-wheel buckets, the breech blocks rose and fell and the hammers drew back and then fired. All was in order. The large hand of the clock was on the nine. If the magazine had been full, the cavern would now be filled with smoke, with the harsh smell of powder, with the echo of how many shots: a dozen? A score? Half a hundred? Time to find out.

I gave the order: "Load the gun machine."

Paracelsus Max inserted the rolls of tape. Bacon Jack filled the mill with ball and powder.

"Youths!" I cried. "All ready?"

The battery mates nodded. Against the walls, with their fingers pressed to their ears, the Angus lads nodded too.

"Aim."

Elbow Frank peered along the barrel to the notch at the far end. We all saw how the hands of the clock, as if flinching, jumped a moment ahead.

"Fire, my dears!"

There was an astonishing roar and a flash of fire. The trouble, as I instantly noted, was that the flame came not from the Sharps muzzle but from the breech. Instantly the sound of exploding powder was replaced by the gunners' screams. They had been burned, scorched by the backfire of the hot gases and flame. Through the choking dust and smoke, I saw that none had been seriously harmed. The eyebrows of Paracelsus Max were singed and his face was black as a minstrel's. Most of his hair had been burned away. Elbow Frank, in the line of fire, was temporarily blinded. "Speak, laddies," said he, peering sightlessly through the coiling fumes. "Dinna we give that clock a mighty wallop?"

We did not. The brassbound clockwork was steadily ticking away. I felt, in my breast, a surge of panic. These were not merely the sounds of seconds: they were drops of ice, drops of blood, the last gasps of the Modoc tribe. We must on the instant return to our task, which was to close the gap between breechblock and bore. The solution lay in a gasket, which we cut from one of the vulcanized rollers. This magical ring of rubber, forced over the rear end of the barrel, was both strong enough to act as a gas check and elastic enough to allow the six locks freely to revolve.

But the next test revealed new trouble. Upon firing, the flame came properly out of the muzzle, like the flickering tongue from the mouth of a snake. But the bullets, issuing one after the other, flew in every direction save at the target. The tremendous recoil of the machine caused the stream of lead to glance off the roof of the cave, its walls, even the floor by our feet. When the chattering weapon ceased its fire, only one voice broke the disheartening silence.

"Question: what law of I. Newton have we seen demonstrated here?"

The Sons of Galileo all cried out: "Third law o' motion! Action! A reaction in kind!"

Thus even more time went by while we sank each of the tripod's three feet into a large chunk of porous stone. The third test, and the fourth, and the fifth, disclosed a problem far more difficult to solve than that of vibration. For at none of these firings would the gun operate for more than a half-dozen full revolutions — that is, not once did it fire more shots than my old navy Colt's — before coming to a sickening halt.

The difficulty was in the two-o'clock position. The debris from each shot, the unspent powder, was clogging the mechanism, forcing it to jam. What to do? To halt the crank after every detonation would defeat the whole purpose of the multifiring machine. But we had neither skill nor time to manufacture an automatic sweeping device.

It was the clever Newton Mike who found the way out of our dilemma. Why, he wondered, when both Paracelsus Max and Elbow Frank had been so close to the discharge of gases, had the former's hair caught on fire while the latter's remained unburned? Simple: the cranker's hair, smoothed down, shiny, had been pomaded with fish fat, while the coarse hair of the aimer had not. If the Sharps cartridges were also soaked in grease — so asked the keen thinker — might they not be as thoroughly incinerated as the hair on the older boy's head?

"*Ja!* Definitely! *Prima!*"

And such, when the Sons of Galileo fired a fat-dipped ball and sack from an undismantled rifle, the case proved to be. Even after three rapid shots, and then after six, there was not a trace of linen left in breech or bore. We had invented the self-consuming cartridge!

With a mixture of confidence and trepidation we approached the sixth crucial test. The hands on the target, the brass alarm, now pointed to sixteen minutes past five in the afternoon. Fifty of the dipped cartridges were inside the hopper. The gasket was in place. The legs of the tripod were set in their stones. The Angus lads lined up against either wall, while the battery mates, the half-blind, one-armed Elbow Frank, the black-faced Paracelsus Max, and Bacon Jack, took their places at the Pinto gun, which smelled faintly of fish fat and coffee. I gave the command:

"Fire!"

A deafening din broke out. It was like a hundred carpenters hammering a hundred nails. At the rear wall of the cave the clock exploded, its springs, hands, escapement, its double-domed bell, flying off in every direction. Then the oilskin bags began to disintegrate, spilling a great cloud of pumice into the air. There were ten seconds of continuous fire, then fifteen, then twenty. The balls began to strike bare rock, and to ricochet wildly, zigzagging like bats from wall to wall of the cave. The Archimedeans did not even duck. They sprang about like Saint Vitus's dancers. They shouted and waved, their faces ruddy with excitement. The three marksmen continued to cling to their machine. After half a minute the drum still revolved, the muzzle spat fire. Not only fire. I took a second look: gobs of molten metal dribbled from the open end. The length of the barrel had begun to glow a dull orange. Overheating!

"Stop! Stop! Attention!" But none of the gunmen heard my call. Even if they had, it was unlikely they could have obeyed. Impossible for anyone looking on to determine whether the battery mates were turning the gun machine or the machine was turning the mates: stooping, standing, cranking and cranking, clinging and aiming, they seemed to have become living cogs, human handles, in endless motion. More seconds went by, and with each second another five shots. The steel barrel was now a bright, brilliant red.

Horrified, I wheeled about and ran full speed to the side of the den. Bending low, I wrenched up the block of ice. Then, in my long, loping strides, I dashed back. At once I dropped the whole frozen load upon the melting machine. There was a hiss, as loud as a steam locomotive, and a thick white cloud rose into the cave's atmosphere. Everything was covered by a murk, a miasma of dust, powder, and pumice. Through this fog the scholars gazed down at their weapon. The barrel, dark purple now, drooped at the angle of a horse's exhausted member, some forty degrees to the ground.

* * *

In the cave there reigned an uncertain silence. No one knew what to say. Was the experiment a success? Or a failure? Should we cheer? Or fall to weeping instead? Certainly we had created a thing, a weapon, never before seen by men — not even by the masses of archers at Agincourt, or those who had released Archimedes' ten thousand darts. The trouble was, this splendid invention sat smoking, not operable, with a series of bullets jammed one behind the other in the barrel's bend. Worse still, we had wasted the last of our water — which for the tribe of Modocs might just as well have been the last drops of liquid on earth.

I glanced round at my dehydrated disciples. Wilting with weariness, they sank down, staring at the cavern walls, onto which the light from the smoldering fires cast their wavering shadows. To me, the scholars resembled those prisoners in the cave of Plato who mistook just such mirages for the perfect, ideal, unchangeable forms that dwelled in the world of light. The world of light! Nonsensical notion! Who better than I could attest that the thirst for knowledge was as nothing compared to that for plain water? And was not the sun as blinding as the shade? Certainly I had been led astray by an ideal form: the Colt's revolver. All along I had been trying to deduce our weapon from the paragon of pistols, when, according to the Baconian system, I should have built upward, from particular examples toward the general class of the machine. A pox, as Burns would have said, upon Plato! We would have to begin again from the start.

"Please, gentlemen. Do not sit in despair. We must put on our thinking caps!"

No use. The stupefied scholars were, one after the other, closing their careworn eyes. It was as if the very fluids of their brains had run dry. Only Newton Mike, rabbit-faced, buck-toothed, had the strength to move about. The rest could do no more than watch as he took up a fresh Sharps rifle, one that had not yet been dismantled, and begin to saw through the wooden stock. Then, with the lead solder, he struggled to fix the rest of the ten-pound weapon to the circumference of the vertical tub. No one rose to help him with the difficult task. To us the sight of the molten lead was a kind of exquisite torture. Here was the only liquid anywhere within the great bed of volcanic rock, and it turned out to be as hot, as scorching, as lava. Then the intelligent Indian turned wrathfully upon us:

"Dinna sit, lads, like mangy sheep! Ye are not fit to wear the plaid. Arouse, my cocks! Dinna ye see? The whole of our fiery weapons, lock an' stock' an' barrel, must turn round on our mighty machine!"

Here was the undeniable solution. Six complete Sharps, each with its own barrel, its own lock, would revolve on the outer rim. The hopper would need no alterations. Nothing could jam. The heat would be reduced by a factor of six. With a groan the Archimedeans roused themselves, one and all. With their last strength they set about affixing the rifles to the chassis drum. By midnight they were done. Then we all, teacher and pupils, inventor and gunsmiths, dropped down exhausted and closed our eyes. Only Paracelsus Max remained awake. In our dreams we could hear him turning the crank and the crankshaft, so that the drum moved about in its endless circle, round and round, like a prayer wheel in the land of Tibet.

Up came the sun again, in the world of light. Inside the cave, in the land of appearances, we shadows rose too. In spite of our thirst, our black, swollen tongues, we could not suppress a sense of excitement. If the gun machine worked — and why should it, how could it, not? — we would launch our attack. We might break through to the lake, to the water, within the hour! That, the idea of drinking our fill, of floating weightless on the feather-soft waves, revived us, refreshed us, as if we had swallowed our thoughts. The Archimedeans darted about, filling fresh sacks with pumice, setting up a new clock for a target, and dropping the cartridges that Bacon Jack had already rolled in fish fat into the open hopper. Then all stepped back together to give a cheer — except that the noise that came from our dried-out throats sounded like the rustle of brittle paper.

The final test began. The three gunners, loader, aimer, turner, took their positions, while everyone else pressed against the walls of the den. I raised my right hand. I tried, through my parched throat, to utter a command. At last I managed to bark out a single word:

"Feuer!"

All went as planned. The clock exploded like a bomb. The thick bags of dust, as if raked by invisible claws, turned to tatters. The roar of the machine was louder than ever. It sounded as if a whole regiment had gone into action. I fixed my attention on the revolving barrels, looking for the first signs — smoke wisps or a change in color — of overheating. There were none. Nor could I see any hints of jamming, or extreme vibration, or backfires from the breech. The gun simply went on shooting, five shots to each second, until after a full minute the priming tapes ran out. During this pause each man knew precisely what to do. While the gunners snapped in new rolls and the loaders new ammunition, I dashed forward to test the temperature of the metal. Too hot to touch, I discovered, but not too hot to continue.

Why, then, did the shooting not resume? When I looked up from the barrels, I saw that my co-workers had ceased their efforts. All stood stricken, with their mouths turned down. On the black cheeks of Paracelsus Max, I saw what looked like the pale trail of tears. The Pioneers were weeping! From joy? No: sorrow! Their chests heaved. Their shoulders shook. Some had their fingers in their ears, so as to muffle the echo of the clattering gun. Others had thrown their arms over their eyes, as if they could thereby blot out the memory of the flame-spitting muzzles. Someone, something, was pulling on the cuff of my checked gabardines. Elbow Frank. I knelt by his side. The youth put his mouth to my ear. A hot rush of air, the boy's breath, blew by me:

"Och, Mister-r-r Pinto. Wha' have we done? 'Tis the work o' the Devil sure!"

I understood. What the lads sought to muffle, to erase, was not the sounds and sights of the Pinto gun, the roar and the flames, but the cries of its victims, the imagined field strewn with invisible men.

It was incumbent upon me to speak. "Do not, friends, make an error. This is not a weapon of war. It is a weapon against war! *Ja!* How many men have I seen return from the battlefield, only to die from sickness, from mortal wounds? Here is a gun that allows one man to take the place of a hundred. *Hundert!* Never again will vast armies have to be raised. Tens of thousands of soldiers will be spared exposure to the wounds of battle, to death, to disease!"

It was true! Everything was becoming clear. The gun machine was not merely a Modoc weapon, a way of breaking the siege. Here was a gift to all mankind. It would save as many lives, more lives, than the vaccine for smallpox, the vaccine for rabies, combined!

Humboldt Johnny, however, shook his head. He opened his mouth to speak, but made only a clicking, a clacking, like the sound of Modoc laughter. Toward him, too, I bent closer, to grasp his words:

"I hae me doots."

But I had none! On the instant I felt carried away. I heard my own voice rise to a shriek. Blood came from my blistered throat, my puffed, parched lips. "The Peacemaker! Thus we shall name it. Do you not understand? This means the end of war! Not only will large armies be unnecessary, even small ones will refuse to expose themselves to such fire. We shall offer this gift freely to all parties. No patents! No profits! Thus one side cannot gain an advantage over the other. No offensive can succeed. When there is no hope of winning, only the certainty of slaughter, all conflict will cease. Come, friends! Let us march! We are the army of peace!"

From the Pioneers of Progress there did rise a feeble cry. They seized the gun machine, the rolls of tape, the boxes of ammunition, and tramped to the front of the cave. They were not, however, an army of peace — or an army of any kind. Nor was their cheer a martial roar, so much as a creak, a croak, a husky whicker. They rushed forward to fight not for an ideal but for an instinct. It was as if the breeze had shifted and they, like the outcasts before them, the old men, the squaws, had picked up the scent of water. One by one they staggered from the shadowy cave, to blink in the light of day.

2

There was no time to work out a plan of attack. General Jack would simply lead what fighting men he had — the Modoc police, the remaining converts, some ten other braves — down an easterly ravine, onto the black slab of glass. The gun machiners, meanwhile, would set up their weapon on the western edge of the same obsidian flow. The idea was once more to draw the infantrymen out of their trenches and decimate their ranks with enfilading fire, a hail of bullets from either flank. Then all the able-bodied Modocs would make a dash for the lake.

The sun was still rising as we went on the attack. The grown warriors began to thread their way downward, northward, through the narrow crevices and cracks. For a moment I watched from above while my students, the Pinto gun on their shoulders, moved off as well, circling down and to the left. I paused a moment more. The sun was sending its splinters through the crown of my sombrero. Beneath it my brain felt as if it were filled with bubbles, like the pockets of air in a boiling stew. Once more sparks were flying from the stones. Was all this, I asked myself, a dream, or was it really going to happen? A fight? Bloodshed? Three hundred bullets fired in a single minute? Three thousand in ten? I glanced down to the field of battle. This was no dream. Stretched on that stone, like so many broken umbrellas, were the black shapes of the outcasts, old men and squaws. I hurried to join the Highland band.

Everything happened rapidly after that. The Archimedeans came out of the lava on the western edge of the slatelike slab, and set up the Pinto gun on a small outcropping of stone. Simultaneously Two-Toes Tom led the first of the police onto the glassy gap. A shout went up from the infantry lines. Soldiers were running, some to the rifle stacks, some to the forward trench. Judge Steele appeared on his mare, gesturing toward the foe: Hooker Jim, Split-Lip Sam, Sardine Frank. Now a cavalry troop came dashing forward, onto the glass. The hooves of the horses struck more sparks against the flinty stone.

Still no shot had been fired. From our spot, well off on the west, I thought I saw Scimitar Sal wave his sword. I looked again. From the tip of that weapon something was hanging. A white handkerchief? A white shirt? A flag of surrender? The horsemen had seen it too! A shout, a cheer, rose from their ranks. They took out their sabers. They spurred on their horses. They bore down on the Modoc band.

Did the charging white men mean to capture the policemen, or cut them to pieces? Moot question. My lads had opened fire! With the Pinto gun! Outdoors, with no enclosing walls, the revolving rifles made only a steady grinding, a bearlike growl. Ahead, the horses began to stumble. Two, three, four of the steeds went down. The troop reined in, amazed. They milled about in confusion. One man, and then a second, threw up his arms and slipped from the saddle. Another horse toppled. It rose, riderless, only to have a butcher's blade of bullets chop through its legs. The cavalry split into two sections. The one retreated toward the camp; the other, the larger, wheeled westward, into the raking fire, where the smoke and the noise gave away our position. The natural scientists, the attackers, were now under attack.

"Take heart!" came the cry from Cavendish Sam. "Here is the turf where hallow'd Wallace lies!"

I stared, wide-eyed, at the boys. Boys? My men! Some stood by their clacking, clattering machine. Others clung to the feet of the tripod, to hold it steady. The remainder crawled over the smooth, dark stone, dragging fresh ammunition behind them. As the seconds went flying by, the whole scene, the entire clump of rock, became enveloped in smoke. The only visible thing was the flickering tongue of flame that darted from each successive muzzle. Suddenly there was a hollow churning, and all six barrels went silent. The minute was up. The priming tapes had run out.

Involuntarily I hunched my shoulders against the shower of steel, the blunt breasts of the horses, the bullet blows that were about to fall upon us. But that storm did not break. I peered to the east, through the thinning smoke. The troopers had been defeated! To a man! Here and there a lone horse struggled to raise its head or thrust its stiffening legs into the air. Not a single soldier was standing!

Priestley Bill rose recklessly above our tiny rampart of volcanic rock. "Coom, detested death! No terrors hast thou for the brave!"

Foolish boy! A shot rang out from a distant trench and struck the scholar in the breastbone. He dropped into the arms of his friends. From the soldiers' ranks a cry went up, and a company of infantry leaped from the ditch and began to run forward, toward our band of flat- and round-headed youths. They covered perhaps a third of the ground that lay between us before the Peacemaker went into action again. The white men in the van seemed to trip on an invisible wire. Those behind closed ranks and sprinted on. To the rear, a second company emerged from its trench, and after it, in support, came a third. Thus was the battle joined.

Not a battle. An execution. The gun barrels turned: ahead, on the blood-splashed stone, the men seemed to fall almost as rapidly as the bullets were fired. They looked like toys, like wooden soldiers, one stiff form knocking over the other until the whole row was flat on the ground. The danger to us became acute when, at the end of the second minute, the rolls of percussion caps again gave out. In that sudden silence there was nothing to hear save the gasps, the choking sounds, from Priestley Bill. Seizing the chance, the infantry made a dash for the unprimed machine.

They rose from the field; they jumped from the half-empty trench. In no time they would be upon us.

Just then a series of shots rang out from the east. Gentleman Jack and his men, and the converts too, had opened fire from the rear. For an instant the infantry faltered. That was time enough for the desperate battery mates to load fresh tapes into our machine. Then Paracelsus Max gripped the crank, and spun it around. Once more a blade seemed to cut through the advancing ranks, like a scythe through wheat. A wind of bullets blew the soldiers down. All around me the half-crazed scholars gave a cheer.

Of all the gunners, only I failed to join in. I had cause enough for concern. First, I had noted that with each pause in our fire, the enemy, drawing up its reinforcements, was growing ever nearer. The battlefield was covered with white puffs of smoke: but underneath these foam flecks, the dark blue tide of soldiers continued to advance. True, the wave of men broke, and broke again; but each time the troops reformed, regrouped, and hurled themselves forward. Second, more serious, I had seen the faint pink blush, and then the orange blur, about the spinning crank-shaft. The metal barrels were beginning to overheat. At the next priming break, I stood aghast: the steel had turned the color of plums. Indeed, I could feel the heat radiate outward, as if from andirons left in a blaze.

Instantly, wordlessly, I stripped off my frock coat and began to wave the worsted over the glowing rods. Kepler Jim, also grasping the danger, did the same with his cutaway jacket. And while Bacon Jack and Paracelsus Max snapped in the rolls of caps, the others fanned the red-hot metal with their hats.

"Goddam!" shouted Boston Charlie. He pointed to where, on the black rock, the assault had resumed. "Here come the bloody buggers!"

The battery mates could wait no longer to cool their machine. The full force of infantrymen had come out of the trenches. They dashed past the bodies of their fellows to no more than eighty, sixty, fifty yards away. Once more the Pinto gun erupted — too high at first, sending a cracking lash, a whipstroke, over the soldiers' heads, Then Elbow Frank lowered the smoking muzzles, so that the line of bullets caught the charging men at mid-section, folding them over, spilling their bowels. For a few fleeting seconds, the barrage kept the army at bay.

Alas! All the scholars knew the Peacemaker could not sustain the fire. The crankshaft now glowed as bright as cherries. The spinning of the barrels made the light dance like Saint Elmo's fire. Above the growl of the gun Cavendish Sam gave a shout. "I have it! Here's tuppence worth o' nappy to wet his whistle!" In a flash he dropped his striped trousers and directed a stream of urine onto the chattering machine. A cloud rose from the weapon, and hot sizzling gobbets flew off to all sides. In no time Boston Charlie and Kepler Jim and Newton Mike had their banker's breeches down as well. They, with Humboldt Johnny, sent their weak waterfall onto the hissing steel.

Meanwhile the three gunners remained at their stations, even as the hot urine, like molten metal, spattered upon them. How long could this shower from the withered bladders, the dehydrated bodies, last? Not long. A four count. The count of five. Then the thin threads of liquid gave out, and the Pinto gun jammed. But the cooling fountain had saved the day. The charging white men lay motionless below, while the reserves followed Judge Steele and his mare in flight. The battle was over.

Immediately a cry rose from the lakefront. General Jack was leading his fighters into the waves. They splashed there. They played. To my surprise, a number of the hurdy-gurdies, and many of the grandfathers too, were crawling across the hard obsidian toward the shore. Indeed, the Archimedeans were the last of the tribe to reach the cool waters. They had to move slowly, supporting Priestley Bill in a stretcher made from their interlocked hands. Everywhere about them the infantry lay. The clothing of those at the front, the ones shot at near point-blank range, had caught fire. Some, further off, still gasped and sighed. The Heirs of Harvey picked their way through these crumpled figures until they, too, came to the shore.

"Sonagun!" cried Boston Charlie, and dashed into the lapping waves. Then he ducked entirely under the water. "Goddam!" he shouted, as he came up for air. He splashed then. He cavorted. He floated on his back and sent up a spout like a whale. Suddenly the young man stood up. The water streamed from his flat head, his plastered hair. Then he began to thrash back toward the shore with more urgency, even, than when he had run into the lake.

There the Sons of Scotia were waiting. For all the pangs of thirst that racked them, not one had taken a single sip or put so much as a toe in the water. Instead, they knelt about their colleague Priestley Bill, who had breathed his last.

"He's gane! He's gane!" cried Cavendish Sam. "He's from us torn fore'er!"

Said Newton Mike, "He has bade the world guid-night."

Boston Charlie pushed through his grieving comrades. He fell on his knees. He kissed the dead youth on his full, smooth brow. Then Paracelsus Max folded the arms and hands on the chest, to cover the gaping wound. Bacon Jack closed the lids of the sightless eyes. From behind us, high in the lava, there came a strange moaning sound. The wind had sprung up and was blowing over the crater of the hollow fumarole, the way a boy will blow across the top of a bottle. The note it made was long and low, and filled with the sound of mourning.

3

Following the battle came a period of truce. The Modocs took over the south shore of the lake. The army withdrew to the fort on the north. Each side agreed to let the other bury its dead. The military sent its little steamer to pick up the flat-bottomed barge, onto which the bodies of the fallen infantrymen had been loaded. The Modoc dead — Priestley Bill, of course, and the five old men who had succumbed to heat and thirst — were carried through the twists and turns of the lava to the hidden burial ground at the base of Wigwam. After that all was peaceful and calm. Even the flies abandoned their stinging assault and, like bees filled with honey, droned above the smooth, unrippled waters of the lake.

There was, however, no peace for me. I took no part in the burial, not even that of the poor Pioneer. Nor did I assist my protégé, Kepler Jim, as he tended to the Modocs still suffering the effects of exposure. In my mind there was room for but a single, fixed idea: the Pinto gun.

The immediate problem was to restore it to working order, lest there be a sudden counterattack. This proved less difficult than might be imagined. Only one of the Sharps barrels had bent out of plumb, and it was easily replaced by another. We took the locks apart and cleaned them one by one. The great problem, that of overheating, remained. How did we know that in the next invasion the Peacemaker would not jam again? Against that possibility we surrounded our emplacement with reserves of water. We even constructed a small tower with a flexible hose attached to the tank, much like the sort constructed by the side of railroad tracks.

But my primary preoccupation, the root of my obsession, did not involve such matters of technology. What was the purpose of developing the Peacemaker — even a liquid-cooled, fully automatic model — if it were not used in the cause of peace? If my vision of mutual deterrence were to come true, the weapon must be deployed on both sides of any conflict — beginning, of course, with our own Indian war. The problem was how to get the machine, weighing as much as a full-grown person, to the camp across the lake.

It was this quandary that came to dominate every waking moment and even my dreams at night. The odd thing, the worrisome thing, was that even though I now had all the water I could wish to drink, the flights of sparks, the tendency of solid objects to fracture in flashes of light, had not abated; if anything, the symptoms grew. It was as if my brain, busily turning over first one solution, then another, were also overheating.

At last I decided that the only sure means of transport was a raft, one strong enough to ferry the invention over the water. I also resolved to build that craft alone, from twigs, from scraps, and to do so in secret. The Disciples of Bacon might grasp every mystery of nature; yet in the realm of politics, diplomacy, the relation of nation to nation, they remained as innocent as babes.

Would the Angus lads resent being left out of my scheme? Perhaps. But I knew they would come to understand later: if not after the peace treaty between the Modoc tribe and the United States Army, then after the general cease-fire that must spread over the entire land. Though a non-citizen, a Habsburg subject, I had no intention of allowing my adopted country to destroy itself in civil war. After delivering the gun machine to the Union forces, I would offer it to the Confederate side. Why stop there? For as long as I could remember, the nations of Europe had sought to annihilate one another, as had the various peoples of that crowded continent: Catholics against Protestants, Serbs against Croats, France against England, not to mention my own revolutionary party against king, emperor, czar. But once every faction possessed the wondrous new weapon, none could hope to vanquish the other. It would be an era of harmony! Of universal progress! Pax Pinto!

Furtive now, sly and secret, I began to assemble the bits of wood, the planks and rifle butts I meant to lash together in lieu of logs. It took me a full seven days to complete the work. The most difficult part of my endeavor was hiding it from my disciples. At the southwest corner of the lake, some three hundred yards from the Peacemaker, stood a tiny stand of tules, some half charred from the fire, the rest newly grown. That was where my vessel lay concealed. I would have no choice but to drag the dismantled gun machine part by part over the distance. The question was, would I possess the strength? Every day I felt more fragile, more feverish than the day before. The sparks, the zigzag lightning flashes, were multiplying inside my brain.

I could not, I knew, afford the slightest wait — not even for the luxury of an overcast sky. Hence, on the very night that the raft was completed, I roused myself to crawl up the inner surface of the fumarole, where the tribe lay sleeping. Stealthily I crept through the lava until I came to the black obsidian, whose smooth surface was now stained, as if by horrible paint, with soldiers' blood. Crouching, I made my way to the clump of stones that marked our emplacement. How quickly all my plans were then confounded! For no sooner did I peer through to where the gun machine nested than I was amazed to see, plain in the moonlight, two human forms. Bacon Jack! Paracelsus Max! Asleep. Loudly snoring. In despair I pulled at the wisps of my sparse, six-stranded goatee. Impossible even to approach the weapon, much less take it apart, without waking both battery mates. My scheme was all undone.

While my head swam and lights, like glowworms, wriggled before my eyes, I pondered. When an idea came, it was so simple, so obvious even, that I nearly laughed aloud. What a fool I had been! There was no need to disassemble my weapon, drag it to the raft, and then, before Judge Steele's eyes, put it together again. All the pieces were under this Mexican hat! Inside this head! The plans, not only for this rude prototype but for the perfected gun, the Adolph Automatic, were in my brain. *Dummkopf! Dummkopf!* I had only to present myself, intact, with my wits about me, at the gates of Fort Webb.

Minutes later, while the yellow stars shone overhead in what looked like a pot of indigo dye, I pulled my vessel out of the rustling reeds. The makeshift pontoons tilted, dipped, and swung into the current. The trouble was, the tide moved southward while my objective was the far-off northern shore. For a paddle I had nothing more than a rifle with a square of wood nailed to the stock. I dug this into the water, first on the left side, then on the right. In minutes my arms began to ache. The rough planks bit into my knees. Alternately I rowed, then sank forward to rest. Whatever headway I made in each burst of activity was largely erased as I lay panting on the wooden deck. An hour went by. Waves broke over the side, soaking me from sombrero to bluchers. The sky, I saw, had grown darker. Was there to be a storm? Onward I paddled, a hundred yards forward, eighty yards back.

Then, disastrously, the raft lurched and the paddle slipped from my grasp. I looked round: blackness above, blackness below, blackness on every side. Not a single light on the shore. No longer a star overhead. Even if I possessed any idea which way to row, I had only bare arms and cupped hands with which to paddle. Wearily I lay myself down. All about the waves seemed to be smacking their lips. The flat craft wobbled. It turned, as if in a whirlpool — either that, or the motion, the circling, was in my spinning head.

Suddenly, from above me, there came a tremendous rip, as if an enormous pair of hands had torn the black fabric of the sky. At the same time there was a bright flash of light. The storm had broken! But it was not a storm. Once again, from overhead, came the sound of cotton cloth tearing asunder. I jerked about in time to see that the flash of light came from behind, at the center of the lake. There was a boat there. The flat-bottomed barge! It loomed out of the water less than fifty yards away. Now, from the opposite direction, over the land, came two explosions, one after the other. Shells — artillery shells! The army had returned! With mortars!

For a brief second I remained breathless, frozen. That was long enough for a third round to go off. Again the hand seemed to part the dark backdrop above, and a simultaneous flash lit up the anchored barge. In that quick glare, and the shuddering afterglow, I could make out the round barrels of the cohorn mortars, like a row of gaping mouths. The dark shapes of the soldiers moved about in the smoke. A few seconds later came the echo, the boom, of the exploding ball. I felt on my cheeks the weak shock wave, like a breeze of light.

The next instant I was in motion, churning back to the shore. My arms slapped the water. My legs kicked the wake of the raft into a froth. The path of these shells was different from that of the howitzers, the Napoleons, the mountain guns. They went directly up, almost, and came straight down. Into the mouth of the stronghold! Into the fortress! Bombs were exploding inside the fumarole!

I reached the shallow shore. The shells were passing directly overhead. They sounded like bird wings, like a pigeon's *flap-flap*. I staggered southward, past the trenches, onto the obsidian plate. Beneath my feet the ground shuddered from the force of the distant blasts. I raced for the lava crags. Heedless of the jagged rocks, I pushed through the twists and turns. Suddenly I halted. Voices came from above me. A group of Modocs were coming down the same ravine I was ascending. It was Two-Toes Tom! And all his band! I flattened myself against the arrowlike stones. Here were Hooker Jim, Rock Dave, Sardine Frank. Scimitar Sal held his curved and glittering blade. Foolhardy fellows! How could they, alone, with their knives, their tiny guns, fight back the white man's invasion?

"Hola!" I cried, stepping into the center of the ravine. "Where are my sweet students? The Heirs of Harvey?"

But the plodding police did not halt. They tramped by me, their faces dark, grimacing, resolute. Only the last man, Split-Lip Sam, looked back over his shoulder. "Inna hideout," he said, pointing up to the fumarole rim. "All blow up! All inna pieces!"

"*Nein!* No! *Gutt Gott!*"

Scrambling now, clawing upward, I reached the stronghold. The scene within, lit by flickering flames, with its sulfurous smoke and the heart-wrenching cries of the sufferers, was like a vision of the hell pit. Even as I stood at the rim another bomb came whirling down. At this range it did not rip the air so much as beat it, as a woman might a hanging rug. The invisible missile rushed by me to explode below, with an awful concussion. Hot metal whizzed away, sizzling, sighing. All around the slopes of the giant bowl, basalt boulders began to roll, as if attracted by sudden suction.

No sooner did the roar of that bomb die away, to be replaced by the wail of Modoc voices, than another shell dropped straight down out of the fiery sky. It sounded this time like cards being shuffled in a pack. The fuse was shorter: the shock of the blast knocked me off my feet, so that I tumbled, like a loose stone myself, into the depths of the crater. I was not wounded. It was not lifeblood that I struggled to keep from losing, but the last drops of sanity. I wanted to hide. I wanted to howl. I felt as if I were inside a kettledrum on which a drummer was beating. The worst of it was, the stone walls, like the iron sides of a caldron, trapped the bomb blasts, concentrating their force, so that the crack of the air was itself enough to crush a man's lungs or a man's bones. We might, the Modocs and I, be fish in a pond: another such blast and we would all float to the surface.

Below me I heard a cry. Was it an Archimedean? An Academician?

"Achtung!" I hollered. *"Jungen! Söhne von Galileo!"*

But the Indian I discovered was no Child of the Enlightenment: just the reverse. Curly-Headed Doctor lay on the ground, his legs crushed beneath a jagged slab of stone. I ran to the spot where the savage was pinned. I tried to lift the heavy block. Immovable. Not even a team of horses could drag it away. I leaned toward the medicine man. "I regret. Amputation is required. Through the bones of the leg. Do you understand?"

But before the shaman could respond another mortar shell dropped into the crater, bursting deafeningly above us. The ground rose and fell. Stones turned and toppled. Hot shards, white-hot slivers, flew by us, miraculously close, like the knives of a performer in the Circus Prague.

In the light of that blast I had seen something, a human form, standing at the bottom of the fumarole. Again I dashed downward, to where the bomb bursts had tossed the ten-ton slabs as if they were pieces of eggshell. Wandering in these twisted alleys, the crumpled corridors, was a figure itself as white and smooth as an egg. It was the mine owner, the daguerreotyper! I rushed to join him. The apparition vanished. I dashed beneath a ledge of teetering rock. There stood the idol, stark naked, fat-bellied, in the remains of his inner sanctum. Chewed bones littered the floor, along with gnawed animal hides, and dry excrement. I shuddered. I forced the words from my mouth.

"Mr. Frank Townsend!"

There was no reply. My old colleague stared blankly ahead. I took him by the shoulders. The bones beneath the skin felt soft, like rubber. "Do you not know me? A. Pinto! Former partner! Also a Harvard man!"

Suddenly I drew back. It was clear from his blank look, his unblinking eyes, that Frank Townsend was out of his senses. He had been mad, surely, from the moment he had been pulled from the Neptune Mine. Heaven alone knew what he'd seen in those depths. Or what he had done. I looked round at the litter of bones. These belonged to the Modoc cattle. But underground, in the darkness, had he eaten Modoc flesh?

"Frank Townsend! Where are my little ones? My poor folkish people! All killed? Every one? All?"

Again, no reply. Instead, from above came the dread sound, a slap, a clap, like hands striking each other in mocking applause. The shell was falling directly upon us! I dove back, behind an upright rock. There I cowered, waiting for the inevitable blast. Strange to say, there was no discharge, only a hissing sound. Cautiously, carefully, I peered round the protective wall. What I saw made my heart stop.

Townsend had not moved an inch. At his feet, spinning and sputtering, was the undetonated bomb.

"Run, sir! For your life!"

But the daguerreotyper would not budge. Instead he leaned over the device, which was spitting out a shower of sparks. Then, amazingly, he reached down for the spinning ball, the way a boy might reach for his teetering top. In horror I watched as my old friend and colleague seized the shell and clutched it to his naked breast. With even greater horror I heard him speak.

"Adolph."

"Ich? Adolph?"

He looked straight at me. His brow was contracted, actually distorted, so that the omega mark seemed stamped upon it with the force of a red-hot iron.

"Everything was dark. Utterly dark. What was I touching? What was that smell? What did I eat? Months of blackness! It has not ended yet."

Could this be? Was I to have a conversation with a madman holding a bombshell? One that sputtered and sparked in his arms? *How you have suffered!* These were the words I would have spoken. But my voice box was frozen, as if in the grip of an icy hand.

Townsend, toothlessly, and with no mirth, smiled.

"Light, Adolph. Light."

Slowly, deliberately, he took the metal nut that held the fuse between his teeth and gave it a twist. No discharge. No detonation.

"Ho-ho," I laughed. "A definite dud."

The flash of light that erupted then was as dazzling as the sun. I was knocked flat to the stony ground. For a moment I lay stunned, my ears ringing from the boom of the blast. Then I leaped to my feet and scrambled over the barricade. Nothing of Frank Townsend remained — not a hair from his head, a nail from his finger, or a scrap of his pale white skin.

"Mister-r-r Pinto, mon!"

"Mister-r-r Pinto!"

It was the Highland band! I looked up. There, against the burning sky, were the waving, shouting silhouettes. Immediately one emotion, sorrow, was driven out by another: joy. The Pioneers of Progress were alive! With a gleeful cry I jumped upward. Hopping, skipping, I retraced my steps to the crater's rim. What a joyous reunion then, between schoolmaster and schoolboys! The pity was, our embraces were so brief. For no sooner had we greeted one another — "Are ye hale?" cried Cavendish Sam; "Are ye hearty?" — than yet another shell came fluttering by us, to explode in the depths below.

The youths were eager for action. Speaking together, as one, they explained their plan. General Jack had already led most of the tribe out of the crater. They were retreating from the lake, southward, where they could hide at the base of Wigwam. The boys themselves, the brave band, were about to join the Modoc police. Together they would put up a desperate defense against the invasion. They meant to fight to the last.

"Arise, Scots!" said Humboldt Johnny. "Wha' right hae we to eat, to sleep, to light o' day, while these dogs hae warm bluid in 'em?"

Boston Charlie shook his fist in the air: "Kill the bloody buggers!"

For a moment we paused on the edge of the fortress. We could see, down at lake level, the lights on the barge, and we noted the sudden flame of a mortar muzzle, which was followed, a few seconds later, by the sound, like shook sheets, of the falling shell. The same thought was in each of our minds. The enemy craft was well within range of our deadly machine. And the invention was primed and watered and loaded. Kepler Jim waved his arm. He gave the command:

"Coom, Scots! We'll bring havoc on 'em with our darling gun!"

Difficult, almost impossible, to find the words to describe what happened next. We defenders raced through the ravines and onto the flat plate of black rock. Boston Charlie, taller, speedier than his fellows, was first to reach the nest of the Pinto gun. With one great bound he leaped onto the outcropping of rock.

"No! No! No!"

At this cry we all sprinted forward and sprang like goats onto the emplacement. Boston Charlie was waiting. "Goddam bomb," he said, pointing to where the Pinto gun had been.

Overhead the clouds must have parted. A thin trail of moonlight lit the spot. The weapon, the marvelous machine, lay smashed: the hopper was flattened; the drum was crushed; the six rifle barrels were scattered like sticks. But it was not the ruin of their creation that wrung the gasp of horror, of dismay, from the throats of the Highland band. The force of the bomb had killed two of their number. Bacon Jack had been flung twenty feet to one side, and lay on his back, legs and arms outspread. Paracelsus Max was closer by, his face turned down and his mouth open, as if in his death throes he were gnawing the ground.

I pushed through the dazed scholars and knelt by the sooty-skinned boy. I saw in an instant that the youth's throat had been slashed, right through the windpipe to the cervical vertebrae at the back of the neck. The blood that flowed from the wound was still wet and warm. I rose and strode to the body of Bacon Jack. Stabbed in the belly, stabbed again through the nipple into the heart. No bomb had done this. These were not wounds of war. I threw back my head and opened my mouth to scream:

"Scimitar Sal!"

Stunned, speechless, the Disciples of Bacon gathered the pieces of the Pinto gun. It had not been blown apart by shock or shrapnel. The weapon had been sabotaged. Two-Toes Tom and his men had been at work here. But why? When? They had descended from the stronghold to fight off the army. Why would they attack their own tribe? Or had this been the white men, after all? Had they disguised the crime to make it look like a raid by the Indian police?

One of the rifles from our machine remained intact. Boston Charlie snatched it up. The soft linen cartridges lay everywhere under foot, like snails after a storm. He scooped up a handful and loaded the Sharps at the breech. Then he turned, aiming at the lights of the anchored barge. With amazing speed, like a human gun machine, the flathead fired three rounds.

No one could have guessed what happened next. The fire was returned: not by a single marksman, not in an infantry volley, but with a series of shots, unending bullets in a stream. They struck the obsidian in a shower of sparks, and moved steadily toward us like stitches put down by the needle of a sewing machine. At the end of two or three seconds—during which a score of balls landed about the thunderstruck Modocs—the sound of the weapon itself, a steady *tat-tat,* a kind of chatter, floated over the water. Impossible! Not credible! The United States Army possessed its own Pinto gun!

Luckily for us, the battery on the gunboat was shooting blind—or else at the tiny flame, the winking light, that had been attached to the end of the rifle held by Boston Charlie. That lad now leaped from our clump of rock and, throwing down his weapon, raced for the safety of the lava. One by one the surviving members of the Highland band followed his example. All, that is, except Elbow Frank. Halfway back to the basalt, he halted. He whirled about.

"Alack, laddies!" he shouted. "Professor Pinto hasna budged an inch!"

True. Entranced, thunderstruck, I stood alone upon the embankment. Suddenly, as if those on the far-off barge had seen me too, the army's weapon began to chatter again. *Tat-tat-tat-tat,* it went, while a series of bullets probed along the lakefront, moving steadily closer to the spot where I stood upright, utterly exposed.

"Hark, mon!" cried Cavendish Sam, from the protection of the pumice. "The deadly darts are hurtlin' a' about!"

Humboldt Johnny: "Coom! Speed wi' us away!"

I made no movement. I made no reply.

Now Elbow Frank ran to where Boston Charlie had thrown down the Sharps rifle. "Mister-r-r Pinto!" he called, even as he stooped to retrieve the weapon. "Are ye daft?"

Then, awkwardly, steadying the stock with the stump of one arm and aiming the barrel with the other, he fired three times at the dark shadow of the barge. Instantly he was answered. A swath of minié balls hummed through the air, making a diagonal line, like a sash of honor, across the poor boy's chest. Then the gunfire ceased.

Instantly all five of the Angus lads burst from the lava and sped back to their teacher. They reached for me. They grasped at my bluchers, my gabardines. They were weeping, beseeching, begging me to accompany them to their refuge. But instead of responding to their pleas, I began to laugh, to point, and to shout in what was to them an incomprehensible tongue:

"Papa Pinto! Die wilden Indianer! Mit den brennenden Köpfen!"

Do you recall how once, in another age, on another continent, I had gone with my grandfather to the Circus Prague? It was the memory of that childhood excursion that caused my outburst. In my crazed state of mind I thought my dear students were the savages I had seen then. The sparks I saw shooting from their hair, the flames that rose from their heads, were like the feathers sewn to the bonnets of the three wild Indian chiefs. The last thing I saw before fainting dead away was my children — Newton Mike, Boston Charlie, Cavendish Sam, and no less Kepler Jim and Humboldt Johnny — twisting in flame. My own burning brain made the whole world seem on fire.

4

Physician! Heal thyself! For all my years of training, my unquestioned skills as a doctor, I had made a serious error of diagnosis. The lights that I had first seen reflected from the burnished surface of the lake, and that then, in sparks, in flashes, flew from every rock, every stone; my spells of dizziness, together with the weakness in my limbs; even my monomania, my mad idea to exchange the Pinto gun — all this had not been the result of sunstroke or dehydration. The symptoms were in fact the culmination of a brain fever that had begun long before the death of Priestley Bill, and even before I had led the old men and squaws across the open obsidian: indeed, the disease might have been initiated by the blow I had received from the butt of my own Colt's revolver, or by the far greater shock of seeing the bodies of Miss Polly, Miss Nan.

An attack so slow in coming on would not quickly pass. Nor was my recovery hastened by the gruesome sight that confronted me when, coming out of my swoon, I opened my eyes. Wherever I looked, to either side, up to the ceiling, or behind, in the shadowy recesses, the tule torches lit piles of human bones, human skulls. The air that filled my lungs was hot — as hot, it seemed, as that of the Neptune Mine. But it was also so dry that the sweat on my body disappeared as soon as it formed. Even the tears, as they poured from my eyes, evaporated upon my cheeks, like a spill on a hot skillet's surface.

And why was the patient weeping? Because I knew that only one of two explanations for what I saw could be true: either I had gone mad, and was suffering from hallucinations; or else I had departed the land of the living for the kingdom of the dead. I lay for a moment, not moving. All was silent. All was still. Then, just as I stirred myself to sit, my hand touched palpable flesh. The body of Bacon Jack! And, just beyond, the cold corpse of Paracelsus Max! I had on many past occasions thought myself in heaven or hell. But this time it was no delusion: the Hebrew had landed in Hades!

Immediately a sob burst from my throat, and echoed in the ghastly chamber. My feverish mind had grasped the very sin that had cast me in this dread abode. I was guilty of murder! Not just of these two scholars and the other departed Academicians, but of all those uncountable thousands whose bones were stacked around me. And who were these victims? I had only to look about to know. There, against the walls, were those who had suffered because I had not succeeded in bringing ether immediately into the public domain. And there, with their tibulas crossed, and crossed femurs too, were the ones who had died because I had not provided the vaccine for rabies. Worst of all, stretching off row upon row, as if into the unseeable future, were the ranks of those who even now, at the very moment, were falling in battle. There was no end to it! I would be haunted forever! The blood of millions was on my hands!

"Oh, heavens!" I cried. "I wanted to do good!"

The shades responded in the only way they could: with a sighing, a soughing. *Shhh. Shhh.*

Then the wraiths of the other Modocs, my own darling students, fell upon me. The ghost of Newton Mike put his hand over my mouth. "Hush, mon!"

The specter of Cavendish Sam: "The least wee sound will undo us a'!"

I wrenched myself backward, away from the touch of the corpses. "*Mein Gott!* Here are phantoms!"

Then the spirit of General Jack appeared. Humboldt Johnny whispered in his ear:

"He holds we are ghaists!"

General Jack grinned. His gold tooth, solid-seeming, gleamed, as did the realistic medals pinned to his chest. "Ain't no ghost. Ain't no spirit. Just old ancestors here. In what-you-call-him: *catacomb!*"

I started. Could it be true? Had my students brought me to

the tribal tomb? But why? From childhood, from Pressburg, I remembered the stories of my own tribe's zealots and how they had slain themselves when faced by the insurmountable foe. Were the Modocs, like Maccabees, to take their own lives?

But General Jack, still smiling, explained. The Indians had moved to this sacred spot not in order to kill themselves, but to survive. The location of the burial ground was a carefully kept secret. The entrance, at the base of Wigwam, could not be detected from outside. Even bloodhounds could not sniff us out. The Modocs must remain silent, never stirring from the spot. They had brought with them food and drink for ten days, for twenty on half-rations. Long before then the pursuers must think the tribe had escaped. The troops would be sent off to fight in their own civil war. Such, at any rate, was the plan.

No sooner had the Modoc chief finished, however, than I realized I could not take part in it. I hissed out the following words: "Curly-Headed Doctor! Poor fellow! I must go to the stronghold. I promised to perform the amputation."

Now it was the turn of Queen Mary to smile. "You don't worry!" she said. "You watch here."

The squaw pointed to the front of the catacombs, where a hole had been sunk in the ground. I crawled to the spot. There I saw a kind of tunnel, with pumice steps leading down. The Modocs had chosen their refuge with care. No need for a guard: the footsteps of any intruder would echo long before he could reach our chamber. Moreover, only one or two attackers could enter the tomb at a time. A single brave with a musket, or even a bow and arrow, could pick the enemy off. Finally, a large boulder, round as a millstone, stood ready to seal the tunnel shut. But how could the medicine man, legless surely, manage to climb these steep steps, even if he had managed to cut himself free?

In only minutes I discovered the means. From below, in the chute, I heard ringing footsteps, and a series of groans. Then, with Kepler Jim pushing him from below and Steamboat Ed hauling him upward by a fistful of hair, the double amputee was brought into our redoubt. The poor savage was barely conscious. Bloody rags had been tied round the place where my protégé had expertly cut through the bone. Instantly the Shacknasty brothers slipped off their shirts and ripped them to pieces. These were not meant for tourniquets, however. They were gags. The Modocs stuffed the thick fabric into the medicine man's open mouth.

Had the rescue party been seen? Or the wounded man heard? No one knew. Steamboat Ed announced that the white men had landed at the lakeshore. The obsidian plate was swarming with soldiers. Many of the invaders had already begun to pick their way through the ravines. At this news the Indians took up their rifles. Big Ike moved round, so as to be ready to tip the massive stone. Then all settled down, some sleeping, some on the alert. In the ensuing silence I, too, closed my eyes. No use. Even in that darkness I saw, grinning at me, gaping at me, a hundred skulls, each with its bones crossed underneath, like the figure on the flag of a pirate.

It was not long before we all heard the noise — a footstep, the clang of boots, which rose up the chute, into our hiding place. The Modocs glanced from man to man. The army must have followed the shaman's bloody trail. There would be a fight. General Jack, clutching a Springfield, moved to the edge of the chute. The signals he made to Big Ike were clear: after he'd fired, the convert was to bring down the rock. Queen Mary, also armed, took up a position by her brother. They'd kill at least two of the foe before sealing the tomb.

The sounds from below grew louder. Too loud for one man. A squad at least. Now a voice, more voices, rose through the tunnel. General Jack cocked his rifle and laid his cheek to the stock. Queen Mary took aim as well. At the last moment there was a shout. I recognized the voice even before I saw the wrinkled face of the man.

"Damn fool! Don't shoot dumb Modoc!"

It was Two-Toes Tom. Behind him were Split-Lip Sam, Hooker Jim, Rock Dave. The Modoc police had returned. There was an outcry. The Indians dropped their weapons and ran forward to embrace their fellow tribesmen. Some wept. Others laughed. They did not think, in their joy at seeing their friends, in their relief at not being discovered, to remain on guard.

Yet I stood apart. How could I forget the image of the two murdered scholars, the slashed throat of the one, the stab wounds to the other? I looked for Scimitar Sal. Sure enough, there was the brave, with bloodstains on his shirt, and more blood on his cavalry trousers. Then, before I could yell a warning, the killer moved between Big Ike and the millstone. Simultaneously, Hooker Jim turned and gave a bloodcurdling shout:

"Come quick! You come! Kill alla stinking Modoc!"

"Attention!" It was I who gave the alarm. "Traitors!"

Too late. Before anyone could move, the hidden infantrymen rushed up the last steps of the incline into the catacombs. For a moment pandemonium reigned. Big Ike moved for the boulder; Scimitar Sal cut through his hamstrings. Queen Mary raised her rifle. A soldier — for some reason I noted his blond hair and blond whiskers — put his musket muzzle to her rib cage and fired. Someone hurled a torch toward the invaders. There were screams. There were shots. Smoke filled the air.

One of the Angus lads, I could not tell which, took my arm. " 'Tis folly to fight. Coom, dearie. There is another passage. A secret door. Above!"

I stumbled after my student. Most of the Modocs had already dashed that way, extinguishing the torches along their path. The troops, disoriented, halted their headlong pursuit. In the darkness, the turmoil, I lost my guide. All I could do was grope forward, in the direction I thought the scholars had fled. Then, from ahead, from above, I heard the distinct *tat-tat-tat,* the deadly stitching of the gun machine. The soldiers were waiting. They knew the secret exit. The Indians were caught in a trap!

In that last act of treachery the Modoc War came to an end. The warriors, the women, were captured as they emerged into the light. Steele had led the attack up through the lower chute. At the upper exit Ben Piper had manned the Gatling gun. After a few short bursts in the air, the Modocs had thrown themselves down in surrender. Then the former anatomy student led a second party through the secret chimney. The two forces met midway in the catacombs. Aside from the invalids — Curly-Headed Doctor, Queen Mary, Big Ike — they did not find a single living Modoc.

However, the white men did come across one of their own color and race. A line of soldiers, walking warily through the tomb, saw a dim movement, heard a faint sound. The officer, a lieutenant, whirled, and made to thrust with his bayonet. Ben Piper held his arm.

"Wait! Don't you see? It is a white man."

So it was, with chin whiskers, and a dark mole on his cheek. I was sitting cross-legged, in the position of the bones stacked about me. One of these skulls was cradled in my lap. On the floor nearby was a small pile of minié balls, a half-dozen at most. I picked them up. I dropped them. I picked them up again.

"Eins. Zwei. Drei . . ."

Poor Adolph Pinto! Such a dunderhead! Could I truly have thought these lead balls were the currants I had baked into a pudding for my son? And even if I had, didn't I know that the empty skull in my arms had no brain to count with, and no tongue to taste the sweets? Why, there was hardly a chance in the world that it belonged to Dumb George at all. True, it was small enough, delicate enough, to be a child's. And there was something about it — the wide-spaced sockets, the line of sharp little teeth, even the bulge of the brow — that reminded me of the lopsided head of the boy. No! No! No! Not possible! The skull that I held in my lap might have been that of any child, a Modoc boy, a Modoc girl, who had died before its time, in the course of ten generations.

CHAPTER FIVE

Pinto & Sons

1

TWO YEARS AFTER THE CONCLUSION of the Civil War, I returned to the Golden Gate. It was August. A bright, brilliant morning. The river steamer maneuvered among the crowded masts, just as the *Unicorn* had done so many years before. But everything else had changed. Seventeen years earlier the city had seemed a gathering of squatters and nomads, whose canvas tents were scattered about the barren dunes, the muddy flats, the chalk-covered hills. What a metropolis now! As in Boston, the very landscape had been altered, with the tops of high hills lopped off to extend the waterfront into the bay. Streets that had once been piers and docks were now at the center of town. The entire city was graded, planked, drained. Crowds in their thousands filled the roads.

I dashed from the gangway and into the streets that stretched from the wharves to the old Portsmouth Square. Every foot of sidewalk was lined with shops, businesses, auction houses. Here were factories. Here were banks with granite ornaments. Great office buildings, municipal buildings, loomed above me. A hotel, the Palace, took up an entire city block. On one street, Market, a steamcar chugged back and forth. Wherever I looked I saw more kinds of faces — black and Oriental and Indian, Sandwich Islanders and hook-nosed Israelites, with Turks and Hindoos and

Abyssinians — than I remembered from my long-ago visits to Prague and the imperial city of Vienna.

I had already decided to reopen my shop, in San Francisco. The difficulty was that I did not have enough money to purchase a site in the commercial center. Back in Yreka, the Neptune Mine had shut for good. Many of the townsfolk were dead or departed. It seemed my old home was about to become a ghost town. Thus when I sold my fireproof I got little more for the two-story building than the value of the goods inside.

With this sum I chose a lot on Vallejo Street, where the grade of Russian Hill was so steep the trams could not reach and where, it was assumed, no venture would prosper. But prosper the Jew's slop shop did, adding, on average, one new story atop the old every five years. The Jew himself, the merchant of Russian Hill, moved upward too, keeping the living quarters — bedroom, library, small kitchen, the music room of his wife — on the topmost floor. These days, in the '80s, only the gigantic Emporium has a greater selection than Pinto & Sons. For all the steepness of the location — and Vallejo is less a street than a set of steps — customers continue to throng. They ride the electric elevator from one floor to the next. And each one is still greeted by my Frau, as she likes to call herself in our little joke.

A further word about this excellent woman. A Berlin native. Soloist upon the pianoforte. I saw her first at the El Dorado Saloon, where she accompanied the performance of the famed Madame Moustache. That female, full-bodied, with a kind of down on her lip, sang songs, recited *The Queen of the Nile,* based on Shakespeare, and danced to the music that Anna, more spindly, definitely Semitic, provided. During the performance the dark-hued garments of Madame Moustache would melt away, so that gradually, like boulders appearing in the muddy Nile, patches of white skin would begin to show through. At the height of this dance a smell, half almond, half ammonia, wafted over the crowd; the dancer's bare breasts swung wildly, like the screws of a modern steamship. This was for me a stimulation. At that time I had little companionship, save for occasional visits to my old friend Antoinette, who had settled in the crowded Chinatown quarter. Madame Moustache was different. When she danced it was as if the painted Venus of the Sazarac Saloon had come to life.

For all my visits to the El Dorado, the great star and I never exchanged so much as a word. Instead I struck up conversation with the sharp-nosed and curly-haired musician. Her eyes, I noted, were watery, and her bosom almost flat. She was the one I courted, until, after almost three years, she agreed to become my bride. Some things, however, cannot be achieved by diligence, by determination. In spite of our efforts, this good wife has not been able to bear a child. The store on Russian Hill is not named for our sons.

In all other ways, through unceasing effort, I have prospered. In the community I have an honored place, as well as a seat at the Emanu-El Temple, with its minarets, its copper globes. Yet all this hard work was expended not merely to increase my wealth, my standing, but to help me forget. Memories, endlessly rising, are worse to contemplate than the blank wall of the future that stretches ahead. Thus did I distract myself with busyness. The grand store filled my days. Nights were devoted to the study of the American Constitution and the memorization of the governors of the thirteen colonies and the capitals of every state. What an honor when, at the Montgomery Street courthouse, I stood at attention and recited the oath of allegiance. A new country! A new nation! Citizen Pinto!

Let us come now to the present, a day late in the year 1885. On this morning, like all others, I sat down to breakfast. The rain was beating upon the new fourth-story windowpane. My repast consisted of toast wedges and a soft-boiled egg. My appearance? Recognizable: the drooping eyes, the mole on the cheek, the lips pursed whether I was or was not blowing steam from my coffee. But my black curls were now half gray, as was my fullish moustache and the dandified beard that grew along my jaw and over my chin. I opened the newspaper and read — here are the words, dancing in front of my eyes — the following story:

PASTEUR'S LATEST DISCOVERY
CURE FOR HYDROPHOBIA
HUMAN PATIENT SAVED

Such were the headlines. The story began precisely like this:

> More than four months ago a boy named MEISTER, who had been bitten fourteen times by a mad dog, was brought to Paris from Alsace by his mother, who hoped that PASTEUR could save him. Two eminent physicians of Paris agreed that

> the boy was doomed to die a painful death unless some remedy should be found, and they advised that PASTEUR should be allowed to save him.

These are the two sentences with which the article concluded:

> The patient is first inoculated with the virus of greatest attenuation, and then with virus of gradually increasing power, until at last a specimen is introduced whose period of incubation does not exceed one week. After that inoculation the patient is proof against the disease.

In the twinkling of an eye my eggcup shattered. The coffee, as a result of my having jumped to my feet, was spilled across my worsteds. I shouted a word to my wife — "*Auf Wiedersehen!*" — and ran from the room. First to the library, where I pulled down the old volume of Burns. Then, coatless, hatless, without an umbrella, to the stairwell, where I dashed down the flights of stairs. Why not the elevator? Too slow! Out into the roadway. Bent from my years underground, I trotted all the way to the Powell Street pier. Then I hired a water taxi and set out into the bay. The rain plunged down upon the awning above us, and streamed over the canvas sides. The gray seas rose ahead and behind. I stared through the spume. Finally, in the distance, there rose before me the black rock and the yellow lights of my destination. The Island. Alcatraz!

2

With a gasp I turned away, but not before a sharp pain passed from one side of my head to the other, as if an arrow had pierced my temples. I leaned dizzily back. I shut my eyes. Seasickness? A little. But mostly I suffered from an attack of remembrance. This was the same delirium, the same half-trance I had fallen into a quarter of a century before, after the capture of the Modoc tribe. The sounds about me, the slap and splash of the waves, were much like those I had heard then, upon emerging from my comalike sleep. No! Do not look back! Do not dwell! Better, far, to throw myself into the deep! Alas: just as then I had no choice but to awaken, I had none now other than to recall.

Two days after my capture I had roused myself to hear the

sound of waves and the intermittent hum of the Tule Lake flies. That meant that the wooden walls around me must be Fort Webb, and that I had been removed to the northern edge of the lake. I listened more closely. It was not the splash of the waves that had waked me, nor the familiar snoring of the Modocs who lay all about. What I heard was a louder sound: a percussion, a pounding, like sledgehammer blows. It came from outside the walls of this building, beyond the barrier of the stockade.

I shook myself fully awake. The sun, I saw, was streaming through the windows of what looked like a barracks — except that these portals were barred. This was a prison! The single door, to either side of which an armed soldier slouched, had been fitted with a bolt. There were no cots; all the Indians slept on the floor. The tribe had been divided in two: the squaws, with their papooses, and the old miners with them, were at the far end of the room, behind a barricade of flat pine planks. Through the gaps in the boards I could see the women walking about, while the grandfathers sat or stood, softly coughing. The braves were on my side of the room, together with the five surviving members — the adults, Boston Charlie and Kepler Jim; and the lads, Humboldt Johnny, Newton Mike, Cavendish Sam — of the Highland band. The Shacknasty brothers were also here, Jake and Jim, together with Big Ike and old Steamboat Ed. I was surprised to see Queen Mary, in the last bits of her linen, her lace. The wound to her side had done no more than sear the flesh and crack a rib. Who else? Curly-Headed Doctor sat upright, holding his rag-wrapped stumps. And there, against the wall — I hardly recognized him without his jewelry, without his general's cape and tunic and the pants with the yellow stripe — was Gentleman Jack. The gold tooth was left. It flashed in a smile.

"Goddam!" declared the chief. "What-you-call-him-inna-Noah-Webster: *salutations!*"

Joyfully I raised my arm in greeting. Only then did I discover, from the weight of my limb and the sound of the clanking chains, that I was no less a prisoner than any of the Modocs in the room.

Just then the bolt on the door was thrown back, and the two guards jumped to attention. In fact, the tribe had been split into three. The third part was the Modoc police. Split-Lip Sam, Rock Dave, Sardine Frank, Hooker Jim, and Scimitar Sal strode into the barracks. Each was dressed in the fresh new uniform of an army private. Last came Two-Toes Tom. He wore, in addition, a corporal's stripes. Could these murderers be soldiers now? Tom led the others across the room, weaving as he walked. The smell of spirits trailed after. Some of the prisoners shrank back. The youngest, Humboldt Johnny, shook his fist: "Ye traitors!" he cried. "Sold the Scottish name for hireling wages!"

The police walked by the youth. I feared they meant harm to Gentleman Jack. But they passed the chief as well. At the center of the room, Two-Toes Tom halted. He started to laugh. "Goddam," he said. "Smells rotten, you betcher!"

Rock Dave: "Sure stinks a lot!"

Scimitar Sal: "Smell lika bunch of fish!"

The rest of the traitors burst out together: "Must be those stinking Modocs! Ha-ha-ha!"

Then the band, all in blue, and still laughing aloud, wheeled round and went out the way they had come.

I hauled myself to my feet and stretched up toward the bars of the nearest window. The Modocs were crossing to the stockade's main gate, which swung open before them. They were free men. Free as the birds. As the breeze.

It was not, however, that realization that made me tremble, so that the chains on my limbs rattled anew. Through the open gate I had heard the swelling sound, the *bang-bang-bang,* of metal on metal, and had glimpsed the hammerers at their work.

"Run! Run, darlings! Run for your lives!"

With that cry I whirled about and made a dash for the door. At once I was caught short by the taut links of my chains. I tripped and fell. From flat on the floor I looked round at my fellow captives. "They are nailing the planks," I moaned. "They are nailing the frame. For *der Galgen!* The gallows!"

That same day, in mid-afternoon, the prisoners were put on trial. Was I, I wondered, asleep or awake? One minute all had been as before: the empty barracks, with the chained Modocs at one end, the old men and squaws at the other. The next moment a crowd of soldiers brought in a table and chairs. Through the guarded door strode Judge Steele and four officers, led by a colonel— Wheaton, his name was, a plumpish fellow with a riding crop in his hand. These white men sat down at their places and the proceedings began. But this trial was indeed like a dream. Not only was there no courtroom, no judge, and no jury, but there was no lawyer for the defense. There was not even testimony on behalf of the defendants. Steele was the one who told each of the

Modocs what he — or she: Queen Mary's crime was the mutilation of the cavalry corpses — was accused of, and asked how he pleaded. If the defendant tried to explain, or to justify what he had done, Wheaton brought down his riding crop upon the table.

For that matter, most of the tribe remained silent. They had been ordered to stand, and all did so save for Curly-Headed Doctor and Big Ike, who, because of his slashed hamstrings, leaned against the wall. They stared ahead as if they did not understand a word. Only the scholars, the Academy members, dared to speak up. Their crime, according to Steele, was complicity in the murder of General Webb. Yet when Newton Mike pointed out that the white men had first shot Scarface Charlie, Wheaton cut him off. The same thing happened when Humboldt Johnny began to relate how the Modocs, uprooted from their village, toiling underground, had been killed by the score in the collapse of the Neptune Mine. Down came the crop on top of the table. Still the natural scientists persisted. Cavendish Sam noted how it had been a white man, not an Indian, who had begun the ghost dance, which had in turn led to the outbreak of the war. At that, Colonel Wheaton rose from his chair.

"You do not understand. This is not a civilian trial. We are not concerned with what did or did not happen between the citizens of California and your tribe. The jurisdiction of this court is restricted to violations of the rules of war — particularly the terms of the Tule Lake truce. What took place before the conflict and what led to the conflict are not relevant. You have heard the charge. How do you plead?"

The Angus lads responded as one: "Na guilty!"

Then the evidence was presented against them. Judge Steele described everything that had occurred on the barge, from the moment he'd boarded until he'd been forced to leap into the lake. After that testimony, the talkative scholars fell silent. The Modoc police entered the room. They did not deny their role in the murders. One after the other, each claimed the idea had come from Curly-Headed Doctor and the then Captain Jack. The converts, they said, had urged them on, too. In the end, all the Modocs, including the top-hatted youths, had agreed to the slaughter. Scimitar Sal and the others had done no more than carry out the decision of the tribe. "Hooker Jim, he gotta do what Two-Toes Tom say do, and Tom, he gotta do what say alla dumb Modoc peoples."

Wheaton turned to the Academicians. So did the other prisoners. I saw how, on the far side of the room, the squaws were pressed to the slats, looking on like Jewesses behind the barrier in a temple. No one spoke. The Pioneers of Progress continued to stare at what was left of their patent-leather shoes. Even I asked myself if what Hooker Jim and the rest had said could be true. Horrible! Not credible! Nonetheless, I could not help recalling how Humpy Joe, for the converts, had taken part in the killings, and how Boston Charlie, the oldest of Harvey's Heirs, had stood by without a murmur of protest. Might it be? Were the lads, the lambs, a part of the crime?

"*Nein!*" I cried, taking a hobbled step toward the table. "What madness! Here the guilty are innocent and the innocent guilty. How can you think to accuse mere children? Attend: before the peace conference I received a message. In code. A dash, two dots. A dot, a dash. Then a dash and a dot. Ho-ho! Do you not realize this? *Danger!* A message from the scholars. A warning! Do not participate! Do not come!"

There was a pause. Suddenly my heart leaped up. I saw, among the crowd of infantrymen standing behind the table, my old acquaintance Sid Christie. With his cane hooked over his arm, the *Ingot* editor was writing on his pad. Hope! Here was hope! Every word was being noted.

Wheaton, however, was frowning. "I do not see how what you say clears your students. It implicates them, in fact. How could they warn you about something they were not aware of? They must have known the Indians would come armed."

"Excellent reasoning, sir! But now we must be with each other candid. Both sides at the conference possessed hidden weapons. Judge Steele surely remembers this fact."

The Indian agent smiled. "Yes. I do remember. You had a Colt's revolver."

"*Ja!* And you a derringer, no?"

"True enough. I used it to defend my life. To what purpose did you put yours?"

"Pardon?"

"Did you not give your gun to the Indians? Isn't that how you managed to survive?"

"What? Give my gun! A non-truth! Falsehood! What can this mean? That I, too, am not loyal? Boston Charlie, tell the gentleman! Tell everyone! I did not in this base manner purchase my life!"

The witness attempted to respond. His words were drowned out in the protests of his fellows.

"Nae!"

"Mister-r-r Pinto is na guilty!"

"He wadna die but by his own hand!"

Wheaton slashed his crop in the air. He pounded the butt on the table. Finally one of the seated officers, a major, leaned forward. "You must admit, the facts seem against you. Coded messages on the eve of the conference. A revolver smuggled onto the barge. Then, not only are you the sole white man not attacked, you manage to escape unharmed."

"Escape? But no! Remember: I was *ein Geisel!* A hostage!"

Once more Wheaton banged his makeshift gavel, striking it repeatedly against the top of the table. I clutched at my head. These sounds were mingling with the blows of the hammerers outside the room. It was as if the nails were being driven into my skull. What sort of trial was this, when the hangman was preparing the noose before the verdict was declared?

With silence restored, Wheaton put the next question. "If you were a hostage, why didn't you get away? You certainly had the opportunity when you came through the lines for water. I am told you were not turned back like the Modoc women and the old Modoc men."

"On the contrary," Steele cut in. "I welcomed you myself. But after you'd drunk your fill and attempted to bring water to your friends, you ran off. This man"—and here the Indian agent turned to address the other members of the panel, and the crowd of soldiers to the rear—"this man made his escape all right: back to the lava beds!"

"What else are we to think," said the major, "but that if not before, then at that moment you joined the enemy camp?"

Now it was my turn to fall silent and stare at my high-topped shoes. The charge was true.

A stir rose from behind the table and chairs, where the infantrymen were crowded together. A shout came from their ranks:

"He's no American!"

"Not a soldier either!"

"He only joined up after the fighting began!"

"A copperhead!"

"A spy!"

The anger in these voices stunned me. Why, for what reason,

did they hate me so? I forced myself to lift my eyes to my accusers. Only then did I note what these men had in common: each was wounded. Some had their arms in slings. There were bandages round the heads of others. The rest leaned on crutches, on canes. One of these soldiers pointed his stick in my direction.

"I seen him! Can't forget him! Waving his coat — that black coat he's wearing now!"

"He was at the machine gun. No mistake. He directed the fire."

"He killed us!"

A frightening growl rose from the men. They seemed ready to hurdle the table.

Colonel Wheaton raised his hand. "The most serious charge, Mr. Pinto, concerns yourself. It is that you, while a sworn member of the United States Army, directed hostile fire against your own race, your own comrades-in-arms."

I was dumbfounded. My mind spun round like the barrels of the Pinto gun. How to explain that my invention was for the benefit of all mankind? That it was designed to bring peace, not war? My accusers would never believe that I had actually attempted to carry the plans for the weapon across Tule Lake and offer them to the army.

Wheaton continued. "We charge you with more: that not only did you command this hostile fire, but you instructed these savages in how to construct the deadly weapon. Will you deny that you stole the secret of the Gatling gun, and in the heat of battle gave it to the foe?"

Now I felt coursing through me not fear but anger. How dare they accuse me of forgery? Of theft? With a clank, I stomped my shackled shoe. *"Nein!* I do deny it! This was my idea, my invention. *Hundert Prozent!"*

At this confession, the infantrymen pressed forward. "That's treason!" cried one. Then the others chanted together:

"Traitor! Traitor!"

In the face of such fury, all the prisoners drew back, pressing against the wall of the Fort Webb barracks. Only Newton Mike stood his ground. He even edged forward. Then, with his sharp chin lifted, the lad began to speak:

"How is it ye dare call this noble soul traitor when so many hae committed the selfsame offense? What of the deceitful rogues, the guilt-bespotted squadron o' the Modoc police? I canna fathom why the deuce ye would reward those turncoats for the very deed ye would punish our bonnie professor! Sirs! Captains! Kill us if ye must. But dinna tie the noose round the neck of our darling teacher. Dinna lay in the dishonored dust so gallant and so gay a friend!"

At these words a lump, as thick as a hangman's knot, rose in my throat. But the soldiers, the wounded infantrymen, stared blankly ahead, as if the brogue of Burns, so musical, so enchanting, was a foreign tongue. As for the panel of officers, they'd spent the moment whispering among themselves. Now Wheaton rose. First he said there was no purpose served in drawing out the proceedings. Next he announced that all of the prisoners had been found guilty as charged and would at dawn's light be hung by the neck until dead.

A cry, a moan, went up from every part of the room.

"A'?" asked Cavendish Sam. "E'en the lasses?"

On Wheaton's white face there was the suggestion of a smile. "We do not wish to appear vindictive, or lacking in mercy— though none was shown to the officer for whom this fort is named. Except for the squaw known as Queen Mary and the old man known as Steamboat Ed, the women and the elderly and all who merely served as combatants will be placed under the jurisdiction of the Bureau of Indian Affairs, for resettlement in the east."

Curly-Headed Doctor said something in Modoc.

"What's that?" asked Steele.

The medicine man translated for himself. "Hooker Jim? Rock Dave? All them fellers? Hang them, too?"

Big Ike turned his large head. He dropped his lantern jaw. "Maybe shoot 'em? Chop offa head?"

From where he stood behind the table, Wheaton replied. "It is crucial that all the tribes of the Northwest know that no harm shall befall those who cooperate with the army. That lesson must spread far and wide. We appreciate the courage it took for these men to destroy the machine gun, and to lead us to the secret redoubt. They put the interests of the country ahead of their people. Let it be known that in saving the lives of many white men, they also saved their own. They are free to go where they please. If it is their wish to be resettled, then Two-Toes Tom will become chief of the Modoc tribe."

At this all the Indians began cursing and wailing. In the commotion someone opened the barracks door. I saw Sid Christie limp through. By midnight, then, the presses of the *Ingot* would be printing the terrible news.

The dawn came all too quickly. Strange to say, I slept through this last of my nights. When I woke, a dew had formed on the bars of the window, and covered the windowsill. Cold droplets ran on the metal chains. The Children of the Enlightenment sat silent. Their teeth chattered — from fear in part, in part because of the chill autumn dawn. Were these boys really about to die? And what of myself, A. Pinto? How many times, in how many ways, had I stood on the verge of extinction? Always, at the last moment, fortune had intervened. Fortune? Impossible not to think I had been chosen, picked out, for some special fate. Even now, with first light breaking, I believed I might escape. But how? Guards stood within the barracks. More soldiers patrolled without. Perhaps a reprieve? An act of mercy? Not likely. Not when the colonel was so clearly determined to hang us all. No: the one hope was Christie. If the telegraph line was still up in Yreka, the publisher would have time to send the news to Wheaton's superiors, to the Department of the Columbia, to the Division of the Pacific, and return to the fort with a reply. I found that I was actually listening for the sound of his horse's galloping hooves. Then I gave a start of despair. Not only were there no hoofbeats, there was no sound of any kind. The pounding, the hammering, had stopped.

A moment later some ten soldiers entered the barracks. They strode down the aisle between the prisoners and pushed through the barrier that separated the tribe. Then they led the women and elders from the building. After that, a chaplain came in to talk to the converts. He told them of the joys that awaited them in heaven: the music, the nectar, the light. All they must do was renounce the evil they'd done. That prompted a response.

"Goddam!" said Boston Charlie. "Sure is a helluva place. You go, mister. This ignorant Modoc gonna stay behind."

The Indians began their clicking laughter; it was cut short when the guards reentered the room. They ordered us to stand, after which they tied our hands behind our backs. A blacksmith moved down the aisle, knocking the shackles from our legs. Then the prisoners — we were an unlucky number: thirteen! — were led outside, across the stockade, where a light rain, more a mist, had started to fall.

As soon as we passed through the gate we saw the gallows. The scaffold, made from unsplit logs, was thirty feet long. A half-dozen nooses hung from the beam. Through these slack ropes I made out the surface of the lake, gray, dull, like iron. To the left of the gallows the soldiers of the fort were assembled. An artillery company crouched before their weapons. A troop of cavalry stood holding the bridles of their mounts. To the other side of the scaffold, on a small rise in the ground, sat the grandfathers, the squaws. The only sound anywhere came from a papoose, crying from hunger, or from the damp, the cold.

The officers — Wheaton, Steele, the major — were standing in the open space, directly ahead. With them was the man I'd been hoping for, Sid Christie. His hat was off. His shiny head was wet with the blowing mist. If he had a message, if he could save us, he gave no sign. The officers did not look up when the Modocs and I walked by, nor when we were brought to a confused halt in front of the gallows. A problem had arisen: how were the prisoners to mount the platform? In novels, of course, there are always thirteen steps leading to the scaffold floor. At Fort Webb there was only a simple ladder. The guards debated whether to untie their charges' hands, so as to permit us to climb the rungs on our own. In the end, two infantrymen were stationed at the top of the ladder. They hauled the first group, in which I was included, onto the untrimmed boards.

I was the last upon the platform. The minute I looked about I discovered a miscalculation. The condemned — besides myself there were Gentleman Jack, the Shacknasty brothers, Big Ike, and Steamboat Ed — stood under the crossbeam, while Curly-Headed Doctor sat strapped to his chair: seven in all. But there were nooses for only six! Hope surged through me like an injection of sugar from needle and syringe. Was I the extra man? Then, while the Modocs continued to stand, shivering, trembling, the warmth of my emotion was replaced by chill despair. There, behind the bulk of the scaffold, was a row of caskets, more than enough for all. Beyond them was a freshly dug pit, its walls stained with lime. Here was the last resting place for Pinto of Pressburg.

Another puzzle presented itself to my busy brain. I saw, leaning against the gallows frame, a steel-bladed ax. At the same time a soldier, a corporal, climbed to the platform, with a long pair of shears in his hand. What did these blades mean? A beheading? Such an end would be a favor to the Modocs, who believed that the tightening noose prevented the escape of the soul. Or were these sharp edges meant for the extra man — perhaps for myself? I turned to the young soldier.

"You are the executioner, sir? The beheader? Better to use the guillotine. This was the idea of a doctor, a Frenchman, at the time of the great revolution. Question: why would a physician invent such a device? Was it to cut off the head of the famed Marie Antoinette? No! No! False surmise. Answer: Monsieur Guillotine wished to allow the common man, and not just the nobility, to escape the sensation of pain."

The corporal, thin-faced beneath his long-billed cap, moved directly to Shacknasty Jake and pushed his head forward. He cut off the hair where it fell below the ears, across the neck. He did the same to Steamboat Ed and, one after the other, all the Indians in the line.

Now the true executioner climbed the ladder. No doubt this time: the man wore a black hood over his head. He placed one slipknot behind the ear of Gentleman Jack and another at the same spot on Shacknasty Jim. Then he paused. The condemned men were all looking off to the right, where the troops were assembled. I turned that way, too. Slouching there, with grins on their faces, were Rock Dave, Sardine Frank, Split-Lip Sam, Scimitar Sal, Hooker Jim. But where was the old man, the head of the Modoc police? The prisoners muttered. They flinched away from the executioner's grasp. All seemed to have the same thought: the man who would hang them was Two-Toes Tom! It was too much to bear. There was a growl of rage, of indignation. Then Shacknasty Jake inclined his head in the other direction. We turned. There was the old man, plainly tipsy, passing his bottle of whiskey round the graybeards of the tribe.

There was no further resistance. The hangman slipped the nooses over the remaining Modocs: Steamboat Ed, Curly-Headed Doctor, Shacknasty Jake, and the large head, the protruding ears, the massive jaw of Big Ike. Then he approached the last victim.

"Ho-ho: a Mexican hat! *Mit* tassels! Too big for your rope!"

But the hooded man — he had a whiff of mint about him — pushed me aside, away from the zone of the drop.

At last the officers looked round. Without raising his voice, Judge Steele asked, "Does any of the prisoners have something to say?"

A second of silence followed. The mist blew over the scaffold, left to right. Then Gentleman Jack said, "How come you gotta steal Jack's clothes? Beautiful cape. Horseshoe vest. Fancy purple braces. Gimme perfume. Gimme pomade. Don't wanna smell lika dog."

A shout came up from the infantry ranks. "Don't worry, Jack. You've got a stiff collar now!"

A ripple of laughter passed over the scene. Even the men on the scaffold smiled.

Then Shacknasty Jim tapped the hollow platform with his boot. He kicked at the boards.

Shacknasty Jake: "Dumb brudder, he wanna cuppa coffee. Black coffee. Hot coffee. Take five minute maybe to make."

Now Colonel Wheaton raised his hand. At the same moment, simultaneously it seemed, the executioner brought down the ax upon the strong hemp that held the trap. The boards fell with a crack. A spray of mist went up from the taut ropes. Two of the men, Steamboat Ed and Big Ike, drew their legs convulsively upward. The rest hung limp. Then Steamboat Ed, shuddering, sagged. Big Ike writhed a moment longer, suffocating from the weight of his body, not the force of the fall. Then his struggles ceased and, relaxed now, he swung back and forth. A brief wail went up from the women. Then all was still.

The major was the first to speak. "Mr. Pinto: would you examine the Indians. We need a doctor's word to pronounce them dead."

Standing stunned, I could only shake my head.

Steele: "You must. No other man has the training."

This time I said, "My hands."

The corporal climbed back on the platform and cut through the cords at my wrists. The executioner, meanwhile, had reset the drop, so that I might approach the corpses. Mechanically I checked each man's pulse. I listened for a heartbeat. There was none. I made the announcement: *"Alle sind tot."*

At that word the guard detail went back to work. The ropes were removed from around the necks of the dead men, so that the nooses hung free in the air. The corpses were dragged to the back of the platform and the second group of prisoners — all the Sons of Galileo, and Queen Mary, too — were hauled up the ladder by the armpits. Once again the dread barber began to shear off the dark locks. Then the executioner — terrible thing for a man to see! — passed the rope over the head of the mother of my child, and tightened the nooses around the necks of my five surviving sons.

This time Steele did not bother to ask if anyone wanted to say a word. But I did! I wanted to howl a protest! Before I could open my mouth, however, someone else started to speak. It was Sid Christie.

"Enough," the editor said. "The charade has gone too far."

The officers threw back their heads. They laughed aloud. The major pointed toward the scaffold and gave an order: "Cut them down."

Immediately the corporal sliced through the rope that stretched over the head of Queen Mary. Then he began to saw at the next in line.

The freed prisoners staggered to the front of the platform and, gasping, with the ghastly garlands still round their necks, jumped to the ground. I leaped down as well.

Judge Steele was there to meet us. "We have this morning received instructions from the Division of the Pacific. The War Department does not find it fitting to execute women or minors. Their sentences have been commuted to lifetime servitude in military prison. As for Mr. Pinto, even if he was not compelled to treachery by his captors, or by his illness, no useful lesson can be learned by the spectacle of white men killing whites. Thus the acting assistant surgeon will be returned to service in the ranks."

Now Wheaton turned toward me and, as if to offer this member of his forces a salute, threw up his hand. Instantly a cry rang out from behind my back:

"Mister-r-r Pinto!"

It was Kepler Jim! And Boston Charlie! Still on the scaffold, and still with the ropes round their necks! Even as I took this in, the hooded killer brought down his ax, the twine parted, and the two Angus lads swung in the air.

I clawed at my own throat, as if hemp had tightened around it. Tears in a fountain poured from my eyes. "Why?" I wailed. "Oh, why?"

But I already knew. The army had separated the flatheads from the roundheads, and cracked the spines of the two older boys.

The major started to speak. "Surgeon Pinto —"

But I did not wait for him to finish. I walked to the ladder, climbed it, and approached my two comrades. No pulse. No life.

Boston Charlie's eyebrows were knit together in a frown. Kepler Jim stared wide.

"Dead?" asked Cavendish Sam, from below.

I nodded.

"The twa best fellows," said Humboldt Johnny, "that e'er were born."

Once more the lament, high and wavering, rose from the knoll where the squaws were seated. When it ended, the major spoke once again.

"We have been ordered to perform an autopsy. The acting assistant surgeon must do it. When you have finished, bring me the report."

Defiantly I shook my head.

"But you have no choice. Nor do we. There is no one else for the task."

"No. Not correct." I turned. I pointed toward the executioner. The hangman removed his hood. It was, as I had surmised, Ben Piper, trained in anatomy at the Harvard Medical College. He smiled, and saluted.

Now the detachment of guards moved forward. They marched the surviving Modocs away. The officers moved off as well. Then the soldiers were dismissed. They ran — the infantry, the artillery, even the cavalry troops — toward the gallows. They swarmed onto the scaffold. All together they fell on the dead men, ripping their clothing, snatching their shoes. Some crawled about on hands and knees to scoop up clumps of the chopped-off hair. Others pulled down the ropes and started to unravel the strands. Nothing was overlooked. Even the buttons of Dandy Jack's trousers were turned into souvenirs.

3

The water taxi shut its engine; we drifted to the dock. I disembarked. The rain, I noticed, had stopped, and the breeze had shifted round. The walls of the prison loomed high. At the far end of the landing, three soldiers blocked my way. In spite of my pleas, they would not let me through. I required a pass, with a stamp. Even if I had possessed it, the hours for visitation did not begin until mid-afternoon. Arguing, gesturing, I held my ground. Useless. The pilot of the tender asked whether he should wait. I nodded yes. Then, full of stubbornness, I squatted on the dock's wet planks.

What was left to recall? Little enough. Ben Piper had performed his autopsies all too well. In his zeal he had severed the necks of Big Ike, Steamboat Ed, and Gentleman Jack. Either that, or the souvenir hunters had dug up the common grave. For years, or so people said, one could find the heads of the fierce Modocs in sideshows, in the traveling circus. I used to scoff at these tales. But the rumor, at least the part about poor Jack-a-Dandy, proved true. Two decades after the hanging, the *Chronicle* carried a story about how the skull of the great warrior — Captain Jack was the rank it assigned him — was preserved at the surgeon general's office in the nation's capital. It might, for all I know, be there still.

The surviving Modocs could not be resettled until after the Civil War, when they were transported to the state of Kansas. But the Indians soon quarreled among themselves, and against the rule of the Modoc police. The greater number were moved again, to land in the Oklahoma Territory. There they remained, until those who had lived through the mining days and the Modoc War died out or moved away. They never seemed to be forgotten quite. As memories of the greater conflict between the states began to dim, the story of the siege, of the murder of General Webb, of the collapse of the mine would surface again. Of late, the Modocs and their war have become a fashion. In the east, or so I have heard, Buffalo Bill has made the storming of the stronghold a part of his show. The invading soldiers are shot at, in pantomime, by Rock Dave and Hooker Jim.

I know for a fact that Judge Steele took three of the squaws on a lecture tour through a dozen cities. On Kearny Street, in the same El Dorado where I'd watched Madame Moustache and first met my wife, I saw one of these performances with my own eyes. There on the dance floor was Steele, a cigar in his mouth, his muttonchops gray. Two squaws, their hair blackened with polish, stood behind him, wearing the kind of buckskins, beads, and fringes they'd never donned in real life. They were motionless, frowning, their arms crossed upon their chests. Only the crowd nearest by seemed to be paying attention. The drinkers went on with their drinking; the gamblers played at their cards. Even the piano player tinkered at a tune. Standing in the doorway, squinting through the smoke of a hundred cigars, I could only make out an occasional word, the odd phrase, of the showman's re-

Leslie Epstein is the director of the Creative Writing Program at Boston University. His other novels are *P. D. Kimerakov*, *The Steinway Quintent Plus Four*, *King of the Jews*, *Regina*, and *Goldkorn Tales*. He and his family live in Brookline, Massachusetts.

marks. Suddenly another squaw appeared on the dance floor, with a knife in her hand. Her black hair was twisted into a single long braid. Her face was covered with warpaint. It was — of this I was certain — Queen Mary. The other squaws unfolded their arms. They too had knives. Steele's voice rose. The women advanced upon him. He had a gun. A derringer. The knives flashed in the lights of the saloon. With weak knees, with a pounding heart, I turned away.

The sun is out. Already steam rises from the damp wood. A captain, in uniform, has arrived on the scene. The soldiers explain. I, too, say my piece. Surprisingly, the young man salutes me. Then he steps aside to allow me to walk from the dock to the prison. But I stand stock still. My feet are rooted. Leaning back, I stare up at the looming walls. Then I wave the newspaper in the air.

"He's done it, lads!" My voice is high, thin, wavering. "The Frenchman! It's foolproof! Foolproof! A definite vaccine for rabies!"

From the ramparts, no response. Only muteness.

Stumbling, breathless now, I make my way to the little launch. On the instant, we pull off, bound for the city. Dare I look back? Dare I not? There is the rock, rising dark and solid out of the blue of the bay. What of my Angus lads? The clever Newton Mike Humboldt Johnny? Cavendish Sam? Who can say whether the are even alive? And, if living, whether they still dwell behind t windowless walls? In my mind's eye I see them clearly: n middle-aged men, but boys dressed in stovepipes, striped par in swallowtails and stiff, starched shirts. Even as old men children will not change. It is as if these surrounding wat sunlit now, and dancing in the wind, had somehow preser them, like a magical fountain of youth.

END OF BOOK THREE